Burke's Soldier

Alan Attwood was born in Scotland in 1957 and emigrated to Australia with his family in 1961. He has worked as an abalone packer, a dishwasher and a mail sorter but, since 1978, mainly as a journalist. From 1995 to 1998 he was the New York-based correspondent for *The Age* and *The Sydney Morning Herald,* and more recently he has been a columnist for *The Age.* He was shortlisted for *The Australian*/Vogel Literary Award with *Sinking Into Winter* in 1990, and his novel *Breathing Underwater* was published in 1997. He lives in Melbourne with his wife and three children.

'The soldier is his own man at the end of this engrossing and utterly plausible novel.' Lucy Frost, *The Age*

'ambitious and energetic' Peter Pierce, *The Bulletin*

'It is when Attwood lets the fiction take control that characters truly take shape and the mood of the expedition comes to life . . . By focusing on one forgotten adventurer, Attwood challenges Australians to continue examining the many versions of our past.'
Andrew Laing, *The Sydney Morning Herald*

'Attwood brings a fresh pair of eyes to an old saga. He does this through the sharpness of his prose and the astuteness of his observation. His is a gentle and thoughtful account of proceedings . . . *Burke's Soldier* does what historical fiction needs to do. It finds the loose ends of an established narrative and tugs at them.'
Michael McGirr, *Australian Book Review*

'The task of the historical novelist is to bring the past alive to the contemporary reader while preserving the feeling that it is not being distorted. It's a difficult trick and Attwood is up to the job . . . *Burke's Soldier* is a satisfying novel on all levels.'
Peter Corris, *The Australian*

'A compelling narrative . . . A must for lovers of history.'
Emily Darling, *Good Reading*

'An excellent read.' Ray Chester, *Daily Telegraph*

'A gripping novel fusing fiction and history in the manner of Peter Carey's *True History of the Kelly Gang*.' *Travel Link*

ALAN ATTWOOD
Burke's Soldier

PENGUIN BOOKS

Penguin Books

Penguin Group (Australia)
250 Camberwell Road, Camberwell, Victoria 3124, Australia
Penguin Books Ltd
80 Strand, London WC2R 0RL, England
Penguin Group (USA) Inc.
375 Hudson Street, New York, New York 10014, USA
Penguin Books, a division of Pearson Canada
10 Alcorn Avenue, Toronto, Ontario, Canada M4V 3B2
Penguin Books (NZ) Ltd
Cnr Rosedale and Airborne Roads, Albany, Auckland, New Zealand
Penguin Books (South Africa) (Pty) Ltd
24 Sturdee Avenue, Rosebank, Johannesburg 2196, South Africa
Penguin Books India (P) Ltd
11, Community Centre, Panchsheel Park, New Delhi 110 017, India

First published by Penguin Books Australia Ltd, 2003
This paperback edition published by Penguin Group (Australia),
a division of Pearson Australia Group Pty Ltd, 2004

1 3 5 7 9 10 8 6 4 2

Text copyright © Alan Attwood 2003

The moral right of the author has been asserted

All rights reserved. Without limiting the rights under copyright reserved above, no part of this publication may be reproduced, stored in or introduced into a retrieval system, or transmitted, in any form or by any means (electronic, mechanical, photocopying, recording or otherwise), without the prior written permission of both the copyright owner and the above publisher of this book.

Design and digital imaging by Debra Billson © Penguin Group (Australia)
Cover photograph by Milton Montenegro/Getty Images
Typeset in Centaur by Post Pre-press Group, Brisbane, Queensland
Printed and bound in Australia by McPherson's Printing Group, Maryborough, Victoria

National Library of Australia
Cataloguing-in-Publication data:

Attwood, A. (Alan).
Burke's soldier.

ISBN 0 14 300082 9.

1. King, John, 1841–1872 – Fiction.
2. Burke and Wills Expedition (1860–1861) – Fiction. I. Title.

A823.3

This project has been assisted by the Commonwealth Government through the Australia Council, its arts funding and advisory body.

www.penguin.com.au

Contents

PART 1   THE SOUND OF THE SEA   *1*

PART 2   DISSIPATED LIKE DEW-DROPS   *157*

PART 3   THE RECKONING   *313*

AUTHOR'S NOTE   *447*

For Harold Attwood,
who started me on this journey

Part 1

The Sound of the Sea

One

The end. They have all wanted to know about the end.

Members of the Exploration Committee and the commission of inquiry. The newspaper men. The people at the railway station, pushing and calling out and gawping at me as if I were a new exhibit at Madam Sohier's Waxworks. And those who, even now, hear my name and pause, wondering why it stirs something in their memories. They have all asked the same questions. Over ten years after it happened, they still need to know about the end.

What did the leader say when he knew he would never see another morning? Was it true he used his last breath to voice the name of a lady? And why did he insist on holding a gun?

They come at it from different places but all head in the same direction, like streams to the sea.

The sea. We went looking for it and never saw it. Never heard it. Perhaps I could smell it, though it is possible the salt tang in my nostrils was nothing more than sweat and fear. Mr Burke declared himself satisfied with what we had done. It was the Gulf of Carpentaria, he asserted. And so it is said we were the first to cross the Australian continent from south to north. Our calamity was also a triumph. Was it? I cannot say, though I was there.

W, with his instruments and journals, was the one who reckoned our position. I never knew where I was from one dreary day to the next. They merged into one another like sand ridges in the desert, shimmering into the distance. Mr Burke and W were the explorers, the gentlemen. I was an ordinary working man. Not much more than a boy, an Irish lad with a sparse beard. I spent my twenty-second birthday trudging north along the banks of Cooper's Creek. Six months and a thousand miles from where we had started – in a park, with camels and wagons and a band and men in top hats wishing us well.

'God speed,' they cried. 'God speed.' The men in top hats went home and we started walking. So slowly. Only four of us, finally, as far as we could go. Into swamps with strangely coloured insects feeding on our skins, trees with roots like fingers reaching out of sucking mud, water tasting of iron and the warm air heavy with moisture. Air twice as thick as anything I ever breathed in India.

I had dreamed of white sand and cool salt water cleansing my tortured feet, but all I saw was a swamp. All I smelled was damp and the stench of death and despair on every one of us. All I heard at night were mosquitoes and the camels moaning and Charley Gray's laboured breathing. Charley was a sailor. He knew what the sea looked and sounded like. But no ship ever sailed upon this bog.

Later I heard W sobbing, crying out to his father. I did not say anything about this to him; we rarely spoke. He never told me what they had seen, the leader and him, when they left Charley and me waiting while they tried to push through to the water. Myself, I never heard waves or cries of seabirds. Just those insects and that scrabbling in the leaves and the human sounds of the four of us so small under all those stars and the moon that sees everything.

I was the only one of us who came back. Charley was the first to go. He died at night in the desert, a sailor far from the sea.

Then Mr Burke. And W, by himself, as he had wanted. I was with Mr Burke when he breathed his last, the life ebbing out of him just as the liquid seeped slowly from our canvas water-bags. His eyes were open, still searching for something he would never find.

I kept vigil by him with birds screeching in trees. The earth cracking in the sun and bone-chilling under the moon. Then I went looking for W. I took some crows I had shot, but he was dead when I found him and the blacks had taken clothes from his body. As best I could, I covered W with sand but could not think of any words to say for him.

Now they were all gone. And the rest of our party, contrary to the leader's instructions and our expectations, had left. I was abandoned – the only white man in the middle of a vast and cruel continent, where my God had never ventured. In the stones and sand and prickling bushes I saw no signs of Him. This was the serpent's land. A place where people walked naked, as they had in the beginning.

For eighty-one days, or so I have reckoned it to be, I didn't live so much as fail to die. I became something less than human. An animal. A black man with a white skin saved by the same wretches we had treated with suspicion early on. I survived and came back. I was a curiosity: the first to cross the continent and live to tell of it. The only one who could say what had happened to the mighty exploring expedition that began with speeches in the park and ended with a white man living amongst natives.

Our tragedy became a triumph for the people of the colony named after Victoria, Queen of Great Britain and Ireland, who watches over us but cannot see into the interior, where the natives walk bare-arsed to mock her. The commission wasn't the end of it. The bones of Mr Burke and W were brought back and put on show, though Charley was left where he lay. There was a funeral, more splendid than anything ever seen before in the colony, and a monument erected in the cemetery as immense as it was meaningless. Still they weren't done. A statue was unveiled, bronze figures that little resembled the men I had known. There are just the two of them in the statue. I'm not there, even though I was the one who returned.

They call me King.

Even at the end, Mr Burke never called me John. Just King. That's how it is in his notebook: 'King has behaved nobly.' The commissioners addressed me as Mr King when they asked their questions. Not because they thought me a gentleman, but rather, I suspect, out of fear that I might say what nobody wanted to hear. In their report I was the 'more fortunate and enduring associate' of Mr Burke and the man he called Will.

The leader spoke to me with the respect owed to a fellow soldier. But W – loyal, meticulous W, who studied his own stools with the same diligence he applied to recording barometric pressure – could make it sound like he was summoning a dog: 'The camels, King, look to the camels. Quickly now.'

W was the journal-keeper. He became the voice of the expedition, though there were many more of us who set out from the park. In his journals, too, I am never more than King, when I am mentioned at all, though Gray is often Charley. And the leader is always Mr Burke. When I look at W's journals, reprinted in full in the newspapers, it is as if I am reading the script of a play in which I have only a minor part. So now that I am intent on telling my own story – having once rejected an invitation to be part of a touring cyclorama of the exhibition – that is what I shall call him: W. Not out of spite so much as an attempt to set right the record.

My name is John King. Now, for the second time, I am dying.

I know what it is to die. I was dying when Howitt's men found me. In my face they saw the same emptiness I had witnessed in Mr Burke's eyes when he asked me to stay with him. But I had no white man to sit with me when my own end was near, which is why I have since marked the day on which I was found – September 15th, 1861, a decade ago in a matter of months – as my true birthday. The date of my restoration to the world has seemed more worthy of commemoration than my arrival on the other side of it.

This is a different kind of death. Abandoned in the interior, my spirit ebbed away less from the want of nutriment than an unshakeable lassitude. You can shrink to nothing in such overwhelming vastness. Nardoo, the plant the natives use to make a rough flour, cannot nourish the soul. Nor the stuff that W described as portulaca and Charley called pigweed.

'We eat grass like bloody donkeys,' he said. Yet he ate it until his mouth became too sore to chew.

Here now I am seldom alone. But still I have trouble with food. Nora, my sister who took me in, and Mary, my widowed cousin, offer soup I can accept only sometimes. Doctor Treacey visits regularly. I hear the jingling of his carriage, then a muted groan and sometimes a fart as he gets down from the jig. He peers into the enamel mug I keep by my pillow for the coughing. With a metal spatula he pokes at the matter I bring up. It feels as if the very tissue of my lungs is being expelled. I know what he is looking for: streaks of red amidst the muck.

Treacey asks about the frequency of the night fevers and insists that I rest and avoid excitement. Yet we both know there is little he can do for me. If I were living somewhere else – in the city itself, or near the Emerald Hill marshes – he might entreat me to move somewhere more salubrious. But there is nowhere better for me to go. I am dying in St Kilda, the seaside place of boats and donkey rides on the beach. At weekends the gentry come in carriages, or ride the new railway to walk along the Esplanade or the jetty. The daring try the bathing machines while invalids suck in sea breezes as a parched man gulps at water.

The ocean scares me. There is too much of it, like sand in the desert.

Our house is in Octavia Street. The beach and its beneficent air are another expedition away and I have not the strength to walk there myself, across the St Kilda Road and its perennial coating of dung. Because of my restlessness a camp-bed has been rigged up for me in the front room, facing the street. But still I disturb the others. Sometimes I talk at night, Nora says. I call out words she cannot comprehend. Both she and Mary attend to me, though Mary also has her work at the café in the Royal Arcade. They deserve some relief in the darkness, so when the coughing wakes me and I have wrenched up some more of my lungs into the mug, I try to keep down some water and wait for sleep to come upon me once again. But as it has become an infrequent visitor of late, I often light a candle and scratch at this account that I have begun belatedly and fear I will never finish.

They have all wanted to know about the end. Now my own ending may leave the tale untold.

Sometimes, if I am too weak to write, I lie upon the damp pillows listening to the night noises. Nora's soft breathing in the next room. Mary shooshing her infants, Albert and Grace, who share her bed. They are the children of a good man killed two years ago. I hear the timbers of the house creaking as they contract in the cool of a new morning. Fowls stirring in a neighbour's yard. The cawing of a seabird. But never any water. No waves or ripples on sand.

Here in St Kilda I still cannot hear the sea.

Two

The footfall on the verandah is unfamiliar. It is not that of Doctor Treacey. Nor Reverend Bickford, whose increasingly frequent visits are, I assume, a reflection of his growing concern about my condition. I know the minister's step. Soft, unassertive – the step of a man accustomed to being turned away.

This footfall is different. It pulls me from the slumber into which I must have descended after another restless night. I wake to find the candle I had lit some hours before burned away; the shades have the morning sun behind them. I can hear the footsteps, quick and confident, pacing the street. They stop in front of the house. A pause, as if this pedestrian is checking the address against a paper pulled from a pocket. Then I hear the sound of boots, heavy-heeled, striding up the few steps from the street and directly to the door. There is a rapping. Once. Twice. Again.

Nora comes from the kitchen, her skirts swishing on the floor. Perhaps suspecting that I may still be slumbering, she closes the door to my room before answering the insistent knocking.

'This is the home of John King?'

'It is, sir. I am Mr King's sister.'

'Ah. Good morning to you. Mr King is within?'

'He is here, sir. But he is indisposed. He is –'

'Unwell, madam? Yes, I am aware of that. It is largely the

reason I am here. I need to see your brother. My time is now spent mostly outside Melbourne, so unless he sleeps or is otherwise insensible I should like to speak with him.'

His voice is muffled by the closed door, but I know it. I have heard it before, though cannot immediately place it. The voice stirs something I have tried to forget. Nora, I can tell, is struck by its tone of authority. This is a man used to getting his way.

Different steps in the corridor. Mary. Who, as she must do most mornings, has been at the trough in the back, trying to beat out stains from my bedding. I picture her hushing the children in the parlour, then wiping her hands on her apron as she investigates this unexpected interruption.

'Nora? What is it?'

'A gentleman insisting on seeing John.'

'I am his cousin, Mary Hill. And you are, sir?'

'Howitt, madam. Alfred Howitt.'

My saviour on earth. The man who brought me back to life and then, his work done, seemed to want nothing more to do with me. I struggle to rise from my prone position.

'Mr Howitt, sir,' says Nora. 'Forgive us. Bless you, sir. Please come in. I will see if John is strong enough to receive you.'

She pushes the door to my room in gently, as if fearful of disturbing me. Seeing my eyes open, she speaks. 'John, you have a visitor.'

'I heard. Let him come in.'

As soon as I say this, I am ashamed. It is as if I can suddenly see who and where I am: a man not shaved for several days, still in a soiled nightshirt on an unmade bed though the sun is well up. The window to the street has been closed since yesterday; the air must be rank. Even as I hear Howitt's boots leaving the verandah and approaching my door, I remember too late the enamel mug half full of muck near the pillow. I pick it up and am seeking somewhere to secrete it when he comes in. I feel like a drunkard surprised mid-tipple. I replace the mug on the bedside table.

It has always been difficult to hide anything from this man.

'Good day to you, King,' he says. 'Don't try to get up.'

The Governor said something similar after Howitt's surveyor brought me back: 'Do not stand to receive me, for you must be rather weak.' And when he asked if my health was now better I answered him, 'Yes, sir.'

I lied. My health has never recovered from my time on the Cooper. There are men of sixty, almost twice my age, sprightlier than I am now.

'Mr Howitt, sir. I had not thought to see you again. You have me at a disadvantage – I was not expecting company.'

But Howitt shows no sign of being offended by the smell of the room or its dingy light or my appearance. If he has observed the mug – and he is a man who has trained himself to notice everything, be it the type of rock in a riverbed or the variety of gum tree on its bank – he does not show it.

'Relax, King. Don't stir yourself. It seems it is my fate to find you in parlous circumstances. Although I would say that your situation now is a decided improvement on what it was, hmm?'

The blacks' shelter. My clothes in strips. The natives excited, calling out. Howitt's men staring at me, incredulous, like children viewing for the first time the platypus or something equally fabulous in a museum, before summoning their leader. Howitt, short of frame but tough as tarred rope, guiding his horse forward, then standing quite still in front of me and gazing at what I had become, while I sought to frame words that couldn't be spoken with bleeding lips.

'You wept, sir.'

He appears discomfited at being reminded of an uncharacteristic show of emotion. 'You were a pitiable sight, King. Completely knocked up. Never before or since have I encountered such a melancholy excuse for humanity – scarcely civilised. Alone and lost. Latitude of 27 degrees, 44 minutes; longitude 140 degrees, 40 minutes. That was where we had camped when we found you.'

'You remember, sir?'

'Facts, King, I always remember the facts. And the fact is we got you before you became a black man yourself. Or worse.'

'You did, sir. I am forever in your debt.'

He gives a dismissive gesture with his right hand. He has not come for shows of gratitude. As if unsure how to proceed next, he probes in a waistcoat pocket, extracts a small, cunningly carved snuffbox – it may be ivory, I cannot say for sure – then sprinkles some of the compound within into the depression formed between his raised left thumb and wrist. He pauses, inhales deeply, once with each nostril, then sneezes into a large linen handkerchief. In one corner I can make out the initials 'AWH'. With unconcealed interest he studies the residue, which has avoided the monogram.

The room lightens. Mary has softly entered and drawn the shades. She opens the window and a warm breeze eddies in from the street.

'Can I offer you tea, Mr Howitt?'

'That would be most welcome, madam. Black. Well sugared.'

Bushman's tea. Mr Burke also liked his tea sweet. When rations ran short he would sometimes scoop handfuls of wild honey from knots in the trunks of trees into our billy.

'Will you try to take some tea too, John? Good. I'll get it. Mr Howitt...' Mary pauses, afraid of causing offence. 'My cousin's condition is delicate, as you can see. Doctor Treacey insists that any upset cannot be good for him. I would hope, sir, that –'

'Mrs Hill, you have no cause for concern on my account. I know Treacey. He has told me how things stand. The only surprise I have for your cousin is my unexpected appearance this morning. I am here to converse, not interrogate.' His smile is civil but also conveys a sense of finality, which is not lost on Mary. She retires to fix the tea.

Howitt, whose eyes seem in constant motion, fixes his gaze on the timepiece that rests next to the pitcher of water I must always have nearby for the coughing.

'Ah, the gold watch. The one given to you, I assume, by the Royal Geographical Society. The Society in London. Not, of course, by the Royal Society in Melbourne, the ones who conceived your expedition.'

My expedition. Never before have I been afforded such proprietorship. From Howitt this is high praise. He knows, more than most, what we all endured. I hold the watch, strangely comforted, as always, by the way it sits snugly in my palm.

'The same, sir. One of my most treasured possessions. And it keeps good time. You knew of it?'

'I read, King. I hear things. I try to keep abreast of events. And your annuity continues?'

'It does, sir. One-eighty a year. Enough for our needs.'

'But perhaps not all your wants. Tell me, King, though I don't wish to be gloomy, what becomes of the sum should you no longer be the beneficiary?'

'When I'm gone, sir? I'm not sure. Reverend Bickford, my minister, has promised to make inquiries on my behalf.'

'I will see what *I* can find out. Mrs Hill, I thank you. Leave the tray there, if you will. I can attend to your cousin. Your own seedcake? It looks excellent.'

Mary, dismissed once again, leaves us, though she seems fascinated by our visitor. Howitt passes me a cup of tea, which I try to balance on my chest as I lie half raised on the pillows. From another pocket Howitt takes a clasp-knife, well used, flicks the blade open with a thumbnail, then uses it to stir his tea, ignoring the spoons Mary has brought in.

We sip our tea in silence, Howitt meditatively chewing on a piece of Mary's cake. There is, perhaps, a little more grey in his beard, but otherwise his appearance has changed little since 1861. His most striking features are still a high and imposing forehead, which seems more dramatic when not shielded by his hat, and his eyes – like those of an emu, intense and piercing. I'm not sure that I have ever seen him blink. I could never hold his gaze long enough. But now, as he takes his refreshment, his eyes appear fixed on my watch, which shows the time as a quarter past nine o'clock.

'So, King, what have you heard of me?'

'Very little, sir. I know that you went back again, to retrieve the remains. And I think I saw you at the funeral.'

'I was there, though one more or less would not have been noticed in that milling throng. Most of whom had less interest in paying respects than having their names recorded in the newspapers.'

'The unveiling of the statue, sir – were you there for that, too?'

'Another fine folly. I hear talk already that the statue will have to be shifted, as it's an obstruction to carriages in Collins Street. No, I stayed away from that one. And I think I've passed by it only a time or two since. I'm a man of the country now, King. A magistrate, up Omeo way.'

A magistrate. Of course. I try to imagine how anyone finding themselves in Howitt's dock could fail to give honest answers when fixed with his gimlet stare, which he has now turned to his nails as he cleans them with the tip of his blade.

'I move around a lot,' he continues. 'On horseback mostly. I rode here this morning; left the colt by a trough in the St Kilda Road. And I find I am more and more interested in the blacks that

I see. Different tribes in different parts of the country, all with different customs. The natives around Omeo, for example, look and sound completely different from the ones up the Barcoo.'

'The Yantruwanta.'

'That's what they call themselves. I believe that Australian blacks are one of the most primitive people on earth. Doomed to extinction, I'll be bound. And yet they have survived all this time. They helped *you* to survive, King.'

'They did, sir. Gave me food and shelter. They seemed to pity me.'

'And Burke? What of Burke and the blacks?'

'Mr Burke was suspicious of them. He maintained that if we were too friendly we might never be rid of them. He would fire his gun to keep them at a distance.'

'Did he indeed?' Howitt's tone is as sharp as his knife. 'What of Wills?'

'He was apprehensive at first. Declared them to be troublesome and contemptible. But later, on the creek, I think he came to see them as our best chance. Though he was lost, too.'

'But not you, King.' His eyes are fixed on me. 'You lived. You lived with them. And in consequence it strikes me that you may know more about the natives and their customs than almost anybody else. Which is why I am here. I wonder if I could speak with you about what you recall of their language and habits and manner of life. Not necessarily today. I see you are poorly this morning. But perhaps we can arrange another time when you are feeling stronger. Imagine, King, you may yet find yourself in the scientific journals.'

I cannot imagine this at all. My intention for much of the past decade has been to live as quietly as possible. I thought I had this in common with Howitt, who seemed to shun the acclamation that could have been his after two trips to the interior and back. He was a man intent on completing his task, then moving on. Now it appears he has moved on to a study of the blacks, though I'm not at all sure I can assist him in the way he expects.

'I will try to help you, sir. Of course I will. I owe you much more than that. But it may be I know less than you suspect. I didn't live with the natives so much as fall in amongst them. There were days, weeks, when I would scarcely see them. They wandered. But then one or all of them would return with some food, to see how I fared. I think we understood only a few words of each other's language even by the time you came upon me.'

My hands are moist on the sheets. My mouth is parched. A look of concern passes over Howitt's face. He gets up, as if to leave.

'Relax, man. There is no need to vex yourself this morning. I can return when it suits us both better. Or perhaps you could record some thoughts when they come to you. Native phrases and suchlike. I see you've been doing some writing already.'

He has spied the pages of my journal by the bed, where I must have let them fall from weariness several hours before. When he moves to pick some up I place a hand over them.

Howitt steps back. He is not a man accustomed to being denied. 'Secrets, King? Or merely a day-to-day diary?'

'Just a record, sir. I am trying to remember while I still can. The expedition...'

His forehead is creased by a frown. 'But you've already told your story. Several times. To me, after we found you, and then to the commission of inquiry.'

'I answered questions, sir. As best I could.'

'You "answered questions"? Meaning there were questions that were never asked?'

I feel as if my bed has become the dock in his courtroom. He looks down at me, pursing his lips. 'Well, well, King. You continue to be a man of surprises.'

He checks his own timepiece, a scuffed silver watch he keeps on a chain attached to the middle button of his waistcoat, then rises, taps at his pockets as if to reassure himself of the presence of snuff and clasp-knife, and moves closer to my bed. I expect a farewell. But instead he says, 'You've been extraordinarily loyal, King.'

'Loyal, sir?'

'To Burke.'

'He was my leader, sir.'

'That he was. The committee appointed him leader. But was he really, I wonder, a leader of men?'

'I'm not sure I understand you fully. He was the leader.'

'Indeed. You followed him. Even in a split party. There were ambiguous orders, incomplete record-keeping... But enough of that now. You need to rest, man.'

He takes my damp right hand, his grip firm and dry. It feels as if I am holding the branch of one of the old coolibahs on the banks of the Cooper. And I am totally unprepared for what he says next.

'You had much in common, Burke and yourself.'

'Mr Burke and me, sir? Oh, no. He was the leader. A gentleman. I was merely a hired hand. The expedition was just another job of work.'

He is unswayed. 'Think on it, King. Yourself and Burke — both Irish, both soldiers, of sorts. Both lost in a country that was still relatively new to you. And I'm not so sure that Burke was a gentleman. Does a gentleman leave his debts unpaid at the Melbourne Club? More than forty-one pounds in arrears, I believe.'

He said he had not come to interrogate me. I wish that Mary or Nora might interrupt us again.

'I know nothing of his personal affairs,' I insist. 'But were we really lost, sir? We knew our position. Knew where we had to go. It was only the want of provisions and strength and equipment that stopped us getting on. You cannot walk if your boots are in tatters.'

'The blacks manage it, King. But it was just you with Burke at the end. A pair of Irishmen marooned in the Australian interior. Strange the way fate sometimes works itself out.'

And now fate has led Howitt to my home, when I had never thought to see him again. Howitt and his questions. One more person wanting to know about the end.

'You know,' he continues, 'I find I still wonder about aspects of your expedition myself. Burke's revolver, for instance. The one you said he insisted on holding. I found that when we went back. Corroded with rust and partly covered with leaves and earth, yet loaded and capped. Why was that?'

The leader's hand too weak to hold it. Eyes too misty even to aim, but still searching for something. Muttering words I could not understand ...

I need air.

Howitt, smelling of snuff and old saddles, is leaning over me, the tip of his ragged beard almost touching my chest. I feel it heaving, convulsing. Then Howitt's face starts to spin.

'Heavens, man, your colour is awful. Take some of your tea.'

The coughing makes it feel as if my lungs are being shredded. Pared with Howitt's knife. While I cough, I cannot breathe. And nothing, it seems, can stop the coughing. There is blood in my mouth. Something warm and wet on my chest. And a grey haze settling over my vision. Or has Mary drawn the shades once again? Mary, I can hear Mary. And Nora. Cool hands on my forehead. Women's hands. Concerned voices.

'John, try to sit up. Take some breaths. Come on, try. Here, sip from this cup.'

'Mr Howitt! What is this? Whatever happened to upset him so?'

The sound of boots crossing the floor. The same confident footfall as before. A damp flannel is pressed against my lips. Water. Then air. I can breathe. The coughs are less painful than they were.

The mist is clearing. Mary is beside me, one hand on mine, the other stroking my stubbled cheek. Nora is dabbing at a puddle on the floor with a cloth. Somehow the pitcher of water has been knocked over. There is blood as well as tea on my nightshirt.

And Howitt has gone.

Three

'Well, King, what are we to do with you?'

Doctor Collis Treacey has positioned his chair so that it is adjacent to my pillow. He is seated but still I must look up at him. He has hold of my wrist, checking my pulse against his fob-watch, which he holds in his right hand. He snaps the lid shut, apparently satisfied, and lets my wrist lie on the coverlet.

Weak. It is as if the blood in my veins has been replaced with a solution of lead. Weak and thirsty. The doctor pours a glass of water and steadies it while I gulp at its contents. By the light, I guess it to be mid-afternoon. I must have been sleeping for many hours.

'Your sister and cousin tell me you took quite a turn this morning. And to think that I impressed upon you just last week the importance of not overexciting yourself. Rest and fresh air and good food offer your best chance of recovery, King.'

'Recovery, Doctor?'

He ignores my question. Treacey prides himself on being a good listener. But he has learned something that cannot be taught in medical schools: sometimes it is best to pretend not to hear something said by a patient, especially when it relates to their prospects for the future.

Collis Treacey is not an old man, perhaps only five years older than myself, and regards medicine as a science that concerns itself with tangible things. His manner is endlessly optimistic, despite his funereal uniform. He favours a black frock-coat with a high collar, many buttons and even more pockets, within which he secretes the tools of his trade. He has listening devices, probes and spoons and spatulas, and tiny glass jars, like something from a doll's house, in which he stores the samples he removes for further analysis at his city rooms in Stephen Street. One pocket is reserved for his cards, which advise that Doctor Collis Treacey is a consultant to the Melbourne Hospital, offers gratis advice two mornings a week, midwifery by appointment, and can arrange for parcels of medicines to be sent 'to all parts of the country and adjacent colonies'.

He has encouraged his side whiskers to grow but their hue is a lighter shade of ginger than the hair atop his head, which is kept in place with a pomade that has a spicy scent. Treacey is proud of his whiskers, but they cannot distract attention from his most startling feature – ginger eyebrows that seem less a pair than a single slash across his forehead. He appears to think with his eyebrows. As he examines the muck in my mug then uses one of his spoons to place a splodge in a jar, the eyebrows rise and bend like the wings of a bird in flight. After secreting the jar in a pocket, he resumes his listening posture, hands stroking his long chin.

'How are you feeling now, King?'

'Tired. Lacking in energy.'

'Any shortness of breath?'

'Only this exhaustion that always follows one of the coughing episodes.'

'Which is why we must seek to avoid them.'

I wonder how much Treacey knows about Howitt's visit. From his travelling case – a neat, concertina-like thing that is also black – Treacey produces a small phial with a purple tinge. He studies it like a man who has never seen it before.

'This, for example, contains a physic that works on the lungs. But there are evidently also triggers within the human mind that act upon the body, as you demonstrated this morning. Indeed, I sometimes wonder if all my years of dissection classes might have been better spent seeking to unravel the mind. It is like that vast inland sea your predecessors in exploration sought to find.'

'But how can you hope to gauge a man's mind, Doctor?'

He looks at me, his eyes the colour of straw. 'Now, that's the thing. The workings of the mind are a mystery.' Treacey's eyebrows form the outline of a tent on his forehead. 'Who's to say what's in any man's mind, eh?' His attention returns to the purple bottle. 'I'd like you to try some of this, King. Chlorodyne. Several of my other patients have reported a measure of improvement after its use.'

I study the label, which promises 'The best remedy known for coughs, consumption, bronchitis, asthma' and ask him, 'You really think it can help?'

'It may afford you some relief. That is my aim: to keep you as comfortable as possible. I would suggest you take the Chlorodyne daily. Save the anti-bilious pills for episodes of indigestion or nausea. And if there is pain, you still have some laudanum.'

'But I am loath to use it.'

'Why ever not? It is the strongest sedative available.'

'The dreams, Doctor. Laudanum seems to precipitate terrible nightmares.'

He gazes at me as if I represent a case that is not conforming to patterns described in his medical textbooks.

'I see. Interesting. Distressing dreams are not a common side effect of laudanum. You may have to choose between two unfortunate alternatives: insomnia, and sleep that is interrupted by some of those dreams you mention. In the meantime I suggest you save the laudanum for occasions when you are experiencing pain. I will instruct your sister and cousin accordingly. Now, tell me, how are your stools? Are you having any difficulties with your movements?'

I cannot help it. I smile. Treacey is clearly surprised. Inquiries to his patients about bowels must seldom cause mirth.

'Forgive me, Doctor. I don't mean to be disrespectful. Your question, following my visitor this morning, has prompted some memories, that's all.'

Mr Burke is tugging at his belt, kicking at the stony ground with the toe of his boot. Admiring something we cannot see.

'A monster, lads. A beast! A behemoth! A titan amongst turds! Come and contemplate the size of it and its firmness of consistency. Feel free to applaud if you must. Any man who can produce something on this scale without rupturing his arse is self-evidently in fine fettle. Rajah, Landa, any of our humped brethren, would be envious of such dung. The interior can pose no threat to a man with such an admirable interior of his own. What say you, Will, do I have here something worth weighing and measuring and recording in your fieldbooks?'

Charley and I exchange smirks. W, who has one of his books open, smiles the indulgent smile one might offer a child frolicking with a new toy, but does not reply. The way they relieve themselves is one of the most dramatic differences between the two men. Mr Burke seems as unashamed of his bowels as any of the natives we encounter. When the need arises, he strides just a little distance from our camp – or our path, if we are travelling – and seldom bothers to seek out a bush or even a clump of grass to preserve his modesty. His trousers are often wrenched loose before he squats, with his subsequent endeavours accompanied by a commentary or sundry exclamations.

'Come on, you dark bugger, I know you're in there. Out!'

Then, with a cry that could be either pain or triumph, he declares his job done and rehoists his trousers. It is not unusual for the leader to invite his companions to admire the product of his labour – an invitation that none of us, to my knowledge, ever accepts. To Mr Burke his stools are another demonstration of his vitality. He is a man whose system is still functioning, still forming waste of admirable heft and hue, whatever privations we might be enduring.

I always wondered if he made such a performance of his bowel movements as a kind of private jest with his second in command. For nobody ever saw W shit. Until the end, that is, when necessity overtook pride and W could no longer wander away to find conveniently placed trees or rocks behind which to perform his toilet. This was something that caused him increasing discomfort, particularly when the nardoo turned to stone in his guts and left him straining in solitary agony, trying to pass turds that couldn't be shifted. In the last days of his journal he discusses the need for sugar and fat in the diet. As if he were dreaming of something greasy, perhaps a plump pork chop from an English dinner table, to lubricate his guts and unplug his bowels.

W was every bit as fascinated by his motions as Mr Burke. But instead of inviting his comrades to a viewing, W privately recorded details of his unproductive straining and the pebbles he passed. Meanwhile the camels farted with every second stride while Mr Burke's pony shat without even slowing down.

We crossed the continent leaving a trail of turds.

'Loose motions when they come, Doctor,' I tell Treacey. 'My appetite remains poor, so it is not surprising I have little to produce.'

'Nothing I might examine – in the bedpan, perhaps?'

'Not today. My cousin and sister are admirable housekeepers as well as nurses.'

'No matter.' Though he seems disappointed that one of his glass bottles will remain empty. 'Have you visited the Esplanade, King, as I suggested?'

'Not for some time. I have been too weak for the journey. But Mary is insisting that when I am strong enough and the day is fine we should engage a carriage and travel to the St Kilda pier.'

'I would recommend it. It is now generally accepted among medical professionals that ingestion of sea air can be extraordinarily beneficial to invalids, especially those with chest conditions like your own. I don't know, however, that I'd suggest you use one of the new bathing machines.'

I cannot tell if he is jesting when he says this.

'That wouldn't be possible even if I had the strength,' I assure him. 'I never learned to swim.'

'Nor did I, King. Although, unlike you, I was born in this country surrounded by water. Which reminds me — there is a school of thought maintaining that some conditions are as much due to history as any contemporary malaise. Your father, King, how were *his* lungs, do you know?'

'I cannot recall my father at all. Only some things he had. A jacket in my ma's chest. A pipe she kept beside her bed, long after he'd gone. He died when I was a babe, you see.'

He nods and makes a note of this in a small pocketbook he has conjured from his coat. 'And your mother?'

Hands red and cracked with toil. Stirring the pot that was never emptied, only topped up with more and more water, leaving a soup that tasted only of the spoon that stirred it. Sprigs of lavender crumbling between the folds of a faded wedding gown.

'Dead when I was just nine. From exhaustion, I think, more than any particular illness.'

'Of course. The hunger. What did you do then?'

'A soldier, Doctor. As my father had been. The 70th Regiment of Foot. Where my brothers had gone before. The two oldest, that is. Another had died. Besides the army, there wasn't much on offer.'

Treacey's gaze is fixed upon me now. Studying me the way he would examine one of his specimen jars. 'How old were you then, King?'

'A boy. Fourteen and one month when I enlisted. Not much older when they sent us off to India.'

'India! Quite a change from Ireland, I imagine. Hotter, certainly, eh?'

Hotter. Bigger. Flatter. The smell of spices and oil and people with skin as dark as mine was pale. The sun, huge and pink, low in the evening sky, reluctant to cede possession to the moon. Giant stick insects I had never seen before captured in the lantern light. Staring back at me, just as Treacey is looking at me now.

'Loosen the top of your nightshirt, if you can, King. Before I leave I'd like to apply some of this balsam. It may ease the congestion.'

From his case he has produced a jar with a violet hue. The paste he applies is thick – he must wipe the residue from his fingers with his pocket handkerchief – and has a pungent smell somewhere between ammonia and piss. Its aroma and the sticky sensation on my chest will linger long after he has gone. This, I suspect, is largely his aim. I have done some doctoring myself. Creating an impression of a lasting remedy can be as important as achieving a result.

The old woman, a lubra with dugs like empty sugar bags, is indicating that she cannot give me any more nardoo because her right arm is too sore to pound the seed. She shows me the arm. Thrusts it close to my face so I can breathe its rancid scent. In the fold of the arm is an angry boil. It occurs to me that if I can ease her discomfort her companions may be more kindly disposed to me.

In the billy I boil some water, then sponge the affected part as best I can. She allows me to do this though my ministrations pain and perplex her. Even after the washing the boil is yet unbroken. I still have some nitrate of silver we carried for warts. I apply a small amount to the boil. The effect is almost instantaneous. She cries out — *'Mokaw!'* — and rises to her feet, waving her arm like a bird with a broken wing. A man I take to be her husband, who has observed our ritual without interruption, appears impressed. The nitrate is some more of the white man's magic. I must hide what I have. The blacks are insatiably curious and I know they investigate my few belongings when they can.

The lubra, still flapping, and her husband leave me. They return a little later with some nardoo paste, which they present like an offering. The arm is revealed for inspection. The boil has broken; much of the pus is gone. Her gestures suggest her discomfort has been eased. She chatters with her husband, who talks excitedly, making many gestures in my direction. Then, biting her lower lip bashfully like a maiden one-third her years, she settles beside me so there is no escaping her scent. Gently she places her left arm, the uninfected one, on my chest. Her name, she indicates with much pointing, is Carrawaw.

Her husband makes some grunting noises and thrusts like a rutting dog. He is smiling. This, it seems, is their ultimate gesture of gratitude.

I feign sleep and silently pray that they will leave me alone.

Doctor Treacey is conversing with Mary and Nora near the door. I cannot recall him withdrawing, but my chest feels damp and reeks of ammonia. Words pierce the mist that is descending on me again.

'Rest is the most important thing for him, ladies. And some sea air if you can manage to get him out.'

'We intend it, Doctor, when he is stronger. There are days when he seems much better than others.'

'That is the nature of his condition. But even on his poorer days you must try to maintain his intake of fluids and nutriment.'

'We do, though his appetite is erratic at best.'

'Ah. Another thing. He mentioned some worrisome dreams. Have you had any evidence of this?'

A pause. As if Mary and Nora are exchanging glances. Then it is Mary who speaks.

'There are bad nights. He is troubled and calls out.'

'Anything you can understand?'

'They are sounds more than words. But these dreams, if that's what they are, trouble him greatly. We find him in a fearful sweat, his bedding quite soaked.'

I imagine Treacey stroking his chin again. 'He blames the laudanum, though I'm not sure that's the cause. Such maladies of the mind are beyond my comprehension, though when his rest is impaired it will produce symptoms we all can see. Tell me, I know you said his cries are impossible to comprehend, but do you suspect that his dreams, his distress, relate to the expedition?'

The response, if there is one, eludes me.

I lie nearby, sticky with balsam, half gone again, fighting the temptation to call out to Treacey an answer that would give him something further to ponder.

Not only the expedition, Doctor. That and more. There were things that happened long before I ever met my leader.

Four

The Colonel liked to do his killing in the morning.

'Do it right. Do it in style. Put on a show.' I heard him say this to one of his officers. 'A spectacle is something everyone understands. And the thing to appreciate about an execution, you see, is that a point is being made. It is the ultimate demonstration of authority. Calculated to impress all who witness it. Which is why you always want as big a crowd as you can muster. You need a band, a bit of a parade. All the men, of every rank. All the prisoners. Empty the cells, get them out there – and not only the feature attractions. One thing I'll swear by, Major, is that those who witness Her Majesty's wrath will not lightly forget it. Have it all over with by noon, that's the idea. Then the normal business of the day can resume after lunch.'

Lunch! I could never stomach food after one of the Colonel's special parades. Firing practice, he called it.

The Colonel himself never seemed the least bit affected. He would sit erect on his favourite horse, which was trained to remain stationary in the midst of mayhem, his dress sabre glinting in the morning sunshine and the scarlet of his parade uniform set off by ceremonial white sashes and gleaming black boots. He seemed barely to notice any of it, managing somehow to appear as if his attention were fixed not on the happenings in the Peshawar square, but instead on a point far away, perhaps even as distant as England herself, where Her Majesty, with her orbs and ermine robes, was resplendent and untouchable on the throne in this the twentieth year of her reign, 1857. Four years after I first set my Irish feet on Indian dirt.

I am facing the Colonel across the hot and dusty square, standing in the front row of the serried ranks along with the other younger or smaller men. If he notices me at all, I am merely another anonymous face in the crowd. But I can watch him throughout the whole ghastly ceremony. And if I keep my attention on him it may distract me, even a little, from what is going on nearby. The Colonel must be able to see and hear and smell all that is consequent to his orders, but he never betrays any emotion. His training at the military academy, or perhaps it is breeding, has instilled in him an air of supreme indifference, even boredom. He could be viewing a march-past of new recruits.

It is only mid-morning but already the sun is huge and heavy in the sky. At dawn the sun was tinged with pink; now all colour has been burned out of it. It seems possible actually to hear the heat, though this may only be the blood throbbing in my temples under my too-large helmet. A throbbing that gives way to the staccato sound of drumming near the blockhouse where the prisoners have been kept. I can see my bunkmate Wilfred Ponting behind his drum, his face pale, trying to concentrate on maintaining the rhythm. And then the band begins to play as the first of the prisoners are led out from their confinement, flinching from the harsh light.

Because they are shackled together, the prisoners must move in a clumsy dance, as if they are a strange circus act. A caterpillar with many heads. The guards' bayonets prod them to a place near the centre of the square as the band, its numbers thinned by recent casualties, strikes up 'God Save Our Gracious Queen'. The

Colonel stiffens on his horse. The prisoners are ordered to halt and stand straight. After the anthem come hymns. The Colonel appears to be mouthing the words to 'Soldiers Of Christ, Arise'.

Any doubts the prisoners might have had about their imminent fate are shattered now by what they can see through their raised hands, cupped against the sun. In a neat row not far from where they stand, hobbled by chains, are the regiment's three field cannons. They have been wheeled into position, a semicircle of soldiers around them, so that they face west – the one side of the square on which there are no spectators. Beside each gun stand three men: one attending to the charges, one with the primer, one holding a smouldering portfire. The prisoners – I can count twelve of them – react slowly to what they see. Then the noise starts: a discordant chorus of wails, imprecations, and cries to their gods with words I cannot understand.

They do not look like mutineers. Until recently they were considered loyal sepoys, obedient and reliable. They moved amongst us fully armed. Although housed in separate quarters, they were deemed to be part of the regiment, participating in all ceremonial occasions. They had taken oaths of loyalty to the Queen. But events of the last months have changed everything. Unrest is like a contagion sweeping across this arid land, and the Colonel is taking no chances. I do not know if these men have even been given a chance to prove their loyalty. Perhaps their sins amount to nothing more than tardiness in handing over their arms. Perhaps no sin was even required to precipitate this retribution, the Colonel having decided on a demonstration of will and force, knowing that word will spread quickly of what is about to transpire here. Hence the crowd, which includes other sepoys – under guard but not yet condemned – watching sullenly from a spot near the quartermaster's building.

I should not be here. I do not belong. I am in the army,

though not yet a soldier. Not really. I am an assistant teacher at the regimental school, a school for the children of officers. But now I am eighteen and the situation all around us is becoming more acute every day, so it cannot be long before I become a fighting soldier like my brothers William and Samuel, of whom I have had little news of late. The school cannot last, besides. Already many of the officers' wives and their children have been sent away, far from the troubles. Yet I can see some of the womenfolk assembled in the party behind the Colonel, sheltering under parasols that provide only meagre protection from the relentless sun.

If the Colonel himself makes any signal I do not notice it. Maybe there is a curt nod or a dipping of his sabre. More likely, his senior officers know the required routine; know also that their prospects for promotion and higher salaries are contingent upon impeccable performance in this ritual. Above all else, they know they must not question their orders.

The band falls quiet. The faces of the trumpeters seem as ruddy as their uniforms. It is hot work playing under this sun. But Wilfred still looks pale as he stares fixedly down at his drumsticks. One of the more senior bandsmen nudges him, instructing him to look up.

As there is no music, we can all hear the sounds as the first three mutineers are unshackled and separated from the group. Then each of them is forced by two soldiers towards the cannons. Because of their time in the shackles, or perhaps simply due to fear, the feet of the mutineers do not seem to function properly. They must be dragged across the dry stony ground. After the clinking of chains comes a scuffing noise, accompanied by the incessant drone of prayers, and then, from the leading man – the one who has seemed to be urging his companions to maintain their composure – curses and even spitting as their arms are thrust apart and tied, one hand to the rim of each cannon's wheels.

When the tying is done and the soldiers have resumed their position near the prisoners, one of whom appears to have fainted, the back of each condemned man rests on a cannon's gaping mouth. The last thing each one of them will feel through their thin tunics is the barrel of the gun, made hot by the sun, the gravel under their bare feet, and the rope cruelly tight across their wrists.

Drumming. A low roll. Wilfred staring down at his blurred hands. His lips twisted where he is biting them.

The gunners apply the portfire to the breeches of the guns. But because the fuses are never of identical length, the explosions are slightly discordant. First the middle cannon and then, almost as one, those on either side. Thunderous in the leaden air.

Explosions. The cannons bucking like horses scared by snakes. The gunners crouching, backs turned to protect themselves as best they can from the residue of the firing. Thick black smoke curling from the barrels of the guns, where there were men just a moment before.

The men have gone.

In their place are mere bits of men.

An arm, as if bitten off just below the shoulder by some savage beast, still attached to a wheel of the third cannon. The lower half of one man, legs folded as though seeking rest, intact some fifty yards from the guns. Pieces that cannot be identified strewn in an arc across an empty section of the square that is changing colour as a crimson mist settles. Oddest of all: fragments of fabric, pieces of clothing, eddying slowly down like paper tossed from the upper storey of a building.

Screaming from some of the women under the parasols. A soldier is ordered into their midst and reappears holding, with hands outstretched, something unidentifiably dark and dripping. The soldier drops his load by the side of the square and crouches, retching.

The Colonel's sabre gleams magnificently in the sunshine. His lips under his splendid white moustache form a thin tight line. I try to fix my gaze on him but cannot help looking away.

Three more times the bloody ritual is repeated. Drumming. Scuffing. Dragging. Firing. It seems that the tempo quickens, as if all concerned want only to get this grim event over as quickly as possible. Perhaps it is just that the drummers have lost their rhythm. Even before the last firing of the cannons, they are one drum short. Wilfred has subsided to the ground, weeping.

I do not cry. I am hollow. Void of feeling. I am glad there are other men on either side of me. They are holding me up; I cannot feel my legs. My nostrils sting with the smell of gunpowder. My ears are full of the cannons' dread thud, women's cries, the shrieks and curses of the prisoners, the gasps of the gunners as their uniforms are sprayed with nameless bits after each firing. I am trying to watch the Colonel, whose expression remains fixed throughout the ceremony, rather than the event being enacted in front of him. And even though the band has stopped, over and over in my head I keep repeating the words of the last hymn it played:

> Soldiers of Christ, arise,
> And put your armour on,
> Strong in the strength which God supplies...

I am a soldier of Christ. A soldier of the Queen. But I have no armour to protect me, just a soiled and threadbare uniform. A uniform spattered crimson after the fourth firing. Something warm and wet thudding against the left side of my face, across my mouth, almost knocking me over.

The boy next to me looks my way. 'Oh Jesus,' he says. 'Lord Jesus.'

I raise my hand to my cheek. I bring it away holding a piece of raw meat.

The band, minus a drummer, is playing once again to mark the end of the ceremony. I know the tune: 'There Is A Green Hill Far Away'.

The Colonel turns his horse around neatly and departs the square at a measured trot. In my mouth is the taste of blood that is not my own. All the strength which God supplies is gone.

I scream and scream and wake up screaming, my bedding damp and rank.

In the early mornings when I awake like this – after Mary or Nora or both of them have wiped my face with wet flannels and quietened me before returning to their slumber – I lie in my room listening to the sounds of the still house.

If the previous day has been hot I hear the wall-boards groaning. I listen to Mary's clock, one of the few family belongings she brought with her from Ireland, trying to slow my breathing in time with its rhythmic ticking. I hear it strike the hour, the half-hour, then the hour again. And in all that time I barely move. Sometimes I light a candle, raise myself with some extra pillows, and try to write. Or I read my most recent entries, which often seem like the scribblings of a stranger.

But there are times when reading and writing hold no appeal for me. Times when I rise, pausing when I am out of the bed until the shaking subsides and I become accustomed to standing again. I relieve myself in the chamber pot, my water the colour of rust in the candlelight, and then, as quietly as I can, walk on bare feet down the corridor to the door leading into the room that Mary shares with her children. I halt in the doorway until the sound of steady breathing reassures me that it is safe to continue.

If they are all sleeping I enter the room, quiet as I can, and approach the end of the bed where the children lie. Mary has her head nearest the fireplace, barren of coal at this time of year. Albert and Grace, aged six and three, lie entwined near Mary's feet. Many times they are off their pillow completely, having shifted in their rest.

I know of nothing more soothing than watching them sleep.

I stand and watch them, barely daring to breathe, guarding the candle flame with my cupped hand. Or, if it is near dawn, waiting until my eyes are accustomed to the weak light and I can discern the children's faces and forms. When it is cool I sometimes pull the sheets over them. But usually they seem not to need any bedding; their nightshirts, pulled into odd patterns, are enough for them.

I have heard them talk in their sleep, heard Grace use words I cannot comprehend as she passes her little hand over her face. But mostly they are quite still. Ineffably peaceful. I look at Albert, his left arm thrown carelessly over his sister, and ponder how different his life will be to mine. At six, like him, I had no father. But his mother, I feel sure, will live well beyond his ninth year. There will be food for him to eat – not the fare of gentlefolk, perhaps, but sufficient – and at fourteen he will not have to travel far beyond the only home he has known. God willing, he will never know a hell like India and experience such madness amongst men, nor see brutality on a scale he could not imagine possible.

Albert, sweet sleeping Albert, never become a soldier.

And Grace, with your head tucked down between your shoulders, what do I wish for you? I wish that you never have a brother whose demise or continued existence is a matter of daily debate in the newspapers. A brother who allows himself to be led into the interior of an untamed continent, far from the ken of civilised people. A brother who was lost and then brought back to a world that would never seem the same to him again.

As I watch over Albert and Grace, my cousin's children, the words of a different hymn come unbidden into my mind. It is a hymn that was a favourite of the Colonel's, though even he recognised it was not a suitable accompaniment to his dreadful ceremonies in the square. A hymn about the Lord God making all things bright and beautiful.

The Lord God made children and the slumber that succours them. But the God who created these sleeping babes also made men who can shoot their fellow creatures from the mouths of cannons. The Creator of streams and shady trees also made barren deserts where thirst turns the tongue to a strip of leather.

And he made camels. The beasts that caused me to travel over the ocean to this dry, flat land.

It all started with camels. And a lie.

Five

'Do you have any experience with camels, soldier?'

'Yes, sir. A little.'

That's what I told him, though all I knew of camels was the dreadful stench they made when dead, their carcasses lying unprotected from the sun in the dirt outside Cawnpore. Near them, bloated corpses of elephants and newly ploughed strips in a field – the hastily dug graves of men. When dogs and scavenging birds got at them, the bodies were exposed and the smell became thicker still in the stifling air.

Some regiments used camels as pack animals, their loads teetering and swaying like coconuts atop palm trees. But our colonel scorned them. They were an Indian beast, he said, and the conflict in which we were engaged represented the assertion of British superiority over a coffee-coloured race.

Now the mutiny was over. A new decade had dawned and Queen Victoria was sovereign still from Delhi in the north to Bangalore and Madras in the south. I was in Kurrachee, on the north-west coast, discharged from the army and trying to recover from the shaking and fevers that racked me. Wondering where the breeze might blow me next. I was barely one-and-twenty but had already lived on two continents and survived a conflict that had taken many others even younger than myself. I had come through, yet felt as brittle as a dry twig.

In the kitbag that carried the sum of my meagre belongings I still had one of poor Wilfred Ponting's drumsticks. The bag was in the tiny room I had taken in the market district, near the docks. On a steamy morning early in April I was at my usual place on the boarding-house porch, where I liked to position a seat in the shade so as to watch the never-ending swirl of people flow by me on the street. There were sailors and traders, stallholders and shysters, women with their heads covered and their children tied one to another so they couldn't stray in the crowd, and religious men engaged in rituals ignored by most who passed them by. I was watching a snake-charmer laying out his mat for a show when I heard a loud and angry voice yelling in English close to where I sat.

'I'm awake to your game, you shameless beggar! You're out to rob me!'

Then I saw him: a heavy-set white man with a broad-brimmed hat and an unkempt beard spilling down his shirt. He was leaning over a native trader who was selling trinkets and stretches of bright-coloured cloth, which were laid out on a blanket on the ground. The trader's eyes were wide with fear and amazement as the stream of abuse continued.

'Two bandannas I paid for. Two! And now you want me to walk away with just the one.' In his left hand the man flourished a small parcel. His right hand was reaching down towards the Indian, who called out urgently in his own dialect. But this seemed only to antagonise his accuser further.

'Stop your damned noise. It means little more to me than monkeys chattering!'

'He says he gave you both,' I put in.

The two men turned on hearing me. The trader, very excited, kept speaking and I understood enough of it to rise from my seat and move to the balcony railing.

'He insists he placed one of the bandannas inside the other,' I said. 'Perhaps if you were to examine the parcel more closely...'

The bearded white man looked at me, straightened up and tugged at his package. I saw a crimson cloth and then, as he pulled further, also a flash of bright blue. He grunted and spat on the dusty ground, narrowly missing the blanket of the trader, who was now trying to pack up his goods. Then the white man moved nearer to me and leaned on the balcony, breathing heavily in the heat.

'A Paddy, eh? Yet you can fathom their language?'

'A bit, sir. Enough to get by.'

'Useful, I'm sure,' he said, studying me closely. 'I swear I find it damned hard work trying to get the duskies to understand me.' He was mopping his face with a bright red handkerchief.

He told me his name was Landells. George Landells. He'd come to the bazaar seeking leather harnesses. The strongest available, he insisted. His breath reeked of onions, which I later learned he crunched like apples to protect himself from Oriental contagions. He was a man inordinately proud of his boots, which were buffed to a sheen even when the rest of his person was scuffed and dirty from the road. Although he said he could never fully trust Indians after their savagery at Delhi and Lucknow, he still affected some of their dress. Over his shirt he wore an embroidered silk jacket, fit for a maharajah, which he claimed to have traded for one of his horses shipped from the colony of New South Wales.

'That's my business, soldier,' he told me. 'Horses. I can sell every horse I bring over in the wake of the mutiny. Or exchange them for the horses with a hump: camels. That's what they now want in Australia. There's an exploration party being put together in the southern colony, biggest thing ever attempted there. Men, wagons, scientists. They want to cross the country from south to north. Some in authority – and I'll wager most of 'em wouldn't know a rock from a root – maintain that camels are just the thing to carry all the gear. I'm not so sure of that. Seems to me that camels are accustomed to sandy deserts; the deserts they're destined for are strewn with stones. But if it's camels they want, camels they'll get from me. And pay damn well for it, too.'

He spat on the ground again, between his feet, neatly avoiding his boots. 'I despise camels myself. Treacherous, stubborn brutes with habits that would make a bawd blush. A kick that can kill a man without his wits about him. But this is the place for them and I'm a businessman. Grafted myself from England onto the dry dirt of a virgin land because I sensed business opportunities. And there are plenty of those, mark my words. There's money to be made by those with eyes to see it. I'll trade silk stockings if there's a demand. 'Tis all the same to me. Ship horses here, take camels back. Plus men to look after them.'

He paused, appraising me as if I were something in a stall for sale. Then came his question. 'Do you have any experience with camels, soldier?'

'Yes, sir. A little.'

The lie that changed my life.

'Well, there's money in it. Good money. A decent wage for a young man like yourself. The committee behind the exploring party has gold money. I'll tell you something . . .' He looked around us as if the nearest stallholder, chewing nuts and appearing likely to succumb to sleep at any moment, might be listening in. 'If I can get this committee the beasts they want, I stand to be one of the top men in their expedition. On a good wage, too. I shall stick them for a salary of six hundred pounds, nothing less. They'll pay it, God's eyes they will. Plus my expenses, for they'll need men like me – and you if you're interested. Who else will take charge of their blessed camels?'

Six hundred pounds! I had never imagined such a salary. Did anyone in the army, even a colonel, earn that sort of money? I knew I'd get nothing like it, but what else was I to do? I was weary of soldiering and the heat and the smells and all the killing and misery I had known. Sick to my bones of India and the 70th Regiment, what remained of it. I had just enough money saved to pay my way out. Now this man Landells with the onion breath and fancy jacket was offering a route away to another continent.

In Kurrachee I had wandered down to the docks and stared out at the ocean, trying to picture distant lands where English was spoken instead of the native jabber that wearied my ears. I thought of South Africa and the promise that lay in a place called the Cape of Good Hope. Thought too of Australia, a vast new country I had heard was populated with strange animals and many of my countrymen.

One lie and it was done.

Landells engaged me for the passage to Melbourne – the name of an English Lord, a place I struggled to find on a map. So the soldier became a camel man, on a level with the coolies and the beasts they attended. I would be useful: after more than six years in India, I had a much better knowledge of the native dialects than Landells, and I warrant he saw in me a man accustomed to taking orders. A man trained not to question authority. During the voyage away from the land of spices and savagery there would be time to learn about camels, just as I had learned about teaching and soldiering. Once we were landed in Melbourne, Landells said, he was confident he could procure for me similar employment with the exploration party.

Exploration! Was there ever a more bizarre idea?

In a country in which I would be a stranger I was to help find places that white people had never seen before. But what else was I to do? I would rot if I remained in Kurrachee, while army life held no future for me.

Our ship was the *Chinsurah*. Creaking timbers. Cooking smells seeping through the cramped sleeping quarters. These smells, however oily or noisome, were preferable to the stench in the hold where Landells had configured his modern-day ark: camels in improvised stalls and, screeching and chattering in a pen, some monkeys that had amused Landells when he spied them in the market. The camels did not travel well. They snorted and belched up their feed and pissed and spat until green muck sluiced around the hold no matter how much straw was laid about.

In Kurrachee Landells had also engaged some Indians and Afghans accustomed to handling camels. As if preferring their own company — and that of the animals — to other passengers, they strung hammocks between beams in a corner of the hold. Heedless of all the aromas, they tended to the beasts between games of dice and dominoes. As long as the animals were looked after, I had no reason to interrupt their recreation.

The senior Indian, Dost Mahomed, a former sepoy in one of the native regiments before the mutiny, took it upon himself to school me in the ways of camels, employing a mixture of his fractured English and my rudimentary Hindi. I noted the way he talked to the camels, the beasts responding to his tone more than the words. And in case his meaning was ever unclear he carried with him a piece of timber the length and heft of a spoke from a carriage wheel. With this he delivered ferocious clouts to the camels' noses, necks or flanks if they were tardy in obeying his instructions. The sound of wood on bone or gristle was startling, but even more impressive was the indifference that greeted these assaults.

On receipt of a crunching blow to the snout, a camel would shake its head, as if more surprised than stunned, and appear to suffer no greater injury than might follow an insect bite. But such treatment produced the desired result. The beast would move as instructed, invariably in a way that suggested it was doing so of its own accord and not because it had been beaten into submission.

Dost Mahomed alternated force with affection. I watched him talking softly to the animals, scratching their noses and stroking their ears. At such times the camels would let their huge, blue-tinged tongues loll in a kind of ecstasy, or close their eyes, their long lashes strangely feminine. But the Indian was always wary of the beasts' long legs. Nothing during the six-week sea voyage caused him more amusement than the sight of one of the other sepoys, Samla, prone in the muck of the stalls and nursing an angry bruise in his side after allowing himself to be caught by a sideways kick from the camel called Landa.

Even when apparently docile, the animals could never be fully trusted. I learned that. Also that no two camels were completely alike. Each had its own personality – timid or tetchy, dominant or submissive. And, just as I was, they were travelling to an unfamiliar land to trek in country the likes of which they had never encountered before. I learned to be wary of their moods, especially if a bull ever got a sniff of a female in season. I learned some of their tricks, such as a propensity to roll on whoever was working alongside them. And I learned that, when unfettered, camels will always wander. But in all the time I came to spend with them I never got used to their rank breath, which made even Landells and his onion fumes smell sweet.

As for Landells himself, he spent most of the journey on deck playing cards, though he found it increasingly difficult to find partners after winning money from the captain and most of his crew. When not at the card table he would take a rag to his boots, applying wax or spit to the leather with the tenderness of a mother washing her babe. Or he would position a chair so he could rest his boots on a railing, looking out at the waves. Sometimes he would sleep thus. Sometimes he would just sit and stare. Sometimes it seemed as if his condition were indeterminately between these two states, especially when he had been taking some of his rum. He left the daily care of the camels to Dost Mahomed, his Indians and myself, appearing indifferent to the welfare of the animals he had travelled so far to obtain. Only once did I see him in the hold itself – early in the voyage, when he wished to satisfy himself that the number of camels tallied with the invoice he was preparing for the committee.

'The Ex-plo-ra-tion Com-mit-tee,' he said derisively, drawing out each syllable of both words. 'The Exploration Committee of the Royal Society of Victoria. Formerly the Philosophical Institute, most of whose members have seldom ventured further afield than an outhouse. Did you ever hear of any exploring worth threepence being done by a committee, soldier?'

He continued to call me that even though I was now in his employ. It made sense, as the few clothes I owned were mostly remnants of my army uniform. And I was still a man taking orders – from Landells now, rather than the Colonel or any of his officers.

Landells, like his camels, seemed content to save his energy. For now, his work was done. Until the *Chinsurah* reached Melbourne there was no cause for him to labour. Perhaps he appreciated that ahead of him lay days and nights of toil and privation, a time when several weeks' idleness on a swaying deck would come to seem like unimaginable luxury. Certainly there was a dramatic change in Landells' mien as soon as the *Chinsurah* came within sight of Melbourne. He slapped his cards together and buttoned them into the breast pocket of his shirt. He hacked at his beard with his clasp-knife, inspecting the results in a small hand-mirror. He spat on his boots and from his trunk produced another Oriental waistcoat even more exotic than the one he had been wearing when first I met him.

It was thus attired, a mixture of dandy and dervish, that he greeted the spectators drawn to the Melbourne docks that morning in June of 1860 when the *Chinsurah* unloaded its bellowing, snorting, sniffing cargo. He was on the camel he called Rajah, leading a parade of beasts away from the dock into the settlement. I was towards the tail of this strange procession, trying to become accustomed to a camel's rolling motion. My slips and sudden lunges at the bridle straps caused constant merriment to Dost Mahomed, riding effortlessly on the camel to my rear.

Because of my uneasy passage, my first impressions of Melbourne were only fragmentary. Wide streets of gravel and dirt. Buildings, two storeys at most, with verandahs like gaping jaws. Painted signs: WAREHOUSEMEN, ROOMS, HABERDASHERY, SMITH AND BLEW: IMPORTERS OF MILLINERY, SUPPLIES, STORES, BOOK BINDING. I had a sense of impermanence, of a place thrown together in haste. There were no fewer than five rickety wooden jetties poking into the rubbish-strewn water of the docks, as if nobody had yet decided which of these might, in time, become more substantial structures. By the jetties were piles of lumber and banged-together huts, many already in service although there was still work to be done on them. In the palaces and massive stone structures of India human figures had seemed insignificant compared to the venerable walls around them. Here in Melbourne men were in a hurry, trying to build a city that was growing to fit their swelling numbers faster than anyone could plan it.

The colours were new. The soft greens of Ireland and the yellows and reds of India had given way to faded hues – shades of grey and brown and cream that appeared to have been too long in the sun. The smells were different again. Something sharp and enticing that I would learn came from the pointy leaves of gum trees. Plus a pungent whiff from the rivulets of refuse and waste water trickling from habitats into gutters, or directly into the town's brown and sluggish river. There was dung in piles on the roadways, left by horses and massive bullocks straining at the halters of drays laden with timber or stones destined for the grander buildings under construction along the main streets. To this scene our strange cavalcade made its own singular contribution: the camels shat their way along the route from the docks, over the Prince's Bridge and into the city.

The arrival of the *Chinsurah* and its odd cargo was evidently quite an event in Melbourne. So many people had assembled to witness our progress that, once our cavalcade was into the city, police were employed to ensure we had a clear passage. The Indian coolies had dressed for the occasion, wearing turbans of red and white not seen during the voyage. Landells had contemplated donning a turban himself before concluding it might be deemed unduly frivolous by those gentlemen he was seeking to impress. On Rajah, whom he rode with ease, he made do with his gaudy jacket and tipped his hat at the ladies. As if also on his best behaviour, Rajah dipped his long neck, though this was only to ascertain if the spectators had anything edible with them.

Although I heard some urchins mocking my uneasy carriage, I doubt that people paid me much mind at all. I was the drabbest figure in the parade. The best I could manage as a festive touch was a blue kerchief knotted around my neck. And mine was not a face or name anyone knew. Besides, it was camels, not people, the spectators had come to see: these huge, humped beasts with their yellow teeth and lolling tongues that supposedly carried the key that would unlock the secrets of the Australian interior.

We were all of us upstaged by camels.

Even on the day of the departure of the expedition, some two months after our arrival on the *Chinsurah*, camels caused the most excitement and problems. Their alien smell and noises upset the horses. And the loading of the beasts, stacking and securing their cargoes, was the main reason that no progress was made until more than three hours after the scheduled starting time. As spectators grew bored and dignitaries, awaiting their cue for speeches, sweated in their formal attire, the police had increasing difficulty keeping people away from all the equipment and pack animals. One of the camels came adrift from its companions and went running amongst the crowd, lips turned back in what could equally have been a grin or a grimace. Before it could be caught and subdued, it caused havoc in the horse pens and panic amongst the assembled women. But most people, especially those not in the runaway's immediate precinct, welcomed the entertainment as some relief from the tedium.

This breakaway now seems like a portent of the camels' contrariness. I ended up in charge of them: I came to know their moods. When we finally left the Royal Park late on that August afternoon, we had with us twenty-six camels. More camels than horses. More camels than people, coolies included. And many of them more trouble than they were worth. South of Balranald, not even a month into our journey, one of them grabbed Ludwig Becker the naturalist by the seat of his trousers and hoisted him into the air with an evil gurgle. We all learned some German oaths that day, until the doctor's trousers gave way and he was dropped face first in the dust, silencing his abuse of this vexatious species. Poor Becker – the old gentleman had joined the expedition as its scientist, his greatest desire being to unveil some of the mysteries of his adopted country, but he found himself drafted into the loading and unloading of beasts that treated him as a plaything.

At night, any camels left unfettered wandered away. Whole days were wasted searching for animals that would inevitably be found mimicking the furtive expressions of truant schoolboys.

And every evening Landells doled out rum to the camels. He insisted it was good for them, warding off the scurvy and other ailments that could slow them down. I saw no proof of that, but no patients ever accepted their medicine with such lip-smacking enthusiasm.

The rhythm of our movement was dictated by the camels. As we headed towards Swan Hill I heard Becker plead with Landells to call a brief break, for he was feeling faint.

'I cannot stop,' Landells replied. 'Loaded camels won't rise again when allowed to lie down.'

There was much rain in the early months of the expedition. Bred for sand, the camels struggled wheezing and groaning through mud and running streams. Landells, no longer with a ship's deck to use as a sanctuary from his charges, became increasingly short-tempered and surly, even though, as he had hoped, he was a leading man in the expedition. Second in command.

'Three cheers for Mr Landells and the officers!' the Lord Mayor had cried out when we left Melbourne.

Landells, without his Oriental waistcoat this time, doffed his hat.

But as we laboured north, our progress slowed by poor weather and mishaps, it seemed as if all those reservations he had expressed about camels were being borne out. Yet even as spirits sank and his mood more and more resembled that of his humped charges, Landells strove to maintain some of the swagger he had shown on our disembarkation from the *Chinsurah*. He continued to lavish more attention on his boots than on the animals. South of Kerang, when our slow-moving caravan was mired by torrential rain, we spent the night grateful for the shelter provided by hospitable squatters. Landells placed his boots in the chimney so that the warmth from the dying fire might dry them. But the nocturnal deluge was unusually fierce, and he awoke to find his prized footwear awash. To dry them, he employed a technique I had never seen before, dropping glowing chunks of charcoal from the rekindled fire inside the boots until there was no more moisture to evaporate. He did this in the slow, methodical manner of a watchmaker.

So when I first noticed that Landells' boots were showing signs of disrepair and neglect, I knew that all of his original dash had been dissipated by the daily tedium, our tardy progress, and the disagreements between the leading men that were an inevitable consequence of this.

By the time we reached Menindie, four months into the expedition, Landells had left us. But to this day I have reason to be grateful to that avaricious Englishman, to whom every new dawn represented another commercial opportunity. It was our chance meeting in Kurrachee that led to my being hired as a camel man on a salary of one hundred and twenty pounds — surely enough for a start in a new country when the exploring was done with.

And it was George Landells who introduced me to my leader.

July 1860. Royal Park. Where the expedition is being assembled. Where the camels have been requartered after being housed in temporary stables near the colony's new Parliament House. Where I have been living under canvas, my main responsibility being to prevent curious locals from coming too close to the camels.

Landells has told me he is awaiting an opportunity to speak on my behalf to the expedition's leader, a former inspector of police from Castlemaine, in central Victoria. But he is proving to be a devilishly hard fellow to catch. A man in perpetual motion. So it seems appropriate that my first sighting of the man whose fate will become entwined with my own is not so much a face or a figure as a blur.

He passes by on horseback and dismounts before his steed has fully stopped. He leaps off, dropping the reins over the head of his mount, which proceeds to sniff for feed in the scuffed surface of the trod-upon park. He appears to be apologising for his late arrival to suited men from the Exploration Committee who have been waiting for him. I observe him from the back, shaking hands, banging shoulders, even bowing extravagantly as if to reinforce a point he makes. I hear a burst of laughter and watch the manner of the committee men change in the face of this effusive onslaught.

John Macadam, the tall, red-headed secretary of the committee, who had been checking his pocket-watch and shaking his head impatiently only minutes earlier, is now smiling indulgently at his head explorer and sharing a joke with him. I see Macadam remove a document from a satchel and present it to the leader as if its contents are of the utmost importance. Barely glancing at it, Mr Burke crumples it into the back pocket of his trousers, which are held up by a pair of sagging suspenders. He makes a gesture that suggests to these gentlemen he has no time to study its contents forthwith. He has too much else to do.

The committee men, surprised to find themselves dismissed so abruptly, shake hands once again with the man in whom they have invested so much faith and return to their waiting carriage. The leader moves to remount his horse, which is now sniffing suspiciously at the breeze blowing from the direction of the camel pens. But he is stopped by Landells, who has seen his opportunity and hurried ahead, urging me to follow without delay.

'Quickly, man. Before the bastard's off again.'

I stand ten feet distant, trying to maintain a respectful gap between myself and these men who are determining my immediate future, observing but only imperfectly hearing their exchange.

The leader has his back to me once more, his left hand holding the reins of his horse. Landells does most of the talking. He nods in my direction. The leader momentarily turns towards me but I catch nothing more than a glimpse of beard and flashing eyes beneath his broad-brimmed headgear. Then a quick nod. Agreement seems to have been reached, another item of business attended to. Landells signals that I should come forward. Clutching my hat, I approach.

He wheels around. Eyes of the palest blue locking on mine and then scanning all of me. I take the hand he thrusts forward. It holds mine in a tight grasp that is maintained longer than I expect, as though this, too, is a kind of test. And then he speaks, his voice surprisingly gentle.

'A soldier, eh?'

'Yes, sir. The 70th Regiment of Foot, sir. In India.'

'Saw action in the mutiny, I hear.'

'Yes, sir. At Peshawar. And Cawnpore.'

'I envy you, soldier. There are few things more glorious than fighting for your sovereign. But this is one of them – unlocking the secrets of an unknown land, bringing glory to Queen and colony.' His eyes never leave mine. I find it hard to hold his gaze. And when I waver under his stare I notice a scar high across one of his cheeks and a tangle of spit in the beard under his lower lip.

He considers me again. 'Not much of you, is there? How tall d'you stand?'

'Five feet and two inches, sir. Actually, an inch and three-quarters.'

'Every bit could help, soldier. Small stature, small stomach. Supplies may run short, in which case I'd rather fill a pint pot than a gallon jar. And Landells tells me you've proved yourself adept with the camels –'

Landells himself interrupts on my behalf. 'Learning all the time, Burke. And he can converse with the coolies.'

The eyes swivel towards my superior. '*Mister* Burke, if you please, Landells.'

The Englishman takes a step back as if struck, unaccustomed to this tone. And then the leader returns his attention to me. 'I am Robert O'Hara Burke. You are?'

'King, sir, Mr Burke. John King.'

'King? An appropriate name for a soldier of Her Majesty. How old are you, King?'

'One-and-twenty, Mr Burke. Twenty-two this coming December.'

He swings away from us, surveying the park but seeming to look far beyond it as he makes a sweeping gesture with one hand. 'By which time we should be well on our way to the Gulf. 'Tis a fine thing to be so young, in sound health, and undertaking such a grand adventure.'

His mind is made up. He turns, wanting to move on. One boot is already in a stirrup. 'You have your assistant, Landells.'

Another handshake, more peremptory than before. The matter under debate has been settled. His parting words: 'You'll do me, King. You'll do me.'

And then he is gone. Turning with a nod, remounting his horse and dashing away through the park in the direction of the city. Leaving behind him Landells, surlier than before, and, in the air where he has been, a lingering scent of sweat, leather, and something unmistakable but decidedly incongruous.

Women's perfume.

Six

'Look, John, it's Abraham Lincoln.'

A tall, upright figure made to seem even taller by the stovepipe hat he is wearing. He has been depicted as if speaking – one hand extended, reinforcing a point, the other tucked into the front of a black waistcoat. It is not a bad likeness, though the late president's beard is patently black fluff pasted onto his face, which has an odd yellowish hue. Beside Lincoln, in keeping with contemporary taste for all things ghoulish, is his murderer, John Wilkes Booth. No attempt has been made to replicate his heinous act in Ford's Theatre these six years past. Instead, Booth, a small, fine-featured individual with a neat moustache, is amongst the crowd listening to this finest of orators. Only a disdainful expression on Booth's face and the way he seems to be turning away from Lincoln suggest the dark scheming in his mind.

Nora studies the figure, glances at me, then looks back at Booth. 'Isn't that odd. The assassin looks a little like you.'

'Surely not. The same height, perhaps, that's all.'

'More than that, I think. But don't fret on it. There's more to see. Here, the Civil War hero, Ulysses S. Grant.'

Nora guides me to the other side of the Hall of Leaders. President Grant, all whiskers and dark brooding brows, appears oppressed by the burdens of his office. By contrast, the English

Prime Minister, William Gladstone, seems more relaxed, though of a suitably serious demeanour. As if in deference to the historical enmity between their two countries, there is a respectful distance between Gladstone and Napoleon Bonaparte. The model-maker — maybe Mr Heinrichs himself, whose waxworks museum this is — has portrayed the Corsican as a short, stout man at the height of his powers, Emperor of France and much of Europe, one hand resting on a globe of the world as if considering new countries to conquer.

In such august company the figure of Sir Henry Barkly, KCB, is rather incongruous, but it seems that Heinrichs is keen to have local representation in his figures. And so the former Governor of Victoria stands much as I recall him, a full-faced figure wearing an extravagant cravat, his hair brushed over lush whiskers. Nora pauses.

'Do you remember him, John?'

I remember. A musty smell. A handshake. His hands soft and white. While I was faint and fearful I might fall even as he addressed me: 'I suppose you were in a very reduced state when you were at Cooper's Creek with the blacks?'

'Yes, sir, very much.'

Nora keeps glancing at me to judge my condition, although she must get a much better idea of this from the extent to which I have to lean on her as we move about the museum. We stop often to rest on the seats Heinrichs has thoughtfully placed for patrons in his waxworks attraction on the St Kilda Esplanade. It is not, I have heard, as splendid as Madam Sohier's famous city establishment in Elizabeth Street, or the recently reopened Kreitmaver's Waxworks in Bourke Street East, which advertises exhibits of giants and dwarfs as well as its gruesome Criminals' Room. But it is popular with those, like ourselves, who have come to the Esplanade for diversion on a sunny afternoon.

This is my first outing from the house in Octavia Street for a month or more. Doctor Treacey has urged me to inhale deeply the salt breezes from the bay: an antidote to all prevalent miasmas, he swears. And although the day is warm he insisted that I be covered with a blanket during the carriage trip from our home, which I found far less taxing than anticipated.

I suspect that Albert and Grace have enjoyed the journey more than the waxworks. They are too young to be interested in generals or emperors, and Mary is adamant that they be allowed nowhere near the Hall of Horrors, devoted to some of the colony's most notorious murderers and their victims. Now, having shown the children some kings and queens, she has taken them outside in search of ices and perhaps a donkey ride near the beach. If the donkeys are absent, there is amusement to be had watching intrepid souls using the cumbersome bathing machines drawn down to the water's edge.

There is now just one part of Heinrichs' museum we have not visited. Nora glances at me; I softly squeeze her arm. 'It's fine,' I tell her. 'Let's take a look.'

'If you say so, John. But I'll not let you stay if it distresses you.'

And so we enter the Hall of Explorers.

There they are. Men whose exploits Mr Burke studied in preparation for the expedition. 'Learn from the past, King,' the leader said to me. 'Learn from the past and apply its lessons to the present. Learn from the mistakes as much as the triumphs.'

Augustus Gregory. Bearded, dark — rather in the fashion of General Grant — who charted the Victoria and Roper rivers in the north. Charles Sturt, a smaller man than I'd imagined. Presented as confident, resolute, scanning an unseen horizon. Not the man who returned with his eyes ravaged and skin blackened after his final trip into the interior. And there — the German, Ludwig Leichhardt. Thin, stooped, aloof. Wearing a gentleman's cravat. Staring into the distance. A keeper of secrets.

'He vanished, King. Good men went looking for him and found nary a trace. It was as if he'd been swallowed whole by the deserts he sought to cross. Or struck down by the Lord for his arrogance in trying to conquer His creation.'

Nora tightens her grip on my arm. 'Look, John. Oh look.'

Black bunting around the diorama. A title in elaborate Gothic lettering across the top: 'Our Heroes'. A crimson rope extended across the front to prevent a crush of spectators coming too close. But there are no other spectators this hour, just Nora and myself. Only us to study the tableau, which is a more elaborate presentation than the others.

An attempt has been made to place the figures in a natural setting. Sand, some branches and several rocks have been positioned. Also a pair of rather scruffy birds of indeterminate species — probably parrots, although it is hard to say with certainty — which look to have been obtained from one of the cheaper taxidermists rather than the new Natural History Museum. The birds have been placed on a horizontal branch from which some dry leaves droop, and appear to be looking at the two bearded figures below them.

Just two figures. Although there were three of us there.

The first is depicted standing with a scrap of paper in his right hand. Near his boots is a bottle and a depression in the sand. On the side of the diorama from which the branch extends is a painted tree. Upon this — in very large letters, so as to be visible to spectators unable to obtain a vantage point near the crimson rope — is the word 'DIG' and a date, 'April 21st, 1861'. The figure, hat pushed back on his head so as not to obscure his features, is looking upwards as if seeking reassurance from the heavens. The news in the paper is clearly not good, but his expression is one of defiance rather than despair.

The second figure, of smaller stature than the first, is crouching head down near his companion. His face is turned towards the front but the modeller has been liberal with the whiskers, so only some of his features are visible. His eyes are closed, suggesting either prayer or exhaustion. One hand is holding a bound book of some sort, the other is raised so as to rest on the knee of the other man. It is a gesture of fellowship and support. This pair is in a fix, but they are not giving up. They are resolute white men in an untamed interior.

The taller one, it must be surmised, is Mr Burke. His companion can only be W. The scene is undoubtedly that which has come to be regarded as the climax of their story — *our* story — the return from the Gulf to find the expedition's relief party gone. Instead of men and succour, we found only a message and an inadequate cache of provisions.

The waxwork-modeller has probably based his figures on Charles Summers' city monument, which is now some six years old. Perhaps he had no idea that Summers strove for an idealised representation of the protagonists and the virtues they represented, rather than individual likenesses. And it seems the modeller also took heed of Mr Burke's summation of this event in his last despatch to the committee, as reported in the newspapers: 'Greatly disappointed at finding the party here gone.'

Greatly disappointed? The leader cursed. He tore at the tree with his broken nails. He sank to the ground with a ghastly wail and sobbed. I had never heard such unearthly sounds. It was some time before he could compose himself sufficiently to speak. I watched him, wanting not to listen, awaiting an order.

And W? There was no journal in his hand, not then, but the sculptor has one thing right. He was on the ground. We all were. Our legs were quite spent. W was a man in prayer, addressing his father rather than God.

The scene I am surveying in this hall, with Nora nearby watching me, bears little relation to what actually happened. Yet my memories are like one of those kaleidoscopes parents buy for their children from vendors on the Esplanade. They change with the light and angle of viewing. Shake it, and you see a different picture altogether. Even so, this diorama is as distant from the reality I recall as Melbourne is from Menindie.

Never mind that I am missing. In the public's mind this was *their* expedition, not mine. And this, so people think, was the pivotal episode in the drama: the 'DIG' tree. But there is no smell here. No stench of sweat and despair and spent animals. We reeked as badly as the dried meat we gnawed like starving dogs.

There are no sounds. I remember birds, their cries echoing Mr Burke's unearthly wails. Pelicans and crows and parakeets. And always insects thrumming and rats scuttling over fallen twigs and bark. The breeze moving through dead leaves. Frogs droning in still ponds, falling silent only when our footfall came too close.

And the light. Such a strange light. Like the yellow-grey glow that casts no shadows just before a storm. It was about half past seven in the evening when we reached the tree at the abandoned depot and found the message. I remember the light was like a pearl. The place seemed completely different to when we had left it early in the morning more than four months before. But was it only the light, or had it already struck us that this could be the last place on earth we might ever see? I cannot say. But it didn't look or smell or sound like this diorama.

I feel Nora's hand on mine. 'Are you all right, John? You've fallen terribly quiet.'

'I'm sorry...' I reply. 'But this is like a place I've never seen before. Somewhere I've never been.'

I note that Howitt is not featured in this exhibition, though few could dispute the merit of his claims for inclusion. Should I tell him of this when I reply to his recent letter asking if I've considered any of his questions about the blacks? Probably not. His omission might vex him, though he professes to be a man who puts little store in public recognition of his achievements. I suspect he would regard these displays as mere fripperies.

'Shall we go now?' Nora asks. 'Mary and the children will be waiting outside.'

'One moment. Look. There's one more.'

The Scot. John McDouall Stuart. Whose journeys were strangely entwined with those of Mr Burke. Who tried and failed and continued to venture forth until, finally, he crossed the continent and came back. The effort nearly killed him, but he lived. Stuart returned to tell his own story. In one of those macabre twists of fate, he returned to Adelaide at the same time as the pathetic remains of Mr Burke and W, all that Howitt could find to disinter from the sands of the Cooper, were passing through the South Australian capital on their melancholy trek back to Melbourne.

Stuart too declared himself perfectly successful in his endeavours. But at what cost?

Here in the Hall of Explorers most of the adventurers are depicted with the sap of excitement rising in their veins. Even Leichhardt seems in fine health and appears not to doubt where he is. Mr Burke and W are shown in a moment of torment, but their carriage suggests a valiant refusal to surrender to their fate. Yet Stuart has been portrayed as a broken man. He is in civilian dress and looks very old. White-haired. White-bearded. One eye almost closed and the other strangely cloudy. He is frail, not triumphant. I can only assume that Heinrichs has presented him thus in deference to the lingering sense of competitiveness between the two colonies, Victoria and South Australia, over the race to cross the continent. A contest between Stuart, a Scot who favoured horses, and Mr Burke, an Irishman lumbered with a cavalcade of camels.

'He looks defeated,' says Nora, as if reading my thoughts.

'Yet he was supposedly the victor.'

'Was there really a race, John?'

Not officially. But papers and journals discussed it, published poems and cartoons about it. The Exploration Committee was obsessed with it. This was to be a Victorian triumph. Damn the South Australians and their Scot. And the unseen figure of Stuart was like a burr in Mr Burke's shirt, an irritant he could never shake free.

Evening camp. Swan Hill.

'He's to go again, King. The Scot. The drunkard. I have heard from Macadam that Stuart will get money to make another attempt. He knows the way, King, he knows the way. And look at the map! He has less ground to cover. Nor, I suspect, will he be burdened with so much baggage. Or scientists. Did a botanist ever discover anything worth his boot leather? I have resolved to tell them – our twin Bs, the doctor and the naturalist – that there will be no time for science from now on. Beckler and Becker can be working men, like the rest. They will trim their supplies and I care not how much they bleat about anything left behind. If they cannot stick it, they can fall back. But I'll not wait for them, I want us to be like soldiers from now on. March light, march fast.'

Mr Burke is pacing about. Gesturing so that tea is leaping from his tin mug.

'John McStubborn Stuart. I don't know if he can do it. He craves drink, King. When the craving gets too strong he turns back. But he keeps trying. There's a relentlessness in his blood. A Scot's refusal to accept defeat. Which is why I must respect him as an adversary. Y'know your Shakespeare, King? What did they teach you at the Hibernian School in Dublin? Consider the Scottish play. Final Act, the climax, Macbeth to Macduff: "Of all men else I have avoided thee..."'

Now he is like an actor mimicking a sword fight, thrusting with his mug, completely emptied.

'"Of all men else..." But I'll not avoid you, drunkard! Lay on, Stuart, "and damn'd be him that first cries, Hold, enough!"'

'What happened, sir? Between Macbeth and Macduff?'

'They fought it out, man.' Leaping and turning, kicking over a stool. 'A fight to the death. And Macbeth was slain.'

He stops. Puffing mightily after his exertion. Chest heaving. Landells and some of the other men have come to discern the source of the ruckus. W peers out from his tent, looking concerned. Mr Burke repeats what he's just said as if hearing the words for the first time. '"And Macbeth was slain..."'

Mary, Grace and Albert are sitting in the shade of some palm trees near the entrance to the waxworks museum when Nora and I emerge. The children, their tunics stained with flavoured ices, are chattering about donkeys. Our driver, surly after being awoken from his slumber in a quiet place near the gardens, opens the carriage door so we can settle ourselves, Mary and her children along one bench seat, Nora and myself facing them. The horse, bothered by flies, twitches its head.

Mary instructs the driver to take the long route back to Octavia Street, via the foreshore. He doesn't object; it could be worth a few extra pennies to him. And for all of us this is a rare outing. Who knows when we may have another? We set off, the carriage wheels crunching gravel, small bells on the horse's bridle jingling.

Even after ten years I still find it odd to travel like this, to be carried along rather than trudge beside equally weary animals. It reminds me of the slow journey back from the interior with Howitt and his party after they rescued me. Then I was like a fragile piece of cargo to be wrapped up and nursed along the trip. Sometimes I had to be strapped to one of the horses, being too weak to hold on by myself. In my mind that journey is like a book with pages torn out. Whole sections of the story are missing, though I recall the movement — a swaying motion that often lulled me into slumber. Lurching over stones and fallen branches. Amidst the discomfort a pleasing sense of no longer needing to make any decisions about my destiny. None of it was up to me now.

I have a similar feeling today as the carriage takes us down towards the water. Past the mansions, painted white, of the wealthy people on the hill. On the beach, which smells of seaweed, a pair of fishermen are tossing a net into the water. Nearby a small group of natives in mismatched items of clothing — one of the women has her pendulous breasts only barely covered by a gentleman's waistcoat that might once have had a tartan pattern — are chattering amongst themselves. But when the fishermen haul their net in, I suspect they'll suddenly find some extra helpers, hoping to cadge a fish or two. Perhaps Howitt should come here and learn about the way of life of natives who have watched a settlement spread ever wider, like a river in flood, over their forebears' land.

Our carriage continues along the track until we are opposite the St Kilda pier, which extends like a multi-legged insect into the sea. Along the pier are amusement stalls and vendors selling trinkets and sweets. A schooner, its sail a vast triangle, is passing the end of the pier, heading towards Williamstown. The road heads inland not far from here. At Mary's instruction, the driver pauses so we can see the bluff — Point Ormond, in Elwood, with its beacon for vessels on its summit. On sunny weekends, St Kilda to the point has become a popular walk for people taking exercise. I couldn't do it now, not even on one of my better days.

I walked most of the way across this continent, but now struggle to last more than a few hundred yards before the breathlessness or coughing and that strange sensation of weakness overtakes me. If I were an animal I'd get a bullet and be left behind.

Nora seems captivated by the scene before us: the pier and wave-capped sea and the ship under sail. She reaches across the carriage and takes Mary's hand. 'Remember when you arrived – how we came to meet you? Like a lost lamb you were, all alone and blinking in the light.'

Mary smiles. 'Course I remember. I'd never felt or seen sun like it. And I feared you were going to fall, running so fast towards me in yer best boots.' She shakes her head and then seems to become aware of my silence. 'Penny for your thoughts, John?'

'I was thinking that what you're talking of was before my time. Before I came back.'

'And what of the exhibition? Y'were in there long enough. Worth the twopence admission?'

'Heinrichs has earned his money. But it's odd the way the past is presented.'

'What ever do you mean?' Mary asks, reaching forward to tuck the blanket over my legs. Nora, meanwhile, is trying to quieten Albert and Grace, who want to comment on all they can see from the carriage: waves and seabirds and a man charging people for a look through his telescope.

'Booth, for example. Just a commonplace actor, wasn't he? But because he was the president's assassin his name is remembered and his likeness put on display along with emperors and generals.'

'There's always a grisly fascination in such things, John.'

'I know it. But there's a tendency to ascribe the shaping of complex events to one or two individuals. Think of the way the expedition has been commemorated.'

Mary casts a puzzled look at Nora, who says, 'John isn't in the waxworks display —'

'That's not what I mean,' I interject. 'The scene it depicts was influenced — you might even say caused — by two men who rarely figure in any telling of the story. But without them I'll wager there wouldn't ever have been a "DIG" tree. And Mr Burke could still be alive...'

The two women exchange glances again, concerned that I'm once more working myself up. And perplexed by what I'm saying.

'Two men?' says Mary. 'Yourself and...?'

'Not me at all. Gray. And Patten.'

They don't respond immediately. Both Mary and Nora have read the accounts, though they know I went for years when I found it difficult to speak about any of it at all. It was like a wound that needed time to heal.

'I know of Gray,' says Nora finally. 'Charley Gray. He were with you on the trek to the Gulf. Didn't he perish before you reached the depot?'

'Just four days before we got back. When we were only about seventy miles distant. We spent most of a day trying to dig a grave. We were weak, the ground was stony and hard, but Mr Burke insisted we should try to give him a Christian burial.' The stores and houses are passing in a blur. 'I think he might have felt some guilt about the way he'd treated him.'

'Guilt?' asks Mary.

'None of us appreciated that Charley was as sick as he made out. We thought he was no worse than we were ourselves. Thought he was gammoning. He stole some flour, remember? And Mr Burke remonstrated with him. Struck him.'

'That didn't kill him, surely? But if you hadn't stopped to bury him, the depot party wouldn't have left by the time you got back. Is that your point?'

'We could have made it. But Charley died and we buried him. If we hadn't done that, Mr Burke would still be alive, as sure as the children here love donkeys.'

'Hush now,' says Nora, taking my hand. 'You can never be sure. Had Charley Gray still been with you, your progress to the depot would have been slower anyway.'

Mary is frowning. 'And Patten? Which one was he? I don't remember a Patten.'

Nobody remembers William Patten.

Early morning on the Cooper. December 1860. A stillness that is a portent of the heat to come. Parakeets noisy in the trees, attending to their business before the air becomes an oven. Along the creek and into the distance, the colours all merge into one another. Water becomes soil. Soil becomes air. It is as if we were heading off towards the painted backdrop of a theatrical production. And we have no way of knowing what we will find when we pass through the canvas at the back of the stage.

Mr Burke has split the party once again. He, W, Gray and myself are to head north to the Gulf, travelling light. We will take with us just one horse, Billy, and six camels. They are to be my responsibility. The other four in our group, which has now established a depot on the Cooper, are to remain behind and await our return. William Brahe, Thomas McDonough and the Indian, Dost Mahomed, seem not to mind this division of responsibility. Their lot will surely be easier than ours. We must push further than white men have ever been before. They have a tolerable camp here, ample supplies, and the means to take fish and even ducks. The natives may cause them problems, although they have not so far proved unduly vexatious. I suspect they will have more difficulties with the rats, which have become so fearless and voracious that all supplies must be parcelled up and suspended from trees.

But the fourth man, Patten the blacksmith, is inconsolable. He is weeping when Mr Burke calls the group together to issue instructions and shake hands and make his farewells with those who will stay. Patten does not release his grip on the leader's hand. He slumps forward and breaks down. The rest of us are embarrassed by this unmanly show of emotion. We attend to baggage and tighten girths rather than watch his sniffling. Patten is older than I am, yet crying like a child.

'Mr Burke. Please, sir. Me too. Let me come along . . . I'll do whatever you ask of me. But don't order me . . . to . . . stay.' His words come out between choking sobs.

Mr Burke seems unsure whether to console Patten or clout him. He releases his hand and produces a handkerchief, the one he sometimes knots around his neck when it is hot. The one which, and it is possible I am the only one who knows this, he sometimes splashes with the women's perfume he carries with him in a small glass phial. I have spied him, alone at night, holding the fabric thus treated to his face. 'A harmless reminder of one of the finer aspects of civilisation, King — communion with the fairer sex. If I can't touch her, I can smell her, eh?'

He thinks better of the handkerchief. Replaces it in a pocket of his breeches and moves closer to speak with Patten. 'Come on, man. You must not fret; I shall be back in three months.' He pauses, as if considering something that hadn't occurred to him before.

'And if I am not back in a few months you may go away to the Darling.'

Worse now. Patten is on the ground before the leader. On his haunches. Begging. W, aghast, takes a step forward, as if intent on pulling the blacksmith up on his feet and back into line. Mr Burke raises a hand to stay him.

Patten does not cease his babbling. 'Please, I... beg you. I want to be... part of it. Want to remain with you. Don't... make me stay.'

Mr Burke's manner becomes more brusque. He wants to be away. 'Enough, man. We each have our part to play. Your skills are needed here. There is still work to be done on the depot, and the horses will need to be shod. We must all get our jobs done and then meet up again — here, at the depot.'

'Never. I'll never see you again. Any of you... Leave me here and I will die. I know it.'

Mr Burke is silent. We all are. Death is unmentionable. It lurks in the darkness beyond the camp like an animal we can hear stirring but never see. Patten's outburst has turned our leavetaking into something unpleasant that is now cut short. The leader steps back from Patten, who slumps forward on the sand, and gives a gesture that is both a wave of dismissal and a salute.

The last thing we hear as we head along the bank of the creek is the screeching of birds. And Patten's forlorn cry. *Never...*

Seven

Nora

He were the runt of the litter. The youngest, the smallest, a quiet one. Lost his da when but six months old. All he had of him after that were a uniform jacket still hanging in a cupboard and some lead soldiers, the only things his da left him. And the smell of his tobacco what had seeped into the furniture. A lot less furniture after the bad winter, when most of the chairs went into the fire.

Four brothers he had. And me, the big sister. His brothers never paid him much mind, they had each other for fun. He were like a pup struggling to keep up with their games, wanting to join in. But his ma doted on him, her last one, and with his da gone there would be no more. She clung to John, doing what she could for him, making the move from Moy in County Tyrone to Dublin in the hope of more work. Sitting up late, straining to see in the candlelight, darning trousers that had already done for his brothers so he could cover his bony rump at school. Hands bleeding from the needle pricks.

Then she were gone too. With him but nine, a scrawny thing in too-big breeches, already with that faraway look in his eyes. Tracing with his fingers the letters on the stone in the cemetery. 'Ellen, Beloved Wife of Henry'. Ellen who were worn down by tiredness and loss of hope. Me all of fifteen and now the eldest.

I tried to take her place. Kept up her wash, took in some more for extra pennies. My hands grew twice as old as the rest of me. I were like one of our grey sheets being forced through the wringer. But then there were less wash, less pennies, less food. Even the potatoes gone. Not enough for four boys growing up too fast. I couldn't hold them for long.

Hannigan our landlord were a good man. He knew how it went with us. Let it go for a while when I were late with the rent money. For he reckoned I would pay when I had it. But then came a time when I didn't have it. Couldn't make it up though I tried. Even with the boys carting the peat and all.

— I'm sorry Nora, Hannigan said, and he had no need to say the rest for I'd been waiting for the words. You'll have to go, child.

Though I hadn't been a child since before Ma went.

— Do you have anywhere to stay?

Aunt Catherine Richmond, Da's sister. She took us in, across the town from where we were. It were a long hike for John to get to school but he liked his school, he were a reader. John had a place to sleep, not a proper bed, in the hall. I shared a room with my cousin Mary and learned to live without taking up much space. Knocked on doors for whatever work could be done, Mary too, but most everyone were doing it as hard as us.

His brothers never made the move. We were blown apart like chaff in the breeze. One went to sea. One drowned in Limerick in ten feet of water, paid a penny to impress his girl in a rowboat and never told her he couldn't swim. The others went to be soldiers like their da in the army. Damn fools, both of them. They thought soldiering a grand game and went to war. With me never even knowing where Crimea were. All I had heard of were Sister Nightingale. I prayed for her to look after the King boys William and Samuel if ever they came into her care.

We got a letter from them when John were but fourteen, just a lad, not even fuzz on his face. A letter no more than a page long passed on to us from address to address. The boys made being soldiers seem like such an adventure. Brass buttons, guns, people talking strange languages. And soon they would be off to India, where it were never cold and rich men rode elephants and food were full of spices. I knew John were lost to me when he read the letter. He read it again and again, closer than any text from school. He were gone even before he saw the notice tacked to the porch of the Town Hall. The 70th Regiment wanted recruits.

He must have lied about his age to get in. John were always good at lies. Like he believed them himself. He could look you straight in the face, eyes all wide and innocent, if there were something he wanted. Food, a favour, books. Now he wanted to go away.

I tried to keep him. Told him to finish his schooling so he'd have better prospects than my own, but the army offered him more. Places he'd never seen, his first pay, meals three times a day, mayhap a chance to see his brothers again. The boy without a da would have generals to guide him.

He were surprised I wept when he went to go. The runt of the litter now running away.

— Hush, sis, he said. We'll see each other again. Just you wait and see.

I thought it another of his lies.

Then he were away, taking with him all I could give. Half a loaf and a shilling I'd been trying to keep. His quick kiss on my cheek like the wings of a butterfly had brushed me.

I never heard from him, never knew for sure where he'd got to. If he wrote at all I never saw anything, and I left just a few years later myself. There were nothing to keep me now, no Da or Ma and the brothers all scattered. Ireland itself were sinking in sorrow. No food, no future.

It were Mary who saw the notice first at the post office. The colony of New South Wales were offering assisted passage to young women, wanted for places as domestic servants and governesses. In the schoolhouse Mary and I cleaned three times a week we found a map on the wall.

— Look, said Mary. How far away it is! New South Wales. Clear over the other side of the world from us. And what a peculiar shape, like a rabbit hunched over asleep.

A big place it were. With names only on the edges of the map, British names. Melbourne. Sydney. Brisbane. And no names, not anything, in the middle. Just an empty space.

I wanted Mary to come with me but she said she had to stay with my Aunt Catherine, her ma.

— Tell me how it is, she said. Then I might come join you. Who knows, perhaps the gentlemen are all rich and handsome and lonely in this New South Wales.

She were laughing as she said it. Laughing until the pair of us were crying, holding on tight.

I'd never left Ireland, never been on a ship before, and now I were leaving to go over the ocean clear across the map. Mary gave me a bonnet when we parted. I'd need it for the sun, she said. The last I saw of her, hurrying away so I wouldn't see her face, were a small figure pulling her shawl up over her head against the misty rain. The rain that would surely keep falling until even the Irish clouds had no tears left to weep.

It all turned to water. Soggy sky above, grey sea below, and no way of saying where one started and t'other ended. For weeks after leaving Portsmouth that's how the whole world seemed to be, grey and heaving and wet. I saw a lot of the sea doing some heaving of me own, hanging onto the railing. There were times, wrung out like a dishrag, when I thought of letting slip the rails and sliding into those angry waves, just to be done with it. Sure to God there could be nothing still inside of me.

A dismal lot we were. Women throwing it all in, the little that we had, to start again in a country that were as foreign to us as a Zanzibar. We exchanged skerricks of knowledge about our destination. English were spoken. Victoria were Queen there too. Gold had made many rich. The lure of it had pulled people from America and all. There were weird animals, heads like rats and tails like monkeys. They jumped.

– Jumping rats! They sound like God's experiments, giggled Brigid Ryan from Aughrim. She were but seventeen and shared my bunk.

And there were blacks, it were said. Savages. We all went quiet when they were mentioned. It didn't bear thinking what they might do to white women should we fall amongst them. God save us all, said Brigid. She cried at night, face down in her sheets so we mightn't hear her. And in the dark, hearing the sighs and sobs of women as wretched as me, I felt my faith slipping. If God were looking out for the Kings, for any of us aboard the *Kilkenny*, it seemed he were making our road cruelly long and hard.

We started in water and ended in sun, hotter the further south we went. Skies I'd never seen before, pink in the evening, cloudless in the day. The sun bleaching all the blue out. A stillness settling on us, sucking the air out of our sleeping space between decks. Always the damp feeling of clothes sticking to skin. And me with a sense of having rolled my own life like dice. Nothing I could do till they stopped tumbling and I knew what had come up.

Sydney Town. Everything so hard and clear and bright, I had to screw up my eyes to see. The noise of banging and building and pedlars calling out their wares. A group of blacks sitting near the docks, staring at us all, wearing odd clothes thrown together without thought to colour or style and no shoes. One of the women in a skirt and a man's shirt missing buttons, careless of a nipple poking free. Brigid and I looked away.

They took us to a place on a hill overlooking the water and

the town spreading fast all around it. A place made from sand-coloured blocks near a sign saying Macquarie Street. Soldiers were stationed in the outbuildings.

— Have you heard? Brigid said, all atwitter. There used to be convicts here. See those rings set in the walls? To hang their hammocks.

In the corners and behind some of the beams were names carved by men with time to leave their marks. JAMES CAMERON, 1810. EDGAR HIGHSMITH, 1807. Then, one day, beneath a balustrade black with time and sweat, I saw it. HENRY KING, 1831. My father's name. I knew it were not him that wrote it twenty-six years past, but still it were strange to find this. I shivered, though it were warm. Had some relative been in this place before me? And where were the other Kings, my four brothers? In this place I felt further from them than ever I had in Dublin. In Ireland they might know where to find me, but I could die here without any of them even knowing I'd breathed this air.

They said we were to stay behind these sandstone walls until places were found for us. Them were the rules. Mrs McAlpine, the supervisor, a woman always half hidden behind several aprons worn at once, insisted we keep up our duties. Cleaning, mending, needlework. So she could tell prospective employers what we were capable of, she said. Keeping clean and busy would be all to our advantage.

Brigid were one of the first to go, as governess to the family of a timber merchant. A hard-faced man with dirt beneath his nails, Mr Benson. I saw him studying her, gazing all up and down and front and back and then the front again, like she were a new plank and he were judging her grain.

— You have experience with children, girl? he demanded.

— Yes, sir, she replied, dropping a curtsey like Mrs McAlpine had trained us. Then giggled when she came to say goodbye.

— Experience? Seven younger brothers and sisters. Shouldn't that be bleeding experience enough for him?

She clung to me. And looked awful young and small when she went away on the back of Benson's wagon, wedged in near the front by a load of lumber.

Mrs McAlpine sent word for me to come to her office on a Wednesday morning. From an upstairs window I had been watching the soldiers parading in the grounds below, a bunch of robins in their scarlet jackets. We'd been warned to be careful not to let the soldiers see us watching them, else there'd be winks or crude gestures made with the ends of their rifles.

I could hear voices from the office before I went in. Mrs McAlpine and a visitor, an Englishman, that much I could tell. He stood up when I entered. I were not used to gentlemen standing for me. He were tall, nudging six foot I guessed. In black, with a churchman's collar. Whiskers like sooty marks upon each cheek, a button gone from his waistcoat, and a smear of something on his chin which had been shaved in a hurry, missing bits. Mrs McAlpine spoke first.

— Nora, this is Mr Taylor. Reverend Taylor, Nora King.

— Theophilus Taylor, he said.

He offered his right hand like he were asking for a dance. I fancied he were as unused to this procedure as me. Mrs McAlpine nodded approvingly as I curtseyed and kept my eyes lowered. I could see the soles of Mr Taylor's shoes were worn down uneven at the backs, like his weight were not balanced when he walked.

— I am very pleased to meet you, sir, I said, all polite.

— Ah. And I you, ah, Miss King. He paused. Or is it Mrs King?

— Miss King, sir. I've not married.

Mr Taylor nodded. Then at last remembered to release my hand.

— Reverend Taylor has a position for a housekeeper, Nora, said Mrs McAlpine, her hands clasped before her. I have suggested you would be well suited to his needs.

I nodded, my eyes still down.

— We are bachelors, Miss King, he said, men of God. But also men in need of a woman's touch around our lodgings. With his right hand, long and bony, he fingered the space for the missing button on his waistcoat. As I fear you can see. I have mentioned this to Mrs McAlpine, but I must tell you direct. We are not wealthy men, Miss King, and our house is not grand. But you will have your own quarters and adequate personal time, as well as such pay as we can manage.

— I would be honoured, sir.

My own quarters! An address on the wrong side of the world. In transit no longer.

— Splendid. Ah. Now, one thing. You *are* a Christian, Miss King?

— I am.

— We are Wesleyan Methodists, Miss King. God's footsoldiers, ha ha! And you?

— We were raised Catholic but I feel sure I can accept your God, sir.

My own one having done little for me.

— Excellent, he said. Well then, if you can get your things together, we can go. There is much to be done.

And then, sudden-like, he were singing.

> Forth in Thy name, O Lord, I go
> My daily labour to pursue;
> Thee, only Thee, resolved to know,
> In all I think or speak or do

Even Mrs McAlpine seemed startled by this, perhaps because Mr Taylor's singing voice were much higher than his speaking tone. Higher and very flat. I thought he might continue on through more verses, as he appeared to enjoy his singing, when he stopped short.

— Oh. Another thing I must ask you. Looking straight at me, his eyes a watery brown. Do you indulge, Miss King?

I blushed.

— Indulge, sir?

— In strong drink? Spirits. Wine.

— No. No, I never, sir.

— Excellent! For there is no drink in our house. We preach against the drink, you see. The drink that is bringing despair to far too many hearths in this colony. Drink and the lust for quick riches.

I had neither drink nor gold, so the position suited. It did not take long to gather together my few things in the small trunk, dented a bit from the voyage. At the bottom, wrapped in paper, the sewing kit that had been my ma's, also one of the toy soldiers from his da that John had left behind. I would look at this toy, its nose chipped away, and think of the King boys still playing at soldiers. Wearing Mary's bonnet, I made my farewells with Mrs McAlpine, who used her topmost apron to dab at her eyes. Seemed like I were always saying goodbye.

Mr Taylor's place were in Darlinghurst, a building of sandstone at back of the church. There were him and Reverend Jenkins and Reverend Usher. Others, too, would stay a while after they'd come from England, waiting for their postings to the Queensland heat or, like Reverend Butters, to Ballarat in Victoria where men were mad for gold.

The ministers were never anything but polite to me. Grateful that I could bring some order to their lives. They could speak to

God but not boil a turnip. Looking after them were no different to caring for my brothers. Better, there were a bit more money, so not everything had to be turned to soup that were more like water as the week wore on.

If my duties were done I would sit near the back of the church to hear their services. Marvel at the way that kindly but awkward Mr Taylor could find passion in his pulpit, like he were transported someplace else, his long arms swinging. And he could sing, loud as he liked.

> Hail the day that sees Him rise,
> Ravished from our wishful eyes!

They were learned men. There were more books in their home than I had ever seen before, and not just the Bible and books of hymns or prayers, but also books in leather bindings from England, and newspapers. Mr Taylor took *The Sydney Morning Herald*. One of his joys were to pore over it during breakfast, folding its large pages lengthwise so they wouldn't cover the entire table. Sometimes he would comment on reports that caught his attention, not always with his mouth clear of his breakfast.

– Ah, Mr Jevons has published his report on the Rocks area. See, he calls it a social cesspool. Quite! I may write to commend him. God rest his soul, Sir Charles FitzRoy has died. A good governor for this young colony. An enlightened man.

I cleared the table after they had begun their daily duties. Often I would find bits of Mr Taylor's food scattered over the newspaper. Crumbs of cheese, bread. I would brush these off as best I could, then put the pages back in order and leave it on the table. Sometimes I would look at it, though I were never a great reader. But it had notices for entertainments. Perhaps a concert at

Mr Paling's music centre in Wynyard Square I might keep in mind for my afternoon off.

It were in the newspaper that I first read of the mutiny in India. There were a headline, bigger than the usual. MASSACRE IN CAWNPORE. And another, TERRIBLE LOSS OF LIFE. In the report, one line caused me to sink to a chair: 'Horrors inflicted too ghastly to report. The casualties included civilians as well as soldiers of the Queen.'

Queen's soldiers like my brothers, wherever they might be. And nothing I could do for them but pray.

I heard the ministers talking that evening, their tone sombre.

— Women! And babes too! Cut down without mercy. And we imagined this to be a Christian country. The Lord's vengeance will be dreadful indeed.

Then the mutiny were over, the leaders hanged. The year of 1858 ended with Queen Victoria's soldiers still stationed in India, and me, well past marrying age, settled into a life far from all I'd grown up knowing. Five brothers I'd had. Now I were sister to none.

Near three years I had there. Long enough to believe this were how God meant things to be. My drifting had stopped in Sydney. Then I saw it. August 1860 I reckon it were. A dismal mid-winter day with rain on the windows in Darlinghurst. Mr Taylor, eyes streaming, his throat wrapped in a scarf to ward off the catarrh. Me clearing the table, putting away his newspaper, seeing the report on a page inside. 'Exploration Expedition Assembles in Melbourne'.

What made me read it? I have often wondered. Mr Taylor said later the Lord led me to it. I don't know. Perhaps it were just luck. Good and ill luck in equal shares. On the page a long list of names of those in the party. Landells, Brahe, Patten, McDonough. Last of all, John King, Assistant.

Could it be? I had no way of being sure. And yet...

— My dear Miss King, you must calm yourself, said Mr Taylor when I went to him with the newspaper, interrupting his writing time. Something I had never done before. But he did not reproach me, being so startled by my urgent manner. He dabbed at his nose with a handkerchief as he read the report.

— Well, well, a huge undertaking it is. Camels as well. But little information on the men involved. And, Miss King, it *is* a common name. Wait, there's a little more. *Mr King, formerly a soldier...* Hmm.

— It *is* him, I know it. I just know.

— Well, then you must see if you can find him. Ah, though it seems the expedition will be leaving within weeks. We must make haste. This is so wonderful, inspirational! He was lost but now is found.

He fumbled on his desk for a pen and a clean sheet of writing paper.

— A familial quest, marvellous! Though we all will miss you. I shall prepare a letter for our brethren in Melbourne. Perhaps my old friend Daniel Draper, Reverend Draper, head of the diocese, can help find a position for you there.

They were good men, the ministers Taylor and Jenkins and Usher. Coming together, pleased as children on Christmas morn, when I opened the package they gave me. Inside, a coach ticket to Melbourne, plus my wages till the end of the month, though it were yet early in it, and a book of hymns. Inscribed by them all.

— Perhaps, Miss King, they will help bring to mind my singing, said Mr Taylor.

Another farewell.

I have their hymn book still. I cannot look at it without recalling the journey from Sydney. Five days and swaying nights. The road awash with puddles, the coach bogged. Myself sick from the motion and a gnawing restlessness inside, impatient to be where I needed to go.

Then Melbourne at last. The coach stopping on a rutted street. Horses slurping from a trough, begrimed bags tossed down from the rack. I saw men pushing barrows, stores with notices calling for staff to replace those gone for the gold.

The talk in town were all of the exploring expedition, the size of it, the grand plans. But it were gone already, just a few days before. A boy with a cloth cap told me this near the coach stop.

— I saw them go! he said. Climbed a tree to get a view and to keep clear of all them camelans. Phew, the smell of 'em! And he twisted his face.

The article in the Sydney paper had made mention of an Exploration Committee of the Royal Society. With my bag in hand that were less heavy than my heart, I walked to its office near La Trobe Street. A pedlar pointed the way.

— Look for the pillars, he said.

Pillars and the grandest door I'd ever seen, polished wood with carvings. The man behind it, gold watch-chain drooped across his chest, looked at me like I were a pedlar myself, selling something.

I told him I had a message for a member of the expedition. He seemed to find this odd. A message? Despatches were only to be sent to the expedition leaders, he told me. He studied me again, noted the mud on my shoes, then asked me if I had this message.

I had to beg of him some writing materials, a paper and envelope, pen and ink. He made me stand to write it, then stood close by, looking at his watch, as I sought the right words for all the things I wanted to say. 'Dear John King, If indeed you be my beloved brother...'

I addressed it to him as part of the exploring expedition. On the back of the envelope, just my name, care of Reverend Draper, Melbourne. The minister I'd not even met.

I left the envelope with the man with the watch. I don't know what happened to it. My letter never reached John. Much later I learned that even letters to Mr Burke himself from the chairman of the committee went missing.

The expedition had departed Melbourne to the banging of drums. Then it were like it had vanished out of sight, with seldom any word of it.

I had no money to go back to Sydney and in Melbourne I knew nobody.

I could only wait.

Eight

On the day of my rescue the natives were unusually excited. *'Nunanga!'* they cried. *'Nunanga!'* The word they used for white fellows.

I could not match their animation. I was too weak. There had been false sightings before, my increasingly feeble hopes dashed time and again. I had come to believe my days would end there on the Cooper: a white man abandoned in the interior. I had even started to think that I was inexorably becoming a native myself.

All of my skin that I could see was darkening. I had long since lost my glass — my own face was a mystery to me. But it felt strange to the touch. Pitted with unhealed sores. The rasp of a beard around lips that easily bled. Eyes sunken into deep sockets. Cheekbones that I could hold between thumb and forefinger, obtruding like the ribs of Billy when we shot him on the return from the Gulf.

I was living like the blacks, sleeping in their shelters, trying to eat their food. Managing some rudimentary communication with them. Since I had shown them the spot where the remains of Mr Burke lay, near one of the waterholes in which they cast their fishing nets, their manner had been more kindly to me. They seemed genuinely affected by the sight of the leader's remains, weeping and covering him over with branches in a reverent manner.

So as to prolong their solicitude, I had tried to make them

believe that other white fellows would be coming, bringing presents with them. They would come within two moons, I indicated. This seemed to satisfy them. In the evenings, when they brought me fish or, more often, nardoo plants or their seeds, they would point to the sky. '*Nunanga!*' There seemed also to be much discussion about what form the promised presents would take. Our tomahawks were especially prized – *bomay ho*, they called them. Any man with a tomahawk seemed to attain extra status amongst his fellows, but they had an insatiable curiosity about all of our belongings. They were meddlers. I knew this, so I hid those items Mr Burke had left with me. His watch and a notebook. And W's things. I enclosed them in a small canvas pouch I carried around my neck.

My eyes had misled me before. White men who turned out to be flashes of pelicans glimpsed through trees. But on the day I was found the excitement was immense. The native woman whose arm I had healed, the one called Carrawaw, came to me pointing away from the creek. And one of the young men who had brought me fish gestured that I should come with him, even assisting when he appreciated my weakness – I tried to walk with him, but couldn't. This prompted much discussion between the woman and the fisherman. Then signals to me. The woman let me sit once again on the sandy bank of the creek, even contriving for me a kind of support with some animal skins in front of the gunyah.

The fisherman left, leaving at a trot. Carrawaw and I waited like royalty prior to an audience, though I'll warrant Her Majesty never felt so wretched.

When the fisherman and some of his fellows returned, bringing with them two of Howitt's men – blacks in white men's clothes, trackers – they showed more animation than I could manage myself. They smiled and slapped at each other, a gesture of extreme satisfaction. Amongst the babble of chatter, I heard it again: '*Bomay ho!*' Already there was a high expectation of reward.

Then came another man. A white man, though his face and neck were red from the sun. A man who looked at me and then grimaced and swore, disgusted by the sight or smell of me, or perhaps the sounds I tried to make.

By the time Howitt himself arrived, many more blacks were there, all looking most gratified and delighted. Howitt stood quite still, studying me as if I were a species he could not identify.

Then he wept. And I had no words for him. My lips were bleeding.

Now, once again, I am waiting for Howitt. Unlike his last visit to Octavia Street, this time his arrival will not take me by surprise. Nor, I hope, will the impact of his coming be quite as dramatic.

Mary read his latest letter to me, smoothing it out on her lap and struggling to decipher his script. The writing of somebody who puts message ahead of manners; less legible, indeed, than W's own hand, which retained its style even in his last messages.

It was postmarked Omeo, Mary told me, before reading:

My Dear King,

I trust this finds you in good health. Business will bring me to Melbourne two Weds hence, and I shd like to take the opportunity to call on you once again; around noon.

Re the matters we discussed: I note that you have not responded to some of the questions I sent you re native customs. I have attributed this to yr weak constitution rather than any unwillingness to assist. I remain hopeful that you will find some conversation less taxing than consigning yr thoughts to paper. To this end I propose to visit you.

Regards to yr sister and cousin.

If the proposed appointment is inconvenient leave word for me c/o Melbourne Club, 137–141 Collins Street East.
Yrs, A.W. Howitt

As the appointed hour approaches I am ready for him, propped up with pillows on our narrow porch bordering the street. It is the posture of an invalid and my hateful mug is under the seat, but I am nonetheless out of bed, having determined that my one-time rescuer will find me more hale than when he last saw me.

I am indebted to Howitt. To him I owe my return to humanity. But I do not know that I can assist him. From our last, truncated conversation I gained the impression that he is now studying natives in the same clinical manner that he recorded latitude and longitude and weather conditions during his several expeditions to the Barcoo region. He imagines there is much I can tell him about natives because I lived amongst them, but I was simply trying to survive. And as the days unfolded one into another I knew little more of what was occurring around me than does a young child. All that mattered was food and shelter, and I was reliant on the blacks for both. I kept no journal. Those eighty-one days and nights before my release have become like fragmented glimpses of the country I later saw during the trip back to Melbourne with Howitt's party.

But I know I was lonely. More than hungry or tired or ill, I felt lonely after both Mr Burke and W were dead and I was the only one left. Even the natives seemed to have gone. The gunyahs I found were deserted. I slept in empty shelters of bark and branches, forsaken to my fate. Then, near one of the gunyahs, I found a bag of nardoo and some other food items. Yet still I dreaded the blacks returning and taking this little food away.

Nobody came back. When my stock of nardoo was running low, and finding myself too weak to gather the seed to make some more, I resolved to try to track the natives down the creek. I shot at crows and hawks that I saw. Hearing the gun, some natives came to meet me and took me to their camp, giving me nardoo and fish. They appeared to feel great compassion for me when they understood that all my companions had died.

So I had food — crows, balls of the nardoo dough, fish scorched on their fires on the outside but raw, gelatinous, inside. I became weaker despite this sustenance. I lay on rank animal skins, trying to understand in the jabber of conversations and gestures parts that might relate to me. A helpless spectator as my future was debated. Always scared that the blacks would become bored with me and leave me by myself again. Parrots screeched. Pigeons in clumps on the end of branches made an unearthly whistling sound. A lone pelican soared up from a waterhole and made several passes overhead, as if checking whether the abject figure I had become was something it could swoop down upon and carry away.

And once more I am lying back, waiting. My eyes are fixed on a place far distant, which is why Howitt surprises me this time too. Or perhaps it is just that I have been listening for his footfall, his boots on the gravel in the street, and instead he arrives on horseback. A smart grey colt that, I suspect, is stabled at the Melbourne Club. Suddenly he is there, black jacket dusty from his journey. He nods when he sees me but does not speak until he has tethered the colt to one of the verandah posts and given it a handful of oats he produces from a pocket.

'Good day, King. You're looking a little stronger. Bit of colour in your cheeks.'

'Thank you, sir. I hope I may be better company than last time.'

Howitt settles himself in the seat that Nora has placed ready for him, opposite me. He swings his legs straight out from him and contemplates his travel-scuffed boots in a way that reminds me of Landells. 'You were expecting me, then? Which means you got my letter.'

'I did, sir. Should I see if we can get you any refreshment?'

'Not now, King. No need. After all my wanderings, a gentle trot down the St Kilda Road from the city is nothing.'

His knife again, probing at his fingernails while he seems to be considering his line of inquiry. His horse raises its tail and releases a pile of dung close to the porch. Howitt appears not to notice. Nora will be aghast when she sees it.

'Ethnology, King. The word mean anything to you?'

'I'm afraid not, sir.'

'The science of customs. Of how different peoples live and behave. It is one of my abiding concerns these days.'

I seek to look interested but can find nothing to say.

'What about Darwin, Charles Darwin — have you heard of him?'

'That I have. Reverend Bickford has mentioned him several times in his sermons. And during his visits here.'

'I imagine the Reverend may not be in accord with some of Mr Darwin's ideas, especially his concept of evolution.'

'He cannot accept it. I do remember him saying that. He says the beginnings of the world and its creatures are best described in the Bible, not Mr Darwin's book.'

'You believe him?'

'I am a believer, sir. In the Bible. I haven't read Mr Darwin, only a little about him.'

'I consider myself a man of science now, King. And Darwin's ideas about progressive development are in accord with all that I noted myself on my expeditions, including those up the Barcoo, to the Cooper. Could anyone who has seen them at close quarters deny that our natives are inestimably a more primitive race than white people?'

'You and I both know how they live. But they do live, sir, while many white men who have sought to travel in their country have died. As I nearly did. They saved me.'

'*I* saved you. They merely kept you alive. Had I not come along, you would have been dead long ago. Or at least scarcely civilised.'

'I was terribly weak when you found me. Less from want of food than something lacking in the diet. And a strange emptiness of spirit.'

Howitt is watching me carefully, having turned his attention from his fingernails to my face. Again I have the sense of being studied, and try to alter the course of conversation.

'I was thinking on the blacks, just before you came – their love of presents. The great excitement that could be caused by ordinary items. *Bomay ho!*'

Howitt smiles. A sudden split in his beard. Have I ever seen him smile before?

'*Bomay ho.*' He seems to be rolling the words on his tongue, like a man savouring a draft of madeira. 'They did like the tomahawks, didn't they? But I think the looking-glasses surprised them the most. On seeing their faces – many, I would imagine, for the first time – some seemed dazzled. Others opened their eyes like saucers and made a rattling noise with their tongues expressive of surprise. My watch amused them greatly, though I was careful to retain it. And when I gave them some of the sugar to taste, it was absurd to see the sleight of hand with which, at first, they pretended to eat it. From a justified fear of being poisoned, I would wager.'

'You treated them well, sir. Rewarded them.'

They come to the camp early. Men, women, piccaninnies. Chattering excitedly. Howitt has tracked down some of their number the previous day, distributing a handful of gifts as samples and leading them to understand there are more to be had if they all come. So they arrive not long after sun-up. Thirty or forty in total, more than I have ever seen together, though I recognise many of them. The uproar is deafening, as the blacks have also roused all the birds. Carrawaw is there with her husband. He has adorned himself with a hawk's feather in his hair and his beard is greased to a point. Howitt is able to get them all sitting before me.

I have been in the care of Doctor Wheeler, from Howitt's party, for over a week. He has fed me rice and butter and sugar, things I have craved. My strength has much returned, though my days pass slipping in and out of sleep. Now, at this gathering, I am reminded of the headmaster of the Hibernian School, Mr Kilpatrick, waiting to address an assembly. Yet no group of Dublin schoolboys was ever as animated as these natives. Howitt has tried to make them understand that any gifts bestowed are in recognition of their kindness to me. And so great shows of solicitude are made, many blacks approaching, clicking their tongues sympathetically and trying to stroke me. Carrawaw, who has coated herself in oil in my honour, has made it her job to stand near me and shoo away any visitors who, as she decides it, overstay their welcome.

As much as I am able, I help Howitt hand out the gifts. Tomahawks, knives, combs — many of which are left stuck in hair as decoration. Looking-glasses. Carrawaw, who is well rewarded, is especially taken with hers. She sneaks looks as if trying to catch her new-found twin by surprise. All these items are received with great delight. And it is touching to note the way some blacks point out others who they feel have been overlooked. Even the little ones are brought forward by their parents to have ribbons tied in their hair.

The sugar is exceedingly popular, once the blacks have overcome their suspicion. A fifty-pound bag is divided between them, and they carry away their shares in another gift: Union Jack handkerchiefs. Then sundry items of clothing brought by the relief party are handed out, leaving many of the blacks adorned in an odd mix of apparel: a calico shirt topped by a fishing-net or Union Jack wrapped around the head. Some of Howitt's men, including the black trackers Sandy and Frank, conclude proceedings by joining in an impromptu corroboree ceremony. Making signs of farewell and gratitude, the blacks then leave as they have come, in a noisy group, carrying their presents. On the trail behind them lies a red ribbon, dropped by one of the children.

Howitt appears pleased by the way his ceremony has been conducted. Henceforth, he declares, these blacks will look upon whites as friends. Those who come after us can be confident of the kindest treatment at their hands.

Howitt snaps shut his clasp-knife. 'Yes, I rewarded them. Just as Charles Sturt recommended. A good man, Sturt. Sound ideas. Do you know if Burke read any of Sturt's journals?'

'I would think so. I believe that the committee, in its instructions to him, made mention of routes taken by Sturt and Gregory and others. And Mr Burke himself suggested to me he had studied some of the earlier explorers, though I don't know to what extent.'

Learn from the past, King. Learn from the past and apply its lessons to the present...

'I ask because Sturt is unequivocal about the blacks. He insists that they will respond well if treated kindly. He made it clear he meant them no harm, and in return, by and large, they helped him. As they helped you, King. But I cannot shake the feeling that your beloved Burke regarded all natives he encountered with suspicion, if not outright hostility. And by doing so doomed himself and many of his fellows.'

I would guess that Howitt believes he is not so much interrogating me as thinking aloud. But he still has the manner of a magistrate, though far from his courtroom.

'As I told you last time, sir, Mr Burke was concerned that undue friendliness to the natives would lead to meddling. There were many instances of pilfering. And haste was of the essence. Stuart was on his mind. Nothing should be allowed to slow us down.'

'Of course. The Scot. Who learned a lot himself as a hand on Sturt's first expedition. All the nonsense in the newspapers about a race between colonies – what did they think this was, a sodding overland Melbourne Cup? Exploring is not about speed. It should concern itself with careful progress and thoughtful observation, not with splitting the group into separate parties and shedding supplies all over the country like a tinker with a broken wagon on a bumpy road.'

Mr Burke is in Howitt's dock. And I am the only one who can defend him.

'With great respect, sir, Mr Burke had his instructions. And remember he was a soldier by background, a man accustomed to taking orders as well as giving them.'

Howitt snorts like a horse coming upon a snake in its path. 'A soldier? More of a copper and wild-boyo cavalryman. Do you know he took leave from Beechworth to go all the way back to Europe to fight in the Crimean War? But he was too late, it was all over by the time he got there. It's a brave soldier who misses a war – I'm not even sure if he ever saw any real action at all. Hmm?'

He stares at me, chin down, so that I have a better view of his eyebrows, which form inquisitive peaks, than the eyes themselves. Did the leader see any action? I know the answer to this, but don't care to travel that path with my hectoring guest. So I seek once more to change the course of the conversation.

'You suggested in your letter there were some particular topics you wished to discuss with me. About the natives?'

Howitt seems faintly amused. He knows what I am doing. But he nods and extracts a notebook from one of his waistcoat pockets, then flips to a blank page with a thumb stained by tobacco. He exchanges his knife for a pencil, the tip of which he licks like a secretary preparing to take down a letter.

'Very well, King. Ethnology it is. So tell me – the tribe of blacks you were with, would you say there was obviously one head man? Or a number of leaders?'

'The older men. Authority seemed to come with age. Let me see if I can recall any names. Tchukulow was one. And Mungallee. Another – I have it, Pitchery.'

Howitt smiles again. 'Ah yes, Pitchery. That rogue! I remember him. Small fellow. Always with a bird's feather stuck in his beard. He made out that he hadn't got his allocation of sugar when we were doling it out. I swear he'd secreted the first lot somewhere and was just after some extra. What of the women?'

'The wives of the head men appeared to have extra status, too. But you would have observed all this yourself.'

'Mostly, King, but perhaps not all. Always be open to new information, that is the scientific method. Observe, record and learn – Darwin, I think, said this. And the hunting, the food-gathering – the job of everyone, or specific individuals?'

The food. Unfamiliar seeds. Birds imperfectly plucked. A parrot with its beak open in a silent squawk, as if it had been not quite dead when tossed on the fire. The entrails of a giant lizard scooped from its belly before me and offered like a prized delicacy. God help me, I ate them. I ate anything offered.

Howitt lowers his notebook, looks at me with concern. 'King, your colour is dreadful. Can I get you anything?'

'A little water, perhaps. Your question prompted some nasty memories.'

'I can imagine there're quite a few of those. Let's leave that one.'

'No, it's just I'm not sure how to answer. Food was often brought without my noticing. Or it was left where I might find it. The men, I would say, did most of the hunting. The women gathered the seed for the nardoo. And I saw some fishing with nets.'

'Which also doubled as an item of decoration, as we saw at our little presentation ceremony. We distributed some trinkets, packed up, and turned around to head homewards the next morning.'

He closes the notebook, perhaps noticing my increasing fatigue. Or has he become weary of his own questions? He studies his fingertips, lost in thought. 'We headed homewards,' he repeats. 'The object of my mission had been fulfilled. The fate of the mighty exploring expedition was a mystery no longer. I had you with me, King, to bear witness to what had occurred. But think of what *could* have been achieved!'

He looks at me, his eyes bright. 'I still carried some five months worth of provisions. Our party, except from yourself, was in sound health. The animals were in good order, both the horses and the camels. We were on the edge of country well worth exploring – and I mean exploring properly, not rushing through like madmen – in a tolerably kind season. With such means at our disposal, *think* what might have been done.' He is leaning forward on his seat. Almost out of it. More animated than I have ever seen him. And it seems to me that this is the issue really preoccupying him, rather than any questions of ethnology.

'Mr Howitt, I am sorry if my indisposition precluded you from achieving what you wanted to do. But I –'

'It wasn't you, man,' he interrupts. 'It was my task to find you. We should all be grateful the blacks delivered you to us.'

'Was it the blacks who delivered me, sir, or God?'

'Tell me yourself, King. Where was God when you were stranded for almost three months?'

His bushman's thumb has pushed straight through my blistered skin into the sensitive flesh beneath. *I looked for Him, called to Him, but the stones and sand and prickling bushes showed me no signs of Him.*

'I confess His presence was hard to discern at the time, but I try to believe there's a purpose to all things.'

'And what was Burke's purpose, do you reckon?'

'To cross the continent, sir, as he was instructed. And he did, too.' Howitt gives me a quizzical look, but lets me continue. 'Had we not been abandoned, had Mr Brahe and the depot party stayed put, as they were ordered, all of us would have got back. Not Charley, perhaps, but the rest of us.'

'Interesting word, that. Abandoned. Originally used by Burke himself in one of his last notes to the committee. Then crossed out in the notebook that you preserved so diligently. But tell me, King, might not Brahe and the other poor souls at the depot also have felt abandoned? Two months. Three months. Then four months gone and still not a word from their leader. At least one man, Patten, sick and others failing. What were they to do?'

Again, an inquisition. 'They had instructions to stay,' I reply.

'For how long, man? How long? Any orders were vague. Unclear. Certainly not committed to paper.'

'We all had our assignments. We were to push on to the Gulf. They were to man the depot and await our return.'

He shakes his head as if he can make no sense of it. 'And my job, it seems, was to tidy up after all of you. When so much else of practical importance could have been done.'

'*What* could have been done, gentlemen? A singularly serious debate for a mild afternoon, I must say.'

As always, Reverend Bickford has made an unobtrusive entrance. It seems that he simply arrives without approaching, so soft are his footsteps. Even Howitt has been caught unawares. He rises to greet our visitor, an inordinately thin man whose professional garb gives him the appearance of a black beetle.

'James Bickford,' says my minister, making his own introduction. 'And you, King, are faring as well as can be expected, I hope?'

'Howitt. Alfred Howitt.'

'*The* Alfred Howitt? But of course. The honour is all mine. I have heard much about you. Allow me to express my own personal gratitude to you for bringing Mr King back to us. He is an active member of my parish. That is, as active as he is able to be.'

Howitt seems uncomfortable, not least because Bickford has made his opening remarks while continuing to hold, and occasionally shake, Howitt's hand. He politely prises it free. 'My expeditions were a long time ago, Reverend. Much has happened to us all since then.'

'Indeed it has, I'm sure of that.'

I am glad of Bickford's arrival. The session with Howitt has sapped much of my strength. 'I mentioned you to Mr Howitt earlier, Reverend.'

'Did you indeed? I am flattered.'

'I told him we had shared some discussions about Charles Darwin.'

'Darwin. Of course.' He places his slim black carry-case on the porch, as if to better expound on a favourite subject. 'He has caused quite a stir with his ideas, hasn't he? Though I suspect his theories will be forgotten, or discredited, before very long.'

'I'm not so sure about that, Reverend,' puts in Howitt. 'They seem to me to be gaining increasingly wide acceptance.'

'Evolution, Mr Howitt? An illogical concept. It all had to start somewhere, eh? And what better starting point than the Creator? Who created, I'll wager, Mr Darwin himself. Though perhaps He now rather wishes that He hadn't!'

The minister seems very pleased by his jest. Howitt consults his pocket-watch. A man with other appointments. Mr Bickford takes his cue. 'Perhaps we can continue this discussion some other time, Mr Howitt. On finches and fishes or whatever you will.'

Howitt nods as if the prospect is an enticing one, though I suspect he would much rather ride in the rain than debate evolution with the minister.

Mr Bickford picks up his case and makes to go inside. 'The ladies are within, King?'

'Mary is working at the café in town, Reverend. But Nora is at home. Caring for the children.'

'Excellent, excellent. I hope we shall have a chat a little later, King. Good day, Mr Howitt. Now, if I may...'

Howitt waits until the minister is inside. He remains standing but makes no move to leave himself, though his tethered horse, which appears to have been slumbering on its feet, has stirred. He rubs at his beard with the back of his hand.

'I'll let you be, King. You've been helpful. I appreciate your efforts, and I do understand that much of your life with the natives must now seem lost in the fog of time. I find it hard to fathom myself what you endured... Tell me, are you making progress with your journal?'

'A little. More progress on some days than others.'

'And why exactly are you doing it, man? After all these years? So long ago, much of it.'

Why? The same question Mary has asked me. The question I find difficult to answer.

'Because... because I never did before. Tell my story properly, that is. And others did. You kept a journal yourself, sir.'

'I did. Standard practice, King, for any expedition leader. Though clearly not for Burke.'

'I explained that at the commission, sir. Mr Burke thought it unnecessary.'

'Yes, yes, because Wills was doing it himself. Wills was the journal-writer, the taker of notes. There's another thing I find odd.' His magistrate's stare again.

'What, sir?'

'You rarely mention him.'

'Who?'

'Wills, man, Wills. Your second in command.'

When I do not reply he becomes more insistent. 'Why so silent about Wills?'

I get up, slowly. Lean on the railing to counter the dizziness I feel. Ignore his question. 'That's a fine-looking horse, Mr Howitt.'

'That he is,' agrees Howitt, who has evidently decided not to push his point. Having stepped down from the verandah, he allows his mount to nuzzle at the back of his hand as he unties it and prepares to leave.

'He's a spirited young colt. I only use male horses now. Remember the trouble we had with the mare on the way back from the Cooper?'

A rocky gully. We are camped by a waterhole that is almost empty, little more than a muddy puddle. Forced to stop for the day because one of the packhorses is in foal. Her eyes wild. Foam on her lips. Legs thrashing at the ground as she rolls to ease her discomfort. Howitt impatient to get on, yet talking to the mare softly, his tone soothing. Making one of his men kneel on her forequarters to steady her while he thrusts his bloodied arm into her, up to his elbow, to untangle the foal's legs and lever the animal out. Gently, speaking to the mare all the time, he twists the foal and prises it out in a sluice of blood and other fluids.

The foal trembles, makes as if to open its eyes. But even as the mare is moving her head around to lick it, Howitt speaks to his man in a different tone. Harsh. Urgent.

'Hold her steady, Frank. Keep her away.' With his hand still bloody he drags his gun from his waistband and once, twice, knocks the foal between its ears with the heavy handle. It sounds like a rock on a melon.

The foal twitches and lies still on the ground. Howitt rubs the handle of the gun on his breeches. 'Now we can move on without this to hold us up. Attend to the mare, Frank. She'll be right soon enough.'

The wind, from the north, is hot and dusty. No rain for weeks.

Nine

Strange how you can spend so much time with a man yet never get to know him. W liked it that way. Could seem alone even when you were with him. Happiest with his instruments, taking his measurements and observations, he was intent on charting and recording every step of our path across the continent. I was there for the camels. He concentrated on turning the country into numbers, crossing it with pencil marks on a map. Confining it between lines in his books of tables and charts.

He preferred numbers to people. There was order in numbers, he could control them. People swore and belched and farted and drank and didn't always adhere to instructions. Not W. There was never an order he didn't obey, even when we might have been better off had he demurred. He was the only one who knew how all the numbers added up. And yet, like me, he was following the man who was his senior by a good many years.

W was with his fieldbooks, his journals, more than he was with us. He would rather write than speak. While Mr Burke spoke like a river in flood, W was stingy with his words, hesitating when he spoke as if unsure what to say. For him words were like rocks on our path: obstacles to be tripped over. Landells said this was due to a childhood illness. The fever took his tongue, he claimed.

Yet in W's journals the words came easy. He would set

himself up at the end of each day, book on his knees, a candle and spare pencils by his side. His writing could occupy him for an hour or more, and in that time he would neither speak nor eat nor drink. He wanted for nothing when he had paper and pencil for company. Sometimes Mr Burke would speak with him before he worked at his journal, passing on something he had scribbled in his own notebook, though it was rare for the leader to jot anything down. More often he would leave him be. Waiting to jest with him when his labour was done and the books put away again.

'Well, Will, where did we get to today? What did we see? Any clouds worth mentioning?'

Sometimes he would accompany this with a thump on W's back, which he accepted with a smile, though once I spied him rubbing at the spot later as though Mr Burke had left a bruise. But W never complained about this rough treatment, even though he generally wouldn't stand for people touching him or any of his scientific equipment.

We got off to a bad start, W and I, because of this gear.

It was in Royal Park, before we left. Our caravan — and that's what it was at that stage, a vast, sprawling parade of wagons and animals and unwieldy bales and crates and stacks of supplies — was being assembled. Landells had instructed me to get the camels used to carrying loads. This was no small task, as some of the Indian beasts were unaccustomed to straps or the bundles that had to be balanced so that they stayed put despite the swaying motion when the camels walked.

The way I see it now it is a mild morning in August. The sky is low and threatens rain. Already much of the park has been churned into mud by the animals and the wheels of the drays. The animals must be kept apart. Our horses are terrified of the camels, which fight amongst each other and try to rut anything. The oxen that the committee has insisted we take to pull the wagons maintain a mournful bellowing in their improvised pens. There are sheep, too, tormented by Landells' dog, which gets into their stalls and nips their legs. Their future is a sorry one: when we leave, the sheep will be packed on a wagon, their legs tied together as with parcels. When we need meat, they will feel a blade upon their throats.

Amongst this zoo the men of the expedition try to go about their tasks. Policemen from the city are employed to keep back the spectators who, every day, congregate to witness the final preparations of the expedition they have heard so much about. The police have rigged up a line, secured on stakes, to restrain the onlookers – a mix of street urchins and city toffs and, on some evenings, whores hoping for business before we go.

'Breeches up, boys,' says Mr Burke with a guffaw when he spies these women. 'Breeches up. Or else it'll be an itchy trek ahead of you!'

People in the crowd give Mr Burke a cheer when he speeds by on his horse Billy. He tips his high-crowned hat at them, though he never slows down. I do not know where he goes, though he always seems busy. Landells suggests he has a lady in town.

'It's breeches *down* for him, I'll wager. Ploughing the field of his actress bint while the rest of us untangle this knot of stuff here.'

On this morning I am working with the camel called Datchi, a cantankerous male who often seems to delight in mischief. He will look down at me, all innocence under those ladylike eyelashes, then let loose a stream of foul brown spit. Or simply yawn and refuse to rise. On such occasions I belabour him about the nose with a plaited leather crop, as I have seen Dost Mahomed do with impressive effect, but he is little more concerned than a man pestered by flies.

Today Datchi is well behaved. He has accepted his load, comprising two large travel cases with a great many pockets and buckles, and has allowed himself to be led, his splayed feet making a sucking sound as he steps over the wet ground.

I am complimenting him, pleased by my success – 'Good Datchi, good Datchi!' – when he farts hugely and with a sigh lets himself down to the ground, legs folded neatly beneath him. He keeps sinking, and before I can prevent him, my cry of 'Stop, Datchi!' making no impression at all, he rolls, kicking at the air.

There is a grinding, cracking sound from the cases now underneath him. And the slightly built man who has been watching me from outside his tent comes running, arms flapping like a nightgown on the line. 'Do something, man. At . . . once. Get it up!'

Hair parted and brushed. Top button of his shirt fastened, like that of a man studying in a library rather than camping in the park. An alarmed look in his eyes. 'My *instruments*! Get the animal up, man.'

I say nothing, though his tone irks me. Does he not see I am doing all I can? I thrash Datchi about the head with the crop, pull as hard as I can at the rope tied to his nose ring. He bares his yellow teeth in a smirk. Another grinding roll. I call out, 'If you could help me, together we could –'

'I cannot. Look to the beast, man. That's *your* job. Oh, for . . . pity's sake.'

A smashing sound from the nether pack.

'Up, you bugger! Get up, or I'll bury my axe handle in your backside.' Landells' face is pink with rage. Or perhaps from the effort he's made rushing to the scene of this disaster. He punctuates each word with a kick to Datchi's rump. These, or his tone alone, do the trick. Datchi rises, unhurriedly. Feigning that this had been his intention all along. As he stands up, pieces of glass tumble from one of the cases, the top of which has been loosened.

The thin man rushes forward with a cry of anguish. He

retrieves the pieces from the soft ground at his feet. 'My barometer! My best an-aneroid barometer. Broken. Quite useless now. From Sydney, too. And we... can't wait for another.'

Holding the shards of glass, he turns to me. Blame must be apportioned. 'You there. What's your name?'

'King, sir.'

'And your role here?'

'Camels, sir. I'm with the camels.'

'He's under me,' says Landells, who has ordered a now docile Datchi to kneel so he can inspect the case.

'That's as may be, Mr Landells.' The man's tone is more polite now. 'But what happened just now is unacceptable. I need these instruments... for my work. Work that is crucial to the success of this expedition.'

'No doubt,' says Landells, 'but you can't have camels without an occasional crisis, and you won't have an expedition without camels. Besides, I think you're in luck. Apart from your pieces there, I can't see anything else broken. You should say a prayer of thanks for the mud.'

The thin man seems only a little mollified. 'I hope you are right, about nothing else being broken. For your sake... K-King. But I want you to unstrap both cases now, so I can complete an... inventory of the contents. And I shall have to report this to Mr Burke.'

'As you wish, Wills,' says Landells. 'Though I'll wager he has other things on his mind. And I'd remind you that King is one of *my* men. *I* will deal with him.'

The thin man turns towards his tent. His intention, it seems, is to lay the broken pieces inside before returning to inspect the cases.

I get to work on the straps. Landells assists me while Datchi chews contentedly on some rubbish he has found on the ground, appearing mightily pleased by all the fuss he has caused. I gesture in the direction of the owner of the gear.

'What's his story, then?'

'Wills,' Landells replies, looking the way he has gone. 'William John Wills. A young Englishman. A great favourite of Professor Neumayer, apparently, from the committee, and a former assistant of his at the observatory. Mr Wills is to be our surveyor. And astronomer. And meteorologist.' Landells' manner suggests he cannot imagine what use a meteorologist will be in the interior.

'Just try to keep out of his way, King, these scientist coves can be prickly buggers. I don't know how he'll manage when things get rough. You don't need a fancy barometer to tell you it's topped a hundred in the shade and your brains are frying. I'll see to it that nothing comes of this. I am, after all, second in command of the expedition. But King, keep his precious cases off that playful brute Datchi next time.'

I tug at the straps, my heels sinking in the mud.

Something was said. By whom, I don't know, but the next time I saw Mr Burke he was aware of this incident.

I was with the camels, hobbling them for the evening. From behind me I heard the snorting of a horse and turned to see Billy's nostrils flaring, sniffing the camels' pungent scent, wanting to be anywhere else. Mr Burke slid off in one motion — he was totally at ease in the saddle — and looped the reins over a post before stooping between rails to enter the pen. He showed no fear of the camels but nor did he seem fond of them. He was like a host with dinner guests he hadn't invited.

'Are they settling?' he asked me.

'Seem to be, sir. Growing accustomed to their loads, I think.'

'They'd better. Or they'll be on the supper plates. If they cart their bags and don't slow us down, I'll put up with them. Not my idea, though. Stuart has always favoured horses.'

He gazed at the animals, all the while sucking at the longest hairs of his moustache, pulling them into his mouth. The resulting sound was not dissimilar to the camels chewing. Up close I could see his scar, the thin pink line across his right cheekbone, pale and prominent against his weathered skin. I'd heard talk about this mark. One of the men said it went back to Mr Burke's cavalry days in Austria, a sabre duel over a lady. Landells snorted when he heard this tale and insisted he'd got the wound walking into a window ledge after too many drinks one night in Beechworth.

'I'm desperate to go,' said Mr Burke, 'but always it seems there's more to be done. More discussions to be had with the gentlemen of the committee, most of whom have never ventured further afield than Moonee Ponds.' He sucked again on his moustache and looked at me curiously, as if suddenly unsure who he was talking to. 'You're the soldier, right?'

'I *was* a soldier, sir.'

A pause. Mr Burke struggling to remember something. 'I have it! You're King?'

'I am.'

'King. That's right. I was told about you . . .' To my amazement he reached out for the side of my head. Instinctively I ducked, thinking that he planned to grab hold of my ear like one of the schoolmasters in Dublin, but all he did was brush his hand heavily against my hair. I couldn't tell whether this was an odd gesture of affection or he was brushing an insect away. But I was relieved to see that he was grinning. His teeth were even but stained.

'Ah yes! You're the one who broke some of our surveyor's equipment.'

My heart sank on learning he had heard of this. 'Just the one piece that I know of, for sure, sir. And I wasn't –'

He dismissed my concern. 'Quite animated about it all, he was.

He's like a child with his toys, is our Mr Wills. But I'll let you in on a secret, King. I'll be damned if he doesn't have a twin of the instrument that was broken tucked away somewhere. When he came up from the observatory he had three or four cases of stuff with him, most of it the likes of which I'd never seen before. He's very organised, carries an inventory of all that he's got. Though now he's got a bit less than he had.' He tossed his head back and chuckled. The camels stirred, unsure what to make of this loud man in their midst.

'Should I try to speak with him, sir? Apologise?'

'Not at all. Get about your duties. He has plenty to do, too, and he'll forget about this incident before long. Don't mind Mr Wills.' He paused. Something had just occurred to him. 'Wills. William Wills. Strike me, how's that for lack of imagination at a christening! Will Wills! He'll be all right, I think, though I'll be watching to see how he fares once we're off the tracks. We need him, King. The surveyor, the one who'll tell us where we are and where we're heading. That's more than I'd know without him!' He guffawed, wiping his lips with the back of his hand, and cleared his nose by pinching first one side then the other and snorting. He poked at the residue on the ground with the toe of his muddy boot. Gazing down, his manner grew more serious.

'He can amuse himself all he likes with his weather observations and whatnots, so long as these don't hold us up. But none of them, him or Becker or the doctor, will be free of camp duties. They must pitch in like everyone else. And if their scientists' gear becomes a burden, we'll ditch it, just like that. So you see, King, you might have done me a favour already. Lightened our load.'

He studied the camels. A general inspecting his troops. 'Which is the animal that rolled on our surveyor's gear?'

I pointed. 'The big one there, sir.'

Mr Burke advanced on Datchi, who backed away while sniffing at him.

'So *you're* the troublemaker, eh?'

Datchi lowered his head, inquisitive. This was a mistake as, with no warning, Mr Burke landed a looping blow to the animal's chin with the back of his right hand. Datchi grunted and backed away as fast as his hobbles would allow.

'There, King. Show them who's in charge, eh? I can now tell the aggrieved Wills I have dealt with the matter.'

He headed back to Billy, retrieving the reins and vaulting onto his back with surprising grace. But as he turned to go I noticed him shaking his right hand and sucking at the middle knuckles. They appeared to be bleeding.

Mr Burke was right. W never spoke of the incident with Datchi again. And I have a suspicion that W might even have come to wish that Datchi had broken more of his gear than he did, for after all the waiting and preparations W missed the start of the expedition.

We got going from Royal Park, Mr Burke on Billy at the head, Landells on Rajah close behind, me on foot towards the tail of our procession, stomping through mud in my expedition outfit of scarlet shirt, thick flannel trousers and broad-brimmed cabbage-tree hat, trying to keep the camels in line. But W was left behind with the American, Charles Ferguson, still stacking his equipment on one of the wagons.

I'd heard Ferguson suggesting, none too gently, that some of the gear should be abandoned. To which W replied insistently that every piece was necessary and that if the wagon were unpacked and packed again, more carefully this time, everything could be accommodated. I saw Mr Burke watch them for a while, then leave them to it.

'Catch us up,' he called, 'but I'll not wait for you.'

As it happened, W had little difficulty rejoining the caravan late on the first evening. Urchins from the park could have followed us, so slow was our progress. All that gear we had! Some twelve months' worth of supplies. Spare shoes and harnesses for the horses and camels, medical equipment, cots for the sick, signals, a Chinese gong, rockets and blue lights, a mountain of firewood, heavy tents lined with green baize, seven hundredweight of oatmeal. We were like pedlars heading off to the goldfields. No wonder the pole of one of the ox-wagons failed as soon as it took the strain of starting. Another broke down between the park and Moonee Ponds, an unevenly stacked load causing the axle to snap. In preparing for every contingency, giving us everything they imagined might be necessary, the committee had made it difficult for its exploring party to move.

Mr Burke rode backwards and forwards from the front of the caravan to its dragging tail, impatient, anxious to get on. He was like a swimmer, arms flailing against the current, with a rope tied to his waist securing him to a river bank. There were occasions, as on the first night, when none of us knew quite where the leader was. The talk in camp was he'd turned around and ridden all the way back into town. I heard Landells say he'd met up with his actress friend, Miss Matthews, but I don't know the truth of that.

Things went wrong.

The horses couldn't abide the camels and they had to be kept apart. One of the colts broke loose and ran off the first night. We got him back the next morning but it wasn't until early afternoon that we got going again — without Landells' dog, of which he was very fond. He had trained it to sit up on the camel beside him, but from Essendon he rode alone. The dog went missing, having wandered away, or been bitten by a snake. This left Landells in a foul mood, not helped when the weather darkened and we had to push on through rain.

It was very early on the second or third morning, just beyond Bulla, when I saw W again. I was looking for a camel that had strayed overnight and came upon the surveyor by himself, sipping steaming tea from a mug and gazing at the sky. Dawn had not long passed; there were streaks of clouds to the east, pink and orange. He glanced at me, showing no sign of recognition but evidently a little irked at having his solitude interrupted.

'Good morning,' he said. 'Everything in order?'

'Morning. Yes, sir. Just the one camel to attend to.'

'Oh yes.' His tone was terse. 'The camel man.' He tipped out the dregs of his tea, leaning first one way and then the other in a stretch.

I looked at the sky, where he'd been staring. 'Will we have more rain today, do you think?'

At once his manner became more animated. 'Rain? I think not. Those clouds you see, high up, they are cirrus. Pretty things, aren't they? No rain will come from them, but should they thicken and become lower ... well, stratus. If all is grey, that's nimbostratus. And you can expect to have d-damp boots again tonight.'

He smiled, pleased by his little lecture, then walked away without a farewell, whistling softly. More relaxed than he'd been in the park, clearly happy to be on his way, albeit slowly.

I had found the camel I was after nosing at some bushes not far from the camp, when I saw a lone figure walking back the way we'd come the day before. It was Samla, one of the sepoys. I had got to know him a little during the voyage to Melbourne but I had never seen him like this before: quite abject, weeping. When I asked him the matter he could barely speak.

'The Sahib, Mr Landells. He has ... discharged me.'

'Discharged? You're leaving? Whatever for?'

'I am a Hindu. I cannot eat any of the food that is given to me. The mutton I cannot touch unless I can kill it myself, in our way. My gods do not allow it. All I have eaten for these past three days is bread. And the work is hard. So I must leave.'

'Crazy bugger,' said Landells when I asked him about Samla a little later. 'I would have thought he could work out there'd be a problem before we left. Or get around it, however Dost Mahomed and the others manage. Damn him! Just a few days out and we're a man down already. A good man, too.'

He was right. Samla had a gift with the camels. They seemed to respond to the way he spoke to them. Landells turned his eyes in the direction that Samla had taken. 'Don't mind saying it gave me the willies the way it happened. He was so upset, I couldn't even be rough with him, though I had a mind to at first. Leaving us in the lurch and all. I even gave him the wages he was owed. But then he did something very odd, King. He bent down to touch the earth with the fingers of his right hand and brought them to his forehead. After that, before I could stop him, he touched me on *my* forehead. Some kind of blessing, I guess, before he got on his way. And the man was crying.'

'I know,' I said. 'He was that way when I saw him, too.'

What I didn't tell Landells was that W had also seen Samla. When I parted from the distressed Indian, I saw W on a rise some distance away. He must have heard some of our conversation, carried his way on the gentle breeze, and stopped to discern its source.

This sighting of W stayed with me: a thin figure standing alone against the feathery pink clouds, watching us.

Watching Samla, a man he had never spoken to, walk away from us all.

Ten

Doctor Treacey insists I give up the dugong oil.

'Get rid of it, King. It will do you no good at all. And it will do powerful good to those of us who must deal with you to be without its appalling smell.'

He picks up the green bottle from its place on the cabinet in the front room and reads the label aloud. '"Dr Hobbs' Own Dugong Oil: Guaranteed To Replace The Essential Fatty Elements Deficient In The Chyle Of Consumptive Patients. Distilled From Queensland Dugongs." Nonsense! Tell me straight, has it done anything for you, apart from induce nausea?'

'Nothing of note, Doctor,' I have to admit. 'Though I have only taken it on a few occasions. But Mr Howitt, who gave it to me, assured me he had read some glowing testimonials.'

'All composed, I'll warrant, by Doctor Hobbs himself. The man is a fraud, though now a well-to-do fraud on the strength of this stuff. Howitt is a wonderful bushman, but if your health is the issue, leave the prescribing to me. Are you still taking the Chlorodyne, as I instructed?'

'I am, though I cannot report any improvement.'

'Give it time. It's a slow process. But no ill effects? Good, good. Persist.' He gazes at me speculatively. 'I wonder... Electricity, King. I have read that galvanism is producing some remarkable results. Perhaps we should arrange a visit to the Galvanic Baths in Lonsdale Street, Mr Knight's establishment. Judicious application of mild electrical shocks to the body can prove extremely efficacious for some patients.'

'Even patients in my condition, Doctor?'

His hand moves from his chin to the top of his head, where he tugs at his hair. 'Ah, now that I cannot say for sure, but it is an interesting concept. There are those who claim that the body has its own rudimentary electrical circuits, so there may indeed be some basis to galvanism.'

'Perhaps. Though if I am to try any bathing it will be in St Kilda, I fancy, rather than Mr Knight's establishment.'

Silence. We both know I am unlikely to be doing any bathing at all. Treacey then leaps up, a man with other business to attend to. He snaps shut his case.

'St Kilda? Well, that's certainly an enticing prospect. You'll get a prettier walk here than in Lonsdale Street. May I?' He takes the bottle of Doctor Hobbs' oil between thumb and forefinger, as if its contents were repugnant to him. I can only hope that when he disposes of the contents, as I am sure he will, none of the local animals — the horses or dogs and the chickens in the house next to us — get at it. Dugongs may disagree with them.

Did we have any dugong oil with us when the expedition left? I cannot say for sure. But we seemed to have everything else. It was extraordinary the things I came upon when loading the camels early in the morning, or retrieving what had tipped out from one of the wagons after its load had become unbalanced. Or when another axle had broken. Or the whole clumsy apparatus had got bogged once again. We had flat-bottomed boats in case we came upon the inland sea that men talked about, guns to defend ourselves against the blacks, and trinkets – mirrors, ribbons, tomahawks, tobacco – to pacify the blacks so that the guns would not be necessary.

And a babushka. Mr Burke had one of those. A Russian doll. Wooden, prettily painted in bright colours. You took the top off one and there'd be another inside. Then another doll within that and yet another, until all that was left was a tiny thing on its own. Mr Burke's had been sent to him by his younger brother James, the one who died in the Crimea. The babushka was in the last package Mr Burke ever received from him.

'James had gone by the time I got it, King. Cut down by sabre thrusts on all sides of his body while charging the enemy front on. A soldier's death! Though I didn't know the boyo was dead for a while after that. Picture it. Me prancing about with a dead man's gift, wondering which skirt I could give it to. Thank God I hadn't parted with it when I heard the dread news.'

The doll was meant for a present. Mr Burke's brother knew he was one for the ladies. From what I heard, he was a bit the same himself. Mr Burke carried a likeness of his brother with him in his bags. He adored him, though I wonder whether this was largely because his brother had died fighting in the Crimea, whereas the war was over by the time Burke himself tried to get into the action.

Neither the picture nor the doll was there at the end. Mr Burke must have got rid of them. We crossed the country leaving objects and people behind all the way. Our expedition was like Mr Burke's babushka – as we went on, it grew smaller and smaller, bit after bit being taken away, until finally all that was left was a single tiny figure on its own. Me. The only one left from everyone there at the start, nineteen men and tons of baggage. The committee could only guess at our requirements; there had never been an expedition like it.

Mr Burke chafed at the delays. 'Come on, lads. Move yer lazy arses! If you can't find it, leave it behind. If you can't mend it, we can do without. Just keep on.'

I heard William Brahe the foreman explain a hold-up by saying some packs had shifted on the horses, a problem that would soon be rectified. It would be all right, he said. To which the leader replied, 'It's not all right. It's all *wrong*.' And rode away.

He was being squeezed by the committee. Such messages as he received in the early stages expressed concerns about costs and slow progress. After a month, we'd made it to Balranald, still in the settled part of the colony. We were an exploring party that hadn't explored anything. All we'd done was labour over old ground.

'See here, King,' said Mr Burke, poring over his map. 'Balranald. And over there, Adelaide. Much the same latitude, eh? If Stuart is to set off again, as I hear he will imminently, where will he leave from? Adelaide. And look –' slashing a line south to north on his map – 'if he's seeking to beat us to the Gulf, he's got a shorter distance to go. All this time and trouble and we're still behind. Further east, farting around with randy camels and a naturalist who wants to stop constantly to paint his pictures.'

This was harsh on Ludwig Becker. He was older than most of us, older than Mr Burke himself, and had done his best to cope with the work required. If I was near him in the mornings, I tried to help him with the loading of his camels, as clearly he was a man more comfortable with paints and specimens than the spitting, kicking beasts he had to deal with. Ruinous work, Becker called it. But he never said so to the leader; he was too proud for that. He was caught between opposing forces: the committee, which had engaged him for scientific work, and Mr Burke, a man with a restless spirit driven to keep moving forward.

We were pushing towards Menindie, on the Darling, when I

heard Mr Burke instructing Becker and Doctor Hermann Beckler that they would have to give up their scientific investigations and get on like all the other men. They didn't like this, and muttered to each other in German – unhappy, it seemed, that men of science could be treated like mere labourers. But to the leader, anything that might slow us down even more was a sin, and the men had a choice: keep up or go.

Yet I think Mr Burke had a soft spot for Becker. He showed no interest in his sketches or specimens, but respected the way he tried to do his work – often struggling into camps late, then staying up for hours diligently writing his reports to the committee on the plants and animals we had trudged past. And painting – fixing on paper what we had seen. A native wearing a coat of animal skins, a brilliant light in the night sky near the Darling that he said was a meteor. In the seconds it burned, it etched the silhouettes of the camels straining towards camp. And Becker, despite all his problems, got it down with his colours.

Mr Burke had less time for Doctor Beckler. He thought him a grumbler, a teller of stories against him. He regarded W as a man who could take over medical duties if required. W's father was a doctor; W himself had done a couple of years' training, plenty enough to dispense pills or medicines or roll on some bandages. Besides, on those days when all around us was a shimmering waste, a featureless landscape similar in every direction, it was clear to each of us that such privations as we might endure would not be much eased by pills or medicine or bandages.

Mr Burke shed impedimenta like a snake losing its skin. Stores were dumped – sugar, lime juice, tents and their poles, medicines, bottles, bandages, some of the guns. Men left, including the disgruntled Charles Ferguson. Others came on board. Charley Gray got talking with Mr Burke at the Swan Hill hotel, told him a bit about the conditions he was likely to find as he pushed on north towards Menindie. Mr Burke offered him a place in the party. Gray, the former sailor marooned far from any sea, accepted. There was a salary to be earned, and perhaps Mr Burke's talk of the Gulf filled Charley's head with images of the ocean. Once again he might taste salt water on his tongue.

The leader liked Charley because he went about his work without fuss and didn't disagree with him. Unlike Landells. They were never a good mix, George Landells and Mr Burke. Vinegar and oil. English and Irish. Second in command and a commander who never countenanced his authority being questioned. The man in charge of the camels – Landells would have had a hundred on the expedition if he could, and a commission to himself for each animal provided – and a leader convinced that camels were more trouble than they were worth.

In Swan Hill Mr Burke played the gentleman to some of the local ladies. He described his grand plans to unlock the interior so that their children's children would have verdant pastures to till.

'Farmland as far as you can see,' he told them, 'rolling into the distance . . .'

Even as he talked, some of the camels hobbled nearby went at each other. One of the males tried to mount another. Thwarted in its endeavours, it turned towards our visitors, groaning most crudely and thrusting with its member, which was obtruded and pink and dripping. The ladies went into a flurry with their fans. Landells, irked by not being invited to be part of the party to greet the ladies, laughed at this obscene display.

Mr Burke never forgave him for that.

And I heard the talk. The griping in camp. Whispers that Landells thought the leader to be unhinged. Rumours that Mr Burke and Landells had argued. It was said that words had been exchanged between the two over the camels' rum ration. Mr Burke declared the beasts perpetually pickled, to which Landells replied that the camels were *his* responsibility. The rum, he said, was to ward off the scurvy, and Mr Burke was ignorant when it came to animals.

Ignorant! Had he scoured a dictionary for a week, Landells could not have found a more insulting word to toss at the leader. It struck him like a woman's slap upon his cheek. Charley Gray, who claimed to have heard this exchange, said Mr Burke had stormed away, his face mottled pink above his beard, then ridden off on Billy. Fast and furious.

Rum and camels made a bad combination. Perhaps, as Landells insisted, it was good for them, but no amount of the spirit could entice the camels across the Darling River, near the Kinchika sheep station. In the end we had to unload them, punt the equipment across, then coax and wallop the beasts to get them through the water. Snorting and bellowing, nostrils agape when their feet no longer touched the river bottom, they were pulled the rest of the way. They were half drowned, but made it.

It was Landells' idea to use some of the shearers from Kinchika to help get the camels across. Mr Burke had left it to him – he wanted the camels over to the north side of the river without delay. The Kinchika shearers were a rough lot, with the manner of men too long away from the regular company of women. What Landells promised to pay them, or whether rum was their reward, I know not. All I can say is that rum meant for the camels went to the men from Kinchika that night. And to some of the men with the expedition party, too. Charley Gray, and me. But not Landells.

He wasn't there when the fire was lit, the barrels broached and the music played. One of the men had a fiddle, another a squeezebox. While I didn't see Landells, I cannot believe that the rum – which, like the camels, was in his care – got there without his knowledge. Indeed, I wonder now if this bacchanal by the Darling was devised by Landells as a deliberate flouting of the authority of

Mr Burke, who had ridden ahead to organise the expedition's camping place in Menindie. Landells let loose anarchy that night, knowing what the likely consequences would be.

I can wonder about this now. Back then I was senseless. Witless. Wondering only how and why I was waking in the dirt with Salah the camel licking at the vomit dried upon my shirt.

I have never had much of a stomach for strong drink, and for many years now haven't touched it at all. But it had been a brute of a day on the Darling. Evening was settling in when we got the last of the camels out of the river and secured them, dripping and foul-tempered, near a stand of she-oaks. A dipper – I don't know whose – was passed around. I thought it was water, maybe tea, until I tasted it. Sweet and fiery, like burning syrup. I gasped and slurped, wanting more. And there was more to be had.

Kennedy, one of the Kinchika men, had the dipper in and out of a rum barrel like a doctor dispensing medicine. Despite what came later, how wretched and ashamed I felt, I remember how the rum seemed to cure all the expedition's ills for a few hours. Charley became different from the man who had been trudging alone from Swan Hill, quiet, cowed by the distances. This Charley was downing the dipper in one draught, staggering in a crazy dance to the squeezebox music, swinging his hat around and around as if it were the handle of a stockwhip, his face turned up to the stars, streaming with sweat in the light of the campfire.

'Into it, matey,' he said. 'Get amongst it. Into the syrup while you can, for we'll never be back. Never be back. Never be back . . .'

It became his crazed refrain as he spun himself in circles, continuing even when the squeezebox stopped for a spell. 'Never be back, never be back . . .' Spinning until, like a child's top, he slowed and sank to the ground. One of the shearers roughly poked him back to safety with a boot when Charley rolled too close to the fire. I laughed as if it were the funniest thing I had ever seen.

Would have laughed even if half of Charley's leg had gone up in flames.

Still the dipper was being passed around. Between doses, Kennedy used it to thump the emptying barrel, a rough accompaniment to the discordant music. Then came cheering from the other side of the fire. A black girl the shearers seemed to know. Barefoot in a blue checked dress, torn along one side. Downing the whole dipper while the men clapped in time and laughed. Her teeth white in the darkness. One of the men took her arm and led her away from the fire. Then another, while those who were left yelled crude oaths and waited. I remember Charley spinning and the black girl tripping over something and calling out – in surprise or pain, I couldn't tell – her voice shrill like a child's, and the fire and the music and the thumping on the barrel becoming a drumming in my head and feeling cold and parched and so weary and then nothing until there was warmth on my face and the snorting of Salah and dirt behind my head and a terrible brightness when I opened my eyes and a pain in my side where somebody was kicking me.

Mr Burke. Shooing Salah away. His face silhouetted against the sun, already well up in the sky. I could tell it was him by the shape of his hat. Then his voice, different in tone to anything I'd heard from him before.

'Up! Up, damn you. Useless logs, the lot of you. Up!'

This to Charley. Who was kneeling, head down, like a dog mutely awaiting the whip's fall.

I groaned as I tried to rise. Mr Burke wheeled around as if at first he hadn't recognised me, my face all smeared with dirt and spit.

'You, soldier! I had thought better of you.'

It felt as if he'd kicked me again. I tried to speak but my throat and mouth filled with something bitter and I had to turn away.

His words throbbed in my head like the drumming from the night before.

The wreckage was everywhere. The campfire still smoking. The Kinchika men slumped on the ground as though poisoned. Kennedy still with the dipper in one hand. Another of the camels kicking at the rum barrel, then butting at it with its head to get at anything that might be left. The black girl was gone, but there, on the spines of a spinifex bush, what looked to be a piece torn from her blue checked dress. A smell of smoke and drink and piss and spew. And Mr Burke whirling around this sad assembly like a man possessed, taking long strides, kicking at any body not moving, his beard shiny with the spit he sprayed as he tried to urge us into action. One of the Kinchika men, eyes red and angry, rubbed at the spot on his side where Mr Burke's boot had thudded home, and swore after him.

'Damn your hide, you mad Irishman! We're not your sheep to be rounded up.'

Mr Burke spun around and let fly with another ferocious kick that landed just above the Kinchika man's belt buckle. The sound was like a stave on a bag of grain. The man gurgled and groaned and rolled into a ball, hands at his belly to protect himself, like one of the spiny anteaters we sometimes surprised on the trail. Then, as if realising how the numbers lay, Mr Burke drew his revolver from his belt and fired once, twice above his head.

The report was shocking in the still morning air. A flock of lorikeets, green and yellow, rose screeching from the branches of a nearby gum. With smoke issuing from the barrel of his gun, Mr Burke shouted at the bedraggled assembly.

'Right! The next sheep-shagger who says a word gets a dose of lead in his guts. On yer way, you useless drunks. You there, King, Gray, retrieve any of the camels that have wandered and lead them back to the main camp. That way, a mile or so down the river. We leave in two hours.'

We didn't.

The sun was merciless by the time Charley and I led Salah and Rajah and the other camels into the camp. I can't speak for Charley, but I felt more wretched myself than at any time since we'd left Melbourne. My throat was as dry as the ground beneath our boots. My eyes hurt in the sunlight. I wanted nothing more than somewhere cool and dark to lie down. The only thing that stopped me doing so was the certainty that I had let down the leader. If I now failed to return to the camp I'd be discarded like another bit of unwanted baggage. Stuck far from anywhere, with little future other than to become another station hand like the dissolute men from Kinchika.

Charley looked wretched but still seemed to find something funny in what had transpired. As we trudged up the river, the camels snorting behind us, tugging at their lead ropes, there was a faint smile on the sailor's cracked lips. And he was singing, over and over again, his refrain from the night before: 'Never be back, never be back...'

At the camp Becker had his sketchbook out, but his attention had been diverted by something happening a hundred or so yards away. We heard the voices but didn't see the figures until we skirted around a pile of rocks.

Mr Burke and Landells facing each other, having it out. And all the others — W standing outside his tent, Doctor Beckler to his side, Brahe and Patten and Dost Mahomed and the rest — keeping their distance as if repelled by an unseen force. Charley and I came a little way into camp and then stopped. On hearing the angry voices, Charley ceased his singing. His smile broadened. 'Jesus, this'll be good.'

Mr Burke had his hat off. His brow shone with sweat. The hat was in his right hand, an aid to expression as he swept his arms about. Billy was tethered nearby, ears pricked, alarmed by the raised voices.

'One night! One night, y'lazy whelp of a whore. One night I leave you in charge and it all falls apart. All discipline gone. Drink running free. The damned rum! Seems the only ones who didn't get at it were the fucking camels. And where were *you*, all the while, I wonder.'

Landells looked hot and tired. Gone was the dashing figure who had ridden away from the *Chinsurah* on Rajah. His beard was matted, his boots that he had looked after so carefully were coated in grime. 'I was here!' he said, his voice even angrier than when he'd tackled Datchi the camel. 'Here, trying to hold it all together because you'd disappeared again. Riding ahead like a madman, though we'll all make it to Menindie today anyway. Racing off, as you do, leavin' the organising to the likes of me.' He moved closer to Mr Burke, who took a step back, appalled either by Landells' onion breath or what he had said.

'Mad? Who're you calling mad? Don't forget, yer money-grubbing English camel-catcher, that you're addressing the leader of this expedition.'

'*Leader?*' Landells spat on the ground, not far from Mr Burke's feet. 'Your *prick* has a better idea where it's heading than the rest of you. A leader would never have ditched eight barrels of lime juice in Balranald just to lighten the load. What do you have now to save yourselves from the scurvy? The only place you'll lead this expedition is straight to the devil!'

Mr Burke's face was crimson. I thought for a moment that he was about to reach for his gun again. Landells, it seemed, had the same idea.

'You're not *fit* to lead. One day soon your hand'll leap ahead of that nut you have in your head instead of a brain and you'll kill someone with that gun of yours. 'Twould be a blessing to us all if you put a bullet through one of your own ears. You don't need 'em, that's for sure. You haven't listened to me all the time we've been gone.'

'Why would I listen to you? Your idea of discipline is to let loose an orgy as soon as I'm away. If I hadn't come back to move things along, we'd have lost another day of travelling time.'

'Orgy my arse! Just some of the men letting off steam. Men you left it to *me* to find because you had no idea what to do. Without those men, most of the camels and much of the gear would still be on the wrong side of the Darling. So don't talk to me about lost time. Without the camels, you'll be going nowhere.'

I saw Beckler nod in agreement.

'Sod the camels!' Mr Burke replied. 'I never wanted them. The camels were *your* idea, Landells. And you've done very well for yourself out of them, taken the committee for a pretty ride. But now it's over. I won't stand for insubordination or cowardice. This grand task ahead of us' – he seemed now to be addressing all of us, not only his second in command – 'demands discipline. Discipline! Landells, you are dismissed.'

If he had expected remonstrations or abuse, he was disappointed. Landells simply laughed in his face. 'Dismissed? No! I leave on my own accord. I'll not put up with your cockamamie posturing a day longer. And be assured that the committee in Melbourne will know of your erratic behaviour. They too must bear some responsibility. How they appointed you is a mystery to me. And, I'll wager, to a good many others.'

He turned, made as if to go, then swung around to once more face the leader, whose body was tensed like a man expecting a blow. 'I'll tell you one thing, Robert O'Hara Burke. Something for nothing. You have some good men on this expedition, honest men, but you'll lead them nowhere except straight to hell. I pity them. But you – God speed there, I say!'

And then he was away. Mr Burke stood quite still, watching him gather up his gear, saying nothing. Then he studied his hat, which remained in his right hand, and replaced it on his head. Suddenly he seemed unsure what to do or say next. He was like an actor come to the last page of his script with the hall lights still on him.

It was Doctor Beckler who broke the silence. He took several steps towards Mr Burke, shaking his head as a medical man does after attending to an unusually vexatious patient.

'Mr Burke. I . . . I really must protest.'

'Must you indeed?' The leader's voice was quieter now, but somehow more threatening.

'Mr Landells is – was – the expedition's second in command,' said Beckler, very animated. 'He was formally appointed to that position by the committee. It is intolerable that he should be spoken to as you have done. Intolerable! Mr Landells has, er, had important responsibilities. His absence could put us all at risk. As a senior man and the expedition's medical officer, I urge you to sort out your differences like gentlemen.'

Mr Burke heard this while brushing some dust from his jacket, apparently giving the task his full attention. He waited until Beckler had finished speaking, then a little while longer, before replying.

Perhaps Charley had seen something similar before. Perhaps he simply read the signs. Still smiling, as if this were all a show being staged for his entertainment, he whispered to me, 'The bloody dam's about to burst!'

At first it seemed he was wrong. For Mr Burke started slowly, softly. A man seemingly puzzled by what he had heard. 'You must *protest*, sir? What I've said is *intolerable*, sir? Well, well.' He shook his head as if everything had just been made clear to him. Then he advanced towards Beckler, standing as close to the medical man as he had been to Landells just a few minutes earlier.

'Well, what do you say to this, Doctor Beckler — fuck you! Fuck you and your pompous fucking protest! Fuck your *grandmother*, sir. There is one thing — one thing! — that I cannot abide. And that is anyone, *anyone*, regardless of their position, questioning my authority. I am the leader of this expedition. And, damn it, Doctor, I intend to lead it in the way I see fit. If that's intolerable to you, I suggest you consign your protest to paper and ram it up your fucking German arse!'

Beside me, Gray was wheezing. Either having trouble breathing, or trying to stifle his laughter.

As for the doctor, he reeled back from the verbal assault like Mr Burke's words were blows. He muttered something I couldn't discern. All I caught were 'outrageous' and 'untenable' amongst a stream of German phrases. The swagger with which he had faced Mr Burke had gone. All the air was out of him, his authority squelched. He headed to his colleague and countryman Becker, who put down his sketchbook and led the doctor away from the camp.

The leader was left alone again. Breathing heavily. Still pink in the face. Billy was whinnying, anxious for attention, and nuzzled at Mr Burke when he approached, talking to the horse calmly and allowing it to sniff at his shirt. Then he looked around him, at all of us standing at a distance, as if he'd only just become aware of the spectators to his performance.

'Well, come on,' he said. 'The entertainment is concluded. No call to loll about gawking, there's work to be done. I plan to break camp by noon and push on to Menindie. And I'll not wait for stragglers.'

But his words lacked their usual conviction. Nobody moved. Mr Burke's authority was like a branch he held before him. Anyone forcing it, hard and decisively, could snap it in two.

'If I may, sir...'

Without any fuss, W had stepped forward from his position on the side, moving like a penitent in church. He approached Mr Burke and addressed him directly, but his words could be heard by all of us. Mr Burke studied his surveyor as if trying to assess whether he, like Doctor Beckler, was reporting a grievance.

W halted a little distance from Mr Burke. His fingers checked and rechecked the buttons on his shirt and he seemed uncomfortable to be voicing his words rather than writing them in his journal.

'If I, er, may, sir. There is something you should know. About, ah, Mr Landells. He has been p-playing a fine game, trying to set us all together by the ears. Am I right, sir, in suspecting that in his comments to you Mr Landells has been finding f-fault with all of us?'

The leader said nothing.

'You told me, sir,' W continued, 'that Mr Landells had ex-expressed to you some, ah, disappointment in me. But to me he has always presented himself as a . . . staunch friend, while abusing *you* most intemperately. He has spoken ill of the doctor and of Mr Becker. But to them personally he has been all m-milk and honey. I would venture, sir, that, er, there is sc-scarcely a man in the party whom he has not urged you to dismiss.'

Still Mr Burke was silent. But his expression had softened, and there was even the ghost of a smile playing around his lips.

'It is a double game he has been p-playing,' said W. 'One that could only have jeopardised the success of this expedition. To which, ah, all personal ambition should be secondary. Discipline must be maintained. Without discipline there will be . . . dis-disintegration. I must say that I, er, support your stand on this. Sir.'

His uncharacteristic speechifying concluded, W made to return to his place. But before he had taken two steps, Mr Burke wrapped him in a huge embrace, thumping him on the back.

'Will! Capital fellow! I thank you.'

Both men appeared moved. Indeed, there looked to be tears in W's eyes, whether from emotion or the pain of Mr Burke's buffeting I could not tell. But the moment of crisis had passed, the leader and his surveyor had come to an accord. Men drifted away to get about their duties, Charley and I tending to the camels.

'Shall you tell them or shall I?' asked Charley.

When I looked puzzled, he went on, 'Tell the camels there'll be no rum for them from now on. Mr Burke will see to that, after last night.'

'No rum for anyone, I'll be bound.'

Charley looked aghast. 'No rum, 'tis the truth. God strike me, King, can it be that we've had our last drink for a good while? What a long, parched slog lies ahead of us!'

I made no reply. There was no need. The answer seemed as clear as the late morning sunshine. Clear and hot and dry.

Menindie was the last settlement before the interior. And not much of a settlement at that. The main building was Paine's Hotel, where Mr Burke and W took rooms. Mr Burke had appointed W his second in command, replacing Landells. Talk in the camp was that William Brahe was put out by this appointment, believing his seniority gave him first call on the position. But having witnessed Mr Burke's treatment of Doctor Beckler, who had announced that he, too, intended to leave the expedition just as soon as a replacement could be found, Brahe wisely concluded that the time was not right to question the leader.

In W, it seemed, Mr Burke believed he had a man who would follow without fuss. Not strain in the opposite direction as Landells had done. W was a different kind of Englishman, and much younger, which made it less likely for him to question Mr

Burke's judgement. And I wonder now if the leader saw in W somebody who would complement himself — someone quiet where he was voluble, thorough and methodical while he was careless of detail.

In Menindie the rest of us camped on the banks of the Darling while Mr Burke and W stayed at the hotel. W was studying maps, trying to determine our course. Mr Burke was chafing at another delay, waiting for wagons to catch us up. A steamer had already arrived by river, bringing yet more supplies. We were two months in and still far from the interior, let alone the Gulf. In the hotel, Mr Burke spent time talking with William Wright, a sullen fellow recently dismissed from one of the local stations, who claimed to know the country we were due to cross next.

It was to the hotel that I was summoned one warm night when pelicans rose from the river and flew away south with slow, effortless strokes of their broad white wings. Patten brought word that Mr Burke wished to see me. Overhearing this, Charley Gray whistled and shook his head.

'You're for it, mate. Can only be bad when the boss calls for you.'

I had learned that jests were Charley's preferred form of communication, but still I wondered if there was some truth in what he said. The leader had never sought me out before, and I knew he was trying to reduce the size of the expedition. Had I now been deemed to be expendable, perhaps because of the episode with the Kinchika men?

At the hotel, a low building with a wide verandah, Paine the publican directed me to Mr Burke's room. The door was open, so too a window overlooking the river. The habits of a man accustomed to sleeping outdoors.

He was seated at a table near the window, writing. His candle had burned very low and was sputtering. The table seemed too small for him, or perhaps the chair was too high. Whatever the explanation, he looked uncomfortable, his legs thrust out to one side as if they were perpetually in the way.

My knock on the door seemed to startle him. He rose to his feet while trying to replace a paper – a picture of some sort, it seemed – into a drawer under the tabletop. But the sudden movements were too much for his cramped surrounds. An ink bottle was upended and a dark stain spread over the document on which he had been writing. He swept it up and waved it in the air. I think he meant to dry it but the action only caused the ink to spread still further, running in outstretched black fingers over the paper's surface. I paused. Was this another mishap for which I could be held responsible?

Mr Burke turned towards me, frowning. 'Ah. Come! Come forward. Yes, soldier.' He studied the ink-smeared paper, his distracted manner suggesting he was trying to recall why he wanted to see me. Then he looked directly at me and it was all I could do not to look away, so intense was his gaze.

'Camels, King. You *are* the camel man, are you not?'

I nodded. 'One of them, sir.'

'And now we've one less than we had. Landells has left us.'

'Yes, sir.' I had seen Landells near the steamer landing. He had been drinking, and was telling anyone who would listen of the doom that awaited all members of the exploring party while 'that crazed Irish idjit' was in charge.

'So, King, I have decided. I want you to assume Landells' responsibilities. You will be in charge of the camels.'

I was a soldier: this was an order. 'Very well, sir. I will do the best I can. One thing, if I could. The other night, with the shearing men, and the drink. I just want to say –'

He waved one hand at me dismissively. The subject held no interest for him. He was looking at the paper again. 'Expunge it from your mind, King. Between you and me, one soldier to another, I have passed some riotous nights myself. Nights when the blood is hot and music is playing and it is grand to be alive and in the company of women. And I tell you, there are few finer women than my sister in Ireland. Hessie. It is she to whom I am writing. But look at this! Ruined, quite ruined. I must begin over again. I shall give up the ink, I think. Useless in these conditions; dries even while a man is gathering his thoughts.'

He studied me across the table. 'You have a sister, King?'

'I do. Though I have not seen her for close to eight years now. In Ireland, sir. Name of Nora.' I recalled how she'd been when I left her – hands pressed together, eyes moist with tears.

'Nora! A grand name. A name for a poem ... I do not think I have known a Nora. At least, I cannot recall one. Hear this, King. It is what I was writing to my sister just now.' He held the stained paper before him and read aloud with expression, as if his words were lines from a play. '"I am confident of success, but know that failure is possible; and I feel that failure would, to me, be ruin; but I am determined to succeed, and count on completing my work within a year at furthest." What d'you say to that?'

'I think we shall succeed, sir.'

'I must, King. I must. The alternative is unthinkable.' Passing his hand over his face, overtaken by weariness, he sat down again at the table and resumed his writing. He took a new sheet of paper and looked to be beginning again on the letter to his sister, using the ruined original as his guide. I waited for several minutes but Mr Burke did not glance up. Our business, it seemed, was concluded. I quietly backed out of the room and hurried away to tell Gray my news. Fearing dismissal, I had instead been promoted. I suspected that Charley would see some humour in this.

It was not until I was almost back with Charley that I was struck by something in my exchange with the leader. 'I must, King.

I must.' Our expedition was an intensely personal mission to Mr Burke. Failure, he had written, would be ruin. No wonder he was so driven to get on.

So now I was in charge of the camels. Dost Mahomed greeted the news with an extravagant bow. As I'd expected, Charley snorted and asked me whether, like Landells, I now planned to wear a bloody dandy's jacket.

But it was a horse, not a camel, that did for Becker before we left Menindie. Poor Becker: he was one of those men to whom bad things happen. Somehow he managed to get his feet in the path of his horse's hooves. Knowing a little of the naturalist's odd ways, I suspect the German had stopped suddenly, distracted by something he had seen — an odd species of bird, perhaps, or a goanna, which he called *guano*, basking in the sun. He stopped, but the horse kept going and trod on the end of his foot. The nail on his biggest toe was rent apart; one half was forced down into the flesh, leaving Becker in agony, barely able to walk.

He was still limping a day or two later when Mr Burke asked him his intentions. The leader had resolved to split the expedition. An advance party would head into the interior to establish a camp at Cooper's Creek, which W reckoned to be four hundred miles or more to the north. William Wright, the local man, had undertaken to guide us the first part of the way. Then he was to head back and join up with the rest of the party. They would establish a depot in Menindie and follow with the remainder of the animals and stores as soon as practicable.

Mr Burke asked Becker to decide between staying and going. 'Well, sir, do you like to stay in the depot, or go on with me now to Cooper's Creek? If you like to be with the party, you are welcome, but I must tell you, there will be no time for scientific research. Nor a horse or camel to ride on. You will have to tramp all the way and work like the other men.'

Becker looked first at Mr Burke then down at his foot, muttered something in German, and threw up his hands as if the decision were not his to make. 'I am not afraid to work, sir, although you will find men possessed of greater physical power than I can boast of. But to walk all the way, Mr Burke, is impossible in consequence of my accident. I am lame at present and can hardly stand. It is better for you and me that I remain here for some time in the depot, where I shall work up the material I have gathered in reference to the natural sciences.'

Mr Burke, who had listened patiently to this speech, appeared satisfied. He knew that Becker was a favourite of some members of the committee. He could tell them now, quite straight, that he had given their man of science a chance to accompany him. 'Very well,' he said to Becker. 'Hear this. I intend to look for a trail up to Cooper's Creek. Once I know where it is, and how it is with water, and once I have found a spot to form a depot there, I shall send for you to come up with the others with such things as are wanted.'

And so the party was divided. Nine of us trudged out of Menindie. Eight kept on, once Wright turned back. Becker stayed behind with the others, consorting chiefly with the grumbling Doctor Beckler.

Mr Burke's babushka was getting smaller.

Nineteen men we had been. Now, of those, we were down to eight. Pieces of the wooden doll, so prettily painted, were being discarded and left behind. Ludwig Becker would have been better served doing his paintings in the city, with somewhere soft to sleep of a night. Somewhere without rats and stagnant water and intractable camels. The learned gentleman never made it to the Cooper. He died from exhaustion and the fever on the way there.

Died in a delirium, speaking sentences that made no sense. He was laid in a shallow grave in the vast and ghostly countryside he had tried to sketch. A good man, gone.

I did not know this at the time. Like a great many other things, I found out only later.

Eleven

In truth, there is much I don't remember at all. It's a decade ago now. More. Much of it has become indistinct — footprints in sand once wind has smoothed the surface. I can only write what I recall and what I have learned since. Sometimes they do not fit together well, like pieces from different jigsaw puzzles.

I must try to lay them on a table. One piece: the trip from Menindie to the Cooper after Mr Burke had split our party the first time. It took us the best part of a month. No, the worst part.

It was late in the year. There were days we could hear the heat. A cracking sound, as if the rocks themselves were splitting. We took to breaking camp before dawn, at five or six by W's watch, but always the sun would surprise us and the earth seemed to hum like a violin string stretched taut.

We must have looked so small to the birds that circled us in the limitless sky, their easy motion mocking our slow progress. Kites they were, or perhaps a kind of hawk. Near the Torowoto Swamp, as arid a swamp as ever I saw, I shot one to try to bring some difference to our diet. A lucky shot, as it was high above us. It came to earth still alive, one wing smashed and the other thrashing. Hissing when I approached it. Eyes still open, glaring at me even after I'd clubbed its head with the rifle butt. Days later there were fragments of skull, wafer thin, set hard in blood on the butt. A useless meal it made, too. Imperfectly plucked, what wasn't burned over the fire was undercooked – bitter and stringy, the eyes melted into a yellow paste. It felt like bad luck to have brought down such a graceful thing. I let the hawks be after that, just as Charley said sailors left the albatross alone.

I can still recall that hawk. And the heat. And the way that most afternoons, when we could hear the blood banging in our own heads, we'd seek out shade – from saltbushes maybe, or rocks, or even within a depression in the ground – cover ourselves as best we could and try to wait out the worst of the sun. But Mr Burke never liked to stay still very long, reminding us we were yet to cross any land that other white men had not travelled before. So at sundown we'd push on some more, if we could get the animals to move. When the heat had been unusually intense, the camels would simply refuse to rise. They preferred a thrashing to more miles with their loads.

Water, it all hinged on water. We each had water-bags, but these did not hold as true as we had expected, and our precious liquid seeped away like the contents of the baked riverbeds we passed. Even when the waterholes still held something, they could be hard to find. On the dry plains the water turned the same colour as the yellow soil all around, and often it was only the glint of sun on a still surface that led us to them.

All those days have merged in my mind to become one vast bleak expanse through which we toiled. There was sand. There were stones that made every step awkward. Trees contorted into strange shapes, and tussocks of grass with prickly seeds that worked their way inside our boots no matter how much strapping we wound around them. Whenever we stopped, the sandflies sucked at our sweat, so that we had to wear netting while we ate or drank to avoid ingesting them.

And always there was the relentless and unforgiving sun. It

left me squinting, reluctant to look up. I paid more attention to the animals that were my responsibility. I was there for the camels, watching for signs of the scab. We carried brimstone and grease for that. The navigating was not my concern and I was glad of it. We could look around and see no horizon at all. It was as if the land and sky had been bleached into one. Our world was quite flat. Sometimes I wondered if we had moved at all, so little did the landscape change. I kept my eyes on the stony ground before me so I wouldn't stumble. Or concentrated on the animals. I crossed half the continent staring at camels' arses.

We didn't talk much. There was nothing to say, or it had already been said. After Wright turned back to Menindie to prepare the party that would come after us, it was W who gave instructions about the route to take. Whenever there was any kind of a rise he would take out his instruments and make his readings while we sat, grateful for a stop. Then W would consult with Mr Burke, whose face had taken on the same scorched hue as the ground we covered. Mr Burke would nod and point ahead.

'Those three dead trees way up ahead, lads. Look hard and you'll see 'em. Fallen together in the shape of a church spire. Straight there. We'll give the animals a break at the next water — I'll wager a sovereign to a turd that there's water beyond those trees. I've seen birds heading on there. If it's bigger than a billabong I'll name it and Mr Wills can add it to his chart. How does Lake Gray sound to you, man?'

Charley just grunted. He had bigger expanses of water in mind than the stagnant ponds we usually came across. He sang shanties to himself as he trudged along, the words running into each other, becoming a drone.

But we were lucky. There was water. Scum-covered pools, some of it, and there were times when the animals got to it before we could put our dippers in, but we seldom had to break into the barrels of water that the camels carried. I think they caught the scent of it sometimes. When the thirst hit them – even though they craved water less than the horses – the camels' nostrils would flare and a grinding sound came from deep within their throats. They could smell the water, hear the slopping sound the barrels made when they rose up, yet not taste it. This was a strange sort of torture. But their cargo could turn out to be more precious than gold where we were going.

In his fieldbooks, which he kept current with the assiduity of a teacher marking his rolls, W recorded the location of all the water we found. When we came back, he said, we could retrace our steps and know where there was water.

When we came back? That prospect seemed more remote than the vanished horizon. And we knew, too, that despite the heat the season had not been unusually harsh. Wright even said there'd been good rains. But by the time we returned, the dry would have set in, turning waterholes into dusty depressions that might mock our swollen tongues. By then, would there still be barrels of water? Or camels to carry them? Or any of us left at all? In such vast emptiness we could disappear like putrid water in a sinking pond, drying out until nothing was left but dust. Vanishing just as Leichhardt and his party had done, leaving no traces to tell of our fate.

Years later, long after the end, Doctor Ferdinand von Mueller, who had been a senior man in the Exploration Committee, showed me some of the sketches Becker had sent back up until the time we made Menindie. They were delicate things. The paper could be seen through the watercolour paints. Several had Becker's handwriting, neat and precise, giving details of what he had depicted: 'Gecko, found by me under the bark of a gum-tree; Fisch, caught by natives in a billabong...'

I marvelled that he'd found the time and energy to finish these, with all the labour he had been obliged to do as well. But when I studied the pictures it felt as if I were looking at foreign places. Becker the artist painted things I had never seen. *Crossing the Terrick Plains,* for example. He must have gone ahead to sketch it. Two lines dividing around him. One, the wagons; the other, camels heading towards the bleached skeleton of a cow, or maybe it's an ox. Between the lines – zigzagging as ever, urging stragglers to keep up – is Mr Burke on Billy. The perspective is odd. Billy looks tiny, little more than a pony. Both he and his rider are toy-like and coloured an odd chalk-grey hue. Ghost-grey. They are spectral figures, transparent, doomed to fade away. The column of camels becomes less distinct as it grows smaller. If I am in the picture at all, I am no more than a couple of lines. A suggestion of something in motion far in the background.

This is one of the few pictures by Becker to include any of the expedition members. He concentrated instead on what we encountered. Empty plains. A rocky plateau forming the only feature in an otherwise flat landscape. Roots of trees exposed on an eroded river bank. Natives depicted in the same manner as lizards and plants: curiosities of the natural world.

I recognised none of them. Only the emptiness and the vastness of the night skies lit up with stars more numerous and brilliant than any I'd ever seen before. Diamonds on purple velvet. Becker and I saw the same skies, but that was all. Perhaps if he had done more sketches of camels' rumps, or my dusty boots taking one endless step after another, or Charley Gray rolled up in his blanket at night like a child, his pictures would have seemed more familiar.

Becker and I not only saw different things, we had different reasons for making the journey. He was there for science, to record and describe the country and its creatures, to reveal to the men of the Royal Society what lay far beyond their lecture halls. As for Mr Burke, he had committed himself to succeed. To prove himself to the ladies he had left behind and to all the scoffers and sneerers in Melbourne – all those who thought him no more than an over-promoted policeman. To show himself to be as worthy of memory as his brother James, killed in battle in the war Burke had been unable to fight. And so he waged war against the emptiness of the interior. Success in this undertaking would see him no longer the wild Irishman, but a gentleman explorer. Conqueror of the continent.

Stuart, the Scot, sought the same goal. In the evenings, when the cold settled down from the stars and a breeze stirred the leaves into conversation one with another and the camels' hobble chains clinked in the darkness, I think Mr Burke sensed Stuart somewhere in the inky void. He was an unseen presence, pushing us on. We had no means of knowing Stuart's position but he was there all the way, the spectral member of our party. Mocking us when our progress was slow.

Mr Burke thought of him often. 'You know the worst of it, King? I dream of reaching the Gulf, stumbling on an expanse of white sandy beach, to find Stuart already there, his trousers rolled up, bathing his legs in the cool salt water. In one hand he holds a bottle of champagne – warm from his journey, but he's heedless of that – and in the other the fucking flag of Saint Andrew! He waves it at me, laughing ... And then I wake, King, and all around me is an empty, stony waste, with so much further still to go.'

And W? I cannot say for sure why he was with us, or what he hoped to find, but until near the end he seemed more content than the rest of us. The physical labour appeared not to bother him and he derived great satisfaction from his observations and notations. It wasn't unusual to come upon him late at night, alone with his instruments, fixing our position from the stars. He would seldom talk, just nod and be about his business. His fieldbooks, with their columns of figures for wind and clouds and temperatures, were testament to his discipline. These were tangible things he could show his father the physician on his return. Proof of what his son had achieved when put to the test as surveyor and second in command of the grandest expedition ever assembled in this untamed country.

W's promotion sat easily with him, though it brought little change to the manner in which he related to the rest of us. He was still a man apart. He listened but seldom offered much to camp conversations. Which is why I have no trouble bringing to mind the night twenty-two days out from Menindie, by which time a slow greening of the landscape and a greater presence of birds suggested we were drawing closer to the Cooper, where we would make a base.

W has finished his writing and is sitting on his own on the far side of the campfire, studying the embers as if the coals are something else he might classify and note down in one of his books. Patten is beside him, his smithy's sack at his feet. The camels are settled. I am savouring my last mouthfuls of tea, the sugary dregs at the bottom of my tin mug.

Next to me, Charley is paring a twig with his bushknife, the shavings falling in a pile near his boots, and softly singing one of his songs of the sea. He seems to have an inexhaustible supply of these shanties, though his memory of lyrics regularly fails him after a verse or two. So then he will start again on another song, though often its tune is near identical to the one preceding it.

It is quiet, with no breeze at all. Charley's voice drifts over the camp.

> I dreamed a dream and I thought it true,
> Of my Lord Franklin and his gallant crew.

> With a hundred sailors he sailed away
> To the frozen oceans in the month of May –

'Stop, p-please, Charley. Now.' W sitting quite still. Looking across the fire. His tone brooking no argument.

Charley halts, mid-verse. More from surprise than anything else. It is rare for W to speak at all at these times, let alone issue an order.

'You mean stop my singing?' he asked, bewildered. 'Why, does it bother you?'

'Not your singing. Just that song.' There are deep shadows on his face from the fire.

'"Lord Franklin"?'

'The same . . . I, er, had a cousin on that expedition, you see. Harry. He was a lieutenant. And he, ah, perished, with all the rest. Or so we must surmise.'

'Bugger me,' said Charley. 'I'll be damned. I didn't know. 'Tis just another song to me.'

'You weren't to know. It's no matter. And all quite some time ago now.'

'May 1845,' says Mr Burke. He has been standing a little distance away, staring up at the night sky. He strides closer to the rest of us. 'Sir John Franklin, Arctic explorer and a former governor of Van Diemen's Land, set off by ship from England to seek the Canadian North-West Passage.'

'Two ships, actually, sir,' his deputy interjects. '*Erebus* and *Terror*. One hundred and twenty-eight officers and men.' W speaks briskly, reciting facts he seems to have committed to heart, then pauses. We all wait. Charley's gaze meets mine. He raises an eyebrow. W has just contradicted the leader. But Mr Burke, this once, appears not to mind.

'Two ships you say, Will? Two ships it is, then. I bow to your expertise.' He continues with his story. 'They were sighted by whalers north of Baffin Island several months into their voyage. Then nothing, not a word. After two years, search parties were sent out. Still nothing. 'Twas a confounding mystery. Sir John's wife, Lady Franklin, wouldn't let it go. Twelve years on, she sent out another search mission. But not until 1859, just last year, were there any answers.'

Mr Burke pauses, as if waiting for W's permission to continue. W says nothing. His eyes have returned to the coals. Now this story is coming back to me. I recall some talk in the barracks and mess hall. Muttering and conjecture. A mystery unfolding in instalments in the brittle pages of *The Times of India*.

'Answers? You mean they found out what happened?' Charley asks.

'It seems so, Gray. Some skeletons were found. Wreckage. A written account, and tales told by Eskimos of starving white men in a dreadful way, hauling sleds, falling even as they walked. Their ships had been trapped in ice for near two years. Stuck fast, drifting with the floes, their supplies running out. Seems that Lord Franklin, the commander, and some twenty others died on ship. All the rest, in desperation, sought to trek across the ice to civilisation.'

W rises from his spot near the fire and walks away without another word, leaving behind an awkward silence and a story only half told.

Patten, who has been trying to clean desert grime from his blacksmith's tools, is the first to speak. 'Is it true what was said, sir, about what happened to those men?'

'That they perished, Patten?'

'No, sir, I mean what some did to try to survive. I heard tales. Rumours, like. That they had to resort to eating one another, sir.'

Charley snaps the twig he has been working on. Mr Burke's

voice is very soft, as if he is unsure whether W can still hear, though he can no longer be seen.

'There *were* claims of cannibalism, Patten, yes. But even if true, no condemnation can be made. We can only guess at the desperation that overtakes men, even civilised men, in such an appalling situation. They were heroes. All of them.'

'Jesus,' Charley says, very quiet. And then the only sound is the fire hissing.

I never heard Charley sing that song again. And, as far as I know, after that night the subject was not raised on the expedition. But it stayed with W until the end, when he, like his cousin Harry, was stranded far from aid. His cousin on ice, W on stony ground in the parched Australian interior. Tragedies have a way of raking cold, bony fingers over family trees.

I have heard much nonsense spouted, usually when toasts are taken and glasses raised, about what drives men to be explorers. I have heard speeches made about communing with the heart of a vast continent, opening trails and grazing-lands, bringing civilisation to primitive people. For me, most of this is as worthless as camel shit.

I was young. There was money in it. And, once into it, no way back. Halfway across a desert, it can seem as hopeless to turn around as to keep going.

Twelve

Nora

It were him.

Call it a sister's intuition, but I knew. The details in the few scant references I found appeared right. John King, an Irishman, age twenty-one. Though I had to think back to be sure about this. An assistant with the camels.

That bothered me. What did John ever know of camels? He never saw one in Dublin. But the newspapers said the camels had most come from India, where I believed my brothers had been.

It *were* him, on the exploring expedition. Crossing the country while I were in Melbourne, having arrived with nothing but hope of finding John, and a letter from Reverend Taylor in Sydney to his cousins in Christ, as he called them.

With this letter, and the bag that held my few belongings, I called upon the Wesleyan Church soon after my visit to the Royal Society. I had nowhere else to go. Melbourne were a settlement in which many of the buildings looked to have been knocked together in too much haste, but the church were a splendid new structure of dark blue stones. Its spire towered over Lonsdale Street. I felt intimidated by its size. It were all I could do to go inside.

A man in black took my letter and told me to wait until Reverend Draper would see me. His face had a sour look, like he bathed it in vinegar rather than water, but Mr Draper, when I saw him, were more welcoming. He were a short man with almost no hair on top of his head. It seemed to have slid down his face and then flourished on his cheeks. When first I saw him he had his head down, reading Reverend Taylor's letter. My view of him were a bald pink scalp, spectacles, and white whiskers alongside his ears. Upon finishing the letter he folded it and laid it on the desk. Then he removed his spectacles and waved them to usher me into the seat opposite him.

— Well, Miss King, you have made quite an impression on my old friend Reverend Taylor, it seems.

— I've... I've not read his letter, sir.

— Of course. Did Theophilus tell you we studied together in London?

— No, sir, just that I would do well to see you when I came to Melbourne.

— Indeed. And I am delighted you have, although I fear you find Melbourne in an unsettled state. Gold has been like a magnet pulling men away. Families have been split. Miners are the most unsettled class of persons I ever saw. Many that have gone will never return, perhaps they will leave the colony altogether. Did y'know that some ministers have relocated to tend to the miners? Nowhere is the need for God greater than on the diggings. The lure of Mammon is a dreadful adversary, Miss King.

I nodded, not knowing what to say. So decided silence were best.

— You have a brother on the exploring expedition? Reverend Draper were looking again at the letter.

— I believe so. Though I have not managed to contact him.

— A marvellous enterprise! Quite the talk of the colony. I used it myself as the theme for a sermon. *Seek and ye shall find*... I would hope, Miss King, that you are successful in your own seeking.

— I don't believe there is anything more I can do to find him.

They are well gone now. All I can do is wait for him to return. Pray that he does return.

— I will pray for you also, Miss King.

Thinking he were about to drop down on his knees, I made to get off my chair but Reverend Draper gestured with a palm upraised to stop me.

— No, no. Not now. I will make further mention of the expedition in one of my addresses, and ask the congregation to pray for the safety of all the explorers. I will make a note to myself on this point.

He took a large appointments book, bound in leather as black as his vestments, dipped a pen in a glass inkwell, and wrote on an open page. His attention then returned to the letter from Reverend Taylor, which he had placed on the desk before him. He considered it again while tapping his front teeth with the stem of his pen.

— Well now, what can we do for you? Theophilus suggests that I must try to find you a position. Your timing is excellent. There is a need everywhere for help, particularly experienced help. So very many people have gone to the goldfields hoping to find in an hour what they couldn't hope to earn in wages over twenty years. I wonder ... He broke off.

— Wonder what, sir? Scared, then, that I might be thought impertinent.

— I wonder if the answer for you may lie in St Kilda. One of our more recent plantings, but already showing signs of vigorous growth. Yes, St Kilda. He tapped again with his pen on his teeth. Though conditions may be rougher than you became used to in Sydney, I fear, and the company more lively.

— Lively? I were not sure what he meant.

— Reverend Bickford is a young man, Miss King. That is, considerably younger than myself, which is a good thing, as limitless energy is required to sow God's seed on untilled ground. I like to think of Mr Bickford as a comet in our planetary system, seemingly in perpetual motion but somehow never burning out. On first meeting he can seem meek, but he is a sight to behold in the pulpit. It is as if he is infused with the word of the Lord. He leads his listeners in veritable bursts of joyous praise. Already he is being spoken of as one of the most powerful orators yet heard in this colony. A title I would be proud to claim as my own.

He paused, surprising me with his silence. Talking seemed to come as readily to him as breathing. Then he stabbed at the inkwell with the pen and began scrawling on a clean sheet of paper.

— Miss King, I am writing to Reverend Bickford in St Kilda, introducing you and advising him of Reverend Taylor's endorsement. I take it there is no impediment to your beginning at once?

— Well, no sir, but what would my duties be?

— As they were in Sydney, I imagine. A combination, if I read the reference correctly, of housekeeper and cook, hmm?

Hearing no objection from me, he continued.

— Why don't you wander out and take a better look at our church, of which I am inordinately proud. If that is a sin, I cheerfully confess to it! And once I finish this note I will see if Mr Metherdew, our verger, can organise some transportation for you.

He returned to his writing, giving me once again the view of his gleaming pink scalp. I left him in his office.

It felt odd to be alone in the church. All those pews with no-one in them. The empty pulpit, decorated windows with nobody looking out of them. My footsteps were loud on the cold bare stones, and then I realised I were not the only one there.

The man with the sour face were watching me from near the main entrance. Mr Metherdew, I assumed. He appeared to be sorting some hymn books. Noticing me looking up at the interior of the spire overhead, he asked a question, his voice as sharp as his expression.

— You like it?

— Well, yes. It's wonderful. Huge.

— And unnecessary! He advanced towards me, taking small steps very quickly, still holding several of the books. Unnecessary, he repeated. Reminiscent of the frippery of the Church of Rome.

— You mean the spire?

— The whole building, but especially the spire. I hear tell it is such a prominent feature that some mariners in Hobson's Bay now use it as a marker to adjust their compasses. A church has no call to stand out in such a way. John Wesley himself never sought such grand surroundings in which to spread his message. Why should they be needed now?

— Because, my excellent but wearisome verger, a church can be a symbol of God's permanence in a shifting world, said Reverend Draper, who had exited his office and overheard some of the conversation.

Mr Metherdew took a few steps back, like a dog surprised someplace he weren't meant to be. The minister, striding back and forth with hands raised like he had rinsed them but lacked a towel for the drying, fast warmed to his theme.

— You see signs of Popery in every fine piece of stonework. I see an altar of consecration to God, a Bethesda of healing to all in need, a bethel of God's presence to multitudes gathered together in worship. The House of God! The Gate to Heaven! May this spire, this pointer to the Pole Star, be as a minaret from whence daily shall come the Christian call to prayer. Metherdew, you mention the mariners in Hobson's Bay. It is my prayer that this spire shall guide them, and indeed all Heaven-bound mariners, whether on land or sea, over life's tumultuous waves.

May it be an inspiration, a rallying point, for all who would rise up to a place by the side of God!

— Amen to that, said the verger, banging a pair of hymn books together to shake all dust from them. But his expression, sour as before, did not reflect an endorsement of what his minister had said. It were an amen of conclusion. A full stop.

And Reverend Draper did stop. He let his hands fall to his side, dabbed at his eyes with a large white handkerchief, then removed an envelope from his vestment pocket and gave it to me.

— You must forgive my volubility. Here is your letter to Reverend Bickford. I have described your experience in Sydney and the nature of your journey here. You will be made welcome, I'm sure. Metherdew, we need to get Miss King to the parsonage in St Kilda. Can you arrange a carriage for her?

— I'll take her meself. Mr Bickford wants some more prayer books. Says his congregations has grown of late. I'll take them down with the lady.

Reverend Draper clapped his hands together, well pleased by this outcome, then turned to me.

— I shall leave you in Mr Metherdew's care. I am sure the St Kilda situation will agree with you. Mr Bickford is a good man. Inspirational, if somewhat muddled at times. And once you are quite settled, perhaps we shall see you again here, hmm?

— I hope so, sir. You've been very kind.

Unsure whether to shake his hand or bow, I made a clumsy curtsey. But I don't think he even saw it, having already turned to admire his spire once again, looking up and rocking slightly back and forth on his feet, hands clasped behind his back.

After making up a package of prayer books, Mr Metherdew led me out a side entrance of the church and along a cobbled path to a small stable. Inside stood an old and thin grey horse, head down, apparently dozing on its feet.

— C'mon Bess, my girl, there's work to be done. Mr Metherdew's voice were different talking to the horse. Softer. The horse raised her head and butted it against the back of his hand. He positioned her between the rails of a tiny carriage, like a basket on wheels.

— Mr Wesley loved his horses, the verger said. Rode all over England, he did, sometimes changing horses several times in one day so he could go on to places where people might hear him preach. He would write his sermons as he rode. Could also sleep as he journeyed, trusting his animal to take him where he needed to go, though there must have been times when he took a tumble.

That prospect never looked likely as we made our way slowly through the town. Over the river and along what Mr Metherdew said were the St Kilda Road. We were squashed together side by side in the carriage, so tight there were no room to wriggle, leave alone fall out. The road were pitted with holes and our progress were slow and bumpy. On my lap I carried my bag and the package of prayer books. I were too busy making sure that neither of these slipped away to take much notice of my surrounds, but I recall a group of natives standing near the river. And a foul smell on the south side that Mr Metherdew said came from a tannery.

He spoke little, content with his thoughts. Seldom did he push Bess to increase the pace. The verger seemed happier here, communing with his God in the open, than he had been in the church.

— C'mon Bess. Nearly there, girl.

Our horse had slowed almost to a dead walk. Mr Metherdew urged her on after we had turned off the main road and began journeying down a slight slope on a smaller track. I saw a sign to the jetty. Our destination were a church set back a little way from the track. Built from the same dark stone as the one in town, though on a much smaller scale, its most decorative features were two tall windows on either side of the door. Ivy had been allowed to climb over the stone, giving it a pleasing appearance.

Bess's breath came hard as she got to the church, and as soon as we reached a small yard in front of the building she stopped, sighed, and let her head fall near to the ground.

The verger indicated I should get out first. He took his package and my bag while I eased myself down, then he unfolded his long legs from the carriage and got out. Filling a basin from a barrel of rainwater near the entrance and placing it so the horse might drink, he turned away from the building, raised his head and breathed in deeply.

— There! Can you smell it?

I were mystified.

— The tang of salt, the sea breeze.

I breathed a little deeper.

— I believe I can. The air is certainly fresh.

— Does you good, this breeze. Blows away the evil vapours that cause sickness in the city.

Mr Metherdew filled his lungs with more of the salt air as he carried the package of prayer books towards the door of the church. I followed him inside with my bag. Out of the afternoon sunshine, my eyes had to get used to the change in light. But even before I got through the door I heard a voice. A clear, ringing voice, with all the words standing alone like they'd been clipped with shears. The speaker, I assumed, were the energetic young man I'd been told about, Reverend Bickford.

— Let us devote ourselves to a study of God's handiwork, taking pride and pleasure in all of His creation. May this lead to a quickened adoration of Him whose redemptive love is shown forth in human salvation. And may it inspire us to sing His praises as we see His works!

The voice came from the end of the room, away from the

door. Inside, it did not look much like a church, more like a meeting hall. A large but bare room with benches in rows. Most of the windows were quite plain and there was no colour but for a picture of Our Lord on the distant wall, positioned above a wooden box. Not a fine pulpit, as in the town, but a box. Like a coffin had been stood on end with its open side turned away from the benches.

On the top of the box rested a pair of hands, pale against the dark wood. Above them nothing but black and a face masked by hair that were longer than usual, parted in the middle and let fall down both sides of the face. I had seen such a style before, in a picture of John Wesley himself in a book belonging to Reverend Taylor in Sydney.

— Consider the Psalms! the speaker continued. *According to Thy name, O God, so is Thy praise unto the ends of the earth: Thy right hand is full of righteousness. Let Mount Zion rejoice.* Oh, I am interrupted, William. We have visitors, it seems.

I thought he were addressing Mr Metherdew, who looked to have been enjoying the sermoning, but then I saw another man in the church. A bigger fellow sitting quietly in a corner by the door. I hadn't noticed him when I came in. He rose from his place as Reverend Bickford approached from the other end of the room. It seemed that the verger and the big man had met before, as Mr Metherdew nodded when his hand was shaken.

— Metherdew! Keeping well? And how is our spiritual guide, Reverend Draper?

— Good enough, Reverend Hill.

I stood to one side watching these men come together. Reverend Bickford also greeted Mr Metherdew. The Reverend were a similar height to the big man in the corner but half his width, like he were hewn from one plank while the other came from two. The voice I had heard before didn't fit him. Indeed, the voice he used as he addressed the verger were different, much thinner.

— Metherdew, what a pleasant surprise. Ah! And you have brought the prayer books. All to the good. Our place here is humble but we are reaching more people all the time. And who is your quiet companion?

I took some steps forward, still holding my bag, unsure whether to put it down.

— A lady, Mr Bickford, Mr Metherdew told him. Sent to help. With a letter for you from Mr Draper.

I made to give the envelope to him, but before taking it he clasped my hand. His fingers too were very thin.

— James Bickford, he said, shaking my hand. And this is my friend, Reverend Hill. He is good enough, when he is here, to listen while I work up a new sermon and advise me of improvements I might make.

The bigger man nodded his head in greeting.

— Not that Mr Bickford is ever short of something to say, he said to me. I am William Hill. You look weary. Would you care to sit down?

— Thank you, sir, but no. I have been sitting for some time. In the carriage, you see.

Reverend Hill smiled. His eyes were kindly.

— Now, said Reverend Bickford, the letter. Let me see what Reverend Draper has to say.

He quickly scanned the letter, reading some sections aloud, nodding his head as he did so. Marking the air with the main finger of his right hand like he were counting out notes of a tune.

— William, 'tis indeed a blessed day, he said. It appears that Miss King has been sent to bring some order to my life. Attend to my worldly concerns so I can concentrate on matters spiritual.

— I wish I could share your good fortune, Bickford, said Reverend Hill.

— You are situated here too, Reverend Hill? I asked him.

— No, I am merely an occasional visitor.

— Mr Hill is based on the other side of the river, Miss King. He walks amongst those in desperate need, ministering to the insane and also to prisoners in the Pentridge stockade.

— Not worth your effort, I would have thought, snorted Mr Metherdew.

— Come, Metherdew. We must strive to shine some light even in the darkest corners.

Reverend Bickford were once again scanning the letter. Unable to stay still.

— How extraordinary! William, it seems Miss King has a brother on the exploring expedition.

— Well, I think that's right, sir, I interjected. That is, I feel sure he is, though I have not seen him for many years.

Reverend Hill, who looked older than his colleague, considered me anew. Like I were a painting and he had just seen something unnoticed before.

— We may have a connection, then, he said to me. Some of the prisoners at the stockade were put to work making equipment for the expedition. Leather gear, mostly. Boots for the men, harnesses for the camels and horses, saddles, straps. I saw some of it being made and parcelled up. Perhaps some of the materials I saw made are even now being used by your brother.

Reverend Bickford appeared moved by this.

— Marvellous! Remember what John Wesley himself said: *The best of all is, God is with us!* A bridle blessed by Mr Hill could be assisting your brother. Whose name is?

— John, sir. John King.

— And where is he now?

Three men looking at me, waiting on my answer. Bess the horse slurping water outside. And me suddenly tired and far from anything I had ever called home. Needing to sit down now.

— I don't know, sir. He's gone. They must be well away from here. And nobody can say when they'll be coming back.

Part 2

Dissipated Like Dew-Drops

Thirteen

The blacks had a plant they called bedgery. It caused waking dreams, vivid scenes that seemed real enough to taste and touch. Only the older men were allowed to use it. They would sit and chew the dried stems and leaves they kept in pouches of lizard skin, then slip into a stupor. Usually it left them tranquil, but there was a time I saw one of them leap up shrieking and run to a fire. He plunged his hands into the embers and smeared ashes over his skin with a washing motion, as if he thought it were water.

Carrawaw's husband gave me some of it to try, presenting it to me on a piece of bark like a rare delicacy. Only later did I appreciate what it must have been. At the time I believed it to be a medicinal herb, a native potion like some of the pastes they applied direct to their wounds. My state was so wretched I did as he indicated, taking the stems in my mouth just as Charley had gnawed on twigs to try to keep some moisture coming. The taste was rank and bitter and stung the sores on my gums.

Carrawaw's man nodded with satisfaction as I chewed until I could bear the bitterness no longer and spat out the foul brown liquid. But the tang of it lingered on my tongue and then a mist settled upon me. I placed my hands down, one on either side to steady myself, for the soil on which I was seated seemed to be moving. And the face of the native who was watching me, clicking his tongue in approval of what he was witnessing, rippled like water in the wind.

It was the leader's face I saw now, straining forward, his eyes wide. And he was speaking: 'The sea, King! We cannot stop. We must push on to the sea!'

I knew the face but the voice was not his. It was low, guttural, almost a grunt. And the teeth were odd — large and yellow. The teeth of a camel. It was not Mr Burke at all; it was Datchi, the camel he had struck. Datchi with his lips curled back from those protruding teeth, so close I could smell the rankness of his breath. And even as I shrank away, fearing the rasp of his tongue, W was beside me, anxious, issuing orders.

'Look to the beast, man. That's *your* job. Look to the beast . . .'

I tried to push the camel away but could not move my arms. My limbs were like lead. I jerked my head back and tumbled over onto the ground, Datchi's wheezing breaths coming closer and closer. When I came to my senses I was still on the ground, shivering, even though Carrawaw's husband had draped a possum-skin blanket over me.

I never took bedgery again. The scenes it conjured scared me. And until last night I had never experienced a dream so vivid, not even when dosed with the laudanum that I now shun. I cannot say what caused the dream — if indeed that's what it was. Might it have been one of Doctor Treacey's mixtures or pills? Perhaps, though there was nothing I had not tried before. But as I lie here — a weak man growing weaker, with lungs like a glass half full of silt — all the details of it return unbidden as soon as I close my eyes.

I am with Howitt in the Melbourne Cemetery. We are standing on opposite sides of the memorial to the expedition, a massive block of granite placed above the graves of Mr Burke and W, adjacent to the grounds of the new university and only ten minutes from Royal Park, where our clumsy caravan lurched into motion on that August afternoon in 1860. This monument is squat and ugly and appropriate: like the expedition itself, it is too big and cost the committee more money than it wanted to spend. There is writing on all sides of it:

LEADER

AND SECOND IN COMMAND

OF THE

VICTORIAN EXPLORING EXPEDITION

They are 'Comrades In A Great Achievement. Companions In Death. Associates In Renown.' And on the far side:

THE FIRST TO CROSS

THE CONTINENT OF AUSTRALIA

BURKE

WILLS

Gray

King Survivor

I am the last one mentioned. After Charley, whose name, like mine, does not warrant capital letters.

It is late in the day: the sun changes the texture of the stone as it sinks down, leaving one face in golden light while another is dark, its writing illegible. It seems that Howitt and I are circling the tomb, though I am not conscious of any movement. Perhaps the granite itself is rotating, leaving us always on opposing sides. When he is in sunshine, I am in shadow. Then our positions change. While I am contemplating 'In Memory Robert O'Hara Burke', he is studying 'Comrades In A Great Achievement'.

But no matter how many times Howitt walks around the monument, he will never find his own name. He is not mentioned, even though without his efforts the committee would have had nothing to put under this granite. The bones he brought back rest under a monument; his own grow weary as he rides his magistrate's circuit up Omeo way. The men whose flesh clung in pitiful strips to these bones are remembered as the first to cross the continent. Howitt could cross Collins Street up and down its length, starting from the Melbourne Club and heading west, and never be recognised.

He cannot accept this. He steps forward, touches the stone before him – just as Mr Burke felt the tree at the Cooper with the message on it. Then he starts to run, clumsily in his bushman's boots. And I am running too, though I find that my feet are bare and bleeding. And as we circle the monument, moving from light to shade and back again, I hear the questions he shouts: 'Tell me, man, did you really reach the Gulf? What of Gray – did Burke mistreat him and cause his death?' And this, with a cry: 'What are you hiding from me?'

He is closing on me. I have no strength to keep running away. Every breath is agony. He is almost on me now, so close that I can see he has his knife out. He is paring his nails with the tip of his knife, but it is tears that are pouring from his fingers. A shower of tears leaving the ground damp all around the granite. More damp with every stumbling step I take, until I am splashing through a creek. I am on the Cooper again, taking shelter in a native gunyah. The blacks have left food for me and I can see fish and ducks in the creek all around me, but I leave them be. I have no strength to take them. The level of the creek is rising; water will soon be lapping clear over me. Yet I make no attempt to drag myself to higher ground. This is how it must be – death through indifference, a deep weariness. I have seen it come upon Charley Gray and W and Burke. *Companions in death. Companions in death* ... The words on the monument are the last thing I see as it comes crashing down upon me, toppled over by Howitt as easily as if he were taking down a tent pole.

I need not attribute such fantasies to Treacey and his potions, his anti-bilious pills or foul-smelling balsams. It is Howitt himself I blame. Howitt and his questions, which he asks while fixing me with his magistrate's stare. The one with which he impales the horse-thieves, cattle-duffers and drunkards in his court. Because I am in his debt, I cannot tell him not to come. I am too polite to do so, too weak to push him away. I have not encouraged him, seldom answering any of his letters, but still he comes. I hear his boots, heavy on the verandah. He enters smelling of horsehide and tobacco, his manner more urgent as my strength ebbs, and there are fewer questions about the natives. He has accepted I have little to tell him that can advance his interest in ethnology. It is not his primary interest, anyway.

For it is clear to me now that the expedition is to him like a bush tick. Once under the skin, it is near impossible to dislodge. Only a deep twist of a knife, or probing with the end of a burning twig, can kill it. Scratching merely worsens the itch and causes the tick to burrow ever deeper.

Ten years on, the expedition and its aftermath still eat at him. And it irks him that it was me, not him, who was there at the end. The documents — the last notes and letters — were entrusted to me, not to him. He has the questions; I have answers, which I may or may not share with him. He is the better bushman, but I have walked on ground he has never seen. Deserts of stone. Damp places where steam rises from the ground and rank mud can suck the boot from a man's foot. Ever-shady rock gullies with strange spectral paintings in which the air is always cold, no matter what the temperature beyond. Cold and smelling of death.

We are linked by what happened, Howitt and I. We have been where they died, my leader and W. And then came back. But I was the one people wanted to see. Howitt was the committee's obedient servant, head man of the Contingent Exploring Party. He was the carrier, I was his load. And now sometimes it seems I am his quarry.

'Their notes, last letters: were you there when they were written?'

I do not speak. I cough and allow my lids to close.

'I fear that John is over-tired, Mr Howitt,' says Nora, coming into the front room. 'Can I fetch you some tea or something cool to drink? Or some bread, perhaps?'

He leaves unsatisfied. He has come for answers, not bread. Will he return? Doubtless so. And before then I suspect I may see him again during one of my restless nights, circling around the monument on which there are four names, but not his. Just four of the nineteen men who left from Royal Park and the others, like Wright, who were picked up along the way. Howitt's is not the only name missing. And he is not one of those who never came back. Men like Gray and Becker and Patten.

Patten the blacksmith who wanted so badly to be part of the small group that left for the Gulf. Patten who wept when Mr Burke made his farewells, as if he could see signs in the bark of the trees along the creek telling what awaited him there — the heat, the native rats, the flies and fleas and mosquitoes. The boredom of waiting for Wright and his party to arrive from Menindie, waiting for Mr Burke and his advance party to get back from the Gulf. The constant uncertainty about the blacks. Wondering what the hell they were plotting when they stood looking at the depot camp, jabbering amongst themselves and pointing with their spears.

I knew before Patten did that he wouldn't be going to the Gulf. Mr Burke told me himself.

A December evening on the Cooper, where it stayed light until well after eight by W's watch. W himself was tinkering with his instruments, taking readings or testing calibrations or cleaning the works. He never volunteered much to me about his scientific duties. Charley Gray, Patten and Brahe were playing cards. Dost Mahomed, who seemed quite at ease with the inactivity that had marked our days on the creek since we arrived, was checking on the camels I had already fed.

My work was done for the day and I had taken myself for a stroll along the banks of the creek, which was high after recent rains. With me I had one of the rifles, thinking perhaps to add a plump cockatoo to the pot or to scare away blacks, who of late had become increasingly bold. Some had ventured into the camp when we left it unguarded and made off with whatever they could grab. Matches, a spade, some rope and a pair of Brahe's trousers. Since then Mr Burke had discouraged any friendliness, fearing we would never be rid of them if they began to feel welcome.

The leader, as always, was keen to push on, and also impatient for Wright and the others to arrive. I knew he had asked W to chart a course north to the Gulf but I was in no hurry to move myself. I would do as I was ordered, with no questions, but was content to tarry by the creek a while longer. After the trek from Menindie, we had found blessed relief here. Shades of green after expanses of stone and barren soil. Fresh running water instead of stagnant puddles. And life! You could hear it – possums in the branches, timid wallabies scampering to drink, and those waddling, porcupine-like beasts that rolled up into prickly balls if surprised. Charley said the blacks roasted them, but I couldn't imagine what there'd be to eat save for scorched spikes. And more birds than I'd seen or heard anywhere. My favourites were the pelicans, huge things with their extraordinary beaks: so strangely built, yet serene and graceful when they flew with a slow, rhythmic beating of their black-tipped wings.

By a bend in the creek I had found a giant river gum with a hollow near the base of its trunk. It was a comfortable place to rest awhile, watch the sun sink from sight, breathe in the scent of leaves and mud and animal dung, and be away from Charley's singing for a time. I had taken to escaping to this spot when I could, and would lean back against the trunk, chewing on a twig and watching the circles spread on the water's surface. A fish would rise or an insect would settle and the ring would ripple out until it faded away completely.

I was heading there again on this warm, still evening and was in sight of my tree when a rat scuttled away from reeds near the creek and made for shelter in rocks some ten feet to the right.

It never got there. I saw it blown apart before I heard the noise. One second it was running, the next it seemed to leap up and disintegrate into tiny pink fragments. Close to my left, an explosion. My ears were ringing. Smoke drifted from the creek. As the army had taught me, I dropped to my knees and swung my gun towards the sound, fearing I was under attack.

Then I heard Mr Burke.

'Got yer, y'sneaking little fucker. Go on! Bugger off to rat hell, but before y'go, tell your million little mates what to expect.'

He was sitting in the creek, close to the bank. All that protruded from the water were the points of his knees and the top third of his body. His left arm was mostly submerged; his right hand was raised, holding the revolver he was seldom without. Its barrel was still smoking. His hair and beard were wet. His naked chest and shoulders and knees were very pale, but when he turned slightly I could see that the back of his neck was the colour of oak.

It was startling to see him like this – unusual even to see him without his hat, which I had now spotted resting on his boots near his pile of clothes on the bank. I knew then that Mr Burke was quite naked in the water. Enjoying what I suspected was his first bath since he had left the hotel in Menindie. I was embarrassed to find my leader like this but he appeared unconcerned. His mood, indeed, was splendid.

'A direct hit, King, as you are my witness! One less rat to gnaw at the flour bags or creep over our feet at night. Blown to bits! I had ensured I was armed lest any of our light-fingered black friends took a fancy to my gear; instead I find I am a better hunter than I suspected. 'Tis a pity there is little left to add to the stew, eh?'

'Only some small pieces, sir.'

'No matter. Perhaps if I stay here long enough I'll get us a parrot. But no, things to do.'

With that he stood up, carefully keeping his revolver high and dry. Water streamed off him. It had darkened what little hair there was on his chest, and that around his private parts was like moss clinging to a rock after rain.

He picked his way carefully over the stones in the shallow water by the bank until he came to his clothes. The evening air was still quite balmy and he seemed content to stand and let it dry him, although he rubbed at his hair and beard with his shirt. The first item he replaced was his hat, which was his only item of clothing when a commotion began on the bank opposite.

Four blacks, all men, had appeared through the reeds. As usual, they wore no garments other than a strange assortment of headgear — pieces of fishing nets, feathers, or greasy strips of cloth entwined in their hair. They carried spears but their manner was not aggressive. Quite the contrary. They were chattering loudly, making signals, pointing across the water. It seemed they were even more startled than I had been by the sight of Mr Burke without his clothes. This must have been the first time they had ever seen a naked white man.

On hearing the laughter, Mr Burke swung around so that he was facing directly towards them. This had the effect of doubling the degree of animation. The blacks' laughter became a cackling and they began to make crude gestures in our direction. One, who seemed younger than the others, clutched at his own stump and thrust with his hips backwards and forwards, causing his companions great merriment.

Mr Burke, still wearing nothing but his hat, took a moment or two to appreciate what was happening. Another man, on understanding the reason for the natives' excitement, would have hurried to replace his clothes. But not Mr Burke. He spread his arms and legs wide, looking for all the world like the white cross on the English flag. Then he improvised a sort of leaping dance, the kind of thing the natives themselves might have done. And he shouted at them, though I'm sure I was the only man there who understood what he was saying.

'Go on, y'heathen bastards, feast your eyes! An Irishman in his natural glory, with all that God gave him. Flag pole'n'all. A grand, glorious, civilised white man!'

The natives, stunned by this exhibition, ceased their chatter. They stood watching as the leader kept on.

'And look! There *is* a difference. I have clothes to put on to stop my skin from turning black. More! I have a brain under this hat the likes of which y'will never comprehend. It teems with grand ideas and schemes. There is drive there and determination. It will take me and my men across the continent and back again while you dog-ignorant savages are stuck here with your dusky arses bare to the breeze. So look on me well. You will never see my like again. Here, this is what I think of your damned finger-pointing and jabbering.'

I still find what happened next astonishing. Mr Burke took hold of his member, levelled it in the natives' direction in imitation of what the young black men had done, and sent forth an arc of his pale yellow water into the Cooper. But rather than being offended, the natives appeared to regard this as a game. They responded in kind, pissing over the rocks at their feet.

With no more water of his own to come, Mr Burke seemed suddenly to weary of the exchange from one bank to another. Cocking his revolver, he fired once over the natives' heads, the report causing a flock of cockatoos to fly squawking out of a nearby tree. I could see the blacks' eyes widen at the sound of the gun. Quickly they backed away whence they had come, holding their spears now as if they had half a mind to throw them.

Mr Burke waited until they were out of sight before returning to where I stood by his clothes. He lowered his head and, like a wet hound, shook the water from his hair and beard. Making no comment on what had just occurred, he dressed slowly. The last items to go on were his boots. He eased his feet into them, fingering places where the stitching was coming loose as though reminding himself to attempt some repairs at a later date. When he was done he sat back on a rock and gestured for me to join him. Still he said nothing. He was more pensive than usual, absorbed by his own thoughts as he considered the vista before us.

The sun was now low, giving the water a golden hue. It seemed clear, from the steepness of the opposite bank and its natural ledges, that the level of the creek varied considerably from one year to another. A little way out, a fish of some sort rose at an insect near the water's surface, the ripples spreading almost all the way to where we sat. When I cast a look at him, Mr Burke appeared to be studying this scene especially keenly. His eyes had caught some of the light from the water and burned bright. His hands were pressed together, resting on one thigh. When finally he spoke, his manner was decisive, like he'd settled something.

'A grand spot, King. Except for the rats, blacks and damned flies, it is almost another Eden.'

'It is, sir,' I agreed.

'"Twould be easy to stop here awhile, all too easy. We could sink into idleness and just wait for things to happen. But I'll not do it.' He slapped his thigh with the palms of his hands and got up, pacing about.

'I must keep moving, King. I am resolved to push on to the Gulf immediately. Recent thunderstorms have left me confident there will be water to the north, and Mr Wills has assured me of cloud movement in that direction. Tarrying here longer will achieve naught. I do not wish to lose so favourable an opportunity to achieve what we set out to do.'

I nodded, though I could see a problem with this plan. 'But what of the rest of the party?' I asked. 'Wasn't it your intention to wait here until Mr Wright arrived from Menindie with the rest of the men and animals and supplies?'

'A leader must be flexible, King. He must have the courage to adapt to changing circumstances. I propose to split our group here and proceed north at forced pace, travelling light. No more supply wagons or needless stores or stops for scientific observations, not even any tents. The minimum number of camels only, and just one horse. Billy, of course; Billy must come. Speed is the key, we must hasten! Get the job done before the weather changes or that damned Stuart gets between us and the Gulf.'

It seemed he was speaking not only to me, but also an audience I couldn't see. He was taking great strides across the stones of the creek bank, making sweeping gestures with his hands. I found it difficult to tell if he was revealing a plan he had been brooding upon for some time or, rather, reaching a decision then and there. Convincing himself with his words.

'Those who remain here I will place under the command of William Brahe. I have every confidence in Brahe. There is nothing to prevent the party remaining here until our return, unless provisions run short. But the feed is good, as long as the rats don't get it, and more supplies will come with Wright when he arrives, any day now.'

'Who shall accompany you, sir?'

He stopped his pacing and looked down at me. From where I sat his head was silhouetted against the evening sky, now streaked with fingers of pink. I couldn't make out his features. Tiny drops of creek water still clung to the tips of his hair and beard.

'Ah! Who indeed, King? Well, Wills, naturally, as the second in command. And we will need him to chart our course. Plus a general hand, an assistant, for the packing and heavy work. Gray, I fancy. Yes, Gray. I find him reliable. And one other...'

Was he toying with me, or can it be that the scales of my life indeed hung in the balance right then on a still evening by the Cooper? Was he appraising me, or even smiling? I couldn't tell. It was like looking up at an eclipse.

'One other for the camels... Why, King, that would have to be you! The camel man. You're young and in fine fettle. What say you: can you conceive of a more splendid assignment?'

I found myself speechless. This hairy, erratic man who just a little earlier had been taunting a group of natives was showing faith in me, wanting me with him on the most critical stage of the expedition. Unable to voice the right words, I stood and clumsily made to shake his hand. But he ignored my offered palm and instead cuffed me on the side of my head. He meant it playfully, I know, yet the blow still caused me to stagger.

'Get on with you, lad,' he said. 'There's plenty to be done, and no more time to be lost. Too much has been lost here already.'

He swung around so that his gaze was directed at the place where the natives had disappeared. 'I don't trust the blacks. Has there ever been a more wretched race? But I believe there is no danger to be apprehended from them if they are properly managed, and I'll be sure to impress this upon Brahe. Firmness, that's the key to it, or else the wretches will take advantage of you. Divisions must be maintained between white men and all others. Why would God, in his infinite wisdom, have created men with skins of various shades if not to make clear the differences between them? Like should stay with like. Nothing but strife ensues when men of different colour and background are forced together.' He cleared his nostrils noisily, one after the other. 'I saw it first-hand on the diggings, the way the conjunction of white miners and Johnny Chinaman led to unholy strife. I was sent from Beechworth to deal with it. And deal with it I did, with firmness. Anything less is folly, as I'm sure you appreciate yourself.'

'Me?' I asked, uncertain what he meant.

'India, man. The mutiny. You were there, right? No need to tell you what can happen when the mix of whites and coloureds goes sour.'

Cawnpore. The heat. The smell. Bits of bodies strewn like rags after the animals had finished with them. Half maddened by thirst after marching for most of the day, we made to the well, only to find it had been stacked, near to the top, with corpses. Many of them children. One of whose eyes, wide and cloudy, were frozen with the horror of the last sight before death brought release from the fear and the running and the screaming...

'I understand, King,' the leader said when I made no response. 'But tell me one thing. The newspapers were discreet. They mentioned atrocities too horrible to mention. Is it true, as I heard tell on the diggings, that even white Christian women were not spared by the sepoys when the bloodlust was on them?'

'Yes, sir, that is true.'

In the compound of the former commander we came upon a pile of soiled bedding crumpled in a corner. That's what we took it to be at first, until we came closer and realised it was all that was left of an Englishwoman. A lady, judging by her delicate hands, though the nails and tips were broken and torn, and the fine lace of her petticoat was pierced with countless cuts. She was partly curled up, as if vainly trying to protect herself, and it wasn't until we tried to move her – one hand each, the other shielding our faces from the smell and flies – that we saw the end of a candlestick thrust in down below her belly.

'Damned heathens,' said Mr Burke, his voice low. 'No torture can have been too harsh for them. Yours was a righteous conflict, King. While I was keeping miners and Chinks apart, you were fighting for God and Her Majesty in India. And you prevailed, King. You prevailed with firmness and force.'

'I suppose we did, sir.'

Birds circling the gibbets, which had gone up everywhere like seedlings in a forest. Carpenters complained about a lack of timber to do the work that was asked of them. The Colonel insisted the bodies be left strung up for the birds and rats and sun to take their toll. They turned black within days – bodies of men who had worn the Queen's uniform not so long before. In the end, hanging was preferred to blowing the mutineers from cannons; the Colonel deemed it a waste of ammunition. Besides, the cannons left nothing to serve as a warning to others who might consider taking up arms against Her Majesty's subjects or soldiers.

An uneasy peace prevailed. Amongst the Indians there was a sullenness, an endless suspicion. They were cowed but not conquered. In my dreams, most every night, I saw bodies awaken on the gibbets. They stared at me with eyes that had been pecked at and reached their fleshless fingers towards me, clawing at my face. I would wake up screaming, my clothes acrid with sweat. I was not even twenty, but the regimental surgeon said I had the nerves of a fifty-year-old.

With his course of action determined, Mr Burke was of a mind to leave the next morning, but it was four days before everything was ready. Four more days in which Wright and the others failed to arrive from Menindie, or even get word to us of their progress or position. Still, the leader would wait no longer. Dost Mahomed and Charley Gray butchered two of the poorer horses, cut the meat into strips and let it dry in the sun so it could be packed and taken with us. Like all our other provisions — we were to carry with us enough for twelve weeks — the jerked meat had to be suspended high off the ground to protect it from rats.

I cannot imagine that Mr Burke did not make clear to all in the party his intentions as to who would go and who would stay. But Patten's performance on the morning we left, crying and begging to come with us, suggests he thought the leader could yet alter his plans at the final hour. He did not know him as I did. Once Mr Burke made up his mind he was never one to change it. He thought and moved only in straight lines. If he found a boulder in his path he would try to force it aside rather than move around it.

And so we left, just the four of us. Four men, one horse and six camels. Birds screeched at our departure. Patten sobbed. Mr Burke said he expected Wright to arrive within days.

William Brahe, who seemed satisfied with his promotion to officer in charge of the depot party, rode with us until our first camp. W calculated it to be twenty-two miles from the depot. Unlike Patten, Brahe appeared content to remain on the Cooper rather than head north with us into untravelled territory. He was a man I never knew well, as he preferred the company of fellow German speakers like Becker. And he regarded himself as one of the gentlemen, while I was but a hired hand.

Much was later made of what the leader said to Brahe on taking leave of him, but what these instructions were I know not.

I was seldom privy to their conversations. All I know is that before he left to return to the depot, Brahe turned and said to me, 'Goodbye, King. I do not expect to see you for at least four months.' Which struck me as odd, as we were carrying provisions for only three. And I recall what the leader had said to the inconsolable Patten: 'You must not fret; I shall be back in three months.'

Then Brahe left, returning along the path we had taken, in no hurry at all.

We weren't alone. A large tribe of native men, perhaps twenty in all, had followed us, intrigued by the activity and keen to know if we were going for good. I couldn't tell if any were from the group we had seen on the creek bank. They carried shields and the large boomerangs they used chiefly for killing rats, which they ate. Several bore long spears, yet seemed not to be of a warlike disposition. They kept their distance but pestered us, making signals that seemed to suggest we should accompany them to their camp and join them for a dance.

Mr Burke was in no mood for such distractions. Once again he took his revolver and fired over their heads, causing them to withdraw into the undergrowth.

But they did not go altogether. As we moved along the creek, I could not shake the feeling of being followed. There were blacks gliding softly between the trees and rocks. Whispering to each other. Watching. Waiting.

Fourteen

On my bedside table in the front room I keep a slim volume. Thirty-six pages in all, no more: *The Burke and Wills Exploring Expedition: An Account of the Crossing the Continent of Australia, From Cooper's Creek to Carpentaria.* Published by Wilson and Mackinnon of 78 Collins Street East, Melbourne, 1861. Price: one shilling.

My copy is stained. Albert and Grace came gambolling into the room one morning while I was on the verandah. They ran around, whooping like black children, and knocked the table, dislodging the mug I had foolishly left near the book. Muck spilled over the cover and seeped inside. I tried to wipe it clean but all I managed to do was smear the mess and smudge the print. Some of the pages are still marked with streaks that grow darker with time. I never told Mary or Nora about this, not wishing to cause the little ones trouble. Besides, considering the events it records, it seems appropriate for the book to be less than pristine.

Messrs Wilson and Mackinnon moved quickly. They reprinted from *The Argus* all accounts they could gather concerning the expedition and its fate, which, when it became known, caused theatrical performances to be suspended and grown men as well as ladies and youngsters to weep in the streets of Melbourne. This is what I have been told. So keen was the public's hunger for information that this book – a pamphlet, really – was published long before the commission inquiring into the expedition had even concluded its hearings, let alone released its findings. So little had been heard of the exploring party for so long, over fourteen months having come and gone since the caravan left Royal Park, that many people believed we had, like Leichhardt, vanished clear away in a shimmering void.

Then, quite unexpectedly, there was news. Of tragedy, not triumph. Despatches received in Melbourne from Howitt were published in newspapers verbatim. Along with letters of a poignancy that only the finest dramatists could ever hope to emulate: 'We have been unable to leave the creek . . . our clothes are going to pieces fast. Send provisions and clothes as soon as possible.'

That was W. He always fancied he had a way with words. But all his eloquence was for naught. His words were buried by sand, the provisions and clothes came too late. Knowledge of this sorry fact made the story considerably more compelling. People queued at Messrs Wilson and Mackinnon's Collins Street door to buy a collection of accounts that most had already read in the newspapers.

I am there in the book on page three: 'King's Narrative'. I didn't write a word of it. I talked, though very weak and sometimes slipping into unconsciousness. Over several sessions after his men found me, while I lay recovering in his camp, I gave answers to questions asked by Howitt, who scribbled my responses down in a notebook with a pencil he would periodically moisten in his mouth and sharpen with flicks of his knife. Sometimes he would interrupt with a grunt or an expression of surprise. Or he would fix me with that appraising stare I have come to know again of late. But for the most part he stayed silent and wrote.

On page eleven he puts it simply: 'I have written down King's narrative as much as possible in his words. Shall annex it to this diary. Finished shoeing the horses.'

When I read it now, it seems like somebody else's story. I recall speaking but not what I said. And I suspect that most of Messrs Wilson and Mackinnon's customers skipped over my few pages. I was not one of the leaders. And I was still alive, undeserving of the attention lavished on those who were gone. This flimsy book is replete with voices that are now silent. And few things are as compelling to the public as dead men speaking.

Mr Burke: 'The camels cannot travel, and we cannot walk, or we should follow the other party. We shall move very slowly down the creek.'

W again: 'It is a great consolation, at least, in this position of ours, to know that we have done all we could, and that our deaths will rather be the result of the mismanagement of others than of any rash acts of our own.'

I can picture him writing, writing. The hand perfect, the sentences complete. Condemning himself to death long before he is gone. Wrestling with the question of who will be blamed. Not him. Not any of us.

Mr Burke found it impossible to keep a regular diary and he regarded the jottings in his own notebook as being of little importance. There were times when he handed the thing to me so I could take a leaf or two as wadding for the guns. Whole sections were torn out. The leader perished; his notebook, which he treated so carelessly, endured.

I pity William Archer, the man later assigned the task of making sense of Mr Burke's notes. It was, he noted, 'an ordinary memorandum-book, with a clasp, and a side-pocket for a pencil. It is much dilapidated.' Yet Mr Archer diligently transcribed all that he could decipher, although I can only wonder what he made of one of the first entries:

No 69. – Line of cour i ing on bags 1, 4, 19, 20, 11, 3. Think well before giving an answer, and never speak except from strong convictions.

Near the end Mr Burke entrusted his notebook to me. I kept it safe from the blacks as it contained his last message: 'King has behaved nobly and I hope he will be properly cared for.'

I am especially proud of that.

Those who paid their shilling for Wilson and Mackinnon's special edition no doubt believed they were getting the whole story. Not so. It contained only accounts from *The Argus*, nothing from other publications, which had their own version of events. The absence of any evidence from the inquiry was not a grievous omission. Many of the witnesses – Wright, for example, justifying his tardy departure from Menindie – were intent only on ensuring that no blame should be attached to themselves. I know it was said that this was also my primary concern, and there is some truth in that.

I too paid my shilling, but a good deal of what Wilson and Mackinnon presented to the public was new to me. This is not so surprising. Any minor actor misses much of what is said by the principals as he waits in the wings, yawning and scratching at his ill-fitting hose.

Even 'King's Narrative' seemed strange. It still does. I cannot suggest that Howitt did not record my words faithfully, only that I cannot recall much of what I am deemed to have said. You must consider the way I was. How did *The Age* describe me immediately after my return to Melbourne? Nora kept the paper. I have it here, yellowing and brittle, its account not to be found in the one-shilling volume: 'With lustreless eye, wasted frame, and weakened intellect, in appearance but little removed from the skeletons of his companions which are bleaching in the desert...'

It is many years since anyone from *The Age* has sought to speak to me. If they did so now they would find me, an invalid in Octavia Street, physically little changed from 1861.

I never kept a journal during the expedition. After it was over, I tried to compile something. Mr Wilson himself encouraged me to put down what I remembered, but the results were unsatisfactory. I couldn't get far and only fragments remain in a small pocketbook:

nothing but stony
Desert 4 mostly
mud plains nothing to
be seen not even
a bush we pushed
that day making
51 miles . . .

No better than Mr Burke's notes. I think it was still too near to me.

And during the expedition I was always too tired. At the end of each day — a halt was often called in the afternoon, or whenever we came upon water — there was work to do with the camels. I had to hobble them, attend to their feed. Check their hides for sores from the chafing of the straps that secured their burdens. Charley had his tasks too. He was responsible for the stores and had to set up camp, though there wasn't much to this as we carried no tents.

When we were done we'd often sit together, Charley forever trimming sticks with his knife, and watch the others. W would almost always be away on his own, writing. Sometimes Mr Burke would confer with him about something. He would nod and walk away, then W would resume his labour.

It was not unusual for Mr Burke to remove himself completely at such times. He would leave the camp, on foot or riding Billy if the pony wasn't spent. I always thought it strange that after travelling for so long the leader could still be restless.

One evening, a week or two after leaving the Cooper, I was searching for a camel that had fled the camp after being nipped by one of the others, when I chanced upon Mr Burke. I don't believe he saw me. If he did he gave no sign, and I said nothing to him about it then or afterwards.

From the position of the sun, which was low in the west, I judged that he had walked in a northerly direction, the way we would all be travelling the following morning. There were no clouds at all. The sky was turning from the palest blue to grey and already some stars were alight. Standing quite still on the stony ground, which was flat all around, the leader looked small and terribly alone. His shoulders were slumped. Large white birds with yellow crests circled above him, as if trying to determine what manner of thing he was. From his stance it seemed he was looking straight ahead. Reckoning distance, evaluating routes, calculating our chances — who can say? His eyes might even have been closed. Perhaps this was his way of finding some peace, though Charley had a different explanation when I told him what I'd seen.

'Blowing his bishop,' he said. 'He probably gets away to check his equipment's in working order. Lord knows, I try a tug from time to time meself, though I've barely had the energy lately with all the walking.'

On his own in the late-day light, Mr Burke could have been daring the emptiness to swallow us up, as it did Leichhardt. He could have been praying. Or doing exactly what Charley Gray suggested. I never knew.

This is the thing that troubles me now. I was there but often don't know what I saw. It cannot be that everything has faded or become foggy in my mind since the expedition. Perspective improves with distance. And still there are times when a smell or a sound can come on me in St Kilda – the tang of dung, say, or the jingle of a bridle – and, like a key, open a part of my mind that is still locked in the interior. Once again I am walking, walking, walking; squinting in light I can seldom escape, and trying to ignore the persistent gnawing in my guts.

Ten years on, my journal is as true as I can make it, although there is never a single truth to something like this. Only different versions of the same event. Here, on page thirty-two of Wilson and Mackinnon, Mr Burke's entry for December 25th, 1860, Christmas Day: 'Started at four a.m. from Gray's Creek, and arrived at a creek which appears to be quite as large as Cooper's Creek. At two p.m. Golah Singh gave some very decided hints about stopping by lying down under the trees. Splendid prospect.'

Gray's Creek was named for Charley. He was the one who found it after Mr Burke sent him on ahead. It pleased Mr Burke to name things in this manner, leaving his mark upon a map. I could tell you proudly of a King's Creek, found and christened on the first day of 1861, but I would also have to report that further north we camped near Billy Creek.

I suspect this was after the leader's supply of place names gave out. There is this, in one of his few notebook entries: '13th January, 1860: Names for places: Thackeray, Barry, Bindon, Lyons, Forbes, Archer, Bennet, Colles, O.S. Nicholson, Wood, Wrixon, Cope, Turner, Scratchley, Ligar, Griffith, Green, Roe, Hamilton, Archer, Colles.' Scribbled in haste. He has the year wrong. And in trying to come up with his list of names, he repeats several. It was just a few months later that he abandoned his sporadic entries almost entirely, leaving the journal-keeping to W, whose self-confidence seldom seems to have wavered. Nor his convictions, like his early judgement of the natives on the Cooper:

'They appear to be mean-spirited and contemptible in every respect.'

All that Mr Burke found to be noteworthy about Christmas Day 1860 fills just half a dozen lines in Wilson and Mackinnon's edition. W, however, trekked all day and then covered the stony ground once again on paper: 'We left Gray's Creek at half-past four a.m., and proceeded to cross the earthy rotten plains in the direction of Eyre's Creek. At a distance of about nine miles, we reached some lines of trees and bushes ...'

He continues on for another half-page. Compass-readings. Topographical features. Vegetation. Comments on climatic and geographical features. There is no mention of Golah Singh, though he does say that the day was hot and the camels tired. And of his companions there is not a word. Mr Burke, Charley and myself are out of sight behind the sand ridges. Our only purpose to turn the 'I' in W's journal into a 'we'.

We. The four of us. Rising early. Beginning without any breakfast. Travelling slowly. Every long day the grinding routine of it: securing the loads, releasing the loads, apportioning food. Always, each one of us in our own way, reckoning what there was left and how long it might have to last. Always looking for smoke that might signal a blacks' camp. Always following water, searching for water, or thinking about water. The camels carried up to a hundred and thirty pints of water each, the horse a hundred and fifty – five pints for each man – but we sought to save it for those times when we had no alternative supply. Three pints a day was then our ration. We became expert at holding mouthfuls before swallowing so as to prolong them.

I marvelled at how little water the camels themselves appeared to need. They seemed better suited than humans to the conditions.

Often I wondered what business we had in such country of rocks and sand and scrub. Most of what we saw looked suited only to blacks. You could no more grow crops or raise livestock on this soil than fly over it.

Apart from some stretches, this land we laboured over was good for nothing, though Charley said he had heard it was all to do with the telegraph. A wire for carrying signals clear across the continent. I didn't know about that. Mr Burke, fretful when anything slowed us down, didn't care much for the country. He just wanted to be first to cross it. And Charley reckoned that being first was worth striving for. It could mean extra shillings to the likes of us.

'The leaders and gents in top hats can make their speeches,' he said. 'I'll take my pay and buy brandy for a sweet little Jessie on the corner, then lick it drop by drop from her cherry-pink breasts.' He thought for a moment. 'No! We'll be famous. They'll all be buying *me* brandy. Maybe even a Jessie too.'

Charley imagined himself out of the desert. I could never look that far. The horizon always seemed too distant. Mostly I kept my gaze on my feet, wary of stumbles, while W was forever taking himself away to the nearest rise, however slight, to give himself a new angle for his reckonings. I wondered if he had one of his calibrated instruments inside his head, its workings unaffected by heat and dust by day and the piercing cold at night that left us shivering and stiff. I contrived once to walk close to him to assure myself that he farted like the rest of us. He did. And then apologised. 'Excuse me,' he said, as if the camels would care.

There is little I can add to his journal. Not if your interest is in navigation, or the types of melon we came across or what they tasted like. 'On tasting the pulp of the newly found fruit,' W wrote, 'I found it to be so acrid that it was with difficulty that I removed the taste from my mouth.'

Of that Christmas day, for example, what can I recall myself? Only a little. We started before dawn. I had hoped a halt might have been called for Christmas, but it was just another day like the others. Did Mr Burke shake our hands, to mark the occasion? I think so. Yes. Fragments fall into view. We shook hands and got going in the chill gloom. I had grown adept at securing the camels' loads in darkness, prodding them up and ignoring their groans on being stirred.

What else can I see? Lots of game. Emus, scrub turkeys, crested pigeons wheeling in a cloud around branches of a dead tree. Kangaroos, which would leap away and then stop to study us, as if they had never seen anything so curious: white men in hats and humped animals strung out in a ragged line. They kept their distance. I suggested to Mr Burke that I should try to bag one, thinking the fresh meat would be welcome, but he said we could not afford the labour of a hunt, nor the time to jerk the meat. We had to push on.

Where there was water there were likely to be blacks. Often they seemed shy and would not come near us. On Christmas Day or soon after, before we reached the desert, we came upon a tribe that numbered about fifty and they didn't seem the least alarmed by us. Mr Burke ordered us to wait back. He rode up to them and gave out a few handkerchiefs, which they fought over with much chattering. We continued on but couldn't shake them off, though they kept their distance. When we halted for the day by a fine waterhole, fifteen strong, able-looking men came within thirty yards of our camp. All had spears and boomerangs. Their elderly leader's spear was about twenty-five feet long, the others' much shorter. They made signs to us to leave the place.

Mr Burke went up to them and gave them some beads and other presents, thinking they would go when they received them. But the old man advanced, sticking his long spear into the earth, then taking a handful of sand and rubbing it first on his hands and then the spear.

'What's he playing at?' Charley muttered to me.

The other blacks formed a ring behind their leader.

Still looking at them, without changing his expression or turning around, Mr Burke called out to us, 'Firearms at the ready!'

At his order we let off a volley over their heads. They ran, the oldest man last of all, stumbling over his spear. Mr Burke laughed at his undignified retreat. 'That great pole of his doesn't aid his exit!'

They gathered together again and came back within forty yards of us, holding up their boomerangs. Again we fired. They ran once more, and this time we saw nothing further of them until evening, when they returned, their manner different, very much afraid of our guns, offering nets and slings in exchange for some matches, which they thought magical.

They pointed away to the east, meaning they were heading in that direction. That was the last we saw of them. And there were no more blacks at all once we were into the stony desert. There were few animals to be seen. Barely a bush or anything for shade for days on end, with no new water and just the tedium of the slow moving and early starts after lying on cold ground in our damp blankets. In the darkness Billy and the camels grumbled but we were struck dumb by the size of the sky above us, a million stars for each of us. W was the only one who could make sense of them, the only one with any notion where we were and which way we'd be moving the next day.

It was in this desert, I remember, that Charley first complained of headaches. He would take the grimy cloth he wore around his neck, soak it in a little of his ration of water, and place it under his hat. It gave him some relief, he said. He blamed the sun. The glare on the sand and stones was too harsh. He grimaced, pressed his palm into his forehead, and talked about living somewhere cool and shady when we were done.

'Me brains are being broiled,' he told me.

This must have been January 7th. I reckon the date by W's own journal in Wilson and Mackinnon, page eighteen. We were through the worst of the desert and had camped near some stands of timber. Billy and the camels had decent feed. W, as was his habit, adjourned to take his readings. When he was done, instead of retiring to record the figures in his fieldbooks, he came over to Charley and me, unusually animated. He looked around as if searching for something that wasn't there.

'I should have liked this camp to have been in a more . . . prominent and easily recognised position,' he said. 'With rocks, perhaps, or a st-striking natural feature.'

'Whatever for?' Charley asked. 'We have water. The animals have the feed they've craved. Why would you want rocks?'

W smiled, knowing he'd been misunderstood. 'Not the rocks so much. S-something to mark this place as distinct from the country all around. It happens, you see, to . . . to be almost exactly on the Tropic of Capricorn.'

I looked at Charley to see if this meant anything to him. But he was using a twig to scrape the last dregs of sugar from his tea. 'The Tropic of what? Bugger me. Drinks all round, eh?'

'Charley, you're in-incorrigible. The Tropic of Capricorn. Latitude twenty-three and a half degrees south. The same distance from the Equator as the Tropic of Cancer is to the north.'

'Which means we're heading in the right direction?'

'More than that, Charley. It means we are now officially in the tropical region.'

Charley gazed into his mug, which did not hold the drink he would have preferred. 'A man could die of thirst in tropical heat.'

But W had stopped listening to anyone else. 'I'm almost sure the relevant line of latitude runs right through here. Though I cannot be as certain as I would . . . like. The g-gale we weathered last night prevented me from taking my latitude observation, but I've recorded some useful readings here and my reckoning c-cannot be far out. If at all. Here's a thing, though. When taking out my instruments I saw that one of my spare thermometers was broken. A nuisance.'

He looked at me. But this time I could not be held responsible. Since the incident at Royal Park, W himself had attended to all the packing and unpacking of his scientific equipment. 'Ah well,' he said with a shrug. 'What's done cannot be undone. And now I m-must attend to my journals.'

Which he did. And my guess is that W told Mr Burke, too, about our crossing of the Tropic of Capricorn. But the leader did not mention it in his notebook. He wrote nothing at all on January 7th. Or January 6th or January 8th, for that matter. But he had put this down on January 5th, his last entry for more than a week: 'It is impossible to say the time we were up, for we had to load the camels, to pack and feed them, to watch them and the horse, and to look for water: but I am satisfied that the frame of man never was more severely taxed.'

W, on the same day, made no mention of privation. I must say this for him: he did all that was ever asked of him, and more, without a complaint until very near the end. Even then there was a candle of scientific inquiry still flickering within him. Did ever another man slowly wasting away take such interest in the size and consistency of his own motions? But on January 5th there was none of this. He mentions blades of grass in depressions in the plain, and a waterhole with piles of shells on the banks where blacks had been camping until shortly before our arrival. And he concludes: 'The camels and horses being greatly in need of rest, we only moved up about half a mile, and camped for the day.'

I have no memory of shells or grassy depressions. If the animals were in need of rest, as W says, we must have been in worse shape than them. We did not carry the loads of the camels, it is true, but they, unlike us, were in conditions for which they had been bred. The heat distressed them less than the stony ground. They would tread awkwardly, like city women with gravel in their button-up boots, too modest to remove them and shake free the grit.

I cannot bring to mind January 5th. It must have been a hard day for Mr Burke to write of men being severely taxed. But I doubt it was much worse than the days immediately before or after, and infinitely better than many days yet to come. We still had hope then.

I suspect January 5th was one of the leader's dark days. A cloud descended on him at times, leaving him silent and apart from the rest of us. On these days, and we all came to know them, Mr Burke would lead the way with only Billy for company. Not just for a few hours, as when I had seen him at sunset not long out from the Cooper, but for all our waking hours. He might confer with W about our course but then, with a curt nod of his head, he would resume his position and push on.

Perhaps he was brooding on the possibility of failure, which could find us in any number of ways. We could reach the Gulf and find a blaze on a tree left by Stuart. We could be forced back by sickness or unpassable terrain before reaching the Gulf. We could get there but perish on the return. Of all the possibilities, I think this was the one that oppressed Mr Burke the most. So much depended on success. To achieve his stated goal but then be unable to claim his reward was a prospect calculated to plunge him into despondent silence.

But it is possible I am wrong about this. Perhaps these silences had little to do with the expedition. He might have been brooding upon a lost love, or the wars he'd been unable to fight.

Perhaps – like the rest of us, with the sometime exception of W, who could be fascinated by a particular type of moss or stone beneath his boots – even Mr Burke was ground down by the tedium of our days. The early starts. The endless walking. The smell of us. With little to look forward to after sunset other than reeking dried meat. Then more of all of it again after a bone-chilling, too-brief sleep.

We learned to let him be when it seemed a black bear dogged his steps, but these dark moods never lasted longer than a day and did not impede our progress. There were periods when it felt like Charley or I could have led our party. W determined our course, we proceeded in that direction, the water held out, our health was reasonable excepting for Charley's headaches, and it seemed just a matter of time before we achieved our objective.

But time was something we hadn't reckoned with. Nor had the committee, with all its instructions. Time passed harder than miles. I would walk and walk then finally look up, hoping that the sun had meanwhile advanced a considerable distance on its own daily journey. But it would mock me, staying put in the same part of the sky where I had last noted it, many hours before. It would slouch across the sky by day and then race through the night and appear again when it was unwelcome – a pink-tinged band in the east that forced us to rise up again from the unforgiving ground.

The sun played tricks on us. When we were only a few days into the tropical region, the light became grey and gloomy. The temperature dropped. There were no shadows. Billy whinnied, his nostrils flaring, as if he apprehended some danger. Yet there were no blacks to be seen. Then, with an exclamation of both delight and frustration, W explained it.

'A solar eclipse! As noted in my charts. I have been so absorbed in the country that I neglected to take any readings.'

Mr Burke reluctantly agreed to a short halt while W made and recorded some observations. Slowly the light cleared. The sun returned as if freshly burnished and we kept going, through country that improved the further north we travelled. There was a gradual greening. Flat land gave way to rises and then distant ranges. Creeks became more common and water was no longer so much of a concern. We saw smoke, which signalled a native camp, and we knew they only stayed where conditions were favourable. Instead of scorched red sand at my feet, I could now see new grass and plenty of the vegetable Charley called pigweed. In waterholes the fish seemed so curious we could almost scoop them up with our hats. The finest country I had ever seen. My spirits were good. Exploring, I concluded, was easier than soldiering.

Yet in both there is more boredom than incidents worth recording, which is why I can bring to mind the time Golah Singh the camel was lost to us. I have checked W's journal. He has the date as January 30th. A Wednesday. We were nearing the Gulf, so that seems correct. A month earlier our preoccupation had been the preservation of water. Now we had too much of it. The ground had become ever more boggy and Golah Singh, with his load, strayed into a creek bed.

Camels are inquisitive animals; perhaps he saw something that took his attention. Once in the soft creek bed he could not be moved out. He was stuck fast. I tugged at his nose-rope and belaboured his hindquarters with a strap, but he seemed indifferent to these blows. Because the camels were my own responsibility, the others had pushed on, Mr Burke telling me to make up ground as soon as I could. I was alone with the camel in a creek bed covered in thick green undergrowth on both sides. The air was moist. There was a rich pungent smell, like something baking in the sun. Golah Singh seemed supremely unconcerned by his predicament, but when I sensed movement to one side and heard what I took to be the whistled signal blacks often gave one to another, I confess I was scared. I could be speared without the others knowing what had become of me.

Still I could not shift the camel, despite the increasing strength of my blows. When that failed I tried luring him out, holding a handful of sugar in front of his snout. His nostrils twitched, his tongue lolled greedily, but he made no move to extricate himself.

Another noise. Distinct now, a crashing through the undergrowth further up the creek. I armed myself, checking that the rifle was primed and ready, its firing mechanism free from the mud that got into everything. Then I realised that the noise I could hear was a horse. It was Mr Burke on Billy, his manner urgent.

'Damn it, King. Have you not budged this brute yet? We are well along already.'

'He will not move, sir. Neither threats nor treats can shift him.'

Mr Burke seemed ready to lay into Golah Singh himself, but just as quickly, even as he looked to be casting about for a branch to use as a club, he changed his mind.

'Then leave him. Take such essentials as we can carry and get on. We could waste days getting this obstinate bugger up.'

Wading into puddles of tepid water, careful not to be snared ourselves in the sucking mud, we dragged from Golah Singh's pack some bags of rice, flour and biscuits. I hoped that this slight lightening of his load might make the camel stir. Yet though he seemed interested in our labour, he showed no inclination to move. Even when we made to leave, strapping the bags to Billy, Golah Singh sighed and settled into the water like a duchess taking a bath.

My rifle was still ready to fire and I gestured with it towards the camel. 'Should I?' I asked.

The leader considered this for a few moments. Then he

shook his head. 'Not now, King. Who knows, he may yet find a way to free himself. And the ammunition is more valuable to us than this good-for-naught animal.'

We left Golah Singh in the creek. His eyes, under those long lashes, observed our departure without apparent concern. Mr Burke and I pushed further along until we rejoined the others, who reported having seen blacks in the box trees quite close to them, though they had not determined whether they were hostile or merely inquisitive.

The episode with Golah Singh unsettled me, though I was not fond of the camels. We had left the Cooper with six of them; now there were five. More disturbing was the shifting balance between time and food. Even taking as much as we could on Billy, we still had to leave some provisions behind with Golah Singh. And several evenings after we abandoned the camel, Charley told me where we stood after assessing the state of our supplies.

Mr Burke had reckoned on needing six weeks at the outside to make it through to the Gulf. Provisions had been worked out accordingly. It was now February. We had left the Cooper close to eight weeks earlier. W made his reckonings and maintained we were now close to our destination. But we weren't there yet.

And more than half our food was gone.

Fifteen

Nora

Walter Tregellas believed he were Jesus Christ. He wore sandals and spoke in parables. A tall, slim man of thirty-four years, Mr Tregellas had grown his hair and beard like he were imitating the portraits of Our Saviour. The sole times he appeared agitated were when he could not recall being taken down from the Cross.

Of all the patients at the Melbourne Lunatic Asylum, Mr Tregellas talked with me most often.

— Greetings, my child! he would cry out when I appeared. You have come to walk amongst us one more time. Be assured your devotion will be rewarded. Perhaps not in this world but undoubtedly the next. Come, there is work to be done.

He would take my arm and lead me around the large, bare room with its walls and floor of cold stone. Although I were a regular visitor, Mr Tregellas would introduce me each time to the other patients. Simon Winslip, who never spoke but had his favourite spot in one corner where he sat nodding his head. Michael Hazeltine, whose moods changed quicker than the weather. One week he would seem calm and polite, the next his language would be foul as he strained against the ties that kept his arms secured to a metal bedding frame. Martin Foley, aged seventy but more like a child every time. Mad Martin, the kitchen lasses called him. He could spend days playing with a boy's wooden spinning top.

Often Mr Tregellas would try to minister to these men, attempt some quiet conversation or make to lay a palm upon them. Though this could vex the likes of Mr Hazeltine. It struck me as wondrous that Mr Tregellas seldom seemed put out by such rejections.

— They mock me, Mary Magdalene, he would say to me. But that is part of it, all part of my assigned task. Yet they can be saved. They can all be saved if they will only listen.

I had told Mr Tregellas my name many times. Nora King. He would smile and continue to call me Mary, like this were something but the two of us could understand. I had learned it were best not to argue with him, or any of them. When they were opposed, they might show the disposition that had caused them to be committed.

It were Reverend Hill who got me a position at the asylum. He had made it part of his mission with the church to help those forsaken by society. And so he spent time with prisoners, amongst the folk who slept rough on the banks of the river, and with the wretched souls in the asylum. He said the Pentridge prison were not a suitable place for a woman but believed I could come and go from the asylum without fear.

— They are deluded rather than dangerous, Nora, he told me. Indeed, you will find that many of them speak more sense than you can hear in Collins Street.

So two mornings each week I made the journey from St Kilda directly along Punt Road to the other side of the river. Some mornings Reverend Bickford were able to arrange one of the church's carriages to take me. On other days I would take the railway into the city, though this meant a long walk along the river or another train to catch. If Mr Hill himself had been staying with us, I would make the journey with him behind the horse he called Wesley, a name Mr Bickford regarded as disrespectful.

My time in Melbourne had turned out different to my expectation. When Reverend Draper directed me to St Kilda I thought my duties would be similar to my time in Sydney, mostly housekeeping and cooking. But although I lodged under the same roof as Mr Bickford, adjacent to the bluestone church off Fitzroy Street, there were not the same call for domestic work. Not because Mr Bickford attended to his earthly needs better than his Sydney brethren. He were even less capable. Wise in his reading and eloquent at the pulpit, yet even the act of cutting bread was almost beyond him. He needed attending to, but James Bickford were one of those men other people look after. Members of his congregation would often invite him to their houses for meals, so I had less cooking to do than previous. With no other clergymen, and his needs so simple, there were little housework. Mr Bickford appeared to want little more in the way of furniture than his old sea-chest. As for Mr Hill, he were a regular visitor but still he might stop over no more than one or two nights each week.

There were warmth between the two ministers, like they were stones from the same hearth. They encouraged me to keep busy. There were useful work to be done in their parishes, they said. I also believe they thought it would do me no good to sit idly and worry about John and the exploring expedition. Of which there were little real news, nothing but rumours.

At Mr Bickford's urging I became involved with his Ladies' Benevolent Society. Simple work, distributing bread or clothes or firewood to women in families with difficulties. I learned it were impossible to tell what troubles lay behind the doors in the neat lines of workers' cottages. Mr Hill said I were a good listener, but what I could possibly do to help his lunatics? I never had any instruction on how to deal with such people. He assured me talking with them would be enough.

— The wretches are shut away, Nora. It is as if we are ashamed and must keep them out of sight. They are bound, often beaten, and a tossed bucket of cold water is as close as many get to a bath. But they are God's children still, and like any of us respond to kindness or attention just as flowers welcome the rain.

Mr Hill accompanied me on my first visits to the asylum. It were situated near Richmond, by the Cremorne Gardens, where the moneyed folk used to come from town on Saturday afternoons, arriving on river steamers like the *Pride of the Yarra*. Mr Hill said he had watched from the asylum as some of these people took balloon rides for entertainment, rising high above the ground.

— Isn't it marvellous the way roses can often grow so near to a rubbish pile, he said. Here we have the playground of Melbourne, and behind a bluestone wall close by is the asylum. And in St Kilda, where our friend Mr Bickford toils so tirelessly, John Gomes De Silva builds his grand folly in Burnett Street. 'Tis all pillars and broad balconies. Yet in lanes nearby whole families struggle to subsist in cottages no bigger than one of Mr De Silva's rooms. The Lord does indeed move in curious ways.

But Mr Hill were not at the asylum with me the first time I experienced one of Mr Tregellas's upsets. It were a Thursday morning. I arrived at my usual hour. Mr Tregellas were not near the door to greet me. I found him in a corner under one of the barred windows, set high to let in some light but allowing patients no view of the world outside. Mr Tregellas were squatting. At first I feared he might be moving his bowels, but as I came closer I saw he were rocking back and forth on his haunches, speaking to himself. Hearing my steps, he looked up at me. His face, usually serene, were a mask of agony.

— I cannot see them, Mary Magdalene. Cannot see them.
— See what, Walter?
— The wounds in my hands. Why can I not see them?

He held his hands before him, studying the palms with the expression of a man enduring a ghastly torment.

— I remember Pilate and *his* hands, Mary. The washing of them. I remember the lashing, the pricking of the crown, the roughness and weight of the cross as I carried it. I can hear the jeers of the people I passed. Then the look on the face of the centurion as he made to strike in the nails.

The fingers of his hands stiffened, like he were recoiling from pain.

— He didn't want to do it, the centurion. He was just a man, like all the others, condemned to carry out his duty. He held the spikes in place, raised the hammer ... And then I recall nothing. It is a blank. I died to save them all but remember not a thing!

Taking half a step forward he brought his face to the wall. His forehead struck hard against the stone. The skin split, blood bright red against his pale skin. I thought the shock of this blow might calm him, but instead it seemed to increase his distress. Again he struck the wall.

I must have screamed. Then clutched at one of his arms, but he shook me away like a cow whisks a fly with its tail. Martin Foley were standing nearby watching, laughing like it were the finest entertainment he could imagine. I near knocked him over as I ran to sound the emergency bell.

I would guess it took the orderlies Rupert and Henry less than a minute to rush into the room. Their station were nearby in the corridor. They passed much of their time playing games of chance. But it seemed too long, and there were nothing I could do to stop Mr Tregellas damaging himself even further.

Rupert were a huge Negro from America who had once worked with a travelling circus, helping to erect the massive tent. He got to Mr Tregellas first and seized him from behind in a wrestling hold, allowing Henry to slip restraining straps over his arms, which were soon pinned to his sides.

— Walter, Walter! said Rupert. What a mess you've made of the wall!

The stone were indeed damp with blood. Mr Tregellas's forehead had the colour and texture of raw meat. But he seemed oblivious to any pain and his upset appeared to ease as soon as he felt himself confined. He looked first at Rupert, then Henry, like he had never seen them before. Then he spoke to them.

— Verily, I say unto you, this day you shall be with me in Paradise.

— A wonderful place to be, too, I'm sure, said Henry. But first we must take you to the saw-bones to have that head attended to.

— You too, Miss King, Rupert said. There's blood on you as well.

I raised my hand to my cheek. It came away streaked with crimson. I knew it were nothing that some water could not wash away but still I felt faint, and I were grateful for Rupert's steadying arm as we left the room.

We must have made an odd procession. Mr Tregellas, calm now, between Rupert and Henry, and me, slighter than all of them. They made me sit on a chair at their station while they took Mr Tregellas to see Doctor Bradford. I awaited their return, dabbing at my cheek with a kerchief. Hoping my breathing would soon return to normal.

— You look dreadful, said Rupert when they reappeared. Your colour is quite gone. What do you think, Henry?

— Not a doubt in the world. Some medicine is called for.

The pair of them glanced up and down the corridor like a pair of schoolboys scouting an approaching master. Then, after a nod from Rupert, Henry reached into a bottom drawer in their table and removed a tin marked 'Best's Biscuits'. From within he conjured a tin cup and a bottle. I could see the label: brandy. He poured some into the cup and passed it to me. I tried to push it away.

— I couldn't. I cannot. It's against —

— Tush! All that and more, I'm sure. But the Bishop himself couldn't deny you a drop after what you've endured. A few sips will see you right again.

There seemed sense in what Rupert said. I took the tin cup and gulped its contents like it were syrup of figs or some other prescribed mixture. I coughed. My eyes streamed. I gasped for air. But even so I felt a warmth seeping through my insides. The orderlies appeared delighted by my response.

— That's my girl, said Henry. Just enough to settle you down a bit.

They passed the bottle back and forth between themselves, sucking from the neck with none of the ill effects the drink had caused me. When my eyes stopped weeping I asked after Mr Tregellas.

— Walter? He'll be fine once he's slept it off, said Henry. He'll have an ugly forehead for a time, that's all. He'll be fine. He always is.

— What occurred before is a regular event?

— Don't know I'd call it regular. Rupert seemed surprised by my question. But our Walter certainly takes a turn from time to time. Can't say I blame him. Must be vexing to be who he thinks he is yet be unable to recall the last chapter of his life story.

— You must excuse my friend here, Miss King, said Henry. I'm sure he's forgotten your connections with the church.

— I take no offence. I'm still startled by Mr Tregellas's manner this morning. He always seemed such a gentleman.

— So he is, ma'am, said Rupert, picking at his teeth with a pearl-headed pin from his waistcoat pocket. But that's the thing about lunatics, you see. You can never tell what will upset their balance. Who knows what set Walter off before? Could have been a voice in his own head. There's no saying much of the time.

It seemed this were a favourite theme of the orderlies. I could imagine them discussing it over their cards.

— It is the thinnest line imaginable between lunatics and, say, some of the gents in the Melbourne Club, said Henry, with the air of a man addressing a learned audience in a lecture hall.

This pair had quite restored my spirits. Or perhaps it were the effect of the brandy. But I had to smile at the thought of making one of my asylum visits to the grand building at the eastern end of Collins Street. It reminded me of what Mr Hill had said.

— So you think I should cease coming here and instead look for lost souls at the Melbourne Club?

— No, we'd miss your pretty face, said Rupert. But there's no doubting not all the mad folk are in the asylum.

— Quite right, Henry continued. Witness them folk by the river, eating rubbish and talking gibberish. And those explorers, given bullocks and bags of money and heading off where nobody has ever gone before. What is that if not a lunatic enterprise?

— Lunatic! Rupert nodded his agreement. And what is the blessed Robert O'Hara Burke if not a madman? A gen-u-ine Irish nutter. Crazy as a coot. I've had it sworn to me by those who knew him as a policeman up Beechworth way that he was wont to take baths in the open. Wearing nothing but his hat! And he would raise this in greeting if a lady passed by.

— At least he didn't stand to say hello, laughed Henry. He's no bushman at all, they say. Could lose himself getting back inside from the thunderbox!

Then he saw my face. Heard the tin cup hit the stone floor with a clang as it fell from my skirts when I stood up.

— Miss King, have we offended you?

— You should know. I had to hold onto the table for balance. You both should know. My youngest brother is on the exploring expedition.

— What? Henry asked. Y'mean with Burke?

— The same.

— God save him! And forgive our damn fool clumsiness. We should stick to cards.

I shook my head. Said I were not insulted. Henry took my arm and guided me back to the seat. Considered me.

— How long has your brother been gone?

— Where are we now, February? Getting on to six months, it must be.

— And you've had no word from him? asked Rupert.

— None at all. But, you see, my brother does not even know I am here. If he thinks of me at all, I imagine he believes me to be in Ireland still. It's many years now since I've seen him. And so little has been heard of the expedition of late it is hard to believe he can yet be out there. It's like holding faith in a spectre that cannot be seen or heard.

The orderlies were silent now, nervous of saying anything further. Henry passed the brandy bottle across the table towards me.

— Here. I think you should be having more of this.

But I didn't take another drink. I went back to the room where Mr Tregellas had taken his turn to see if any of the men had been upset by what they had seen or heard. And to show myself, and Rupert and Henry also, that I would not allow this incident to drive me away from my work.

So I visited the asylum again, as usual, the following Tuesday morning. Waiting for me just inside the door were Mr Tregellas. The bruises on his forehead had turned to yellow and purple and the lacerations were still raw, but his manner were calm. He seemed pleased to see me.

— Mary Magdalene, my child! You have not abandoned me. Walk with me awhile.

— I'll be glad to, I replied, giving him my arm. But tell me, how is your head?

Mr Tregellas pulled me close, wanting to confide a secret. The smell of his skin were like a room locked shut without air for too long.

— 'Twas the crown, my child. The crown. Those thorns can rip a man's skin something terrible.

Sixteen

I didn't need any of W's instruments or assertions to know we were in the tropics. I could smell it in the air, thick and warm. Feel it in the oozing silt that sucked at our boots. W called where we were Camp 119 and said we'd advanced just over seven hundred miles north from the depot on the Cooper. Charley called it a bog. I waited for orders but couldn't see how the camels could be pushed on much further. They weren't accustomed to mud.

Mr Burke was speaking with W. I saw the pair of them poring over one of W's little books, then Mr Burke gestured towards something out of sight and sniffed at the damp air like an animal. They returned to where Charley Gray and I sat on a log at the campsite, trying with no success to get a fire going. Everything was too moist to light. There was no hope of our boots drying. W headed directly to his gear, leaving Mr Burke to speak with us.

'I am dividing the party once more, lads.' That was the word he used for us, although Charley was several years older than himself, the oldest of the four of us in the group near the Gulf. 'It seems useless to take the camels any further north. The ground is in such a state from the rain that they could scarcely be got along, and the undergrowth is thick. So Mr Wills and I will take Billy and press on together. Mr Wills calculates that we can only be a day or so distant from the sea. The smaller our group, the speedier our progress will be.'

'So Charley and I will never get there?'

Mr Burke seemed surprised by my question. His eyes widened, though it was not my intention to question his authority. I had spoken impulsively, struck by the realisation that my journey might never be completed. My lot, it seemed, was to come so far and no more; to make the long trek from the Cooper and then, after near to two months' toil, be unable to finish the job. The leader considered me thoughtfully before replying.

'Will you ever get there, King? Who can say? Perhaps another time. There is no certainty Mr Wills and I can even make it through on this attempt. We will take with us three days worth of rations. The rest of the stores I will leave with you. Charley, I hold you responsible for their allocation while we are gone. You know the proportions by now. I don't expect the blacks to give you any trouble. You have guns, and know what to do if necessary. Five shots will serve as an emergency signal. Three, then a pause before the final two. I have little doubt the sound will carry to us.'

It was early morning. We took our breakfast, doing without tea for want of a fire. Then they were gone, both Mr Burke and W carrying small packs, the bulk of their supplies on the horse. Billy appeared not best pleased about going. The constant moisture was damaging his hooves, and a fungus of some kind had proved resistant to any treatment we could improvise. Ahead of him was more boggy ground and long tendrils of plants that would flick at his face as he pushed along. Our five camels, though, were delighted about not moving on. I had secured them so they could graze without straying. They preferred sand to the squelching ground we encountered here, but without loads on their backs they were in relatively good humour.

There were no farewells, no handclasps. Mr Burke had made

his intentions clear. There was nothing more to be said. The leader nodded at us and then he and W headed away along the creek. Charley and I watched them until they had pushed through the undergrowth, thick and vivid green and gleaming with damp.

They went, we waited. We were alone. Charley looked the way they had gone and stretched, thrusting his arms out wide. 'Bloody magnificent,' he said. 'You dopey bugger, did you really want to press on with them?'

'I . . . I had just thought to conclude what we had started. And I have always wanted to catch sight of the sea at the Gulf.'

'The sea? 'Tis a wet desert, that's all. I've seen more of it than I care to recall. And I'll die content if I never set eyes on it again. I say we've done well sticking here. Three days without stomping through more mud? Three days without wondering what manner of biting creature might next drop from a leaf down the collar of me shirt? Three days without belabouring the camels to keep on? I'll take it and call meself lucky.'

'I don't mind a rest. But we're so close. The rocks . . .'

'Yes, I know. The level of the creek rises and falls. Rocks that are covered in the evening stand clear by morning. His lordship has convinced Mr Burke that this is tidal water. Maybe it is, maybe 'tisn't. But who's to say he has our position correct? I've known inlets that extend for miles in from the coast. From where we are now it could be a week before they see any sand, let alone ocean. Especially with all this bloody vegetation to get through.'

'A week? But they've only taken rations enough for three days. And that's to get them back, too.'

'Indeed. Three days. I'll be interested to hear their report when they return. For here's the thing: they'll be the only ones who'll know for sure if they make it through to the sea or not.'

Charley then turned his attention to his feet. He sat down and used both hands to pull off his boots, first one and then the other. He did this with care so as not to further damage the boots, which were already in poor shape. Such socks as we'd left with had been reduced to shreds, so we'd taken to using bandages from W's medical supplies, winding them in strips around our feet as best we could. Between sweat and moisture from the leather, they had assumed a yellow-brown hue. Charley slowly unravelled his bandages, laying them over a branch so they might dry even a little before he put them on again.

I was sitting close by, so the smell caught me. Like something rancid and rotten. It could have turned my stomach were I not used to it. I got the same stench from my own boots when I took them off, sometimes only once or twice a week.

Charley held one of the boots close to his face, as if searching for something inside. Then he grimaced. 'Strike me! This stink could kill a camel. If it says anything about me health, I'm a dead man already.'

He put the boots to one side and studied his feet, which were very pale and streaked with pink and purple bruises. Unfolding his clasp-knife, he set to work on his toenails. To my inexpert eyes, they looked unusually thick and yellow. When he probed at one, I saw a piece flake away like old paint. Without comment, Charley flicked it off with the tip of his knife, which he then used to point at the bruising on his feet.

'You got any of these markings?'

'Don't know that I have,' I said. 'But I've not looked for a while.'

I knew there were sores that wouldn't heal, from the incessant rubbing of my boots. I had dreamed of bathing them in salt water at the Gulf. The best they could expect now was a splash in the creek. But the atmosphere was so warm and wet that I could not imagine them ever drying properly. Like Billy, we'd finish with fungus feet.

'I don't like the look of them,' Charley continued. 'Seems like there are more marks whenever I check. On me legs too. How are *your* legs holding up?'

'Good enough, I'd say. Weary from all the walking, but bearing up.'

'Sure they are. Your legs are many years younger. Mine ache, most of the time. A dull ache. And if they're knocked I'm left with marks that don't go away.' His tone was very flat. I couldn't tell if he didn't much care about the symptoms he described or simply knew there was little he could do about them.

'What do you think it is?'

'*Think?* I don't think, I *know*. It's the scurvy, and that's God's truth. I've seen two-thirds of a ship's crew struck down with it before. Here, look.' He moistened his lips a little with his tongue and spat on a stone near his feet. The clear globule of spit was streaked with red. 'Seems like me gums bleed all the time. I can make holes in me cheek with the tip of me tongue. Can't help doing it. And me teeth feel like they're shrinking in their sockets.'

Even as he spoke I had a finger probing in my own mouth. Was I imagining it, or were some of the teeth loose? But there was no blood I could taste.

'Jesus,' I said softly. 'What can you do?'

Charley shrugged. 'What can any of us do? They say James Cook made his sailors eat the German sour cabbage on one of his long voyages. Tasted foul but kept the men healthy. I've not seen cabbage in any of our packs. And our leader, in his wisdom, ditched the lime juice.'

Now it came back to me. Landells having it out with Mr Burke near Menindie. *Your prick has a better idea where it's heading than the rest of you. A leader would never have ditched eight barrels of lime juice in Balranald just to lighten the load.*

'I'm sure Mr Burke had his reasons. He'll see us through.'

'Maybe he will,' Charley said, giving me a queer look. 'Or maybe we'll all end up grazing like camels on anything that grows. We already smell as bad as them. And grass could make a change for the better after those damned hard biscuits. Perhaps it's them that's wrecking me teeth. I'm finding it harder and harder to chew the things.'

He shook his head and said no more about his ailments. I was glad of that. I'd never before heard him sound so grim.

The morning sun had worked its way through the thick layer of cloud. We could feel its warmth but had to peer through the canopy of trees to see it. We went down to the creek, Charley stepping gingerly over pebbles as he was still without his boots. Finding a boulder with a flat top some three feet above the water level, he said it would do for him and lay back flat in the sun, his hat off, his face turned up to the sky.

It was odd to see him bareheaded like this. Charley was seldom without his hat, even when he slept. Best thing for keeping his nut warm, he said. I'd not noticed before how much hair he'd lost. A patch on the back of his head, twin furrows leading up from his forehead. His beard too. Had it always been so streaked with white? It gave me a strange feeling seeing him like that. He lay so still and spent on that rock that anyone coming on him would have sworn he was dead.

I checked I could hear the camels' bells not far away and stretched out on a log close to Charley for a kip too. What else were we to do? It would be three days at the earliest before Mr Burke came back. Our orders were to wait. Before I dozed – hearing the mosquitoes droning around me, waiting their chance to feast – I thought of Brahe and Patten and the rest of them at the depot on the Cooper. Also waiting for Mr Burke to return. What had they been doing all this time? Charley and I had to sit tight for three days; they'd been told to kill three months, maybe more. They could die of the boredom, if blacks didn't get them first.

All that time they'd been in the one place, while we'd gone from the creek through the stony flat stumbling desert into country that Mr Burke said could be a grazier's paradise, and now these wet forests with mud and waterfalls and the constant rotting scent and plants too thick to push through. I'd only known Ireland and India before this, and couldn't conceive of another land with such startling changes from place to place. Still ahead of us lay the trek back to where we'd been. Now even drier, I'd wager. The creek lower.

But that was yet to come. For now it was warm and I had no duties to attend to. I could close my eyes awhile.

I woke to raindrops like small shot tumbling out of pewter-coloured clouds. My face was wet, my mouth dry. I must have slept with it wide open. Even as I struggled upright, the drops became a torrent. A waterfall from the sky. Charley had been stirred in the same manner. He rose from the rock, cursing, his first thought for his boots, which he had left in the open to catch the sun.

'Fuck it! They'll be wetter now. Full of water.'

Wincing as he stumbled bare-footed over stones, Charley grabbed his boots and the bandages, dripping now, and looked around. The rain was not letting up and we had no shelter. Our tents had been left behind long before, Mr Burke insisting we carry as little as practical. There was no cave or even an overhanging ledge to protect us from this deluge. The best we could do was crouch like wounded animals beside one of the bigger trees, hoping its foliage would provide a little shelter. The camels were nearby, hunched together, Landa with his head back and yellow teeth bared, apparently revelling in this novel way of taking a drink.

'Fucking fuck,' said Charley. He fell silent, like a man who had passed judgement on the situation and had nothing further to add. Even as the rain made everything still wetter, he slowly wound the bandages back around his mottled feet. Then, having upended his boots to remove the water, he forced his feet back into them. This made a squelching sound. I saw Charley's lips twist; the action must have hurt him. But still he tried to find some good in it.

'Perhaps any warmth left in me feet will dry 'em out. Either that or it'll be a regular little swamp in there. Might grow toadstools between me toes. Stand well clear if ever I take the boots off again.'

The rain stopped as abruptly as it had begun. Then came a warm breeze and sun enough to raise steam from some of the rocks. We dried out a little before the rain returned, and this was the pattern for the three days we were there. We sat. We slept. We got sodden, then waited to dry again. Even the food became damp, though it was all wrapped up. Before we could chew on our chunks of dried meat, we had to use our knives to scrape green scum off the surface. Charley worried that our flour might get moist and set solid.

I have wondered since what we might have done if Mr Burke and W had not returned. If, say, they had lost their way or been speared by natives they never even saw. I have wondered about this, though none of the commissioners ever thought to ask me. I was asked if Mr Burke had expected to meet up with a vessel in the Gulf, and replied that I had never heard of any expectation of that kind, but nothing was raised about our being left alone. Both Charley and I had pocket compasses. We had the camels and food for four men. We could have headed south, tried to pick up our old track, and made it back to the depot.

But I don't think this would have happened. We were in the tropics. Tired from all we had done already. Our three days waiting at Camp 119 were enough for us to sink into laziness. It was so warm and wet it was hard to find the will or energy to do anything much at all. And there was nobody to tell us otherwise. There were big birds, wild geese and turkeys and other things I couldn't name, but we made no attempt to bag any. We'd been told to save ammunition and we still had no fire to cook anything we caught. So we didn't try. We waited, sunning ourselves like lizards when we could and huddling beside our tree when the rains came.

If they hadn't come back, we might just have stayed there until something happened. Blacks coming at us. The food turning rotten or running out. Sickness striking us down. Charley was already failing and he seemed as content to do nothing as the camels were. If nobody pushes a camel, it will go nowhere as long as there is feed to be found. Charley and I were like that near the Gulf.

It was too far back to the depot and we knew the harshness of the country. It was February, which meant still more months of heat. Waterholes could have dried up since we first passed them. Where we were, there was water and game we hadn't yet bothered to get. Charley would surely have stayed put, but I like to think I might have tried to make it through where Mr Burke and W had gone. Just to see the ocean and bathe my feet in salt water. Just to feel I'd achieved what we set out to do. I would have sipped some of the sea water to get the taste of it on my tongue and then gone back to Charley.

We knew we were close. But at night, with the sky blacker and more threatening than anything I'd ever seen, I listened and listened but couldn't hear the sea. I heard insects, and Charley groaning, camels slurping in their sleep, but never the sound of waves on sand.

We waited. And then, late on the third day, they came back.

The camels heard them before we did. And smelled them, caught the scent of Billy. Raised their heads to sniff. And there were Mr Burke and W, coming back along the creek the way they had gone. And Billy. All of them half covered in mud, Mr Burke's breeches so thick with it they might have been made of clay. They didn't have the look of victory on them.

In India I had seen men spent on their feet who could still kindle an inner fire when a battle had been fought and won. But Mr Burke and W were as wet as Charley and me, and thin and drawn with fatigue. Not talking at all as they made their way near to us. Charley and I approached them, anxious for their news.

'Mr Burke,' I said. 'Here, let me take Billy for you. So tell us, did you get through?'

Mr Burke looked at W before replying. 'King. Gray. Get ready for our return, lads. We have accomplished our task as far as it is necessary.'

'So you reached the sea? You got through?'

Again it was Mr Burke who spoke. ''Tis not quite as simple as that. It would be well to say that we reached the sea. But we could not obtain a view of the open ocean, though we made every endeavour to do so. And so I'm satisfied with what I've done. With what *we've* done.'

Grey smudges under his eyes. W still silent. Misty rain.

I had expected a celebration of some sort. Handshakes and banging of backs. Instead, only this sense of extreme fatigue and the leader so careful with his words. *It would be well to say that we reached the sea.*

Mr Burke must have sensed my bemusement, for he tried to rouse himself. 'I tell you what I *didn't* see. A fucking Scotsman! Of one thing there can be no doubt: we got this far before that drunkard Stuart.'

'I'll drink to that!' Charley cried. And we all laughed at this. Even W smiled, for there was nothing to drink but the water all around us. Everything boggy. Puddles lying on the mud.

Mr Burke had me busy getting the camels ready. He wanted to head back at first light the next morning. Charley was put to work marking some of the box-wood trees roundabouts, using a tomahawk to cut off a square of bark and fashion a letter 'B'. Just that initial, no date or anything else. W helped Charley once he'd put down his pack, saying they had marked many more trees in a similar manner where they'd gone.

That night, with the insects noisier and even more ferocious than before, Charley related to me a little of what W had told him while they toiled.

'He said it was real heavy going. Billy got bogged several times and they nearly couldn't get him out. They came upon a blacks' camp, with yams that they ate. A group of blacks with a baby who looked so terrified they guessed they must never have seen white faces before. Then a swamp, a flooded marsh, so hard to get through that they short-hobbled Billy and pushed on without him. But the strange thing is, his lordship wasn't clear on what they'd actually reached. Fifteen miles further on, he reckoned, yet only the pair of them know where this got 'em. I put it to him straight: had they made the water? And it was like the leader himself replying: "We accomplished our task as far as necessary."'

Charley paused, looking up at the moon coming and going behind clouds through the overhanging leaves. 'It'll do me, King. Whatever they reckon. I've no wish to follow where they went and search for the most northerly tree with a fucking blazed "B".'

But here's a curious thing. I've only noticed it of late. You can check it in Wilson and Mackinnon, pages twenty-one and twenty-two — W's journal. There's a date missing. Then whole pages gone. Nothing between Sunday February 10th — as I guess it must be – and Tuesday February 19th, when we were on our way back to the Cooper. W the assiduous notetaker, who wrote in his fieldbooks even when he was spent or hot or wet or hungry, is silent on his ultimate destination, the reason for the journeying.

He leaves us at Camp 119 when he and Mr Burke head off for the Gulf, then describes an encounter with a family of blacks and a boggy marsh flooded by sea water. The neighbourhood of their next camp, he notes, 'is one of the prettiest we have seen during the journey'. They hobble Billy and push on. Then nothing. Where they ended up, what they saw, what they left behind, he does not say. I know only what they told us when they came back to camp.

But at the time we had other things to think about. Mr Burke and Charley made an inventory of our stores. It was a matter of such importance to Mr Burke that he recorded the quantities in his notebook: 'Flour 83 lb; pork 3 lb; dried meat, 35 lb; biscuits 12 lb; rice 12 lb; sugar 10 lb'. With the distance we had to travel back to the Cooper – eight weeks, assuming no delays – it would mean even shorter rations than before. Our provisions would have to be reduced.

Thereafter Mr Burke himself took charge of the distribution of food, dividing up our rations – a stick or two of scummy dried meat and perhaps a spoonful of rice and flour – and placing them on plates. These he would cover with our hats or his neckerchief and then attach to each a number. He would shift them around, as a fairground trickster does with cups and dice, and urge us on.

'C'mon, lads, pick a number. One for every man and no favours to any. Say your number and I'll have the one that's left.'

We stared at those scrawled numerals like circling hawks scanning the earth below for something struggling and helpless. Then we'd choose, trying a different order each time. Three, one, four. Leaving the other for Mr Burke himself.

He was different on the way back. I sensed it the evening they returned from their attempt on the Gulf. It was very windy, with misty rain.

'I'll wager those showers come from off the sea,' said W, looking up at the scudding clouds. 'And that breeze — it's a northerly. Also from the sea.'

'The sea!' Mr Burke replied. 'Everything starts and ends at the sea. We finish there and then start all the way back again.'

He was looking north, where he'd headed off with W just a few days earlier. Now he was turning his back on it. All the long way up from the Cooper he'd had a goal — the Gulf. Now he had to retrace steps we'd already taken. We were all more or less spent and the camels would have been better for another fortnight's rest. Charley's feet and legs were in a bad way. But our rations wouldn't allow for idleness, so Mr Burke insisted we press on again.

For what? To proclaim that he had fulfilled his mission? He had nothing to show for it, not even a bottle of sea water from the Gulf. There was no Becker with us to record the scene with his watercolours. I did not hear Mr Burke say they had built any cairns; others would have to get through on their route to find the trees they'd marked and thus verify their feat. Mr Burke and W were now tied together more firmly than ever before. Each needed the other as a witness to whatever they'd achieved.

Charley Gray, however, had no doubts about our success.

'First to cross the continent,' he said as we coerced the camels along a sodden track. 'First white men to gaze upon the Gulf. That will surely be worth a few extra shillings and kisses from a willing bint. We'll be famous, King. All of us.'

'But you and I didn't get there, Charley. We never even heard the sea, let alone saw it.' I said nothing about him having joined the party in Menindie, months into the expedition.

He grabbed at my arm, rougher than mere jesting. 'Listen to

me, soldier boy.' His face was close to mine, his tone urgent. I could see that the whites of his eyes were turning yellow. 'I'm much older than you. Twice yer age. If we make it back, anything that comes of this could be enough to see me comfortable for the rest of me days. I've earned any reward that comes with every sorry step I've taken and all of them yet to come. So don't be buggering it up by arguing the details. We're all part of this, understand?'

I protested that he was hurting my arm. And tried to reassure him. 'Don't worry, Charley. My need is as great as yours. I have no trade other than soldiering. No expectation of money other than the salary I signed on for. It's just – I'm not sure what we've done.'

'That's easy. We've done whatever they say we've done. Now, come on, put your shoulder under this camel's lazy arse and let's get him on a bit.'

It rained. And kept raining. For the first few days heading back we couldn't travel more then four or five miles a day. It wasn't only the sodden ground that made the going difficult, days and nights alike were sultry and uncomfortable. We weren't dry for weeks. All of us had trouble sleeping, though we were bone-weary from the effort of trying to push on. The aches and stickiness and rumbling guts couldn't be ignored sufficient to rest long. W complained that many of his instruments were ruined by the humidity, becoming fogged or mouldy. Yet his spirits held up well, and his enterprise. He was the one who shot a pheasant, bagging it when it got curious and waddled in too close. We planned to eat it at what W christened Recovery Camp, all of us eagerly anticipating a change to our dreary diet. So we were much disappointed on butchering the bird to find it almost all feathers and claws, such flesh as we got off the bones stringy and sour.

It was the hunger, the constant nagging knots inside, that led us to eat the snake. We were crossing a creek by moonlight, Mr Burke having decided to travel by dark to try to escape the worst of the steamy conditions, when Charley stumbled over what he thought was a log. He cursed it, then saw it move. The snake was larger than any serpent we had ever seen. Charley killed it with a stirrup-iron, giving the monster more than half a dozen blows around its head before it stopped moving.

In the morning W measured it: eight feet and four inches in length, with a girth of seven inches around its belly. In colouring it was mostly black, with yellow on its underparts. W said he could discern no poisonous fangs, but there were two distinct rows of teeth in each jaw. Charley hacked away slabs of it with his tomahawk, saying the blacks often prized snake as a delicacy. When we were able to get a sputtering, smoky fire going we cooked it as best we could, holding chunks over the flames on green sticks. Hunger aided our appreciation of it, though what wasn't blackened of my piece still seemed raw and sticky in my mouth. But it helped fill our bellies and for that we were grateful.

The day after we ate the snake, Mr Burke fell ill. He had been silent; we thought he had slipped into one of his dark moods and so let him be. But then he broke away from our track, tearing at his breeches. He barely managed to get them down before his bowels exploded. It was pitiful to see the leader so – squatting like a dog, shitting liquid, his face twisted with pain.

'That damned snake,' he said. 'It's burning like coals in my guts.' And then he was sick, the stuff he brought up an evil green colour. He rested awhile, and said he would try riding one of the camels. But he was giddy and unable to keep his seat. When W said we should break for a rest, Mr Burke did not dispute it. All of us were glad to stop.

There were date trees near our camping place. Charley and W gathered some of the fruit, declaring it safer than snake. Such pieces of the reptile we still had were tossed aside, making an unexpected feast for the crows that descended from nearby trees. It puzzled me that only Mr Burke had fallen sick from the snake, as we all ate it. Perhaps there was something else that ailed him. For myself, I know that my legs ached, though I tried to put it from my mind. Charley let on that he was still troubled by headaches. As for W, he kept his own counsel, and also kept up his fieldbooks and readings and notations of clouds. I never knew what kind they were, but there was always a lot of rain in them.

After a day's lay-up, Mr Burke declared himself strong enough to continue travelling, though his eyes had sunk. Yet he was still able to jest a bit.

'The serpent's revenge, eh, King? The snake was cast out of the Garden of Eden, so ever since has sought retribution on those who caused it to go through life on its belly. At least we are still on our feet. Mostly.' Then he laughed – too hard, as it caused him to wince and clutch at his stomach – and told me to attend to the camels.

We were back to six of them now, having come across the abandoned Golah Singh the morning before Charley trod on the snake. The hapless animal had evidently extricated himself from the bog in which we had left him almost a month earlier, though he was in a decidedly sorry state. He was thin and miserable, his coat stuck fast with mud. It seemed he had fretted much on being left behind, and had made a pathway in the nearby vegetation with his wandering to and fro, always on the same course and apparently never straying far from his original position. He was delighted to be reunited with the other camels and began feeding again immediately on seeing them. For their part, our camels, which had caught Golah Singh's scent before we saw him, appeared concerned about their former companion. They butted him gently with their heads in a kind of greeting.

It lifted our spirits a little to find Golah Singh again. We took it as a hopeful sign. But within a week, even after we'd had a day's rest to allow Mr Burke to regain some strength, it was clear we could not push the beast any further. He seemed to be completely done up and would not come on. I put a light load on him but still he was unable to keep up. Even when the pack and saddle were taken off he did not travel.

So again we left him behind. I removed all his gear and let him loose, thinking he would seek to follow us when we set off. Instead he nosed at some bushes, then sank down as if to rest awhile.

I saw Charley gazing back at him.

'Any party that comes along here after us will pick him up,' I told him. 'And he's already demonstrated his capacity to fend for himself. He must be half wild already.'

Charley just shook his head and licked at his lips, which were split with sores that would not heal.

As we pushed on, though our progress was slow, the days became less humid. This made our going somewhat easier, as we tired less quickly. Conditions were good. We had water. Game was plentiful, but we weren't able to get more than a couple of birds. When we came across it we ate the pigweed. We tried boiling up its leaves into a tea. I never liked its taste but W insisted it would be best to take some. The soreness in my legs eased somewhat, but Charley's condition worsened. He had the trembles most of the time now and seldom sang to himself at all.

W gave him some medicine from his supply, but appeared unsympathetic as to his plight. 'He has caught cold through c-carelessness in covering himself last night,' he told the leader. 'And I suspect the man's constitution is quite gone through d-drink, which was too freely available when he lived in a public house.'

Charley lay with his head propped on his pack. He shivered, though the evening was warm. I made him a cup of the pigweed tea and took it to him. But he wouldn't have it, turning his head to one side when I placed it near his mouth.

"Tis not the kind of drink I sorely need, soldier boy.'

'Come on, Charley, take some of this. It'll help get your strength back. Look, I'll heft some of your gear myself if you think it could help, but you must try to keep going. Think back on what you said to me – all those willing bints waiting to give a hero a good time.'

He turned his head back to me but didn't smile. Didn't say a word. Didn't respond at all. I left the cup near him and had to walk away to hide the fear I felt.

Charley's face was changing. He looked older by the day. And in his eyes, when he turned, I saw the same look Golah Singh directed at me when we left him behind for the last time.

Seventeen

'What's a baron?' Albert asks me.

'It's an honour. From Germany. Like being a knight.'

'A knight like Sir Lancelot?'

'Hush child,' Mary tells him, though she is smiling at her boy. Her russet hair is tucked up under a checked travelling bonnet.

But Albert is too excited to remain quiet for long. 'He must be very important.'

'He is,' Mary replies. 'Baron Ferdinand von Mueller is one of the most distinguished gentlemen in the colony. We are indeed lucky to have been given an invitation to see him today. The fame of his gardens has already spread over the oceans.'

Mary is in a good humour. Delighted to be part of this rare outing. Delighted to have been excused from her work in the Royal Arcade café so she can come. The distraction will do her good.

The day is perfect, sunny and mild, and from the carriage that von Mueller has arranged for us we can see some early pink and white blossom on the trees. The St Kilda Road, scattered with puddles just a few months ago, is now firm and dry. Nora points out to the children the army barracks being built in bluestone on our left as we pass, heading north towards the city. Albert and Grace lean over the sides of the carriage, hoping to catch a glimpse of soldiers in scarlet jackets.

'I can never come along here without thinking of the first time I made this trip,' says Nora, keeping hold of a clump of Grace's tunic. 'I went much more slowly then, travelling in a tiny carriage with Mr Metherdew from Reverend Draper's church in town. He took me down to see Mr Bickford. That were also the day I first met Mr Hill.' She glances at Mary, then continues a little too brightly. 'Dear Mr Metherdew, he's getting old now. Quite stooped. So much has happened since then.'

'Course it has,' says Mary. 'It must be eleven years now since you got here. And near enough ten for me. Things change. People come and go. That's how it is.'

I see Nora take her hand and give it a squeeze.

Having failed to see any soldiers outside the bluestone barracks, Albert is back thinking about von Mueller and his titles. 'Are you very friendly with the baron, to be invited to see him?' he asks me.

It has been a confusing few years for Albert. I think he still grieves for his father. Grace, thankfully, is too young to be troubled by this. I cannot look at Albert without thinking of myself as a boy: an orphan at nine, a soldier at fourteen. Then, almost nine years on, reunited with my sister and a cousin I had never expected to see again. If I wasn't swathed so securely in blankets, I would like to rest an arm on Albert's shoulders, but Doctor Treacey insisted I should be kept warm and well wrapped up. Other than that, he was enthusiastic about the outing. I heard him say so to Nora.

'If the day is fine, I think it's a capital idea. As long as John does not become overly tired. But you have the wheeled chair in which to move him around and you will know, I'm sure, when it's time to go. The change in routine and air will do you all good.'

Albert is irked that nobody has answered his question. He bangs on the side of the carriage with his little hands, then tugs at my blanket and says, 'I *asked* if you are great friends with the baron.'

'Not friends, as such,' I tell him. 'But I knew him some years ago. We were involved in the same enterprise. I saw him on several occasions because of that.'

When was the first time? I cannot be sure. As a senior member of the Exploration Committee, von Mueller must have been one of those well-dressed men who would call on Mr Burke and hand him envelopes before our departure from Royal Park. But I don't remember him. My work was on the stinking side of the park. He certainly would have paid me and the camels no mind. As a botanist, he was always more interested in plants than animals.

I recollect he was one of the few committee men who showed me any concern after I came back. Him and John Macadam. To the others I was just an unwelcome reminder of all that had gone wrong with their expedition. The leaders they had appointed had perished or, like Landells, packed up and left. But a hired man had returned.

Von Mueller, short and whiskery, with spectacles that always needed cleaning, spoke to me before the commission hearings. 'Just tell the truth, my boy. Answer the questions honestly, that is all anyone can ask of you.'

His English was quite good, although 'that' could often sound like 'zat'. And even after more than twenty years in the country, he was still more comfortable conversing with other German speakers. Apparently he had been friendly with Becker.

'It is a remarkable story you have to tell,' he said to me, studying me through his smudged spectacles outside the hearing room like I was a rare species of plant. Then he said it again, 'Remarkable.'

It was only much later, long after the commissioners had released their report, that I learned the extent of von Mueller's role in the expedition. The whole thing had largely been his idea. He had been an explorer himself, travelling in the north of the country with Augustus Gregory. He knew Leichhardt, another German. It was von Mueller who pushed the plan for Victoria to be at the forefront of any attempt to traverse the interior of the continent.

Now, in 1871, he is the director of the Botanical Gardens, near the site set aside for the building of the new Government House. Our driver points this out to us, rolling his eyes at the proposed extravagance – twenty bedrooms and a ballroom, he says – as he guides the carriage off the main road and onto a much rougher track across a paddock. The gardens are fenced. At the gate a sign informs visitors that they close promptly at sunset and insists that all carriages be kept outside.

The driver leans down from his raised seat and talks to the gate attendant. I make out the words 'appointment' and 'director'. The attendant waves him through after giving instructions on where to find our host.

Mary smiles and says, 'I feel like a princess, getting this treatment.'

I have visited the St Kilda gardens, which are within walking distance of the church, but these are grander, like a zoo of trees and plants. I can see labels: oaks from England, palms from the Canary Islands, shrubs with flowers like trumpets from Africa.

'Look,' says Albert, who has spotted a lake at the bottom of a hill. 'Ducks!'

'Ducks!' Grace pipes up. 'Ducks!'

The driver stops the carriage near a glasshouse on the northern side of this lake. Von Mueller appears from inside, where he has been talking to someone in a long dark jacket. I recognise the distinguished botanist by his squat shape and spectacles, which he lets hang from a crimson ribbon when not wearing them. The spectacles catch the morning sun as he approaches.

'My dear King, and ladies, *willkommen*.'

Albert and Grace are the first out, jumping from the carriage without waiting for the driver to place the wooden steps in position.

'Are you a *real* baron?' demands Albert.

The botanist hoists the boy to shoulder height, much to his delight. 'Indeed I am, young man. But you can call me Vonny.'

'Vonny!' echoes Grace with glee.

Von Mueller puts Albert down and takes Grace's hand. With his free hand he holds the carriage door open while Mary helps me down and Nora steadies the special chair, which the driver has untied on our arrival. The effort of getting into it leaves me sweating and breathless. I am embarrassed to be seen like this, so I am surprised when von Mueller says, 'You are a lucky man, King.'

'Lucky?' I ask when I have found my breath.

He lets Grace twirl around his arm, as if she were a dancer. 'I never married, you see. I was engaged once, but had to break it off. Too busy. All my time and money have always gone into my work. Children — I have always loved children. I think I would have been a good papa. Though now, at my age — closer to fifty than forty — I would perhaps be a better grandpapa.'

'It is wonderful what you have achieved with the gardens,' I tell him, looking around.

'Thank you, King. I wish you could tell this to my critics. Some of whom, it seems, have the ears of our newspaper editors. I read that not enough has been established here. They do not understand that botanical gardens are not like statues: they are living things and must be given time to grow. But enough of my grumbles. Ladies, feel free to roam around. I wonder, do you know the name of that lovely specimen there?'

'A gum tree, surely,' Mary says.

'*Ja!* Correct. One of our many fine eucalypts. Did you know that, with my encouragement, eucalypt seeds have now been exported to California, India and Algeria? Threads from Australia stretching clear across the world. I have been in correspondence with physicians who believe that the oil distilled from eucalypts could be useful in combating the malaria. Amazing, I think. So please, ladies, enjoy my gardens. There is just a little business I must attend to with my former associate King.'

Mary and Nora take the children, who are eager to get closer to the ducks on the lake, while von Mueller pushes my chair towards the glasshouse. It is heavy work, the wooden wheels sinking into the gravel. His breathing becomes more laboured as he speaks behind my head.

'It pains me to see you like this, King. I fear your health never fully recovered after you came back. And for that I am sorry. Truly sorry.'

'But you were not personally responsible. Not at all.'

He stops. Steps in front of the chair. Polishes his spectacles. His face pink. His checked waistcoat, pushed forward over his swelling stomach, missing two buttons.

'But I *vas* responsible. We all were, but myself especially. I fought hard for such an expedition. You know, I even quoted Isaac Newton to my colleagues in the institute to sway them. How does it go? *Ja*: "I have played like a child with the pebbles on the shore while the great ocean of truth lies unexplored before me." Fine words indeed! And it happened. We got money enough, but mistakes were made. Although there was much we could not have known in advance, about men we appointed and how things would turn out... Exploring, you see, is not as predictable as botany. If you plant an acorn, you will never grow an elm, hmm?'

He resumes his position behind the chair and pushes me inside the glasshouse. At once it seems as if I am again with Charley, waiting near the Gulf. The air is hot and moist. It smells of soil and growing things. I can see ferns with long thin fronds in pots, piles of strangely shaped seed pods atop a wooden packing-case. I close my eyes, shaken, and realise the sounds are different.

Rather, the lack of sounds. No water trickling in a creek, no whining insects. Only von Mueller's voice.

'Are you all right, King?'

I open my eyes and shake my head as if waking from a dream. 'Sorry. I was distracted for a moment.'

'Ah! I was thinking perhaps you had swooned. And was pondering where I might find some ammonia to revive you. Now, allow me, please, to take you over here.'

He pushes me to a long wooden workbench, navigating my chair between small palms with their lower halves swathed in hessian and tubs of rank-scented fertilisers. Drops of water cling to the windows. He picks up a spindly seedling. 'Do you know this one, King? No, of course not. I named it *Willsia*, to placate the persistent Doctor Wills who sought no end of tributes to his unfortunate son. He kept at us, wanting the pistol Burke had with him, claiming it was his late son's personal property.'

'That's true,' I put in. 'He gave it to us when he couldn't go on.'

Von Mueller considers me through his spectacles. 'Indeed. Was his. But also such a melancholy and interesting relic. So. To satisfy Wills senior, I assured him I would seek to find a plant genus in the Australian flora as noble as the young man who sacrificed his life in accomplishing such a great endeavour.' He gazes at the seedling. 'A little thing for such a large sacrifice, I think.'

He replaces the plant on the bench, wipes his hands on his trousers, heedless of the muddy streaks he leaves, and indicates a pile of small boxes and specimen cases stacked six and seven high. 'I must confess that this was not purely a social invitation, King. I am hoping you can do me a service. You see here some remnants from the expedition, botanical and miscellaneous samples sent back by my lamented colleague Ludwig Becker. To my eternal shame, these have never been properly sorted. Such labels as there were have very often been lost or separated from specimens. I wonder if you could take a look – *ja?* – and see if there are some you recognise. Or can at least place in a region from your travels.'

He positions my chair so I can work at the bench. There is no order to the boxes; they look like they have been tipped out of a bag. I hardly know where to start. The nearest box is open. Inside are tussocks of grass, of different sizes, stacked end to end. I look more closely. No, they are birds. Dead birds. Around their legs is white thread, as if they have been trussed for cooking. Thread for tags that have become detached. Owlet, spinifex pigeon, orange chat.

Von Mueller sees what I'm looking at. 'Ah. Matters ornithological. I keep meaning to move them from here. Conditions are not right. I fear they are rotting. But please, take a look at anything there. And excuse me for a moment, there is someone else here who has been helping me.' I presume he means the man in the jacket I glimpsed earlier. Von Mueller hurries away.

I look at the contents of the next box. Some leaves, pieces of grass, a long-dead lizard with tiny eyes that seem to stare at me reproachfully. Labels, loose, in a neat hand: '*Triodia pungens*', '*Melaleneus*', '*Tympanocryptis*', 'probably *T. lineata*'. A single sheet of paper, its edges curling, with a pencil sketch – a map of some kind, with writing: 'S.36. E point B. S.25. E red hill point'.

I can recall the studious Becker, seemingly always battling an illness or injury of some kind, writing his notes and collecting his specimens. Other than W, he was the only one of us who could become excited by the sight of a particular kind of creeper on a tree. Now he is dead and his work is a jumble. His efforts seem all the more futile, and there is nothing I can do to help. These specimens mean little to me. I know where we left Becker, but not what most of these things are or where he might have gathered them.

I tell von Mueller just this when he returns, wheezing slightly, saying his other visitor will join us shortly. He seems disappointed but not unduly surprised by my admission.

'Ah well, I thought it worth a try. I am sure I could identify the botanical specimens myself, if I had the time. But that is the thing, *ja?* I have so much to do with the gardens, and this herbarium, as well as assisting Mr Bentham with his *Flora Australiensis*. There is too much to do. And my dear Becker's specimens are of limited use to anyone if their origins are uncertain. Ah. Good. Over here.'

The clunking of boots. The smell of stale tobacco. A familiar voice.

'Dammit, Mueller, a man could get bushwhacked amidst all this stuff.'

The botanist seems to find this amusing. 'Ha! I think of all men, you are least likely to be lost, Mr Howitt.'

His fingers on my shoulder, then shaking my hand while those eyes scan my face. 'Well met, King. It's been a while. You're not growing any fatter, man. Though I'm glad to see you've been able to get out.'

Von Mueller consults a large silver watch he keeps in his waistcoat pocket. 'Time slips away! I have enlisted Mr Howitt also to help tie up some loose endings from the expedition.' The old botanist is looking on like a proud parent. 'I remember when you were brought back. Such scenes ... But I must not ignore your ladies, King, or the little ones. Have a look at what is there, gentlemen, and meet us outside when you are done.'

He scurries out of the glasshouse. And now I have no escape. Howitt is pushing the chair to a different part of the bench. More boxes. I can see flowers pressed flat as if they've been stepped upon. Neither of us is much interested in examining them. We move on. The ends of Howitt's beard – which seems longer than ever, as if he has become even more indifferent to barbering – flick at the side of my face.

'I'll not muck about with pleasantries, King. You know me as a blunt man. I confess you are vexing me. My letters are unanswered and the last time I called I was turned away. Politely, but turned away nevertheless. And I can't help wondering why.'

'I am not well, Mr Howitt. You know that.'

'I know it. Yet even so, you are intent on raking over cold coals. Writing that journal. I take it you persist with it?'

'When I can,' I tell him.

He stops pushing. The humidity in the glasshouse is making me unpleasantly warm. Howitt stands in front of me, looking down. The moustache near his nose has been stained orange by snuff.

'Now, here's where I start to scratch at the scab on this business, King. You've been admirably reticent all these years. Kept your own counsel, never sought to inflate your own role in things like Welch and most of the others. I even retained some comments attributed to you.' He dips into one of his waistcoat pockets. Produces his knife, half a cigar, its end well chewed, then a piece of paper, which he unfolds. 'I keep things, you see. Especially anything to do with that jest of an enterprise. Recognise this?'

It is a page from a newspaper. Discoloured. Darker along the folds.

'*The Bendigo Advertiser*,' says Howitt. 'January 1863, after the funeral. You wrote a letter.'

'I think I recall it. Allegations had been made about Mr Burke. And Charley.'

'Indeed. But here's the part that intrigues me.' He holds the paper well out in front of him, as if he would be more comfortable wearing spectacles.

I sincerely hope ... that with the interment of the few sad remains of my late generous leader and friend may be as far as possible forgotten the melancholy incidents of the exploration of the interior of Australia ... To be compelled to live over and over such scenes as those I passed through I find to be depressing to my spirits and injurious to the little health I have yet regained.

'Movingly put, I would say,' Howitt continues. Sounding very much like a man parcelling things up to be put away, like one of the unfortunate Becker's boxes. 'But now you cannot leave things alone.'

'There are some things to be said. Some things to set right.'

'You are a free man, King. You can do what you will, write what you like. But I'll tell you what bothers me most about this business. Burke! That dunderhead led a shambles of an expedition, yet he's been afforded the status of a saint. I appreciate the politics of it – it's never done to accept responsibility for a tragedy – but the truth of it is, he failed.'

'Not so. He succeeded in what he set out to do. What *we* set out to do. Crossed the continent...'

Howitt kneels so that his face is level with mine. I cannot avoid his gaze. 'Did he? See, this is the thing. You're the only one who knows. And I suspect, more and more, that you've been playful with the truth. Not to say strangely loyal to Burke.'

'*Mr* Burke was a fine leader –'

'He couldn't find his own boots without a light to guide him! Listen to me, King. He divided his party. He was rash and intemperate. Assaulted his own men!'

'That's not so. He cared for us all.'

'What of Charley Gray, for Christ's sake! Burke thumped him when he was clearly ailing.'

I can still smell the fertiliser. Or is it the dead things? 'It wasn't like that,' I respond.

'It's all in Wills's fieldbooks, King. You think I haven't studied them? Wills came upon Gray sneaking flour when you were all on short rations. This was reported to Burke, who gave Gray a thrashing. That's how Wills describes it, *a good thrashing*. And within a couple of weeks the poor sod was dead.'

'That's not how it was. I told the commission so. It wasn't an assault. Mr Burke was just trying to enforce discipline, chastising Charley for pilfering from the little store upon which all our lives depended. Six or seven boxes on the ears with an open hand. That's all it was. Nothing more. God knows, I saw much worse in the army.'

'So Wills was wrong?'

'About the punishment, yes.'

'How can you be so sure?'

'It was all over when he came back from getting the ramrod he'd left behind. *I* was there, not him. What I've said on that incident has been the truth.'

Howitt smiles and raises an eyebrow, as if he finds this amusing. 'The truth? I sometimes wonder what *is* the truth of this venture.'

'And . . . there might be another explanation.'

'Meaning?'

'It is possible Mr Burke told him – Mr Wills, I mean – that he had given Charley a thrashing to satisfy him that conduct so dishonourable had been duly noticed and corrected.'

'A neat theory, King. Demonstrating, once again, your allegiance to Burke.'

The taste of blood is in my mouth. I cannot say more. Howitt shakes his head and pushes me out into the sunshine.

'I'm done for, soldier boy.' Charley has the expression of a dog awaiting a whipping.

'What are you talking about?'

'His lordship surprised me eating a porridge I'd made up from flour and water. On the sly, like.'

'On top of your rations, you mean?'

'I'm awful sick, King. The dysentery has got me. Me guts are knotted. I'm shitting slops, been doing so for days. All I was trying to do was clog meself up so I can keep something down. Otherwise I'm a dead man.'

'Did you tell him this?'

'He couldn't care. Never seen him like that, a gent no more. Swore that I'd been robbing him, robbing everyone. Now he says I must tell the leader meself about the flour. But I can't do it, King. Can't do it.'

'Jesus, Charley. Things will be worse for you if he informs Mr Burke himself.'

'But if *you* tell him, King, it could make the difference.' And he clutches at me like a drowning man grabbing onto a floating log.

The leader is tightening straps on Billy's pack when I report to him. At first he says nothing. He finishes the job. Fixes a buckle, tucks the strap in, and turns to face me. 'Does he deny it?'

'No, sir. But he has the dysentery, I think. Says he's sick.'

A muscle in the side of the leader's face is twitching. 'We're *all* sick, damn him. Bring him to me.'

Charley has to lean on me for support. But then shakes himself free and faces Mr Burke alone. When he gets close he tries to stand straight but a pain inside causes him to hunch over, a hand on his guts above his belt.

'What do you mean by stealing the stores?' Mr Burke's voice is cold and hard.

'Just a bit of flour, sir. Here and there. Just so I could keep on going.'

'Sod it, Gray. Did you not receive an equal share of the rations?'

'I . . . I cannot deny it.'

'How long has this thievery been going on?'

'A few days, maybe. Perhaps a week.'

'A week? Damn your thieving hide!' And he hits him. Steps forward and clouts Charley first over one ear, then the other with his right hand. Once, twice, three times. Again.

It is over very quickly and there is no blood. Charley says nothing. The first blow has knocked him off balance. By the last blow he is on his knees. And then he throws up, cloudy liquid trickling on the ground. Ants come at it.

Mr Burke looks down at him. 'I trusted you, Gray. Trusted you. Now we'll all pay for this. Look to him, King. Prop the wretch in the shade awhile, we'll move off as soon as Mr Wills is back.'

'Goodbye, Vonny, goodbye!'

The children squeal with delight as von Mueller lifts Albert then Grace up high, tickles their faces with his whiskers, and hoists them into the carriage.

Howitt – who has been cordial to Mary and Nora, his manner betraying nothing of our exchange in the greenhouse – gently helps me back up into my seat and assists the driver in securing the chair. I cannot resist his aid but try not to meet his gaze.

I am placed facing the rear of the carriage, opposite Nora and Mary. The children, beside me, wave as we lurch away. I can see the figures of von Mueller and Howitt – one who began the expedition, the other who ended it – receding as we pass through the gates of the gardens. Howitt watches us go. The women chatter about the birds and plants they have seen.

'What an interesting man the baron is,' says Nora. 'He asked us if we might be interested in joining his Ladies' Leichhardt Search Committee. Imagine, he really seems to believe that after more than twenty years there are still traces of the explorer waiting to be found.'

'You are very silent, John,' says Mary. 'Are you all right?'

'Tired, that is all. Let me try to rest awhile.'

But when I close my eyes I am more conscious than ever of the motion of the carriage as it lurches over the rough ground we must cross before returning to the St Kilda Road. It is impossible to get comfortable. And I cannot shake the image of another uneasy passenger.

Near the end Charley cannot walk. He tries, but slumps to the ground. W maintains he is sick through his own failings. He has not forgiven him for taking the flour. We wait for Charley to regain some strength, but each time one of us must go back to fetch him. He tells us to push ahead without him.

Mr Burke will not leave him, but nor will he stop. He cannot, he says. So Charley is secured to a camel, hoisted up and strapped to a pack like another piece of baggage. His head jerks with every step the camel takes as we stumble over sand ridges. But he never complains. Never says anything.

On his second to last day it rains. It starts early in the morning, just after we break camp, and rains for much of the day. Not heavy, but unceasing and soaking. The ground beneath us turns to slippery clay. I try to stay close to Charley, fearful he might slide off despite the ropes. His head is sunken. He is hardly human, just a sodden shape.

And yet, near evening, he lifts his face. Holds it up so that the misty rain dampens it. Like a sailor wanting to feel the sea-spray one more time.

Eighteen

The smell of death was on us now. We had been gone from the Gulf forty days or more. W estimated we needed another few days to reach the depot on the Cooper, but he could not be sure. Many of his instruments had been lost or broken or left behind. We were still shedding stuff as we went along to try to lighten our loads.

We were down to only two camels, Boocha having been killed when she could not go on. A whole day was lost cutting up and jerking the meat, laying it in strips in the sun to dry. Billy was gone too. He had lasted almost a week without proper feed by the time we camped near a creek with grassy banks and saltbush all around. Billy was glad of the grass but the next morning was loath to start again. He was knocked up and there appeared little chance of his reaching the other side of the desert. So Mr Burke shot his horse. Took a revolver and put a bullet between his eyes even as he stroked his ears and spoke to him gently. Then he walked away without looking back while we cut Billy up, so he never heard W's dispassionate comments about the meat.

'See here, King. The flesh appears healthy and tender, but is without the slightest trace of fat in any p-portion of the body.' As if Billy were just a scientific specimen, not a living thing that had shared our journeying for eight months.

We were all poorly. The dried meat we had was all that

remained of our rations. That and whatever pigweed we managed to gather. Charley couldn't keep any of it down. Twenty days, maybe more, had passed since W had surprised him sneaking the flour. His condition had become ever more wretched since then.

But still it was a surprise when he died. I had expected him to hang on until we made it back to the depot. There, with rest and better food, he might have survived. W maintained he was gammoning, making out he couldn't walk so he could ride instead, yet he too accepted that Charley was really ill the night before we found him dead. We couldn't stop his shivering even when we laid him under our pitiful blankets — all of them, W's as well — and tried to make him comfortable. His skin was grey and cold to the touch. He could not speak and showed no signs of seeing us. His eyes were dark holes. What little strength he had left was spent trembling. Still I hoped he would rally by morning, enough to take some food, but by dawn he was dead. Lying as we had left him. I doubt that he'd moved at all during the night. Only closed his eyes and stopped shaking.

W gave him a few lines in his fieldbook: 'Wednesday, April 17th — This morning, about sunrise, Gray died. He had not spoken a word since his first attack, which was just as we were about to start.' That was all.

Mr Burke removed his hat and stood for a long time over Charley. He wept. Unashamed for us to see his tears. He said, 'If I had thought I would lose even one of my party, I would never have entered so perilous an enterprise.'

I wish that all those who have sought to blacken the name and memory of the leader had seen him that morning, standing over the still shape under the blankets in the half-light of a new day. Charley was the first of us to die, you see. Others in the party also went, I know that now, but not while they were with us. Not with Mr Burke. And he believed himself responsible.

So he insisted we stop and give Charley as decent a burial as we could manage, even though he would not have been blamed for wanting to push on. We could travel faster now, without a lagging Charley to hold us back. It was decided that Mr Burke himself and W should inter Charley's body after I had dug a grave.

The digging was brutal work. Most of our tools had been abandoned. We only had one shovel and we were all weak. I did not tell the others, as I was much the youngest, but I felt very bad. My arms as well as legs now ached. My gums bled. And two fingernails, what was left of them, just broke away when I scrabbled at the dirt with my hands, trying to clear some stones. Those fingers looked like new-born moles. Bare and blind.

I made slow going on the grave. The ground was hard and the day very hot. There was no other life around, no birds to be seen, and there had been no blacks, not even smoke from a camp, for many weeks. Only saltbushes and claypans and endless sand ridges, and always too much further still to go. It took me until late in the day to fashion a hole big enough for us to lay Charley down in, on his back, with his hat over his face and an oilcloth all around for protection from the stones and sand we heaped back over him.

Before we covered him we paused awhile. This was the moment for something to be said. But we had no Bible and none of us knew any words that suited. All I could think of was the sea tune Charley used to sing, the one about Lord Franklin that W wouldn't hear because of his cousin Harry. Standing beside Charley's crude grave I found I could not properly bring it to mind. Only fragments of lines about poor sailors and cruel hardships. And this, which I silently mouthed as a farewell: 'And now my burden it gives me pain . . .'

Without a proper reading or even a prayer we just stopped, standing around the grave, looking down on the oilcloth and the sorry shape under it, until Mr Burke nodded and we all of us pushed the stones over. The sound was like rain on an empty water tank. The last I saw of Charley he seemed small and shrunken, the husk of what he'd been just a couple of months before. Now he would never get the drink he craved, or tell the girls his tales of all he'd done and seen when he went wandering far from the ocean.

As a marker to the grave, and to rid ourselves of more items, we hung a camel's bag in a nearby tree, in which we placed a tin pot and some of Charley's articles. We also left a rifle in the hollow part of the tree.

We stayed put until dawn the next morning, Mr Burke declaring we were all done in from the effort of laying Charley to rest. For our meal, yet again, we had dried meat — all that was left of Billy — and water. I often wondered if there would be much difference between the meat and chewing the straps we used to secure the loads on our two remaining camels, Landa and Rajah. Water was now also a concern. As we had got closer to the depot, we had found many of the waterholes dried up. And the liquid in those that remained tasted like metal.

It was cruelly chill that night. Our clothes and blankets were insufficient. I felt as cold as Charley beneath the ground close by. Mr Burke never liked leaving a campfire burning, saying it would only attract natives, but on this occasion he kept it going so we could lie close to it. He even sat up by it late, feeding it more wood, the glow from the flames showing how sunken his face had become around his beard. He had said very little since morning.

I never saw any officer in India care so much about the loss of a single soldier. But I cannot believe that Mr Burke's punishment of Charley for stealing flour hastened his death. Charley himself expected to be treated more harshly. He was a condemned man even then. And never was Mr Burke a nobler leader than when he tried to ensure that Charley, dead, was afforded more respect than he had been accustomed to in life.

We could not appreciate then the cost of this delay. Could not look ahead at pages still to be turned. It would have been so much easier to let the sailor lie where he slept and go on. But we stopped to bury him. And then were a day late returning to the depot.

That's how it went.

Mr Burke was silent the night we lay near Charley, but W was unusually talkative. He spoke – to himself, I guessed, as much as to us – as we struggled to sleep in the fire-flickering dark.

'Poor Gray must have s-suffered very much many times when we thought him sh-shamming . . . It is fortunate for us that the symptoms that so affected him have not come on us un-until now, when we are reduced to an exclusively animal diet of such an inferior description.'

Burke said nothing. The camels grunted in their slumber. I made no reply, but was struck by what W was saying. For the first time I could recall, he was revealing some weakness in himself. He sighed. Wheezed. Like a concertina being put down after the tune was done. Grimacing, he said, 'Such a leg-bound feeling I never before experienced, and hope I never shall again. And the lassitude . . .'

That's all I can bring to mind. Sleep came upon us, but our slumber was uneasy. W shifted on the ground as if trying to relieve pains in his legs. During the night he groaned and called out as a child does.

In the morning, early, Mr Burke stirred us. We sipped some foul water and headed off, travelling south-south-east from the grave. The camels most miserable about moving on. In a matter of days, W said, we would be safe at the depot. But those days stretched ahead like deserts we had still to cross. And as we walked away from the tree with the rifle in its hollow, I envied Charley Gray. He had the rest we craved.

For four days after we buried Charley, we forced ourselves on. We seldom spoke. It seemed that any energy saved by staying silent might help us advance just a little closer to Cooper's Creek and the depot. Only the expectation of relief there kept us going. Mr Burke was in the lead, followed by W, who took readings to confirm our course but otherwise abandoned his scientific work. Then me, worse than I let on, my head faint and legs like lead, yet not as spent as both the camels.

Mr Burke would speak of the depot to raise our spirits if one of us seemed to be failing. 'C'mon, King. Keep your strength up. You'll need it to cope with the feast that Brahe and his lads'll have ready for us. A bubbling stew, I'll warrant, and a pile of fresh steaming damper. All you can get into yourself.'

Or, 'Will! Go easy on that meat. I know you maintain that nothing is finer eating than old camel, especially when it has been hoisted in a bag for several weeks, but leave some room for everything that awaits us.'

He was trying to spur us on. Trying to spur himself on, as we must have made poor company for him. W could barely bring himself to make any entries in his fieldbooks. He would write the date, perhaps a line or two, and then put the book aside, staring into the distance we still had to travel.

Even without Mr Burke's comments, our thoughts were always on food. That, and reaching an end point to the expedition. It was a long trek back to Melbourne, but compared with all that we had endured since leaving the Cooper for the Gulf, it would seem like a stroll. Rest and decent food would restore our strength and spirits. As would fresh clothes. We had little more than what we wore: rags, mostly, and boots that threatened to disintegrate altogether. At night everything we had, even the thinnest of camel pads, was pressed into service as cover. Yet still we shivered.

On the last day, like horses hurrying when they scent water, we covered some thirty miles in the expectation of imminent relief. To make haste, we rode the camels, Mr Burke on Rajah, W and I clinging to Landa, ignoring their aggrieved protests. Lurching and stumbling, every mile seeming like a mountain, we pushed towards the Cooper. Over and over in my head, in rhythm with Landa's weary footfall, I kept thinking of what Brahe had said: 'Goodbye, King. I do not expect to see you for at least four months.' Now, if W's reckoning of dates was right, it was a little over four months that we'd been gone.

So confident was he of relief that Mr Burke allowed us to eat as much as we liked of our remaining supply of dried meat. Brushing the flies off it, he said, 'Into it. Chew hearty. There'll be better fare on the morrow.'

The meat was in an awful state. Tough and scummy. When we boiled it, to try to soften it, it was like a slimy dried stool. My mouth was so sore, it was agony to chew. Yet we went at it like dogs. Mr Burke held up a chunk he was gnawing. 'Don't know about you, lads, but my turds look exactly the same,' he said, trying to keep us lively. 'This will take a free ride through my guts and reappear, untouched, out my arse!'

As the light began to fade on the last day, Mr Burke, in front of us, called out what he could see. 'Tents! I think I can see the tents.'

Then: 'No. They must have moved them. Of course – they would have moved the tents to a better place on the creek with the change in seasons. That would explain it.'

Silence.

I heard things. A horse's hooves. Patten, perhaps, riding out to meet us? No. Then I thought I heard bushman's calls, cooees. I listened again: only the squawks of birds in the trees. On a gust of breeze, I caught a snatch of song and voices, as of men at a meal around a campfire. But when I raised my head I smelled no smoke and could hear only the drone of mosquitoes. Perhaps the voices belonged to the blacks who had been following us at a distance since we had come upon the creek.

As we headed down the Cooper – and even I could tell that this was familiar ground, with the depot near – Mr Burke's pace quickened. His legs were sore, his feet cruelly chafed, but he was off Rajah now and pressing on with a loping limp. He was wound tight like a watch spring, a man looking for something that wasn't there. His head jerked from side to side, as if pulled by strings.

'Jesus save us,' I thought I heard him say.

We came upon horse dung, not old. Some tins, not badly rusted. W was the one who saw the tree, with the words crudely hacked into it: 'DIG 3Ft NW APR 21-61'.

'Today's date,' said W, as flat as if he were announcing a reading of humidity.

Mr Burke was staring at the tree. A thick-trunked thing with the top portion of its roots above the sandy soil, like a hand half buried in earth. He ran his fingers over the carved letters, as if he did not want to trust his eyes, hoping his fingers would spell out something different to what he saw.

I let go the ropes of Landa and Rajah, knowing they would not stray. They sank to the ground, apparently sharing our dejection. My senses seemed unusually acute.

W spoke again. Calmly, as if trying to identify something he couldn't immediately recognise. 'Had the party merely shifted to any other part of the creek, they would not have left that mark behind.'

Mr Burke groaned and seemed to scratch at the bark.

W took one stride north-west from the tree, then attacked the soil with the small shovel we had used for poor Charley's grave. Unlike there, the ground was soft. He had not gone far into it when we heard the dull clang of metal on something solid. I helped him get it out. A box, of the sort used for stores on the camels. Inside were supplies, and a bottle near the top. Paper in the bottle.

We ignored the food, though there was more than we had seen in many months. Hunger can be put aside, though it won't go away. W handed the bottle to Mr Burke, who smashed the neck of it in his haste to get at the paper.

It was evening. Daylight was fading. A yellow moon was barely up, but still there was light enough for Mr Burke to read by. I saw his eyes and lips moving.

'Brahe,' he said. 'Brahe.'

Then he appeared to remember us and read aloud, though he missed words in his haste, using a voice I had not heard from him before.

Depot, Cooper's Creek, 21 April
The depot party ... leaves this camp today to return to the Darling. I intend to go SE from Camp LX to get to our old track ... Two of my companions and myself are quite well; the third—Patten—has been unable to walk ... No person has been up here from the Darling. We have six camels and twelve horses in good working condition.
William Brahe

Mr Burke let the paper drop as he slumped to the ground.

'The 21st of April. That's today,' W repeated. 'We can only have missed them by twelve hours or so. Perhaps less.' Then he too went down. Dropping to his knees as in prayer.

'Oh, Father,' I thought I heard him say, 'we have been grievously let down.'

Did I fall myself or sink? I do not know. I was on my arse, hearing frogs and birds cawing and cicadas chirping, none of them loud enough to mask the ghastly sound of Mr Burke's curses.

'Damn you, Brahe! Damn you to hell! You have abandoned us!' Then choking sobs with no words.

Strange. I watched him. Heard him in his agony as if it had no bearing on my own situation, though I fully understood what had happened. The depot party had gone. Wright, it seemed, had never even arrived from Menindie.

But at once I was distracted by a more basic need, my bowels about to burst. I managed to move a little distance away before I tugged my trousers down to squat. The turd was painful to pass. I recalled Mr Burke's comment about the camel meat going through his guts untouched.

Then I went to the box to see what food Brahe and the others had left for us. Flour, rice, oatmeal, sugar, dried meat. My stomach wrenched again, this time from hunger.

In a billy I drew water from the creek. It was an enormous effort to do this. I mixed together heaps of oatmeal and sugar to make a porridge. I took a handful of sugar and gulped it down. I had not tasted anything sweet for many months.

It only took a little time to gather sticks for a fire. With one of them I held the billy over the flames, taking it off to stir from time to time. The bubbling paste smelled so good it was all I could do not to wolf down every bit of it myself.

The tending of the porridge diverted me from all else. I did not even look over to see what Mr Burke and W were doing and I could hear no sounds from them. I remember thinking, despite our situation, how beautiful it was near the creek. The light was tinged with pink. Trees arched over opposing sides of the water as if yearning to touch in the middle. A pair of pelicans drifted past. If we were to die, this was a pretty place for it.

But I was too famished to think much on dying. When the porridge was ready, I doled out two portions on flat pieces of bark and left an equal amount in the billy for myself. Careful not to trip and lose the precious loads, I took the bark plates to Mr Burke and W. They were still on the ground, sitting now, and looked to have been conversing.

'King!' said Mr Burke on seeing what I had brought. 'You'll do me, King.'

'Capital fellow,' said W.

We ate. The finest meal I've ever known. Saying nothing, using fingers to pry loose the last sticky, sweet portions. We ate but were still hungry. Then had the same thought. There was much more in the camel box to be eaten.

'No,' said Mr Burke. 'We must take an inventory in the morning. Assess what we have and determine how best to make it last.'

I knew then that the leader was not giving up. He was looking ahead, thinking of survival. Already eking out our rations. Such pain as he had felt on our arrival was suppressed. His thoughts were on how best to proceed from here.

'Well, lads, what are we to do now?' We were seated around the fire I had made for the porridge. The flames etched the lines on our faces even deeper. 'Mr Brahe, it appears, has proceeded on towards the Darling,' continued Mr Burke. 'South-east. Greatly disappointing, but thus it is. So, it seems to me we have two options. We can try to follow him up, though he says his animals are in good order while ours are spent, and we must assume he will make reasonable speed . . . I fear it could be madness to attempt to pursue him in our weakened condition.'

The flames hissed. A possum, or perhaps a lizard, rustled leaves in a nearby tree.

'You say there is another option?' W was looking at his hands, studying the broken nails.

'Gregory's trail.'

W now turned his gaze directly on Mr Burke. He was frowning, puzzled. 'Gregory? I don't understand.'

'Augustus Gregory was up this way in '58. We can follow the creek as far south as it takes us and then push on to Mount Hopeless. It cannot be more than a hundred and fifty miles. One-third of the distance back to Menindie and the Darling. Before our departure, the committee assured me there was a cattle station in the vicinity of Mount Hopeless. From there it is but a straightforward journey through settled areas back to Adelaide.'

He fell silent, staring at the fire. While I waited for W to speak, the name of the place Mr Burke had proposed sounded in my head like a doleful bell. *Mount Hopeless.*

'If we take the Darling track, there is a chance we may come upon Brahe and the others.' W was addressing the flames, looking neither at Mr Burke nor myself, as if giving voice to thoughts in his head. 'They have only half a day's start on us. Patten, apparently, is ill. This will slow them down. And they m-may have to stop.'

'So, Will, you would rather take that route?' Mr Burke's voice was very soft. W paused before replying. One of the camels moaned as it pissed noisily nearby.

'On balance, yes. Some of Brahe's party may even double back to see if we have returned. And w-we know the track well.'

'And how precarious the water may be. Especially at this time of year. But wait. What do *you* say, King?'

They were both looking at me. I had not wanted this. I was being pressed into tipping the scales one way or t'other. There was sense in what W had said. If we were able to push on, and we now had food to recruit ourselves, it was possible we would encounter Brahe. The track would be familiar. The alternative? *Mount Hopeless*.

They waited. The light had faded.

'I . . . I am in agreement with Mr Burke.'

He was my leader.

'So it is, then,' said Mr Burke. 'Let's rest now, and regroup in the morning.'

W nodded. His lips pressed very tightly together.

Something shifted right there. We all felt it. There were three of us, but from then on W was the third. He was Mr Burke's deputy, but his opinion had been voiced and overruled. His suggestion about the Darling track had merit, I knew that, but to side with him would have been another kind of mutiny. And that first night back on the Cooper, lying with my stomach part full for the first time in many weeks, I realised something else.

My fate was now inextricably linked with Mr Burke's.

Nineteen

In the morning – a glorious morning, warm and still – we all sensed the change in our situation. There was no longer any urgency. From the time we had left the Cooper four months earlier, we had been hurrying. Now, if only for a day, we were in no haste. We had given Brahe and the others up, we would not chase them. Instead we would make for Mount Hopeless. But we could not proceed at once.

Morning brought sunshine but also a realisation of the wretchedness of how we stood. We had rations enough for only several weeks. We felt better for the food the evening before, yet were still very weak. Rajah and Landa were in a poor way and they needed time to recover. So we rested. After more porridge, with salt in it this time as well as sugar, we lay around in the shade.

'Here we are,' said W. 'Waiting like Mr Micawber...'

'Like who?' Mr Burke asked this while placing bark inside his boots to thicken the soles.

'Dickens. Charles Dickens. A favourite of my f-father's. In his *David Copperfield*, Mr Micawber is always looking out for something to turn up.'

Mr Burke studied him with bemusement. 'I've no time for made-up stories. Give me the classics only: Shakespeare, Goethe, Dante. So bugger your Mr Dickens. And his fucking Micawber.

We're not idly waiting, we're preparing for another push. Yet should Micawber and his mates turn up with some claret and cigars, or, even better, some new boots, they'd be very welcome.'

W adjourned to catch up on his writing, which he had let slide for many days. Mr Burke, meanwhile, surprised me by using the time we now had to make an entry in his notebook. I was sitting near him as he did so and watched as he wrote, very slowly, holding his pencil low down. He reminded me of the children I had taught at the army school in Peshawar. His letters were very large, as were my own. Often a line could be taken up with just a few words. He grunted occasionally as he wrote, and then read aloud the result of his labour as if seeking my approval.

Return party from Carpentaria arrived here last night, and found that the D party —

He stopped here. 'That's Depot, y'think that's clear enough?'

— had started on the same day. We proceed slowly down the creek towards Adelaide by Mount Hopeless and shall endeavour to follow Gregory's track . . . but we are very weak, the camels are done up, and we shall not be able to travel more than five miles a day at most. Gray died on the road, from hunger and fatigue. We all suffered much from hunger, but the provisions left here will, I think, restore our strength.

'Well, King? Could Will's Charles-sodding-Dickens have put it any better?'

'All true enough. And it's good of you to make mention of Charley.' But I was thinking, Five miles a day at most . . . If Mr Burke was right, at least a month's travel lay ahead of us. Somehow, we would have to supplement the food Brahe had left for us.

Mr Burke was studying the entries he had made in his notebook. 'Who will ever read this, I wonder?'

'You will yourself, sir. Surely. Another time.'

'Read it myself? Yes, 'tis possible. I can picture myself, King, in a frock-coat and cravat, addressing the august members of the Royal Society.' He was standing now, his eyes brighter than I'd seen them for many days. The pages of his notebook fluttered as he made sweeping gestures with his right hand. 'The hall is packed. Faces ruddy from port. And every gentleman Jack of them there to hear me. *Me!* A very prince of the city. First man to cross the continent and return, bringing great glory to Victoria – the colony and the Queen. I have them all in tears as I describe our privations. The hard going near the Gulf, poor Charley laid in desert stones, then finding the depot abandoned, against my clear and direct orders.'

I could almost hear the calls of 'Shame!' from the audience as Mr Burke continued.

'From the breast pocket of my waistcoat I produce this notebook. Somewhat battered, some pages missing here and there, but so much the more affecting for all of that. A hush is on them as I read my own words. They rise as one, applauding our fortitude and strength of spirit.'

Then, all at once, the leader's mood changed. More rapidly than a breeze swinging around from south to north. He let the notebook fall to the ground and scuffed it with the toe of his boot.

'Or they could find these scribblings next to my bones and dismiss them as the ranting of a madman, a tale told by an idiot. Signifying nothing...' He sighed. 'Who will tell my story if I am gone, King?'

'Don't speak of that, sir. Besides, Mr Wills has his fieldbooks.'

'True. There's no stopping the man when there's writing to do. But the little I've seen – 'tis all science and weather. *Portulaca-*

fucking-*olerasca* and strata cirrus or somesuch. People will think I led a botanical field trip.'

His agitation unsettled me. 'We'll get back,' I said to reassure us both. 'I'm certain of it.'

'Are you, King? See, there's the rub. It was always thought – and I imagined so myself – that the hardest part would be making it through to the Gulf. Now we find that the greatest challenge will be returning to civilisation. There's irony here. I'm like a man with a great golden nugget in his bag but lacking the way to make money from it. You can't eat gold or drink it. All we've achieved is worth naught if we can't get on. Ah, sod it, forget all that. 'Tis time to clean my stinking hide.'

With that he stripped off the clothes he stood in and strode to the creek, quite naked except for his hat. It was startling to observe the change in him since the last time I'd seen him thus. Just like Billy, all traces of fat had been wasted from his body. His ribs, back and front, were like roots in eroded earth. And he could almost have hung his hat on his hips.

He stepped slowly into the water, wincing either from the cold or the sores on his feet. Still with his hat on, he waded out until the water near lapped at his backside and then settled down, having found a rock or submerged log, something on which he could recline. Then he stretched his arms out wide, as if mimicking Our Lord on the Cross, and called to me.

'C'mon, King. Will you not join me? There's no telling how long it will be before your next bath.'

I have always been nervous in water; I have never been a swimmer. But I felt stiff with grime and sweat and salt, so I shed my garments, treating them gently so as not to tear them even further. Unlike Mr Burke, I removed my hat before I trod gingerly over prickly plants and sharp-edged rocks into the creek. The coolness of it caused me to gasp.

Mr Burke found my awkward progress amusing. ''Tis a shame none of our black friends are around again to feast their eyes on this rare vision. I wager they'll never have seen such a bony white arse. Or – the water rises quickly, does it not? – so shrivelled a bag of bollocks!'

To avoid further scrutiny, I let myself sink down on my knees, resting on the mud of the bottom. Allowing the water to soak my aching body. Once the shock of the cold eased, it was not unpleasant.

'I'm afraid this bathhouse doesn't run to soap, King. Let alone hot towels. Cannot be helped, I'm afraid.' He laughed, a deep laugh that bubbled up from his guts like a billy boiling.

How long W had been standing watching us, I do not know. But I think both Mr Burke and I became aware of him at the same time. He was on the bank of the creek, a little distance downstream, observing us like we were some unusual type of water beasts. He didn't call out or signal, he just stood there looking at us. Nor did he respond immediately when Mr Burke bellowed at him.

'Ahoy, Will! Come join us. Get your reeking English skin into the water and give it a wash.'

W gave no answer. He walked along the bank towards us, grimacing as he came, as if his legs or feet or both ailed him. When he was close he sat down on a rock and pulled a small package from a trouser pocket.

'I'll not bathe just now. You two can be the ex-exemplars of cleanliness. I have some mending to do.'

He removed his hat so that he could pull both his shirt and undershirt over his head. His chest and back were very pale and quite hairless. Like Mr Burke's and my own, his ribs were as distinct as if they'd been marked out with a stick.

Something caught the sun. A needle. W had a needle and

thread and was trying to fix the worst of the holes in his top garments. But after a few minutes' labour he allowed all that he had to fall in his lap.

'Useless,' he said. 'In fixing holes I merely make new ones. Our clothing is coming apart. Before long we'll be like the b-blacks.'

'No, Will. Before long we'll be back in the settled region. You can have a hot bath then. Ask some rosy-cheeked squatter's daughter to boil the copper. I'll guarantee she'll want to stick around and soap your back – and anything else! – too.'

While W was succumbing to some uncharacteristic gloom, Mr Burke seemed determined to appear positive about our prospects. He stood up. The creek water sluiced off him. Far from being self-conscious about his nakedness – though I saw W looking away – Mr Burke gave his private parts a scratch and then stretched, like a man just awakened. Stepping carefully, he walked to the bank. But even before he had reached it and started examining his clothes, sniffing the sorry items and scanning them for holes, he was a leader issuing orders.

'Gentlemen, I am resolved. Tomorrow we will start back along the creek, beginning our progress towards Mount Hopeless. We cannot wait until the camels recruit completely. Our pace will not be hard; they shouldn't find the going too taxing. I see little to be gained in remaining here much longer.'

W nodded but said nothing in reply. He put his garments back on and headed off the way he'd come.

I felt awkward being the only one still in the water, so, as Mr Burke had done, I rose to return to the bank. I wasn't far from it when I trod on something that gave way under my feet. It felt like an eel, the sensation horrid on my chilled skin. Jerking my foot away, I lost my balance. Then I was face down in the water.

It wasn't deep. A few feet, no more. It shouldn't have been difficult to right myself and get back up. But the strangest thing happened. Rather than feeling scared or panicking – as I had done before if ever my face was submerged – I felt extraordinarily calm. And tired. Terribly tired. It seemed that my eyes were open. The light was yellow-brown. And in my ears an odd buzzing. I was tired but not scared. Just wanting to lie down. Thinking how silly it was to drown in so little water. Like my brother, the one who died in Limerick impressing a girl in a rowboat. But a rest was not unwelcome after all the walking we'd done. I'd missed the sea but was now enveloped in cool water. I let myself succumb to the creek's embrace.

I suspect I was about to take my first spluttering breath underwater when my right shoulder was jerked. Then a pair of hands had me under the armpits and Mr Burke was pulling me out. Dragging me along the mud of the bank like I was some strange inert creature he had found on the end of his fishing line. I tried to sit up as a burst of wrenching coughs shook me.

The leader, still without his clothes, was crouched next to me. 'C'mon, lad. It'll be right. Don't be giving up on me now.'

As if he knew what I'd been thinking in the shallow water by the bank. My arse was still on the ground but my head was up. He was in front of me, his face level with mine. Water dripping from the tangled ends of his beard.

'I need you, King. Need your help and young bones. They'll last longer than mine. Get your breath back, and when you're ready, organise your gear. C'mon, man. We'll stick together. See this through.'

I was still having difficulty breathing but I nodded to show him I had understood.

He laughed, looking down at me. 'The jest is on you, King. You'll have to step back in the water to get all the filth off you. Any more mud and you'd pass for a native.' He kicked his feet in the shallows. ''Twas lucky for you I hadn't got me boots back on. If

I had I'd have left you there for the crows to pick at. Give me a choice between dry boots and a worn-out camel man and you'll not wait long for your answer.'

He stood in the sun for a few minutes more before dressing. Slowly, carefully, I splashed water over my legs and backside to get the worst of the mess off.

It seemed to take all my strength to put my clothes on again. They smelled as bad as the camels' breath. I resolved to rest once we got back to our gear and I had checked on Rajah and Landa, who would be unimpressed by the notion of moving on the next morning. But that was what Mr Burke intended to do. And despite the shaking that came on me when I recalled the seductive lure of the water, his words gave me the strength I thought I had lost. *I need you, King. Need your help . . .*

The following day, as the leader had proposed, we headed away along the creek.

The 'DIG' tree wasn't the end of it at all. The way our story has been told, and depicted in tableaux like the one in Mr Heinrichs' waxworks museum on the St Kilda Esplanade, the tree is the climax of the tale. A full stop to the expedition. We came back from the Gulf, found the depot party had gone, and languished in despair. Gave up and succumbed. That was it. The finish. That is what people believe.

But it wasn't like that. The tree was just another stopping place. Now W's journal lets me quantify how long we were lost on the Cooper. At the time the days merged into nights like water seeping through sand. W was still counting, still recording days and dates, up until his end. Which didn't come about for two months or more after we'd come back to find the message buried with supplies in the camel box.

We thought to follow the creek as far as possible. We needed the water and no longer had the strength to carry much of it. Only a billy or two. But things went wrong. Landa got bogged and we couldn't dig him out. We shot him where he lay, cut off as much meat as we could and tried to dry it. Then we had to reduce our gear even further, as Rajah was now our only pack animal. And he was near gone. The season had been dry and branches of the creek kept running out into earthy plains. So we would backtrack, find another stream, and follow it along until it too trickled into the sand.

We planned one big push, like the day we returned to the Cooper, but Rajah was very ill. I thought he could not linger more than a few days. Yet that same evening, as the brute was suffering, Mr Burke ordered him shot. I did so, and we cut him up with two broken knives and a lancet.

Now I was a camel man without camels.

Our rations were fast running out, but Mr Burke remained suspicious of the natives. He said they weren't to be trusted, despite some friendly signs. When we were stopped near a waterhole, a group of young men with raised scars criss-crossing their chests appeared carrying some fish on a bark tray. They offered the fish to us, which we accepted. The next day they came again. More of them this time, wanting to converse with us. But as they pointed away from our camp, Mr Burke noticed one of them trying to make off with an oilcloth. It wasn't until the leader fired his revolver over the man's head that he let the cloth drop at his feet. The other natives shifted away, grinning like it was all a game.

'Y'see?' said Mr Burke. 'They'll pinch our cods if we let 'em.'

We didn't see blacks again for some time after that. Lacking their nets, and the knowledge of where to set them for fish, we had to rely more and more on the nardoo. Mr Burke believed that without it we could starve. And when he and W went looking for the natives to find out where the nardoo grew, it seemed to me that this must be very hard for Mr Burke – to ask the blacks where they found their food.

This is what we had come to. How far we had fallen.

Yet still the leader believed we could get through to Mount Hopeless. We made another attempt, taking with us what remained of the provisions: two and a half pounds of oatmeal, a small quantity of flour, and the dried meat. On a plain I saw a plant growing that was like clover. I looked closer and called out that I had found some nardoo. We stopped to lay in a supply of the seed, which W called the staff of life.

'The staff?' said Mr Burke. 'More like chaff. Better suited to horses than men.'

But he ate it just the same.

Gathering it was tiresome labour. We had to find the plants and strip the seeds, which would then have to be crushed as best we could manage. W and I were collecting a supply by the creek late one morning. The sun was near its zenith when we heard an explosion that caused parrots to flee from the nearby trees. We paused, rising from our haunches.

Another explosion. And this time no doubt – gunfire. From where we had left Mr Burke at the camp.

'Blacks!' W said. 'Quickly, or they'll have all we've got left.'

Such nardoo as we'd gathered we left behind in our haste to get back to the leader. Who was standing, when we found him, as if at attention. Rifle in his right hand, still smoking from the muzzle. He seemed puzzled by our consternation.

'We f-feared you were under attack,' W explained. 'The gunfire...'

'A modest salute, gentlemen. All I could manage in our circumstances. Come, Will, what's today's date?'

'I wrote the entry last night – May 24th, 1861.'

Mr Burke seemed exultant. 'Just as I'd reckoned it to be. My celebration was in order.'

'Celebration, sir?'

'For the Queen's birthday, King. Her Majesty, God save her, is forty-two today. Just a little older than myself. Were our situation different I would declare it a day of rest. As it is, we shall toast her with tea and a modest fusillade.'

Again he fired, causing W and me to step back. The sound of the shot echoed between the trees, then a deeper silence lingered. Or maybe it was just our ears in shock.

Mr Burke lowered the gun and looked at us, frowning. 'You're empty-handed. I thought you were getting the seed.'

'We were,' said W, 'but we ran when we heard gunfire. Left the nardoo behind.'

'We will need it. You'd best retrieve it at once, and then we'll proceed.'

W said not a word to me all the way back.

When we continued on, we followed a watercourse from the creek but again it dwindled away in the sandy flat country. There were sandhills in front of us and no signs of water. No birds flying towards a waterhole we couldn't see. Nothing. Just rough ground and scrub. We were all greatly fatigued, as our rations now consisted of only one small johnnycake and three sticks of dried meat daily. We camped early in the afternoon, intending to push on the next day. But if we couldn't find water, we would have to return.

We travelled for a further day and still found no water. The three of us sat down and rested for an hour. Mr Burke sighed. 'Well, lads, I guess there's nothing for it.'

He looked hard in the direction we'd been heading. Then we turned back. W said that if there had been just a few days' rain we could have got through.

In Kurrachee, when I was recovering from my illness, I watched a pair of spiders trapped in a bathtub. The sides were too slippery and steep for their limbs to keep a grip on. They would climb and climb and get close to the lip, but always, inevitably, slip and tumble down the sides of the tub. Then they would try a different part of the tub, though it never made any difference to the result. In the end I reached down with my hand and lifted them clear. They drifted free on gossamer threads.

That's how we were on the Cooper, like spiders trapped in a tub. Desperate to leave but unable to get out, whichever route we took. By the creek there was water and some hope of food, but no expectation of escape or relief. Brahe had gone. Wright had never shown up.

It can be lovely on the Cooper. The sun rises a pale orange through the trees, waking birds that commence a squawking symphony. There are fish in the creek, which at its wider parts better deserves to be called a billabong – the natives' term for it. You can smell crushed grasses and the tang of gum leaves. But there are also rats and flies and mosquitoes and heat that saps all energy. It was our prison. Its plenty kept us there just as surely as if we were chained to its banks. Several times, in different directions, we pushed to the limit of those invisible chains. Each time, unable to break the want of water, we came back.

With Billy and the camels dead we had become our own pack animals. Our provisions near gone and our clothes in tatters, we lived like blacks. Looking for their food. Sleeping in their shelters when we found them. Waiting. Wondering.

Before starting for Mount Hopeless the first time, we had returned to the 'DIG' tree. Mr Burke wished to deposit a message, similar to the one I had watched him compose in his notebook. 'We shall proceed slowly down the creek...'

I was the one who left it there. In a jar in the ground so the blacks wouldn't get at it. There was a rake the depot party had left nearby. I covered over Mr Burke's message, and some other papers, spread dung over the pile, and left the rake against the tree. It did not occur to us to make any further mark on the tree, as we thought the word 'DIG' would serve all our purposes.

I have reflected often on what might have happened if I had left a sign. Even just a scrap of paper with a message nailed to the tree. 'South along creek. Weak. We cannot get far. For pity's sake follow. B.W.K.'

I could have so easily done that, but I didn't. I try not to dwell on it. Because they did come up, although I didn't know this until much later.

Brahe and Wright returned to the depot after we had left and saw no evidence we had ever been there. No note, no new sign on the tree. Nothing. To them, the ground near the tree looked undisturbed. So they stayed only briefly before going away again.

A hand reached down but the spiders were gone.

Twenty
Nora

Where were they?

Whenever I saw a newspaper, and I think Reverend Bickford kept some from me, it seemed there were questions about the expedition. Why had nothing been heard? Had these explorers simply vanished without trace in the empty wastes? The committee were urged to act and find those who had left from Royal Park more than eight months prior.

If he found me distracted by such things, Mr Bickford offered to pray with me. God would watch over John and the others, he said.

A letter in *The Argus* said the problem were plain. The expedition had set forth without any blacks in the party. The writer, who signed himself Sohoben, said blacks had an instinct for finding water and staying on track in the interior, skills beyond the power of white people. This Sohoben offered to start for the Gulf of Carpentaria with a party of eight. Four whites, four blacks. Success were assured, he said. Expense would be one-tenth the cost of the late expedition.

The late expedition. Seeing those words made me shake.

The committee had to do something. There were reports of a search expedition. A Contingent Exploring Party, it were called. Its leader would be a Mr Howitt, said to be a reliable man. He left near the middle of 1861, with winter closing in on Melbourne. Left without all the speeches and fuss lavished on those he set out to find.

In such a situation I were glad of any distractions. I had written to my cousin Mary in Ireland telling her I were settled. I urged her to cross the seas and join me in St Kilda, if she were able, but could only wait on any reply. Meantime I tried to keep busy with Mr Bickford's Ladies' Benevolent Society and my work at the asylum, while the newspapers seemed to weary of talk about the expedition. Instead they had reports from the goldfields, where white miners rose up against Chinamen. Some five hundred were driven from their homes at a place called Lambing Flat. The homes were burned. Mr Hill were particularly distressed.

— 'Tis anarchy, he told Mr Bickford as he read of it. See here: *When police intervened, they themselves were swept aside.* And when ringleaders were arrested and sent to the lock-up they were liberated by the mob. The rule of law has quite broken down.

— It's just as I've said, William. Greed for gold can bring out the basest instincts in men.

But Mr Hill insisted that more than greed were at the root of it. He talked of hatred based on race, resentment at the industriousness of the Chinese. Most miners had come from other countries, he said, just like the Chinese. Now they feared they might be denied all they believed to be rightfully theirs.

Mr Hill were staying with us to help prepare for what Mr Bickford described as the most important event yet in his parish. He called it a Lovefeast. Mr Bickford explained to me that this were a religious awakening.

— We entice all sorts of fish into our Gospel net with a combination of hymns and prayer and powerful speaking, he said. I have seen whole families converted at such meetings. And individuals, hitherto lost, embracing the Lord Jesus as a personal Saviour.

It happened on a cold and damp evening. The church in Fitzroy Street were more full than I had ever seen it, filled not just with people but also a strong sense of expectation.

Mr Hill were the featured speaker. Standing tall before his audience, he began his address quietly, like he were searching for a path to follow. He spoke of the events at Lambing Flat, where greed and intolerance had led people to forget the principle of loving their fellow man, he said.

Then he allowed his voice to rise. I saw the talkers fall silent, the fidgeters become still. Many were people I had not seen before. Sailors from the docks, rough folk from shanties near the river, women that some called fallen but Mr Hill described as luckless. These made up his flock.

— We call this a Lovefeast, so let the praise of God in festive joy rise up beyond this plain ceiling to a place near the throne of God in Heaven!

Mr Hill's face were shiny with sweat. Now I understood what Mr Bickford had meant about his friend tapping wells of passion.

— There will be a new beginning here tonight. A revival is under way. We can all feel it. Peace and goodwill among brethren who have been at strife.

A baby wailed and were shooshed by its ma.

— May our living experience for all generations be the dying words of our founder, *God is with us!* For, as Psalms instruct us, *This God is our God, for ever and ever.*

People were cheering, Forever! And my cheeks were moist with tears.

The success of the Lovefeast meant we were busier than ever at our church. People came calling at all hours, checking on times of services, asking when Mr Hill would be preaching again. Yet it were not so busy that I were ignorant of all else. Mr Howitt were said to be heading for the expedition's base camp deep in the interior on the Cooper's Creek. But nobody knew when he would get there, or what he might find.

Then came a letter with wonderful tidings. Mary were coming. She had been encouraged by my reports of Melbourne and all I had told her of people I had met. She would be coming to link her life once more with mine. Her mam, my Aunt Catherine, had died. There were nothing to hold her in Ireland now.

I would be seeing my cousin again before long. But my brother? I tried to believe what Mr Hill had said at the service, yet still I were nagged by doubts. After all this time, would God still be with him? I wanted to talk to the ministers about that, needed to believe that John were not abandoned. So I went to Mr Bickford's study on a Monday, near to a week after the Lovefeast.

Even before I knocked on the door, which were closed, I could hear footsteps and voices. Mr Bickford and Mr Hill were talking, their voices low and excited, but I could make out words and phrases.

— Extraordinary! . . . A terrible result . . . Meant to run no risks . . .

Then I entered and they fell silent. Mr Bickford were at the table. Behind him, standing up, were Mr Hill. It must have been him I'd heard pacing about. On the table, open in front of Mr Bickford, were a copy of *The Age*.

It were like a scene in a play that had been stopped, the two of them forgetting what they were meant to say. Because of the curious silence, I thought to leave at once. This could not be a good time to ask about faith and doubts. But Mr Hill moved to the side of the table and gently directed me into a seat opposite Mr Bickford. Who smiled at me, though his eyes were not on my face.

He were looking at Mr Hill, seeking guidance from his fellow minister. I were puzzled and asked if I were interrupting.

Mr Bickford's eyes still would not stay on me.

— Ah, Miss King, he said. Please excuse us. There is some news.

I felt Mr Hill's hand on my shoulder, soft but strong.

— News of your brother, Nora.

It were unusual for Mr Hill, for either of them, to use my Christian name like this. They were always very proper in their dealings with me, so this made what were to come seem even more serious.

— There is news of the expedition?

Odd how easily we are distracted. Even as I waited for their answer I were aware of a bird cheeping outside and the sound of a tinker pushing his cart along Fitzroy Street.

— Is the news good? Please, you must tell me.

A look of pain crossed Mr Bickford's face. With both hands he picked up the newspaper before him.

— Ah now, that is the difficulty, you see. The news is equivocal. Quite how it affects your brother is difficult to say.

I did not understand his words. Equivocal?

— Pray don't torment me. Is John alive?

Mr Hill crouched down next to me, his voice now quiet but insistent.

— They are missing, Nora. John, Mr Burke and two others. They have not been heard from for some time.

Mr Bickford pushed the newspaper across the table to me and directed my attention to a folded page. I saw the type, *Melbourne, Monday 1st July, 1861*.

I began, *The unexpected news*, but I could not go on. I am not a strong reader, I never finished my schooling. I can manage if I have time and can concentrate, but there at the table, with Mr Hill so concerned and my mind whirling, I could not properly see the print. And sobs were coming.

Mr Bickford retrieved the paper.

— Of course, how silly of me, he said. Please allow me. He coughed once, to clear his throat, and began.

I kept the newspaper. I kept all the newspapers. I have looked at them like a seamstress studying a piece of cloth, trying to see where the pattern went wrong. So I now know what he read. This:

The unexpected news of Mr Burke's expedition of discovery, which we publish this morning, is positively disastrous. The entire company of explorers has been dissipated out of being, like dew-drops before the sun.

— The entire company? What are they saying?
— Wait, Nora, wait. Listen. Continue, James.

Some are dead, some are on the way back, one has come to Melbourne, and another has made his way to Adelaide, whilst only four of the whole party have gone forward from the depot at Cooper's Creek upon the main journey of the expedition to explore the remote interior.

— But four of them?
Mr Hill now had his left hand over mine.

The four consist of the two chief officers and two men, namely Mr Burke, the leader, and Mr Wills, the surveyor and second in command of the party, together with the men King and Gray —

— Lord save him! John! So he lives?
— It seems so, my child, Mr Bickford said. Listen further:

This devoted little band left Cooper's Creek for the far interior on the 16th of December last, more than six months ago, taking with them six camels and one horse, and only twelve weeks' provisions. From Mr Burke's despatch we learn that he meant to proceed in the first place to Eyre's Creek; and from that place he would make an effort to explore the country northward in the direction of the Gulf of Carpentaria.

The bird and the tinker were silent now. I heard naught but Mr Bickford's voice. Yet I could not fathom all he said. Fragments of what he were reading stuck out like rocks in a fast-flowing stream. Left six months ago. But only twelve weeks of provisions. Mr Burke's despatch.

— I still do not understand. How is this known?

— Mr Howitt, who departed just a week ago to seek news of the expedition, fell in with William Brahe, one of the senior men, on the Loddon. Mr Hill said this like a man trying to soothe a trapped animal. Brahe is now back in Melbourne with Mr Howitt, who has reported that the expedition was split into smaller groups, one of which proceeded to the Gulf. Your brother, apparently, was among them.

— And nothing has been heard from them?

— That seems to be the case.

— But your brother is in the finest company, Miss King, Mr Bickford interrupted, putting down the paper. Both the leader and second in command of the expedition are with him. I know nothing about this man Gray, but Mr Burke must think well of your brother to have included him in such a group.

— What happened to the others? There were so many at the start.

Mr Bickford returned to his paper.

— Ah. Now, there the news is not all positive, he said.

Some of the men were prostrated by scurvy, as well as being additionally enfeebled by the irregular supply of the water. And at length four of their number, worn out by their sufferings, perished by a wretched lingering death in the wilderness —

— Enough of that now, James, Mr Hill put in. The important thing is that you must not abandon hope, Nora. There has been no word from this party that pushed on to the Gulf, that is true, but news comes painfully slowly from the interior. It is possible that Mr Burke, your brother and the others are waiting for conditions to improve before they continue on.

— It talked of them having but twelve weeks' provisions.

— They are resourceful men. You should have faith both in their abilities and the love of the Lord who watches over us all.

We were to talk about faith after all.

— Let us pray, said Mr Bickford.

The three of us joined hands. Mr Bickford prayed for the souls of the brave men who had perished. He prayed that God would give Mr Burke the strength and courage he needed to guide his men, including my beloved John, safe out of the wilderness. I felt calmer after that.

— We must believe that he lives, Nora, Mr Hill said.

Yet still I did not know where I stood.

— What now?

— There is talk that Mr Howitt will lead a more substantial party direct to the spot where Mr Burke and his band departed for the Gulf, Mr Bickford told me. I think we can place our trust in this man Howitt. It cannot be an accident that shortly after his expedition set out he came upon the first solid news of the explorers for some time.

— But it could be months before anything further is known?

— It could, said Mr Hill, squeezing my hand. It will be a difficult time for you, no doubt. We will assist you all we can. But you must have patience and faith. And try to carry on.

I stood up, dabbing at my eyes and nose.

— You are right. You are both right. I am grateful for your concern. I should keep myself as busy as possible. There is nothing else I can do for John right now other than hope.

— And pray, Miss King. Never underestimate the power of prayer.

I begged to be excused, needing to compose myself. I told them I would prepare a cold meat lunch for us all. Mr Hill suggested there were no need for me to bother but I said I would prefer to be occupied.

Once I were through the door, the grief swept over me. A sense of uncertainty and being so helpless. I tried to stifle my tears, not wanting to cause more alarm to the ministers. I stood leaning against the wall, choked by sobs like bubbles rising up in gruel.

My friends must have believed I had moved well away, for again I could hear their voices. Mr Hill said something, then Mr Bickford replied with anger in his tone.

— Incompetence, William. You have to wonder how else it could have come to this. Listen, this is how *The Age* concludes:

The whole expedition appears to have been one prolonged blunder throughout: and it is to be hoped that the rescuing party may not be mismanaged and retarded in the same way as the unfortunate original expedition.

— God save him, said Mr Hill.
But I could not say if he meant my brother or Mr Howitt.

Twenty-one

I never dream about the end. I dream about India. Of children crumpled dead in corners, their arms across their faces as if a tiny limb might protect them from the scything steel approaching them, the last thing they ever see. I dream about what we found in the well near Cawnpore after the siege, and the way the local dogs had circled its sides, desperate to get at the source of the smell within.

I dream about India but never the way my leader died. I have heard it said I simply avoid the topic, that I will leave a room if the subject is raised. So people walk around it like a puddle on the floor. At the commission I lost my composure when they asked me questions about the manner of Mr Burke's end. I wept. The commissioners looked embarrassed. Shuffled papers and studied tobacco-stained fingers.

Out of pity, Sir Thomas Pratt changed the theme. Sir Thomas, the chairman of the inquiry, who smelled of whisky and dust when I passed him, asked if I had seen the letter written by W for his father.

W's letter was the most famous and affecting document of the expedition. It left ladies swooning and members of the Exploration Committee congratulating themselves for sending such a gentleman into the interior. Only a gentleman could have contemplated his own death with such equanimity. Only a gentleman could have penned so eloquent a testament in the face of the inevitable.

Yes, I told the wheezing Sir Thomas, I had seen the letter. I was aware of its contents. W himself had read it aloud to Mr Burke and myself.

Sir Thomas appeared puzzled. 'Why did he do this – was it not addressed to Doctor Wills?'

'It was, sir. But Mr Wills believed we should see that he had not said anything to our disadvantage. He thought we should see it was the truth and nothing but the truth.' Also, though I did not say this, because he knew the singular power of last lines. This was his final speech on stage before the curtain came down.

Cooper's Creek, 27th June, 1861
My Dear Father,
These are probably the last lines you will ever get from me. We are on the point of starvation, not so much from absolute want of food, but from the want of nutriment in what we can get.

Our position, although more provoking, is probably not near so disagreeable as that of poor Harry and his companions –

Mr Burke had interjected here. 'Sorry, Will. But who in hell's Harry?'

W looked at him, his eyes sunk into shadows. 'Harry, my cousin. You recall? A m-member of the Franklin expedition. Lost on the ice.'

'Ah yes,' Mr Burke said. And then was silent. I don't think Mr Burke remembered Charley's song at all.

W continued:

> *We have had very good luck and made a most successful trip to Carpentaria and back to where we had every right to consider ourselves safe, having left a depot here consisting of four men, twelve horses, and six camels, they had sufficient provisions to have lasted them twelve months with proper economy. We had every right to expect that we should have been immediately followed up from Menindie —*

Mr Burke suppressed a noise. I couldn't tell if he was stricken by emotion or angered by the mention of Brahe and his men. W kept reading:

> *The party we left here had special instructions not to leave until our return unless from absolute necessity.*

And more. Much more. The man who said he had no energy left, who insisted that we leave him alone with some water and nardoo and firewood and push on without him, had found the spirit and strength to pen a long farewell letter.

I was barely listening at the end. W's voice grew very faint. It was a pathetic scene. A bearded man in rags lying in a native's shelter — a crude structure, no more than fallen boughs over which branches had been heaped — holding a paper in hands from which all flesh seemed to have been stripped. Before him, two other white men in similar condition, though one much older than his companion, seated on the ground because they were too spent to stand. The older man with his head in his hands. Quite the picture of defeat.

How had we come to this?

It has been suggested that conditions on the Cooper can be tolerable. Howitt and his relief party found it a fine stopping place, though he noted that much would depend on the presence of rain. There were fish in the creek, birds in the trees. But we had nothing for the catching of fish, and though we still had some firearms and ammunition, any birds we potted were gained more through luck than prowess. Our powers of endurance as well as our bodies had wasted away. No-one could have foreseen what had befallen us: to return and be abandoned; to try to push on yet be incapable of moving far from the creek. When it was plain we could not make Mount Hopeless there was nowhere else for us to go. And little for us to do.

We ate, yet were hungry. We slept, yet were always tired. We waited, yet nobody came. We sought the blacks, who vanished between trees like the breeze. Mr Burke remained suspicious of them. He called them miserable wretches and still believed they would pilfer the few possessions we had left unless we maintained our guard. Even if they appeared friendly – as when a group of them came offering us fish on some bark – he kept them at a distance, knocking the fish clear and ordering me to fire over their heads with a rifle. I did so and they ran off. We collected the fish from the ground.

'There,' said Mr Burke. 'That'll show them there's still some life in us, eh?'

But we paid dearly for that. Mr Burke tried to cook the fish on a fire near one of the abandoned gunyahs we were using. The wind was strong and flames caught the shelter. It burned so rapidly we were unable to put it out or save many of our things. We had barely anything left after that, save for what we carried on our persons, and there seemed little chance for us except with the natives. Then W said he could not go on. So he composed his final letter and insisted on reading it to us.

When he was done he coughed and closed his eyes. Leaned back. The hand holding the paper flopped to his side.

Mr Burke lifted his head. 'That is finely put, Will.'

'Wait. There is m-more.' And he read on. Straining forward

like he was having trouble reading his own words on the page. Strange, I had the impression he was speaking directly to me until I recalled to whom it was addressed.

> *You have great claim on the committee for their neglect. I leave you in sole charge of what is coming to me. The whole of my money I desire to leave to my sisters; other matters I will leave for the present. Adieu, my dear Father. Love to Tom.*
> *W J Wills*

He gestured to Mr Burke that he should take the letter. The leader did so, but seemed unsure where to put it.

'Another thing,' said W. 'Here.' He gave Mr Burke his watch, of which he was very proud. From all the instruments he had set out with, all the gauges and thermometers and pieces of scientific equipment, this was the last thing he had. It was still working. And now he was giving it up.

Mr Burke closed his hand over W's. 'I will be sure to get these to your father,' he said.

W nodded. Then he turned to me. His eyes were like coals in a campfire left burning overnight, only the faintest light remaining. 'I want you to promise me something, King.'

I moved closer, so as to hear him better.

'In the event of you surviving Mr Burke, I w-would hope that you carry out my last wish. Give these to my father.'

I nodded, to signal I had understood him. But could not summon any words.

Mr Burke rose to his feet, gasping as if the effort caused him pain. But his voice was still strong. 'Enough maudlin talk, Will. My expectations of relief remain strong. You'll deliver that letter to your father yourself and laugh about the gloomy state you were in when you wrote it. Now, listen to me, man. Are you still determined we leave you here? If you have any doubts on that score we'll not go. We'll stay. Some blacks are bound to show themselves, by and by. The inquisitive buggers are always nosing about. We'll get some food from them one way or t'other.'

W shook his head. His eyes were closed. 'No. You two must go up the creek in search of the natives. It is our only chance to get some food.'

Mr Burke was crouched close to him now. 'We will not leave unless it is your wish.'

'Go,' said W. 'And . . . this.' He held out his revolver, a Colt with prettily engraved metalwork.

Mr Burke did not take it. 'I cannot leave you defenceless.'

W let the pistol fall to the ground as if it were no use to him any longer. 'Take it,' he said again.

Mr Burke leaned forward to pick up the gun, brushed the sand off its stock, and spoke some words to W that I could not hear. Then signalled me to come forward. I wasn't sure what was required. I have never been good at farewells.

I thought W was trying to say something, so I leaned over him. Breathing the smell of decay in his clothes and mouth and hair.

'Nardoo,' I told him. 'I have left you a good supply.'

His lips twisted. 'That is kind. But here's an odd thing, King. Vexing. The nardoo seems not to agree with me. The stools it causes . . . Enormous.'

There – the last words he spoke to me were about his shitting. Then he said it again: 'Go.'

He seemed to be slumbering now.

'How can I leave him?' Mr Burke asked. Then, 'Come, King, we should try to get on a little way before dark.'

After this, there was no looking back.

The weather had been unsettled. We had endured a dreadful storm a few evenings before, huddled together in an abandoned gunyah like shivering curs. I was the only one still with strength enough to search for and fetch the nardoo, but I was able to pound less and less of the seed before my strength failed. After being buffeted by the wind the day after the storm, I told Mr Burke I wouldn't be able to look for food much longer.

'Then we must trust in the mercy of the blacks,' he replied.

But where were they? We hadn't seen them in many days. The camping places we had found were abandoned. Now, as we moved away from W, walking slowly and stopping often, for Mr Burke was very weak in the legs, the evening seemed to be settling in much earlier than usual. The light was odd. Low clouds like purple smoke shrouded the setting sun. There was no breeze at all. It struck me that W would have been fascinated by these clouds. Another entry for his fieldbooks, which we had wrapped in cloth as best we could and buried near the shelter where we left him.

The clouds seemed to signify another storm. We would need to find somewhere we might cover ourselves. A soaking could mean the end of us. As I scanned the creek banks for a hollowed tree, an overhanging branch, anything offering some protection, I realised how far the pendulum had swung. Mr Burke was now allowing himself to be led. Not resisting if I took his arm when he stumbled. Accepting meekly when I found a flattened spot with rocks on two sides and suggested that we stop there and wait for morning.

"Twill do,' he said. That was all.

I think he was glad just to rest awhile. He seemed little interested in nardoo when I made it up into a paste. He took some, but much of it dribbled from his mouth and hardened into clumps in his beard. I wanted to ask if he truly was confident of relief, as he had told W, or if they were just soft words. He removed W's letter from where he had stowed it and peered at it. Quietly mouthing some words. '"The party we left here had special instructions not to leave..." Aye, Will. Nicely phrased.'

Two days we travel together, moving slowly upstream seeking the blacks. As we walk Mr Burke leans on me. He needs to rest often. When I prevail on him to press on after he wants to stop in a place badly exposed to the wind he does not object, although he is still my leader.

At last, some good fortune. I bag a crow with one lucky shot. It falls from the tree, half its head blown away. I am too weary to do more than toss it whole upon a fire that has taken my remaining energy to build. I scrape away charred feathers as best I can when I judge it to be done. I hack some pieces with my knife, grown blunt and broken, and take them to Mr Burke. I have left him propped against a tree.

Light from the fire flickers across his face, making a canyon of the scar high on his cheek. He eats a little of the crow, a small piece of grey flesh lodging in the corner of his mouth, though he seems not to notice. More is left untouched on the bark. I must get at it before the ants appear in swarms out of the sand. He seems not to be in any pain, though he complained of aches before we stopped.

'So this will be it,' he says, peering around as if taking particular note of his surroundings. A heron makes its mournful cry across the creek.

'Sir?'

'I am convinced that I cannot last many hours. So cold. Desperately cold...'

'You should try to eat some more of the bird,' I plead. 'Here. Some food and then rest will see you right. We have a fire. You'll feel stronger in the morning.'

He raises one hand, as if demanding silence. 'You must hear me now, King. My time is near. I do not believe I will see another evening. So listen – I want you to stay with me until I have gone. I could not bear being alone.' His tongue works at his lips, which are cracked and bloody. 'You have been very loyal, King. I am sorry you now find yourself in this damnable state. But . . . the committee would not forget us. Somebody will have come after us.' He turns his head away to try to swallow.

'Would it be a comfort if I recited some Bible verses?' I suggest.

His answer comes direct. Bitterly. 'None of that.' Then he mutters something. 'Late,' he says. Or perhaps it is 'Wait.' He changes position, seeking to get comfortable, then grimaces and reaches down to his side where he has thrust W's pistol in his trousers. He tries to hold it but his grasp is weak. 'Such a pretty thing,' he says. 'I must have it at the end. Be sure of it. Now. I must give you some more instructions while I am able. Poor Will's things you know about. You understand what to do. Now. My own watch. Here. It belongs to the committee – it should go back to them. Ah. And my notebook. I have written some lines in it for Sir William Stawell. A last report, such as it is . . . Damn!'

A page, folded several times, has slipped from his fingers. The cool breeze catches it and it falls near the fire. A corner curls, drawn towards the flames. A look of extreme alarm, panic almost, passes over his face. He tries to raise himself.

'King! Grab it, man, grab it.'

Two steps and I am on it, fetching it even as the corner starts to smoke. A tiny flame flickers. I swat at it with my hand. Very little is lost.

The page has unfolded. It is a picture. A portrait. I catch a glimpse of a flowing gown, a bare arm, but no more before I hand it to Mr Burke. He clutches it as a supplicant in church might grab at the wafer. His eyes turn to water.

'My lovely,' he says. 'My lovely. It was all for you.' He notices me looking at him. 'My most precious possession, King. One thing I have never discarded, through it all. Just as she would never forsake me. I truly believe that. She has been my strength, my inspiration. Love for a lady is a powerful thing.'

I remember him returning a picture to the table drawer in his hotel room in Menindie. How long ago that seems now! I am taken aback by his confessional tone but less surprised by what he says. The men often used to joke about Mr Burke's fondness for the ladies. One time I heard Landells refer to him as Robert O'Harder Burke, making of the 'O' an exclamation – Oh! – accompanied by a thrusting of his hips.

'I crossed the continent for a woman, King. Can you conceive of such a thing? Ah, but such a woman!' He looks directly at me. 'Do you know to whom I refer? Surely you must, man.'

I can think only of the name most often mentioned. 'The actress, sir? Miss Mathews?'

Mr Burke's eyes widen. At first I think he is angry. The corners of his beard twitch with agitation. Then I realise he is simply incredulous.

'Miss Mathews? Julia? A tart, King. Merely a tart. At times, t'be sure, a comfort on a cold night for a lonely policeman, but she could only ever play at being a Princess.'

He turns the page towards me. 'Here, King. My one true love.'

The fire is growing low. The sun has near set. I must take the page to see it. Its surface seems greasy from much handling. The colour has gone along the folds. But the image is unmistakable. The direct gaze, the hair pulled back severely on both sides of the forehead, a hint of plumpness in the shoulders and swell of the bosom. The coronet.

'My God, sir. It is Her Majesty.'

'Aye, King. I would stand if I could. Alexandrina Victoria. Queen of Great Britain and Ireland and all of her colonies. Empress of the waves. My love and my sovereign. I am, ma'am, your most obedient servant.' Mr Burke's lethargy has temporarily gone.

'Do you know her, sir?'

'Only as a pitiful moth can know the most lustrous star. But just the thought of one touch of her milklike skin has been enough to push me on when all seemed impossible.'

His head sinks low on his chest. When he raises it up his eyes are brimming with pain, his voice husky.

'Y'see, King, I had great hopes for what might become of me after this. A measure of fame would be mine, and surely some fortune as well. An honour, perhaps. Was it too fanciful to imagine a presentation at the Palace in London? Her soft hand in mine. The delicate scent of her cheeks as she hangs the medallion around my neck. I have to stoop. Her eyes look up into mine – she is of a modest stature, y'know – and her ruby lips frame a question: "Well, my brave Mr Burke, you must have some captivating stories to tell."

'I bow low. My head near touching my knees. "Your Majesty, I have tales to tell the likes of which you cannot conceive. I need only your indulgence to share them with you."

'She waves me towards her parlour, where two chairs are ready.'

'What of the Prince Consort, sir?' I ask.

He stares as if shocked to find me rather than Her Majesty awaiting his words.

'Albert? The lugubrious German? He is not there, man. Not there. He has taken himself away. Riding, or shooting, whatever he does. He knows better than to compete with the hero of the time. First man to cross the continent of Australia...'

He falls quiet. And then he is weeping. Tears seep from his anguished eyes. His arms fall slack at his sides. The picture is crumpled, but he seems not to care. I do not know what to say to him. Or even if I should speak at all. Never before have I seen my leader's mood swing so dramatically between fancy and reality, exultation and despair.

He meets my gaze and tries to smile through his cracked lips, as if acknowledging my confusion. 'What a damn fool I am!' he groans. 'Nothing but a dreamer. Blethering about London when my bones will rest under this godforsaken tree. If my Queen even hears my name now it will only be a line or two from *The Times* reporting the sorry fate of a reckless Irishman, once an inspector of police on the diggings, who led a party into the interior then lost good men as well as himself trying to find his way back. What wretched folly!'

The words have drained his strength. He lets his head slump back against the tree. His eyes close. His breathing slows. I believe him to be sleeping. He mumbles some words and his arms jerk. I stay with him, though I am very weary. Then his eyes are open. Burning. Anxious, until he sees me there. He stretches out his hand.

'You are . . . You are too hard on yourself,' I protest. 'You – we – were let down. Your instructions were not followed through.'

He shakes his head. 'It's all down to me. I left them waiting, without word, for too long. Too long. And now it's too late. Yet perhaps I can still put something right. Fix my affairs. Here – help me rise up a little.'

His hand when I clasp it feels as dry as paper.

'I must compose a letter to my sister in Ireland. But I am too weak to hold the pencil, King. You must write down what I say. Find a clean page in my notebook. Tear one out if you must.'

I place more branches on the fire and have to sit near to it to see the paper. He pauses for long stretches, then begins to speak again in a voice so soft I must strain to hear him. But this is what I take down:

> *Cooper's Creek*
> *26 June*
>
> *Good bye my dearest Hessie, when leaving Melbourne I foolishly made over what I left behind to a young Lady with whom I have only a slight acquaintance. I hope you will not take it ill of me. I was wrong and I only meant and mean the bequest to apply to the ~~few~~ money accruing to me in Melbourne and not to any thing derived from home. Good-bye dear Hessie my thoughts are now fixed upon you, say good-bye to John for me . . .*

In the silences, while he ponders his words or seems to slumber, I wait with the pencil. I do not understand all that I am writing. Do not know these people he is addressing.

> *I hereby cancel the bequest or will I left in Melbourne, and I leave all I possess to my sister Hessie Burke but I wish her to make over any money derived from my salary or the sale of my things in Melbourne to Miss Julia Mathews.*
>
> *R O'Hara Burke for Miss Burke. To be remembered to Annie Elizabeth and . . . Mrs Taylor . . .*

He stops. Something splashes in the creek. A stick hisses on the fire. Then, very soft: 'That is all for now, King. Show me what you've put down.'

Soon afterwards, when a possum squeals nearby and the leader does not stir, I know he has lost consciousness. Whether he is sleeping or has sunk into something deeper I cannot tell. I try to place the pistol in his right hand, but I can make out no meaning in the sounds he makes. He is restless, as if the pain in his limbs still bothers him.

I sit beside him, waiting for morning. There is nothing else I can do. I have no blankets to lay over him, though he is shivering.

A numbness has come over me. I am tired but do not feel able to sleep. I am hungry but cannot bring myself to gnaw at what is left of the crow. It is stringy and bitter. All I know is that I must keep vigil beside my leader, who may wake and want for something. But even as I wait in the night I wonder what my purpose will be if Mr Burke is gone.

It is dark. The moon is mostly covered by clouds. I sense the creek rather than see it, can hear water rippling. When I look in that direction I see movement. Dark on dark. Then it passes into a narrow strip of moonlight. There, I can make it out now, a lone pelican, its head tucked into its chest, drifting silently on the inky water. Gone now, into the blackness. But this sight is calming. I have a sense of things moving along quietly.

Twenty-two

Mr Burke had expired by eight o'clock in the morning.

I know this because I checked his watch, the one he gave me to return to the committee. Strange, alone in the interior I had clothes that were rags and little food, but two watches. Mr Burke's and W's, both now entrusted to my care. I was later to lose count of the days but I knew the time. I secreted the watches in the canvas pouch I hung around my neck, along with Mr Burke's notebook and W's letter. Though the blacks would not understand the workings of the timepieces, the slow-moving hands and the numerals, they were fascinated by things that caught the sun.

I cannot say exactly when the leader died because his eyes were open. There were no last words – none that I could understand, at least – and no struggle right at the end. It was soft and gentle, as if he just sighed and simply didn't care to breathe again. There was some muttering, a clicking in his throat. Then nothing. Only his unblinking stare. It was like looking into a tunnel with no end to it. Propped against the tree, he seemed to be gazing along the creek bank in the direction we'd been travelling.

I couldn't bear the staring. So I kissed his forehead and softly held the eyes shut. Then I wept. For myself more than him. He was at peace, I was abandoned. I could not even conceive what my next steps should be.

W's pistol had fallen from Mr Burke's hand. I do not think he would have had the strength to use it, if that had been his intention. Why had he insisted on holding it? I imagine he believed this was how a soldier should die. Prepared to defend himself and his Queen even unto the end. Perhaps he believed he might need to use it against any natives who sought to take advantage of his incapacity. Perhaps it was a homage to his loyal second in command. Circumstances might have separated him from W, but he could still hold his revolver.

I had loaded and primed it for him. It occurred to me now that I might lie down on the tree roots, place the revolver to my temple, and then rest beside my leader. I could say I did not do this because of my determination to survive, but that wasn't it at all. I was not strong enough. Too weak even to fashion a grave for Mr Burke. The revolver felt heavy, its trigger stiff. I feared botching an attempt at self-destruction, leading not to release, but lingering agony. Lying with an ear and pieces of skull shot away. The rats and crows drawing closer until they were confident I was no longer able to keep them from my eyes. I had seen men die like that in India.

I lived because I was not confident of slipping away as easily as Charley and Mr Burke. And because I thought it possible that W still survived. If the blacks had given him food, he might yet know what course to take. With Mr Burke gone, he was the leader of the expedition. I awaited his orders. I needed to return to him. And find the natives.

I didn't tell Howitt all of this after his men found me. Nor did I mention the leader's picture of the Queen and what he said about it. You can check what was published in 'King's Narrative'. Howitt wrote that he tried to take my story down as much as possible in my own words. I described Mr Burke's condition worsening, saying he felt convinced he could not last many hours and giving me some of his belongings for safekeeping. Of his last request and end there is this, more elegant than I actually recall it:

> *He then said to me, 'I hope you will remain with me here till I am quite dead — it is a comfort to know that someone is by; but when I am dying, it is my wish that you should place the pistol in my right hand, and that you leave me unburied as I lie.' That night he spoke very little, and the following morning I found him speechless, or nearly so; and about eight o'clock he expired.*

True enough. I told Howitt I went up the creek in search of the natives. I did, though not directly. I was like Golah Singh after he got bogged. On freeing himself he did not stray. Rather, he waited for something to happen; for someone to come by.

For the first time in more than a year — since I had fallen in with Landells in Kurrachee — I had nobody to give me instructions. And there was nothing more I could do for my leader. I was too weak even to bury him. Walking exhausted me. The aching and heaviness in my legs was worse now. They were wasting away and had sores upon them. Muscle was shrinking from the shin bones. Yet when I moved they felt to have great weight in them.

I could not cover Mr Burke, other than to pull some branches over him. I left the revolver where it had fallen. I still had my gun, with which I bagged another crow. I hoped the sound of the shot might attract the natives, for they seemed my best chance if I could not find W. I stayed put for two days, but no natives came. Nor did I hear them. All I had for food was the bird and some nardoo. Hunger I was used to; it was the solitude that was strange to me. I had always had others around me — my brothers and sister, soldiers in the army, everyone else in the expedition. They were all gone now, leaving me on my own in a foreign land. Wondering how best to proceed. Trying to determine the course

I should take if I wasn't to meet the same end as my leader, who no longer had any decisions to make.

Only when the nardoo was almost finished did I go along the creek, slowly retracing the path I had taken with Mr Burke. My hope was that the blacks would be in the region we had left W.

I was not even sure I would know the place where he had lain. Turns in the creek looked similar one to another. I recalled a stand of trees, their trunks bleached white, roots raised above the sand like an emu's claws. But there were many trees like that.

It was the broken limb that served as a pointer. A limb caught in a forked trunk, protruding in both directions. I remembered that as being close by. It was late afternoon. I cooeed, though my throat was very dry and my voice hoarse. No reply. No sound other than my feet on stony ground.

W was where we had left him. He was dead.

I knew that as soon as I saw him. Some of his clothes were gone – his shirt and hat and boots, though these had been in poor condition. Blacks must have come and taken them. It seemed they had tried to place him back as they found him, but the removal of the shirt had twisted his arms into odd angles. The way he lay reminded me of a child's doll, its limbs crudely screwed to its sides.

He must have been dead for several days. His colour had changed and the smell was bad. This young Englishman who guarded his privacy, who had been particular about his appearance, had no dignity in death. But there was nothing I could do for him other than spooning some sand over him with my hands. I knew the wind would shift it off him in time, yet it seemed right to do something.

And it was fortunate I tried to cover him a little with sand for I found, near his side, some of the pounded nardoo we had left with him. I was surprised the blacks had not taken it. Perhaps they were well supplied with food themselves. But all I had was this nardoo and some pieces of the part-cooked crow I had brought with me for a man who would never need it.

Now I was quite alone. I could not see or hear any natives. My main concern was to find somewhere to sleep. There was the gunyah in which W lay, but the smell was too strong even for an exhausted man. As it did not look like rain, I fashioned a depression in the sand and curled into it, my head towards my knees for the little warmth I could create.

I slept well. Without dreams or disturbances. When I awoke it was just getting light. For a few precious moments, while the warmth was still in me and before I remembered where I was and the circumstances in which I found myself, I was not uncomfortable.

Then it all returned. Emptiness of spirit, emptiness in my guts, a great heaviness in my limbs, and, most curiously, an indifference to my situation. I no longer had any place to go.

With W gone, I saw nothing to be gained by moving any further. If a tribe of natives remained in the vicinity of the creek, they were more likely to find me than I them. So I stayed where I was, near the creek, in a stand of trees on the sand. The nardoo could last me for several days. Maybe more, if I did not exert myself.

I was twenty-two years old. An Irishman in Australia for little more than a year. A member of an expedition party that had been scattered like a dandelion in a breeze. I was the only man left, I had no-one to talk to. So I read.

I had helped Mr Burke bury some of W's fieldbooks near his shelter. It wasn't difficult to find the spot, which I had marked with stones. But I had to labour to dig them out, stopping to rest several times. Had the ground not been so sandy, I could never have managed it.

After making a poor breakfast of nardoo, which seemed to

form a clump in my guts, I sat on a fallen branch by the creek. I removed my boots, which were in a poor way, to examine my feet. Most of the nails were gone and the skin was grey. I kept the boots off to give my feet air, and scanned the journals to which W had devoted so much time.

All those pages and pages of writing. And his hand neat unto the end: the last entry, a long one, dated Friday, June 26th. I fumbled at the canvas pouch around my neck to check the letter I was keeping for his father. There: Cooper's Creek, June 27th, 1861. It seemed he had written nothing after this.

Yet as I looked at the previous pages something was not right. 'Monday, June 24th – A fearful night...' Then, 'Tuesday, June 23rd', followed by 'Wednesday, June 24th'. W had confused his dates. The man who measured everything, who calculated distances and direction and the heights of stony outcrops, ended his life unsure what day it was.

But I could only marvel at his facility with words. W wrote without any hesitation or stutter. His final entry read:

> Clear cold night, slight breeze from the E., day beautifully warm and pleasant. Mr Burke suffers greatly from the cold, and is getting extremely weak; he and King start to-morrow up the creek, to look for the blacks – it is the only chance we have of being saved from starvation. I am weaker than ever although I have a good appetite.
>
> Nothing now but the greatest good luck can now save any of us; and as for myself, I may live four or five days if the weather continues warm. My pulse are at forty-eight, and very weak, and my legs and arms are nearly skin and bone...

He had given his watch to us by then. His pulse rate must have been a guess. He was taking readings without his instruments, even at his end still analysing everything:

> *... starvation on nardoo is by no means very unpleasant, but for the weakness one feels ... Certainly, fat and sugar would be more to one's taste, in fact, those seem to me to be the great stand by for one in this extraordinary continent; not that I mean to depreciate the farinaceous food, but the want of sugar and fat in all substances obtainable here is so great that they become almost valueless to us as articles of food, without the addition of something else.*
> W.J. Wills

There was barely enough room for his signature. And no other pages in the little book. It made perfect sense that he should slip away then. W, the man who had to put everything down, had run out of space to write. He signed his name because he could say no more. 'Farinaceous'? I didn't understand it. And about me, just that passing mention: 'he and King start to-morrow up the creek'.

The entries for previous days were mostly about weather and clouds and the state of his bowels, with only incidental references to myself:

> *I have determined on beginning to chew tobacco and eat less nardoo, in hopes that it may induce some change in the system. I have never yet recovered from the effects of the constipation, and the passage of the stools is always exceedingly painful ... King was fortunate enough to shoot a crow this morning ... About eight o'clock a strong southerly wind sprung up, which enabled King to blow the dust out of our nardoo seeds, but made me too weak to render him any assistance.*

Like I was a food-gatherer. A servant. Scurrying about trying to find sustenance for my superiors. A reader of these journals would know more about W's stools than my part in the expedition and the last days of its leader.

It was there, on the banks of the Cooper, with the morning sun on my back and nardoo paste drying in the whiskers on my chin, that I resolved not to sink into a seductive torpor. I would endure, if I could, as the only one able to tell of the last stages of the expedition. To tell of more than W's clouds and camping places. To tell of Charley Gray and myself and Mr Burke, who never told much about himself.

When the stock of nardoo ran low, I would try to seek some more. As I still had a gun and ammunition, I would hunt for what I could find. If the blacks did not chance upon me where I was, I would look for them.

I especially hoped to find one called Pitchery. It seemed he had helped W – who I had heard describe blacks as mean-spirited and contemptible – to a camp. There it was in his journal, from the period weeks before, when he had gone alone back to the depot to see if anyone had followed us up and had encountered a tribe of natives:

> *Monday, June 3rd . . . I was conducted by the chief to the fire, where a large pile of fish were just being cooked in the most approved style . . . I was expected to dispose of this lot – a task which, to my own astonishment, I soon accomplished, keeping two or three blacks pretty steadily at work extracting the bones for me. The fish being disposed of, next came a supply of nardoo cake and water, until I was so full as to be unable to eat any more, when Pitchery allowing me a short time to recover myself . . .*

Such a feast. It made my guts grumble and twist just reading about it. If I found such hospitable natives, I could surely survive long enough for any relief party to find me. But with the author of the journal I held lying dead not a hundred yards away and the leader gone, the prospect of rescue seemed remote. Nobody who might come after us would know where to look for me. And when I scoured the bank, searching for tracks in the sand left by blacks, I found nothing but animal spoor. I felt like the last man alive.

I never told Howitt about reading W's journals, which I covered over again before I moved on further up the creek. I suspected he would regard this as grossly improper. But I did tell him how the blacks found me after I had shot at crows and hawks.

I assumed they had heard the gun and then come to me, seven men with their hunting sticks. But the way they suddenly appeared from behind a stand of trees made me wonder if they had been watching me for some time. They jabbered between themselves in a stream of phrases mixed with clicking noises. When I presented a crow to them as a gift, this pleased them. They took me with them to their camp a little distance away and gave me nardoo and fish, which I hadn't eaten for a good while.

'Pitchery?' I asked. 'Pitchery?'

They found this amusing. When it grew dark, it was indicated to me that I should share a gunyah with three of the single men. My clothes were in such a threadbare state that I welcomed the warmth of these blacks. Their smell was pungent, due to the animal oils they smeared on their skin, but not as bad as W's when I found him. And I was in an awful way myself.

The next morning one of the older men, whose beard was quite grey, commanded my attention. He placed a finger on the ground and partly covered it with sand, at the same time pointing in the direction I had come. He then said a word I did not understand until later – *Nunanga!* – while again making the gesture in the sand. He was telling me a white man lay dead. From this I knew that these were the blacks who had found W's body and taken some of his clothes, though I never saw any of his items being worn. The old man made signals, pointing at me and then away down the creek, seemingly asking about the other white man. I imitated his gesture, placing two fingers on the ground and covering them with sand. This caused much clicking of tongues. They then seemed to feel great compassion for me, and offered me more to eat.

When I recounted this to Howitt I told him how the blacks appeared to grow tired of me after four days or so and made to move to another camp further down the creek without me. I followed them. I shot some birds, which appeared to gratify them so much that they made a windbreak in the centre of their new camp, then sat around me until such time as the crows were cooked. Then they assisted me to eat them.

Soon after, I tended to the woman, Carrawaw, whose boil I treated with nitrate of silver. '*Mokaw!*' she cried. But her pain was soon eased and she was grateful. I told Howitt I hoped that this act of kindness, plus any birds I could bring down, might make me seem less of a burden to the blacks.

But I didn't say anything to him about the time Carrawaw took me.

I feigned sleep. I turned away. Her smell repelled me. But the arm she had placed on my chest, the arm without the boil, slid down my shirt and into the waistband of my torn and ragged trousers. She giggled like a young girl as her hand closed around my part. Which, to my surprise and shame, swelled in her palm. She made a cooing noise, as if of approval, and gently pulled me towards her so I was lying on my back, her hand still in my trousers.

She seemed curious to see what a white man looked like. I did not resist as, still making those strange sounds, she eased my pitiful clothes down and examined me, softly touching the tip of my part with her fingers and then – Heaven help me, before I knew what she was doing – with her tongue.

I could say that I was insensate, that I was weak with fatigue and did not know what was occurring. I could say that I was curious to see if this bit of me still functioned after all the privations I had endured. But that was not the case. It was only the second time in my life I had experienced such a thing. The first was on my eighteenth birthday in India. My friends in the regiment got me drunk on porter and, laughing all the while, led me down the back lanes of Peshawar to a dingy place redolent of candle wax and incense. I recall dark eyes and warm hands and a hot wet softness and then being wretchedly sick on the dirt floor. My friends carried me back to the barracks, singing a song about Johnny being a boy no more. 'Too roo too roo lay . . .'

I had never thought to know such a feeling again, such a mixture of shame and delight. Yet I lay on an animal skin while Carrawaw lowered herself on me, her huge breasts swinging before my head like water sacks. My mouth lurched towards them like a baby thirsty for the nipple. They were dry and tasted sour. I didn't care. For the few minutes it took, until my part throbbed and her soft reeking weight came down upon me, I entirely forgot the hopelessness of my position. And then I slept.

By daylight she was gone. But her husband was unusually solicitous towards me. He brought me a nardoo cake, still warm from the fire, and indicated that there was now a powerful bond between us.

I told Howitt and the commissioners I had forgotten much of my time with the blacks. This was not wholly evasive as I did lose track of days and weeks and phases of the moon. The blacks treated me kindly, though I suspected it would not be long before they took the gun, which I tried to keep with me, or the pouch around my neck. They were curious, above all else, and my great fear was that they would become bored with me and chase me off.

I would not have lasted much longer had I not been saved. I had food, but not of sufficient variety to sustain me. I was becoming weaker, both from a lack of nutrients and an ebbing away of will. So many nights had passed, I could not conceive of any white men finding me – if indeed any were still looking. The days were growing warmer and the blacks were making preparations to move on again. I knew if I was not able to keep up with them I would be left behind.

Then it came. The day of my release. *Nunanga!* By the time I got to this part of the tale I was tired of Howitt's questions. Tired of talking and trying to remember. 'Shortly I saw the party coming down,' I told him, and thus my narrative ended.

I have since heard my rescue described as one of the most dramatic moments of Australian exploration. Edwin Welch became a popular dinner guest around Melbourne, telling his story. Welch was the surveyor in Howitt's party, a fellow troubled by boils on the back of his neck. He claimed to be the first of Howitt's men to find me. In his account – which I suspect grew more dramatic with every telling, every glass of brandy and cigar smoked before the speeches – he related how he'd been out riding along the creek on the morning of September 15th when his attention was drawn to a very animated group of natives who were making a lot of noise and gesturing to him from the top of a sandy bank. He maintained he had kept a diary, later published, in which he describes how these blacks led him on until he observed 'one solitary figure, apparently covered with some scarecrow rags and part of a hat, prominently alone on the sand'. In what followed he was careful to keep himself at the centre of the story:

Giving my horse his head, I dashed down the bank towards this figure. Before I could pull up I passed it, and as I passed, it tottered, threw up its hands in an attitude of prayer, and fell on the sand. When I turned back the figure had partially risen. On reaching him, I hurriedly asked:

"Who, in the name of wonder, are you?"

And received the reply:

"I am King, sir."

For a moment I did not grasp the thought that the object of our search was attained, King being one of the undistinguished members of the party.

"King?" I repeated.

"Yes, the last man of the exploring expedition."

"What — Burke's?"

"Yes," he said.

"Where is he — and Wills?"

"Dead, both dead long ago."

And he again fell to the ground.

The party having come in, we halted and camped. King was put in a tent and carefully attended to, and by degrees we got his story from him. The emaciated survivor of the disastrous exercise looked more like an animated skeleton than anything else and resembled a blackfellow in almost everything but colour...

Lies, most of it. Reading it, I appreciated the gulf between what had happened and what would be said about it. Welch might claim he was the first to find me but it was Howitt's black trackers, Sandy and Frank, who spotted me and directed Welch to me. Then Howitt himself came.

I must attribute Welch's reference to me as 'one of the undistinguished members of the party' to his resentment at the attention afforded me when we returned. Although I do not dispute his description of me as 'an animated skeleton'. I did not recognise myself when I looked in Howitt's glass for the first time.

I could barely speak when I was found. My tongue had not spoken English for nearly three months. My ears had become accustomed to native words, though I still understood few of them. I doubt I could say much more than my name. But I remember the actual words Welch used on seeing me. As well as the horror and disgust in his eyes when he spoke.

'God strike me! Sweet Jesus, you sad sorry bastard!'

Twenty-three

Nora

It all changed then for each one of us.

Early November, 1861. A Saturday night, near eleven. We were all abed. Mr Hill were back at his place in East Melbourne. Mr Bickford always liked to retire early because of the sermons to deliver in the morning. Mary were asleep. The excitement of her arrival just a week before had only just worn off.

We had all gone down to the Sandridge pier to meet her, Mr Hill at the reins of a carriage belonging to Reverend Draper. A carriage big enough for four people and a little luggage.

Both Mr Hill and Mr Bickford made as much fuss about Mary's coming as I did myself, though I suspected that much of their enthusiasm were to distract me from thoughts of the expedition. Nothing more had been heard. Almost four months had passed since Mr Howitt left to take his party into the interior and I had no way of knowing if John still lived. Beyond the tracks, beyond the settled regions on the maps, the unknown country appeared to be as limitless as the oceans must have seemed to early mariners. People ventured into it and vanished.

It were almost summer the morning we went to the pier to meet Mary. The day would be warm. I remembered the bonnet my cousin had given me before I made the same journey more than four years earlier, and wondered if anyone had thought to give her something so practical before she too consigned herself to the sea.

We arrived at the docks a little after the stated time for passengers to disembark. There were few figures on the decks of the *Orion*, out of London. Its three masts towered over the pier like the steeple of a church. Gangplanks had been put in place. Men wearing black caps, with broad leather belts around their waists to support their backs when they lifted heavy cargo, were already scurrying in and out of the ship's hold.

— I cannot see her, I said to Mr Hill. Is it possible she never made the voyage? I have heard naught since her letter telling me she had bought a passage.

— Have faith, Mr Hill told me, placing his hand on my arm. No doubt she is having her papers checked.

We could see passengers coming out of the small wooden huts for officials, near where porters lurked with their pushcarts. They were laden with baggage and walked with the uncertain gait of folk who have spent their past few months at sea. They brought to mind my own arrival in Sydney. There had been no-one to meet me then. Did I too blink and squint in the harsh Australian sunlight? Had I paused, like this young woman with the red hair and long patterned dress, uncertain where to go first, perhaps thinking of returning to the vessel that had been her home for so long?

Red hair! The face seemed different, but it had to be her.

— Mary? I cried. As much a question as a greeting.

She turned in my direction. It *were* her. I ran towards her, not caring that my shoes might trip on the rough wooden planks of the pier.

Her hair were longer than I recalled it and there were lines around her deep blue eyes that I hadn't seen before, but her voice sounded the same.

— Well, look at you, Nora King. Quite the colonial girl. And just look at your colour! Have you not been wearing my bonnet?

It seemed like I were laughing and sobbing all at the same time.

— Mary, Mary, 'tis so good to see you again. Just wait, a year or two in this climate and you'll lose those pale Irish cheeks.

— Freckles on freckles, I'm sure.

Arm in arm, more like sisters than cousins, we walked to where my friends waited for me. The two ministers looked as pleased as parents watching a child unwrap a gift on Christmas morn. Mary wouldn't let me help her with the one bag she had. One bag and a heart full of hope, she said.

Like they'd rehearsed the move together, Mr Hill and Mr Bickford removed their hats in unison and bowed to Mary. She giggled.

— Like I'm Queen Victoria herself!

— Her Majesty would be no more welcome, dear lady, said Mr Bickford.

— William Hill, said the other minister, introducing himself. And I swear I thought at the time that his hand lingered in hers a moment longer than were necessary. Then he gave her a searching look the likes of which I'd not seen from him before. And this time Mary didn't argue when he insisted on carrying her things.

We sat together in the carriage as we headed towards St Kilda, where I had already prepared a bed for Mary in my own room. She were fatigued by her journey and the excitement of arriving, but she were also fascinated by all that she saw. To her everything appeared new and different. The offices for shipping agents and importers, placards for boarding houses and building materials, the railway line heading towards the pier, the group of natives in checked shirts and torn trousers loitering near a tavern. The building work continuing near the army barracks off the St Kilda Road.

— 'Tis indeed a new world, she said. A world being banged together with lengths of timber. And just look at that sky, it's like riding under an enormous bright blue bowl!

I held her arm, buoyed by her excitement. When we returned to our cottage near the church, Mr Hill helped Mary down from the carriage and took her bag inside. Then he and Mr Bickford excused themselves, saying there were work to be done. Before returning Mr Draper's rig, they planned to make calls in the local area, seeking donations to fund extensions to the church.

I had expected Mary to crave some rest. But though she expressed delight in my little room and the bed I'd made up for her, she said she were far too excited even to think about lying down.

— Get on with you, Nora girl. Show me around this new world of yours! And tell me more about how you've fallen in with these Methodist gentlemen.

So I led her on a stroll up the hill to the St Kilda botanical gardens, with its flowerbeds neatly laid out and many of the trees with little nameplates.

— Look, Mary said. Near the entrance, Tennyson Street. Sure it seems like a little England. A colony named after the Queen, though it lies on the other side of the world from where she be.

We wandered along the paths in the gardens for a short while, though we paid scant attention to the plants. There were too much talking to be done. All those years to catch up on. So we sat on a bench in the shade of an oak and talked and giggled and cried like a pair of schoolgirls.

Mary told me that after her ma died she had thought about shifting to England, where there were more work. Things were still very bad in Ireland then. But, she said, it were better to be poor amongst people you know than starve amongst strangers. So she stayed, just scraping by with cleaning and washing jobs.

— That's all I could see ahead of me, she said, turning her face up to bask in the sunshine. Scrubbing and scouring and beating the sheets. So when I got your letter and heard you were doing fine, it was no tough decision at all. I had no-one depending on me. I'm just glad I'd put enough shillings aside to cover the passage, though I've landed on you like a pauper.

— You'll be fine, I told her. There's still work here, even with people coming back to town now that much of the gold has gone. Everything's growing so fast. And my friends know plenty of folk.

— The ministers, you mean? You've fallen on your feet there, it seems. I'm just surprised one of them hasn't made you his bride yet.

— Hush, Mary. They're good men.

— Sure they are, girl. But good men get lonely too. Y'could do a lot worse than a minister, that's a fact. Even a Methodist.

She laughed. A sound I hadn't heard for so long. For all the good fortune I'd had since arriving, I had missed the understanding of someone like Mary. A friend I'd known long before, in another land. As if sensing what I were thinking, she took my hand and we sat together silent like that, watching some tots playing near the side of the pond while their ma kept an eye on them lest they got too close to the water and the swans went at them.

— It's so good to be here, Mary said after a while. There's a freshness to things. Port Phillip is more civilised than I'd thought, with some fine buildings. Can you imagine, we were told to expect naked black men with spears lurking behind trees!

— There are natives about, I told her. Though none have spears and most wear some clothes. Mr Hill works with them and other unfortunates. Says they've been dispossessed.

— Does he indeed? Whatever that means. Will I be seeing him again?

— Of course. We're having dinner in your honour tonight —

mutton, a rare treat. I must be back in time to get the fire going for the stove so I can prepare it.

— Mutton sounds grand compared with the swill we got on board the *Orion* these past few months. I'd never have thought that everything could be the same shade of grey. Meat, vegetables, and the stuff they floated in too. She laughed again. It were all behind her now.

— And your little room is plenty more cheerful than the boardbunks on the ship, she went on. Six girls in a cupboard, that's how it felt, though I guess you had much the same yourself. And now we're together again. Just like the time when you and your John-boy came to stay with us when you'd lost the place y'were in . . . Have you had any news of him, the one you called the runt?

Everything fell silent then. The children by the pond, the birds flitting between trees, the horses outside the park. Mary sat waiting, puzzled by my quiet.

Had I not told her anything about John? I'd written to her but once, mayhap twice. Letters full of my news, trying to encourage her to follow me out. I had told her about the ministers and my work at the asylum, but I must not have mentioned John. What *could* I have said? That I thought I had found him, yet hadn't seen him, hadn't heard a word from him? And still didn't know where he were?

But now, on the bench in the park, with Mary holding me when she saw the tears building in my eyes, I told her what I knew about the expedition. All the fuss made of its going, then the long silences and uncertainties. And the latest news, both good and bad.

— The thing is, I told her, the last information in the newspapers were in July, near four months ago. Since then, nothing. People expected the men in the follow-up party to have had something to report before now. It cannot bode well for them to be silent so long.

— Look at me now, girl, Mary replied. You must trust in him. And have faith. Pray for him! You're in a fine position to do so with your new connections. Tell me, are your friends much concerned which side of the religious fence a girl comes from?

I had to smile at this, which I'm sure is what Mary had hoped for.

— John-boy an explorer! she continued, to distract me. After all his soldiering. I can hardly credit it. Always such a quiet one. I used to imagine that came from him being the youngest, with all those big brothers. But y'know what I reckon? He's a survivor. If he got through India and muddled his way here, he'll find his way back somehow. If only to see *me* again!

— You're such a cheeky thing!

— Quite what all the sailors said. How old would your Johnny be now?

— I've been trying to work that out. Two-and-twenty, mayhap. No more.

— Fancy, a young Irishman trying to cross a huge country like this. Goes to show the unexpected paths we can take.

She were right there. It seemed a miracle Mary and I being together again after all that had happened to us both. But within a week she were starting to wonder what she would do with herself in her new situation. And then, late on that Saturday night, it all turned upside down for every one of us.

I cannot say if I were awake or dreamed I heard it. The sound of horse's hooves coming clattering fast. The crunching of wheels on the dirt track. Dogs barking in the street at the sudden noise. Then a man's voice, urgent, and knocking on the door.

— Bickford! Are you there, Bickford? In God's name open the door, man.

— Whatever is it? Mary raised her head. What's the infernal racket?

I reached for my robe, and thought I could hear the Reverend stirring in his own chamber down the hall. The caller knocked again.

— Bickford!

— Wait on.

I heard Mr Bickford topple something over, then more shouting.

A man were through the door when Mr Bickford, candle in hand, had it but half open. A man in formal dress with a long black coat. Pushing into the hall in great haste.

— Reverend Draper!

Did Mr Bickford say it first, or me? We were talking both at once. Behind Mr Draper I could make out Mr Metherdew securing his horse and carriage in the dark.

— Forgive me, said Mr Draper, talking and breathing hard as he strode direct to the parlour. But I bring astounding news.

— News of what? And is it good news?

— Well now, I would say wonderful news and terrible news all together. Miss King, forgive me, but this pertains to you most of all. Please be seated. I insist on it.

— My dear Draper, said Mr Bickford. You are welcome, always welcome. But do explain yourself.

Mr Draper couldn't sit down. He were pacing to and fro, holding his hands before him like he were warming them at a fire. Odd that I should remember his hands.

— I will try to be brief, he began. I was at the opera tonight at the Theatre Royal. There was an interruption. The manager himself took to the stage, said he had an announcement that would concern us all. Indeed, would concern the entire colony. Seems that a despatch had just been received in the city from Mr Howitt. News from his party sent out after the exploring expedition.

I were staring at his hands, while Mary had placed her own hands on my shoulders from behind me. I hadn't even noticed her come in, or Mr Metherdew, still in the corridor but looking in. The strangest look on his face in the candlelight.

— Tell us the news! cried Mr Bickford.

— Patience please, Bickford. The manager called for calm, then said the rest of the performance would be postponed because it had been learned that the leaders of the expedition, Mr Burke and Mr Wills, were both dead of starvation.

— Dear Lord...

— Gray, too, another man in the party. But Miss King, my dear Miss King, the wondrous news is that your brother has been found alive! He is with Mr Howitt, and recovering. It appears your brother is the only member of the main group of explorers who has endured.

I had forgotten to breathe. Everything had slowed down, like we were all moving through water. Mary were hugging me, smiling, yet weeping too.

— What did I tell you? John-boy's a survivor! Your runt has come through.

— And he's coming here, said Mr Draper. Mr Howitt and his relief party are now returning to Melbourne, bringing your brother with him.

— Praise the Lord! Mr Bickford had fallen to his knees. We must give thanks for this miraculous deliverance. We must give thanks and also pray for the brave souls who have lost their struggle for life. They are at peace now, surely.

I fainted then, Mary said later. Just slipped from my chair to the floor before she could grab me. Next I knew I were lying on my bed, Mary kneeling alongside me with half a lemon under my nose.

— There. I thought that would bring you back to your senses.

My head hurt. I touched it to find a lump on the side.

— You gave it a bump when you slid down, said Mary. Then she placed her hands on my chest to stop me getting up.

— Did I dream it? Mr Draper, his news?

— Not a bit of it. John's been found. He's alive and being brought back. Quieten yourself, sleep now. Things will make more sense in the morning.

She stroked my forehead with her fingertips, just like she were soothing a child into slumber. My last memory before sleep came upon me were of voices in the parlour, Mr Bickford and Mr Draper and Mr Metherdew all talking together.

— I shall refer to it in my sermon, said one of the ministers, I couldn't say which. A miracle! A lost soul found in the desert.

But there were no mistaking Mr Metherdew's voice.

— They say he lived with the natives. Imagine, a white man living like a black!

Mary were wrong. Things did not make more sense on Sunday morning. There were nothing but rumours and half-heard reports. *The Argus* issued a single sheet that gave but the barest details. The remains of Burke and Wills found. Gray, another of the party, perished. And this, near the bottom: *King is the only survivor.*

Not until the following day, when the newspapers were published, did we learn any more. Mr Hill arrived early. He strode into the house, bringing with him a copy of *The Age*, then did something he'd never done before. He wrapped his arms around me in a huge embrace. It fair squeezed the air out of me, from surprise as much as anything else.

— I'm very happy for you, he said. It's the one piece of good fortune in such a tragic tale. He must be a remarkable man, your brother, to have survived after such hardship.

— Come, William, let's have it, Mr Bickford said. Let's see what the paper has to say about this extraordinary turn of events.

We sat round the table, Mary between me and Mr Hill, as he read aloud some of the long columns of print dedicated to news of the expedition. He described a veil shrouding the fate of the explorers suddenly being torn away. Then came to a section he said touched on John directly:

> *The wanderings of the three survivors — their ineffectual efforts to find their way to South Australia — their conferences with the blacks — their return to the camp on Cooper's Creek — their last effort to reach the outposts of civilisation . . . are told by King with affecting simplicity. Who can fail to admire the stolid perseverance of this man? He clung to life as if he felt it was an absolute necessity that he should live. First he sat by and watched Burke breathing out his latest breath: heard and obeyed his last commands. Then, leaving his dead leader stretched upon the sand, he went back to find and endeavour to save Wills.*

It might have been written in French. The camp, South Australia, blacks. I didn't understand much of it at all.

— Stolid perseverance, I said, what does it mean?

— It means he has courage and prevailed, Mr Bickford replied. Now, William, I'm intrigued. This alludes to a tale told by King himself. Is there something else?

Mr Hill turned the page, folding it and scanning the dense stretches of print. There were three separate headlines:

VICTORIAN EXPLORING EXPEDITION
THE CONTINENT CROSSED
MELANCHOLY DEATH OF BURKE, WILLS AND GRAY

Then, in much smaller type, JOHN KING'S NARRATIVE. I read it myself after. Slowly, line by line, not comprehending all of it. I barely moved from the table that Monday trying to fathom it. Could it really be my brother telling this story? My brother eating the uncooked flesh of camels and seeking aid from the natives? And what were this nardoo he depended on?

I did not know this man. This John King relating a story I could barely believe. So many words after such a long silence.

Like a voice from the grave.

Part 3
The Reckoning

Twenty-four

Once Howitt had me, I thought it was all over. I was saved. But I hadn't considered the coming back. The crowds. The noise. The bands. The clamour and smell of everyone pushing and wanting to see me. People raising their glasses for toasts and calling for speeches. I didn't understand it.

Howitt could have done something to stop much of it. He was most considerate to me after I was found, delaying the travelling until he judged me strong enough to last the journey. But in Menindie he too split his party, declaring he needed to rest his animals and men before their final push south. So he instructed Edwin Welch the surveyor to escort me back to Melbourne.

I cannot recall any leavetaking with Howitt. I sensed that he had lost interest in me. Perhaps I represented a failure to him. He had been charged with locating the exploring expedition, but the only member of the main group he had found was the camel man.

Until Swan Hill things went quietly enough. Welch and I stayed with settlers. They were kind, though some of their children stared. But at Swan Hill they insisted on a celebration and Welch went along with it. For the first time, I think, he began to discern his new status: the man who had discovered the survivor of the exploring party that had succeeded in crossing the continent.

That's how it was described. That's the word they used – 'succeeded'. Though it didn't seem like much of a success to me.

In Swan Hill they lifted me off my horse. Rough men with gentle hands and ale on their breath.

'Easy, lads, easy,' said Welch. 'The man's yet frail and easily tired.'

He was looking out for me but already had a bottle of porter for himself.

Then I was in a wagon, being taken to the courthouse for a reception when all I wanted was somewhere quiet to lie down awhile. A man with a chain around his neck shook my hand and insisted I sit near him at a table on a stage fronting rows of people all standing and applauding and looking at me. I couldn't see where Welch had gone.

The man with the chain was the mayor. He quietened the crowd, saying it was his honour to present the hero of the hour, a man who had brought great glory to the colony of Victoria – the intrepid explorer John King. 'Three cheers for the survivor of the exploring expedition!'

As the mayor hauled me to my feet I remembered something Mr Burke had said to me about the glory that would be his if he made it to the Gulf and back again. Now he was gone and I was displayed to the crowd like a prize pig at a show.

'Three cheers for Victoria!'

Their toasts to the colony brought to mind the leader's last evening. His picture ... My legs were shaky. I had to sit down.

'You're overcome, man,' said the mayor. 'Understandable. Not many chaps ever had a reception like this.'

On it went. I couldn't tell if it was light or dark outside. In the courthouse it grew smokier and noisier. I longed for air. Longed to sleep. But every second man there had to make a speech. And then they were singing. 'For he's a jolly good fellow ...'

They insisted I say something, but I was weak with fatigue

and the little wine that I'd sipped had left me dizzy. I'd felt nothing like it since I'd chewed the leaves the blacks called bedgery. I stood up, saw all those pink faces looking at me, said, 'Thank you,' no more, then sat down again.

The mayor jumped up, said I was done in, and started to clap. More cheering. More again when Welch appeared, puffing on a huge cigar. Its smell made me retch. Welch was prevailed upon to speak about how he'd come to find me. He made it sound as if there'd been nobody else there. No Howitt, no Sandy or Frank. Only him, Edwin J. Welch Esq., to rescue me from the blacks.

He sat down, well pleased with himself. I leaned over to him. 'For pity's sake, get me out of here.'

'Soon enough. Who's to say when we'll get another welcome like this?'

When? Why, the next night and the one after that again.

We travelled in a coach to Bendigo. Before we'd even arrived, a stout man, short of breath, who said he was the chairman of the municipality, insisted that we alight from the coach and ride with him in his carriage to the township. There were people all along the route, shouting and waving flags, and lads on horses trying to ride alongside. One of them, a boyo in a leather jerkin, called out to me, 'Did yer spear any of them black bints with yer pole, mate?'

He laughed and turned his horse about even as the chairman gestured him away. I shrank back in my seat, but Welch, who'd smirked at the question, waved at people as we went by like he'd been doing it all his life.

Our parade stopped at a hotel called the Shamrock. A band was playing. Old and young people, women and men, were cheering and gaping. Because I was down in my seat while Welch was more prominent, doffing his hat to the crowd, many thought he was the one they had come to see.

'God bless you, sir!' cried one old crone, dabbing at her eyes with the hem of her apron. Welch blew her a kiss.

When the chairman bent over to ease himself out of the carriage at the hotel, he let loose a ripe fart. Charley would have joked about that. Charley would have loved all this. But I felt like a twig borne along by a river in flood, with no idea when or where the torrent would stop.

On the steps of the hotel the chairman, forehead streaming with sweat, took my arm and told me to turn around. 'Come on, young feller. Give 'em a look. God knows, they've waited long enough. Not every day they get to see something like this.'

Give 'em a look. A sideshow attraction.

In the hotel a long table was piled with food. I saw a pig with a plum in its mouth. Its eyes were open, surprised. Like a second plum had been placed in its other end. And there was shellfish, though I couldn't imagine where this had come from. Oysters. Mussels. I didn't hunger for any of it. Eating had been uppermost in my thoughts for so many months, yet now my guts rebelled at much that I ate, as though I'd become unaccustomed to food in any quantity. All I craved were oranges, which I sucked greedily when I found them. I looked for oranges here but saw none. I saw a fish cut up into sections. A slab of beef seeping pink juice. A goose with its neck twisted around so it seemed to be looking backwards. A buzzing noise in the crowded room . . .

There is a commotion in the reeds by the creek, where the young men have taken their spears to see what they can find. Excited cries. Shouting. Then the one who calls himself Kuparunni emerges, holding away from himself with both hands a long, twisted branch that scrapes the sandy soil. Kuparunni's teeth flash in his dark face. He is proud of himself. And he wants to share his triumph with me, for he is approaching the place where I have propped myself against a tree, hoping the morning sunshine might heal the gaping sores on my arms and legs. As he comes closer, he twists the long branch, the end of it flickering like a stockwhip.

Then I see it is not a branch. It is a snake. Six feet long at least. Its belly a lighter colour than the rest of it. Kuparunni has his hands clasped behind the serpent's head. Now he is standing near enough for me to hear the snake's angry hissing and smell the grease that the native men rub on the scars across their chests. He is naked, apart from a pair of armbands made from twisted reeds fastened above each elbow. His member, dusty as the rest of him, hangs next to the writhing snake like some strange sort of offspring.

Kuparunni is chattering, though I recognise none of his words. He gestures without ever relaxing his hold on the snake, and then he thrusts its head into his own mouth. The snake is spitting even as he clamps his teeth around its neck. Only then does he release his hands, which run a little way down its spine before taking hold again. A tight grip, knuckles together.

Kuparunni's eyes hold mine: a magician commanding attention. Without looking down he gives a sudden sharp jerk with both hands. The snake twists violently then hangs still. Kuparunni opens his mouth. The tips of his teeth are stained with blood. He spits, then smiles and holds the snake towards me for my closer inspection. I can see the puncture holes of his teeth like a crude necklace. The other men make noises of approbation.

Kuparunni rubs his belly. Then I understand. He wants me to share in the eating of the snake. I remember the monster Charley killed on our way back from the Gulf and how sick it made Mr Burke. His bowels turned to liquid. The foul snake taste lingered in my own mouth for days afterwards.

Kuparunni gives me the snake to hold. It is heavy and limp

and warm. I try to look pleased and grateful. What else can I do? I dare not offend.

Welch was tugging at my arm. 'Rouse yourself, King. You're seeming more dead than alive.'

'Snap out of it, man,' he insists when I don't respond.

'I'm sorry,' I said. 'I'm ... finding it difficult to get accustomed to any of this.'

The chairman, seated between Welch and myself at the head table, was attacking his portion of pig like it was the first food he'd seen in weeks. There was grease on his chin when he banged his fork on a glass and got up to speak.

'Gentlemen, I wish to propose a toast to the health of our honoured guests.' (Shouts of 'Hear, hear!') 'I'm sure it is unnecessary for me to remind you of the claims that Mr King has on your interest. He is the only surviving sharer in that splendid enterprise, the great and noble task of crossing the continent of Australia. At the same time, we can only deplore the circumstances, the ill fortune, that led to the untimely demise of Mr Burke, Mr Wills and ...' pausing to check his notes, 'Mr Gray. I trust that when his time comes to appear before the commission of inquiry in Melbourne, which has already commenced its hearings, Mr King will be able to fully vindicate the character of his late leaders. Once such formalities are attended to, a splendid future lies in store for our friend, Mr King. So I would ask you all to stand and drink to his long life and prosperity.'

They stamped their boots on the floorboards. The chairman turned to me. 'On your feet then. Give 'em something to take home.'

I looked at Welch. But he was in an ill humour, and not only because of his boils, which were troubling him.

'It's you they want to hear. *I* didn't even get a mention. And this time, try to get out more than a couple of words. This mob has waited for hours.'

I rose in my place. More cheering. Everyone looking at me.

'I . . . I thank you for this welcome,' I managed to say. 'Such honours are more due to them who are no longer with us, and whose deaths, I believe, were caused by neglect and bad management.' ('Hear, hear!') 'Many lies have been told about my leader, but in time I hope to be able to clear them up, every one.'

I could see Welch watching me, a curious look on his face. 'It has been reported that Mr Burke gave Charley Gray, my companion, a sound thrashing,' I continued. 'This is false.'

'Shame!' called someone in the audience.

'It was Mr Wills who wrote this in his journal. But he wasn't there when it happened. I was. A better leader than Mr Burke I never wished to have.' (Cheers.) 'He proved himself equal to all the difficulties of the task, and had an encouraging word for all of us to the very last. I –'

'Sit down, King,' Welch hissed, grabbing my arm.

I sat, but the chairman hauled me up again to acknowledge the stamping feet.

'What did you mean by that?' Welch asked when calm was restored.

'By what?'

'The reference to neglect and bad management.'

'I meant the committee, of course. Their poor instructions to us. And Brahe and the others leaving. They abandoned their post.'

'You'd best be careful what you say,' Welch warned. 'People'll be listening to you closely, and not all of 'em are friends of Burke. They could use your words as proof of *his* bad management.'

'But I've made clear my opinion of him.'

'Keep calm, King. It's not *me* you have to convince.'

Then the chairman was standing again, a claret stain on his shirtfront. 'Gentlemen, I'm sure there are some questions you would like to put to our honourable friend here.'

I had not expected this. The first two questions were simple enough. What had we done after returning to the depot? How had we collected water? I answered much as I had answered Howitt. But I didn't speak for long, the closeness of the room was making me feel faint.

Then came a voice I couldn't place.

'Why only you?'

I couldn't see the questioner until the chairman pointed him out. 'To the side. Young newspaper chap from the city, name of Clarke.'

A dandy's cravat and matching pocket handkerchief. A pencil held over an open notebook. 'Why only you?' he repeated. 'How was it that you survived while your more experienced leaders perished?'

Murmurs of assent in the room. A hush. Others wondering the same thing.

I stood in my place, my hands on the table before me for support. 'I . . . I hardly know . . . Perhaps the scant food agreed with me better. Perhaps because I was younger . . . In truth, I do not know.'

Then I was seated again. I heard muttering. Coughing. The scraping of chair legs on the floor. When I looked up, the young reporter with the cravat was scribbling something. His expression betrayed nothing of what he thought. With great relief I heard a new voice raised, proposing a toast to Bendigo's other distinguished guest, Mr Edwin Welch, a member of the Contingent Exploring Party and discoverer of the survivor John King.

'Not before fucking time,' said Welch very softly, scratching at his neck.

I do not remember leaving. I was assisted out, by whom I cannot say.

After Bendigo came Castlemaine. Another reception. More handshakes and speeches, and the sense that people regarded me as a fantastic animal come to life from an illustration in a book. Then we were in another coach, heading to Melbourne. Welch said we were expected by evening. It was a curious feeling, heading south to where we had started. I was being carried along, not responsible any more for what happened to me.

'Where will you go after you're back and the committee is done with you?' Welch asked as the coach swayed through grazing country.

'I do not know,' I told him. This was the truth. I had not looked ahead. To be found had seemed beyond belief. Now any other sort of life was hard to imagine.

'Do you have anywhere to go? Any family with whom you might stay?'

The paddocks on either side of the rutted road were brown and dry. Out of the townships we saw few other travellers. There were bushrangers about, the driver had said. He kept a gun next to his seat for protection.

'No family. I had brothers in the army, but I've not heard of them in many years. I have no idea where they are, if indeed they still live. And I've a sister. An older sister. In Ireland still, I imagine.'

'You must look out for yourself then, King. One thing I've learned: look after yourself, as nobody else'll do it for you. Have you brought anything back with you, f'rinstance?'

'Brought what back?'

'Trinkets. Souvenirs of the blacks, and the like. Look.' He pulled his bag down from the rack above our seats, unbuckled its straps, peered within and produced a calico sack, the sort of thing I'd seen Becker use for his specimens. Then he took out what seemed to be a coil of greasy cord.

'Native gear,' he said with satisfaction. 'A girdle of grass rope and a net, what they use on their heads. I did well there. A young fellow gave me these at the creek for a pair of my oldest trousers. City folk will have seen nothing like it. Or this, a nardoo cake. Now dry as a camel's turd. And a bottle of the nardoo seed.'

The glass caught the sun. Inside, W's staff of life that we had laboured to find.

'Wait,' said Welch. 'The prize samples. These I'm keeping with me.' From his inside jacket pocket he removed a pair of envelopes, their openings folded over to guard the contents. 'Lean forward for a look. Careful, I must guard against any breeze.'

At first I thought the envelope he showed me was empty. Then I saw dark shadows. No, fibres. Or fluff.

'What is it, Welch?'

'Hair, King. Hair of the much lamented lost explorer.'

Black hair. Straight pieces, none very long. I could look no more. 'From Mr Burke? But how?'

Welch seemed amused by my shock. He folded the envelope over again. 'Before we buried him. Our little service. You said you were indisposed that day, I recall. I trimmed a few of his locks with my pocket-knife before we covered him up. No charge to the estate for the barbering, either.' He patted the second envelope but didn't open it.

'And the other must be . . .'

'Mr Wills, of course. More of a challenge there. Portions were, ah, missing, as you know, but I retrieved some fine pieces from the place where he had lain. Interesting, too. Much longer. A fetching shade of auburn, the ladies would say. Enough for several samples, too.'

'I can't believe you ... What of respect for the dead?'

He spat on the carriage floor and swivelled his boot on the globule. 'Think of the living first, I say. The dead can't care no more. And don't look so appalled, King. Mr Howitt also took some souvenirs of Wills. I saw him myself. And some native stuff – a possum-skin bag and the like. Though he'll put it down to science, no doubt.' Welch gave me a hard look. 'You mean you've got nothing for yourself? After all that time?'

'Not of that sort,' I replied.

'More fool you, then. And I'll tell you this for nothing: be careful the committee don't leave you high and dry after what you've endured. You could make some pretty shillings with speeches, I'm sure. I can picture the posters: THE ONLY LIVING MAN! But don't wait too long. People soon forget. Something else will take their attention and before long your expedition will seem as distant as Peter Lalor and his stockade.'

I didn't know who he was talking of. But I let it go.

In Woodend we changed to a train. A train decked out like a fairground ride, with Union Jacks draped on the engine and rosettes with ribbons adorning the carriage in which Welch and I were told to sit.

Welch seemed unimpressed with these decorations. 'Fucking flummery,' he said, before turning his attention to a telegram that had been thrust into his hand at Woodend station. '"Tis from Macadam,' he said as the train moved off with much squealing of wheels. 'Preparations have been made for our arrival. We will be met at the Spencer Street station. Macadam himself will be there. Hansom cabs will convey us to the official reception. Where, I sincerely hope, cool drinks will be made available. Between times, King, you can please yourself. But *I* plan to have a kip.'

He propped his boots on the leather seat opposite and settled back, tipping his hat down over his eyes and crossing his arms on his chest. I knew he was slumbering when the match he'd been chewing lay still in his mouth. This left me alone looking out the window.

It was late in the afternoon. The shadows were long. We were rolling into the more densely settled areas, and when the tracks passed near roads there was often traffic on them: riders and carriages and bullock drays lurching along. I remembered the trouble we'd had with our bullocks early on. Heavy wheels stuck in the mud and the beasts snorting as they laboured to move. One dray had simply been pulled apart, unable to handle the strain. Now, approaching Melbourne in a train fit equally for a fête or a funeral, it seemed to me that this was how it had been with our expedition also.

From Howitt I had learned some of what had transpired with the other parties. More men gone, including Patten and Becker. Both, like Charley Gray, left lying in stony soil, while I sat on a soft leather seat thinking on what the man with the pencil had asked: *Why only you?*

We passed through stations with names I recognised – Essendon and Moonee Ponds, where we had stopped the first night. The train slowed and crawled past platforms but did not stop. Melbourne had grown, it seemed. Many of those who had gone for gold must have come back. A crowd of people stood three and four deep along the platforms, children clutching their mothers' skirts towards the front. Men waved flags, and a brass band played when the train passed by. The noise woke Welch, who pushed his hat back when he saw the scene outside.

'Mother of God, will you look at that!'

And only then did it occur to me what was happening. The crowds and the band were there for us. For me.

Cheering. A cry: 'There he is!' An explosion, like a gun had been fired in the air. A series of thuds against the side of the carriage and the window itself. I shrank to the floor, out of shock more than fear. Something came through an opening near the window top and fell on the floor close to me.

Flowers, with a card attached.

'"Hail the Homecoming Hero",' Welch read. Then he laughed. 'You don't look much like a hero right now, I swear.'

'What must I do, Welch?' I asked him. 'I don't know what they want from me.'

'Just a sight of you, King. That's all. The one who came back — that's you. So don't be hiding yourself the whole time.'

More people at North Melbourne. The train slowed and then came to a halt altogether. Faces pressed against the glass. The rosettes! The crowd knew the carriage I was in. Welch stood by the window, the better to see out. Someone called out, 'Mr King!' People cheered. Another band, this time playing the national anthem.

A fearful din nearby. Someone saying, 'Wait on, sir, you cannot —'

Then the door to our carriage was abruptly pulled open and a man entered. A very tall, thin man wearing a long black jacket, the kind favoured by medical or legal practitioners. Under one arm a black case. His hair, which was greying and long, was combed straight back from his forehead, though several strands had come loose and swung free. On his nose he wore a pair of silver-rimmed spectacles. Through these he made a cursory examination first of myself and then Welch, who was reaching for his revolver, thinking, as I was, that we were about to be robbed.

'You are King,' said the intruder, gazing straight at me. A statement, not a question. 'And you must be Welch.'

'Correct,' my companion replied. 'But who in hell are you, and what the blazes do y'mean bursting in like this?'

'I am Wills. Doctor William Wills. Father of the late explorer of the same name. My poor boy.'

W's father. Of course — clean-shaven, though he'd missed a patch near his chin, but still there was a resemblance. The same angled features and lean build. He felt his pockets as if looking for something.

'Gentlemen, we have little time,' he said. 'I must ask you to leave the train with me now. I have a carriage outside, which will convey us direct to the Governor himself. The mail leaves for England on the high tide today. We need all your news.'

'That's as may be,' said Welch, producing the telegram. 'But I have specific instructions from Doctor John Macadam, the secretary of the Exploration Committee, to deliver Mr King to him personally at the Spencer Street terminus.'

Deliver. Like a parcel.

Doctor Wills raised a hand, the gesture of a man who had heard enough. 'The committee? The committee has done too much damage already. I insist you alight with me at once. Time is of the essence.'

He clutched my arm, his grip remarkably fierce. I looked to Welch for instruction but he had sat down again.

'I'm sorry for your recent loss, sir,' the surveyor said. 'Really I am. But I have my instructions. We'll not leave the train before the terminus.'

Doctor Wills pulled at my arm, trying to force me up. A sudden lurch of the carriage caused him to lose his balance and sent him sprawling on the bench beside me.

'Seems the argument's over,' Welch said. 'The train's on its way again. Looks like you'll be travelling one stop further than you'd planned.'

'Damn!' Doctor Wills exclaimed, watching the throng on the platform recede from our moving compartment. I heard a scrabbling sound at the side of the train. Boys were running and grabbing at the rosettes for souvenirs.

'Damn,' said Doctor Wills again. 'Another botched job!'

He still had hold of my arm. As if realising this, he turned, looked hard at me and then, to my astonishment, threw himself upon me in a clumsy embrace. He smelled of pipe tobacco and something sweet: pomade in his hair or cologne on his cheeks. He spoke words I could not comprehend and made choking noises. When he sat up again his cheeks were moist and he had to wipe his spectacles, which had been knocked askew.

'You must excuse a father's grief, King. It has been a most trying time. And you know what he endured. My little Willy . . .'

'I, I understand sir.'

'You were with him, then — at the last?'

'Almost to the end. A brave man, sir. Your son.'

He nodded. Looked out the window. The bump in his throat in motion. 'We must talk at length at a later date, King. When you are quite yourself again and things have settled down.'

Then his manner changed abruptly. He frowned as he produced from his black case a page torn from a newspaper. Unfolding it, he waved it before me, pointing to a section ringed with several black circles. 'What did you mean by this?'

He wouldn't stay still and I couldn't see what he was so anxious to show me.

'This item in *The Argus* yesterday. The meeting in Bendigo. You maligned my son, King. Here: "Mr Wills, who reported this treatment of Gray, was not himself present, said Mr King."'

The man with the matching cravat and handkerchief, Clarke. This had to be his report.

'You called my son a liar, King!' He was shouting at me.

'No, I was saying that versions of the same event can be at odds —'

'Another thing: why all this unseemly spectacle? You are but a common soldier returning after the loss of your officers in the field.' His eyes were wide. His cheeks had patches of crimson.

'Believe me, sir, none of this was my —'

'We're here,' interrupted Welch. And then, 'Madness! Out of control completely!'

Every inch of the platform was crammed with people. Young men hanging onto verandah poles, perched upon signs saying SPENCER STREET. A dark, moving mass that pushed forward as the train slowed. A woman screamed, fearful that her crying child would be pushed over the edge. Even Doctor Wills was temporarily shocked into silence.

What followed still comes back to me on my worst nights. I wake shaking, damp with sweat, remembering the clutching hands and noise and the buffeting while somewhere a drum is beating, beating.

Welch pushes open the carriage door. Urges me to follow as near to him as I can. Doctor Wills is close behind me; I can feel his hand on the back of my coat. We hear voices — 'Welch! Over here. We have the carriages.'

A glimpse of men in dark hats. Long red hair under one of them. 'Macadam,' says Welch. But the press of people keeps us apart. The hats and red hair vanish from view. I have lost my balance. Men have grabbed my legs. I am falling, scared that I will be trampled underfoot here on this station platform. The men are trying to raise me to their shoulders.

'Let's carry our conquering hero!' one cries. Then, 'Shit!'

And he is holding his face, which Doctor Wills has thumped with his case. The fellow who has been hit loses his hold on me. Welch, or Doctor Wills, I cannot tell which, is tugging me to my feet again. We are straining towards an exit. A baby, stuff coming from its nose, is thrust at me. A woman's voice: 'Touch my child, Mr King. Please touch my child to save him!' More hands grabbing at me. Shouting and cheering and calling out.

At no other stage of the expedition — not the Gulf, not the

deserts, not even the last lonely walk up Cooper's Creek – was my progress ever so painful or terrifying.

We finally make the street. A hansom cab, its horse snorting in fear at the noise. Welch pulling me up and urging the driver on. 'Move it, man. Quick as you can!'

'Where, mate? Where?'

'William Street. The Governor's quarters,' says Doctor Wills, who is still with us, though he appears to have lost his spectacles.

Children running after us. Other carriages following. My trousers are torn where I fell. Buttons on my jacket have been pulled off. Welch is breathing heavily. His hat has gone. I reach up. Mine too.

'Bugger me,' says Welch. 'They must be starved of excitement here!'

The streets are wide and dusty. We pass signs for boarding houses, ironmongers, shipping agents. Children playing in the West Melbourne common school. A crowd of people pushing and shouting and pointing near a grand white building. We are stopping by its huge iron gates, which are closed, and Doctor Wills is talking urgently to a pair of soldiers in scarlet jackets. Then he is at the side of the cab, pointing at me and saying, 'See here.' One of the soldiers looks in and whistles softly. The gates are opened and our carriage moves through. I hear a voice – 'Close the gates, quickly now!' – and we have come to a halt by a door.

I think it is Welch who helps me out. It is quieter now. Calmer. We are in an entrance hall with a marble floor. My boots sound noisy and awkward.

I am directed into a room hung with paintings of men wearing medals and sashes. I find a chair by a window and sit. Waiting. Wanting to hide. Welch and Doctor Wills are talking in the hall. Doors open and close. The sound of the gates again. Carriage wheels on gravel. Men's voices.

'Welch, you made it! Thank God.'

Then a Scottish accent, and Welch replying, 'Doctor Macadam...'

A different voice, little more than a murmur.

Then Doctor Wills speaking. 'I must insist, Your Excellency...'

The new arrival replies, 'Not now. Not now.'

They move away. Silence. Then more footsteps approaching.

Welch is opening the door. I try to stand.

As he says, 'Another surprise, King. Someone to see you. Says she's your sister.'

Twenty-five
Nora

Not him. It could not be him. I did not know this man standing before me in the Governor's house.

Such a small man, desperately thin. A young man, yet with eyes become dull and lifeless. A white man, yet his hands and face and the back of his neck burned the colour of the furniture all around him. With sores on his skin and lips. But he looked to have had his hair cut recently and he wore a moustache, neatly trimmed. John never had a moustache. Still, it were close to nine years since I had seen him.

He were most agitated when Mr Welch showed me into the room. It appeared he had been facing out the window, towards the street where a crowd of people were gathered. He turned to see us like a man fearful that something else would be asked of him. He were nicely dressed, a blue jacket and new boots, yet still looked dishevelled. His clothes were torn and buttons were missing from his jacket and waistcoat. And the nails on his hands, when I got close enough to see, were split and broken or gone altogether. He made no move towards me.

— Who are you? he said.

I didn't know the voice. It were soft, suspicious.

— I am Nora King. Your sister, John.

Had I expected a sign of recognition I would have been

disappointed. Indeed, he took a step backwards so he could lean against a chair.

— My sister is in Ireland, he said. If she still lives at all.

— I came out, John. To Sydney for some time, then Melbourne when I learned of a man with your name on the expedition. But I were too late. The expedition had gone already.

He did not know what to do with his hands. They were by his side, together in front of him, then in the pockets of his jacket. All the time he were looking at me, frowning.

— You say your name is Nora. What was your father's name?
— Henry. A soldier.
— And your mother?
— Ellen. Both long dead.

I think he knew right there, but still he persisted, though his voice were faltering.

— I had a brother died early. What happened to him?
— Drowned. In Limerick. Poor fool trying to impress a girl in a boat.

He were crying then, sunk on his knees in his torn trousers on the fine wooden floor by the chair. His chest heaving with sobs that came out like they'd been held back too long. And I knew him now.

I held his head against the waist of my skirts. My hand moved to his shoulders. So little of him. Under the jacket nothing but bone.

— A brother who drowned, I said. And another who came back. Look now.

I held out the lead soldier with the chipped nose, the one left by his da. He took it as he rose to his feet, pulling a handkerchief from a pocket to wipe at his nose and streaming eyes. He studied my face, then hugged me. It were like holding a bird. I were much bigger than him.

— Forgive me, sis. I am in a daze. So much has been happening too fast. I thought it *could* be you from the first. But so many people have been wanting something from me.

Sis. What he used to call me long before he went away.

A cough from the corner. Mr Welch were still standing near the door.

— Forgive me, both. I'm a great admirer of touching family reunions, but the Governor is about to come in to meet with our returned explorer.

— A moment, John said. Just a moment, so I can collect myself.

I had already met the Governor, just a little earlier in the evening. I had Doctor Macadam to thank for that. And without Reverend Draper I would never have seen him at all. I still recalled the sneering man with the gold watch-chain rebuffing me at the Royal Society around the time the expedition left, so after we learned that John had survived I did not know who to contact at the committee. Until Mr Draper were told of my problem.

— Macadam's your man, he said to me. The honorary secretary. He occasionally lectures in chemistry and natural science at Scotch College, which I visit from time to time. Let me have a word with him.

He did better than that. He arranged a meeting with Doctor Macadam at the end of the same week that news of the expedition were received. Then Mr Draper took me to see him. I were glad of that, for Doctor Macadam had a fearful appearance. Everything were red — his hair, which he wore long at the back, his beard, even his eyebrows, like red smudges on his freckled forehead. Yet he greeted me most polite and said I should sit in a high-backed chair opposite his desk. Before he turned to the reason for my visit he spoke to Mr Draper, as men do, about other news.

— Amazing how quickly attention is diverted, eh Draper? On Monday all the talk in town was of the expedition. Now it's yesterday's horse race.

— Ah yes, the so-called Melbourne Cup.

— Aye. You had an interest in it, Draper?

— Of course not! I'm no betting man. But I've seen the reports. A crowd of four thousand at Flemington, it seems.

— The happy ones those who backed the Sydney horse, Archer.

— It's a brutal business though, John. Is it true a horse died?

— Two, after a fall. And a rider with a badly broken arm.

— Dreadful. I'd have it banned.

— Sure you would. But you cannot deny the public their entertainments, and the racing club has high hopes of turning this cup into an annual event. I would that my own committee had such promising business to attend to . . . Which brings us to you, Miss King. I understand you are the sister of our new Lazarus?

— I am. That is, I believe I am. John King is my brother.

Doctor Macadam were looking at some papers on his desk, eyebrows twisting.

— I'm afraid there's not much I can tell you other than the reports we've had from Mr Howitt, the meat of which you'll have seen already. I cannot say for sure I've met the man myself. There were so many men when the expedition began. So very many men . . . And King was a hired hand who signed on not long before they left. Where did he learn about camels?

— It were in India, I guess. But there's much I don't know. It's a long time since I saw him last.

— Well, then. We'll have to see what can be done about that.

But he said I should not try to meet John before he returned to Melbourne. He were very frail, it seemed. Still recovering from his experience, which, Doctor Macadam said, few men alive could fathom. He added that if I'd waited all those years to see him, another few weeks could surely be endured.

Three weeks it were. Three weeks that passed awful slow, though Mary and the ministers tried to divert me. Mr Bickford would read reports in the newspapers. Look, he'd say, he's been met in Swan Hill. Then Bendigo. Castlemaine.

Finally came the day he were due in Melbourne. In the afternoon Mr Metherdew arrived at our gate in the carriage pulled by his favourite horse, Bess. He said he would stay as long as I needed him, and almost forgot himself enough not to protest when I gave him a quick kiss of gratitude.

— Macadam's been in touch, Mr Metherdew said. Insists we go nowhere near the station, as big crowds are expected. You're to travel direct to the Governor's residence, in William Street.

— The Governor! I couldn't possibly —

— All taken care of, he said. Like he always dealt with Governors.

We were early. I couldn't wait. Bess's sedate progress up the St Kilda Road into the city were torture to me, though we were still well in advance of the expected arrival time of the Woodend train. But even as Bess plodded north up William Street, a stream of people could already be seen heading west the few blocks further to the station. Men in fine carriages, women with babes, dogs leaping about and youngsters ripe for mischief.

At the gates of the residence, white and grand, Mr Metherdew talked to the soldiers on duty and showed them a paper he carried. The first soldier nodded and the gates were unlatched. Bess stopped near the entrance and another man in a different uniform opened the carriage door and held it for me. I'd never had such a welcome, or been inside such a building. All that polished wood, stone floors, paintings on the wall. Queen Victoria, tiny in the billows and folds and tucks of her gown, gazed down on me.

I were led down a corridor with burgundy carpet along its middle and told to wait. The attendant, who never said his name, though he knew mine, disappeared behind a huge wooden door. I had nothing to do but listen to the ticking of a hall clock. Just gone seven. The Woodend train would soon be in. I heard voices behind the door, then the sound of footsteps. The attendant returned and told me to follow him into the next room.

— Your Excellency, may I present Miss Nora King. Miss King, Sir Henry Barkly, Governor of the Colony of Victoria.

He had his back to me. He were looking at a picture on the wall. I noticed his shoulders, which were slumped, and a bright red sash across his coat. Then he turned and looked at me.

A sad man. Eyes like a bloodhound's under heavy lids. And about him an air of resignation or fatigue. His face were very long, made to seem even longer by his whiskers, which he had let grow around his cheeks and chin. He were balding on top of his head but sought to conceal this by brushing his dark hair over. Beneath his coat, blue with gold buttons, he wore a white shirt with a high collar. It looked stiff and uncomfortable.

— Miss King, he said, his voice quiet and low.

— Sir, I replied, unsure whether to approach or curtsey or shake his hand. He made no move towards me, so I made a clumsy bob where I stood.

— Be seated. Please be seated.

He seemed diverted again by some business before him. I thought I should wait for him to speak, but he didn't. So I just sat. Minutes passed like this, then he studied me, frowning slightly, and asked my age.

— Turned twenty-nine, sir.

— And how old is your brother, the resilient Mr King?

— Near twenty-three, by my reckoning. His birthday would be next month, December.

— Remarkable. So young to have been through so much. Doctor Macadam tells me you have not seen him for many years.

— 'Tis true. He ran away to be a soldier when he were but fourteen.

— So many do, thinking there is glory in it. Though they learn different soon enough. You've been through much yourself since then, I'm sure. Please tell me.

So I talked about coming to Sydney and learning of the expedition. About the ministers in St Kilda and Mary coming to join me and my work at the asylum. But the Governor seemed not to be listening. He were looking towards me but not seeing anything. And when I fell silent he did not respond at once.

— Please excuse me, he said at last. You remind me of someone, you see. Almost the same age . . . It seems we must all endure things in our time, Miss King. I had a wife. Not unlike you. She was carrying our child, my son, but she was thrown from a pony phaeton not long after our arrival in the colony. The pony was scared by a runaway omnibus carriage. Such a silly accident.

He fell quiet again, looking down.

— She survived the fall but the shock of it brought the infant on early. My son died in delivery. This proved too much for Lady Barkly's system. We laid her in the same grave as her child.

I couldn't think what to say.

— I'm so sorry, sir. I didn't know . . .

— Of course not. It will be five years past before long. But there is work to be done. And we must all carry on as best we can.

Again that faint smile, followed by another silence.

Then there were a commotion. Shouting outside. Children's voices, dogs barking, the sound of metal scraping and carriage wheels on the cobblestones. A man calling out to close the gates. Then rushed steps. The Governor, who had risen on hearing this to-do, glanced outside.

— I think we can assume our visitor has arrived. It may be best if you wait here, Miss King. I'm sure you will be called for shortly.

He moved to the door, checking his hair in a glass as he went by. I stayed by his desk, my thoughts churning, half wanting to flee. On the wall near the window were the picture he had been looking at when I came in. It were a portrait of a young woman in a blue velvet gown, her hair a chestnut colour, tied in a bun. Her hands were in her lap, her skin very pale, made to seem even whiter by a ruby in a gold clasp hanging around her neck. I could only assume her to be the unfortunate Lady Barkly.

I were gazing at this picture, wondering if I could possibly look so fine, when the door opened and a man with side whiskers came in. Said his name were Welch. He gave me a cool stare, then instructed me to follow him. He would take me to see my brother.

— A moment, John said. Just a moment, so I can collect myself.

And then the Governor came in.

— I congratulate you on your safe return to Melbourne, he said. Do not stand, for you must be weak. Has your health quite recovered?

— Yes, sir, said John.

I could tell this were not true. His weakness were clear. Walking seemed to pain him and he had wobbled in his place just before the Governor came in. He returned to his seat and the Governor stood close by, facing him, one hand on John's left shoulder.

— I suppose you were in a very reduced state when you were at Cooper's Creek with the blacks?

— Yes sir, very much. John were overawed, unsure what to say. The Governor turned to me.

— Where is your brother going to stay?

— With me, at a friend's house in St Kilda.

– I think it would be best if we allowed your brother a few days of perfect quiet. You will, I hope, leave your address with me.

– Allow me, Your Excellency.

A very tall man, all in black, approached me from the doorway. Said he were a doctor. Father of the unfortunate Mr Wills. He held out a pocket-book.

– Write your details here, if you please.

While I attended to this, I heard the Governor ask John about India.

– What were you there, may I ask?

– A soldier, sir.

Then John started fumbling at his clothes. At first I thought he were choking, struggling for air. I moved to assist him, then realised his intention were to remove a stained pouch he had around his neck under his shirt, next to his skin. The Governor and everyone else in the room watched as he reached within and then removed two objects. A paper and something shiny. These he offered to Doctor Wills, rising awkwardly from his seat to do so.

– These are for you, sir. I didn't have an opportunity before. All the people . . . Your son asked me to give them to you.

– My son, said Doctor Wills, holding what I could now see were a pocket-watch and a folded piece of paper.

He appeared unsure what to do with them. He just stood there, looking at the watch and paper, his face creased with emotion. Then he took several strides to the side of the room, where he unfolded the paper and read softly to himself. Squinting, holding it close. I heard him say, *My dear father*, before he made a choking sound and rushed out into the corridor.

– A sad business, said the Governor.

John were still standing, though he looked unwell. There were sweat on his forehead and a bad smell about him.

– Some other items, he said. For the committee.

— For the committee? Doctor Macadam said, moving from his position at the side of the room.

John nodded.

— From Mr Burke. His watch also. Which he said belonged to the committee. And something else. Here.

He gave Doctor Macadam the pouch, from which the secretary to the Exploration Committee produced a watch, which looked scuffed, and a small, clasped, black-covered notebook, still with a pencil tucked to its side.

— I shall give these to Sir William Stawell before our next meeting, said Doctor Macadam. You've done well to keep them. There may be much we can learn.

As he spoke he opened the notebook and flipped through its pages, some of which seemed to be loose. I fancied I saw some dust or soil fall out of it.

— Curious, he said. His eyebrows had come together in a frown of concentration. Pages seem to be missing. What's this? A letter, it seems. A jumble. He shook his head. We must study it carefully when there is more time. Ah, but look here. This seems to be a particular message for the committee.

John were overcome. He slumped back into his seat with a fit of coughing, or perhaps it were sobs. He covered his face with his hands, presenting a most abject figure.

— Easy now, soldier, said the Governor. You've done well. He gestured to Mr Welch to fetch him a glass of water from a jug on a silver tray.

Mr Welch did so, even supporting John's chin as he drank.

— You're a man of surprises, King, he said. I knew nothing of this pouch, though I was with you for several weeks. Did Mr Howitt see its contents?

John did not answer at once, and when he did his voice were weak.

— I kept it close to me.

— An eventful evening indeed, said the Governor. I think it would be appropriate for your sister to take you home now so you can rest. In a few days, no doubt, you will feel able to face all the receptions awaiting you.

I were ready to leave with John directly, but there came a clattering near the door. Doctor Wills, perhaps? No, a man I had not met before. Larger in girth than height and made to seem even larger by the scarlet robe he wore, trimmed with white fur. As he approached Sir Henry, I saw the Governor's man, the one who had shown me in, appear in the doorway. He made a gesture of frustration, like he had tried but failed to prevent this happening.

— Your Excellency! said the man in the robe, his voice very loud. Forgive my tardiness. The crowds outside, extraordinary!

— Your Worship, the Governor replied. If anyone could make it through, it would be you.

— Now, said the new arrival. This must be our survivor, eh?

Then he were upon John, shaking his hand in a manner that caused my brother to wince with pain.

— I am Bennett, sir. Robert Bennett, MLA. Lord Mayor of the City of Melbourne. I have much pleasure in welcoming you back to the bosom of the colony. I do so not only on my own part, but on behalf of the corporation and citizens generally. In the meantime, sir —

He seemed ready to launch into a speech, but I saw the desperate look in John's eyes and interrupted.

— Forgive me, sir, but my brother is poorly.

— Ah . . . And you are?

— Nora King, sir. His sister. Preparing to take him home.

— But that's impossible! There are hundreds of people outside in William Street. Citizens waiting for a glimpse of this remarkable man. Listen.

He moved to the window and raised the sash. We could hear the sound of voices, an animated buzz. On sighting the scarlet figure at the window, the crowd began cheering. Then calling out.

— Let's see the hero!

— We want King! We want King!

— No, said John, pleading rather than protesting.

— Miss King is right. Her brother is very weak, the Governor told the Mayor.

— The people won't be denied.

— Would it suffice if *I* made an appearance?

— At any other time, Your Excellency, at any other time. But, with the greatest respect, there's only one man they've come to see today.

The Governor approached John and knelt so he were level with his face.

— You see the situation we are in. I would not presume to order a man in your condition, but if you can make even a brief appearance I suspect that will satisfy them. The people may even disperse then. Are you up to it?

— As you wish, sir.

He tried to walk by himself but looked in danger of falling. So Mr Welch took one side of him and I the other, and we walked out on the balcony with the Governor close behind.

There were cheers when the doors were opened, then an echoing noise as John appeared.

I'd never heard or seen anything like it. People were packed across William Street, urchins hanging onto railings of the Governor's residence itself.

— There he is!

Hats were tossed into the air. Someone called for three cheers. When the last of them were done, a young fellow called out.

— Let's 'ear from him!

— Let's! came a chorus. Some words from Mr King!

We moved him to the railing of the balcony. All those faces looking up! The noise of excited conversation quietened at once when John raised his arms. They thought he were calling for calm so he could speak. In truth he were stopping himself from falling forwards.

He couldn't utter a word.

— We must get him away, Welch said. Is your man still here? Perhaps there's a way he can leave without attracting attention.

While we led John back, sagging in our arms, Mr Bennett the Mayor moved to the balcony edge.

— Friends! he said, very loud. This is an auspicious day for our city. A day tinged by tragedy, yet one on which we celebrate the safe return of one its bravest citizens!

There were more cheers, and because he made no mention of the hero's departure the crowd stayed put. We had reason to be thankful to Mr Bennett after all.

As Mr Welch had suggested, there were a side exit from the residence. The Governor's man got word to Mr Metherdew, who brought Bess around. But the Governor himself saw us out.

— Farewell, King, he said. I hope we will meet again when you have recovered your strength somewhat. Then he turned to me. You have quite a task ahead of you, it seems, my dear Miss King. Take care.

The last sight I had of him were like the first, his back. And those sloping shoulders, burdened with responsibility and sadness.

Mr Metherdew helped get my brother into the carriage. If he were shocked by his appearance he didn't say so, and I were touched by the tender way he wrapped a blanket around him. Like he were but a child.

John appeared to take little interest in the surrounds as we travelled towards St Kilda. Indeed I think he slumbered much of the way. He seemed to me a man who had travelled too far. Seen too much. I do not even know if he heard me when I took his hand and spoke to him.

— You can rest now, John. Your journey's over.

Twenty-six

During my restless nights, when I go into Mary's room to watch her and the children as they slumber, I wait until my breathing slows before I ease myself down near to them. And I do this gently, lest I wake any of them. There are times when the sweat rises from the effort of stifling a fit of coughing. But I must be quiet. I want things to stay as if I were not there. They need never know that I come like this to watch over them. And if they ever feel my fingertips lightly playing on their foreheads, it is nothing more to them than a phantom caress in a dream.

Mary murmurs, then rolls so her face lies on one of her arms. Albert and Grace shift position as if by instruction. Then they are still. It could easily be imagined that life has left their bodies. Slipped away as soft as my entry into the room. And yet there is always something there. A flicker of an eye. A twitch of a lip. Something, compared to the awful void of the dead.

I like to stay close to Mary and her babes when they sleep because it soothes me. Because I have seen too many spent things. Because a force still flickers within them and I know they will wake up.

I know, too, that Doctor Treacey considers me to be a vexatious patient.

'I wish you would desist from your writing,' he says one

morning, removing his stethoscope from my chest. 'It tires you out and leaves you fractious. Miss King tells me you are regularly up in the early hours scribbling in your journals, leaving ink all over your bedding. I'll wager that even the late Mr Dickens never toiled at such irregular hours.'

'I write when I cannot sleep. The coughing rouses me and I am unable to rest. It is the strangest sensation, Doctor, feeling so weak yet still not physically tired.'

'Ah, now that would be attributable to your lack of exertion, due to your condition – which need not worsen if you would just be sensible. You are a young man still.'

'And doubt that I will grow much older. No, don't dispute it. I know the inevitability of this thing. I will soon turn thirty-three. I will have lived some six years longer than the second in command of the expedition.'

'Wills, you mean? I knew his father, another medical man. But something of a busybody; could never leave well enough alone. He returned to England some time back, I believe. No doubt he was responsible for the drinking-fountain erected in his son's honour in his former hometown in Devon. A drinking-fountain! I rather fancy the younger Wills had hoped for a finer memorial than that. But I imagine the doctor felt it incumbent upon himself to promote the good name of his unfortunate son.'

'By rights I should have perished with him and Mr Burke more than ten years ago.'

'By rights, King? There are no rights or wrongs to these things. Several people in a similar predicament will always fare differently. It depends on age, disposition, ability to adapt to conditions – which must have been horrendous in your own case. And I suspect your present state is not unrelated to the privations you endured back then. You survived, it is true, but were permanently weakened, both physically and mentally.'

'You think I'm unstable?'

'Would you deny it? You'd become something of a recluse even before your present incapacitation – seldom venturing out, easily distressed. I have often wondered if any of this is due to what you experienced in India. Were you not on invalid leave when you fell in with that man from the expedition?'

'Landells? Yes. But I was near recovered then.'

He strokes his chin and considers his patient, as he is wont to examine his instruments. 'So you say, but by the time you were twenty you had already lived through so much. Some of my colleagues with a phrenological bent would love to get their hands on your head, King. If experiences and emotions do manifest themselves in bumps, as they insist, your skull must resemble a pineapple.'

'I've never held with that. Besides, they'll have no need of phrenology if I can only complete my journal. And there's not so very far to go now.'

'But why relive it? The expedition is a decade past now. Few people are preoccupied with it still, as you seem to be. The public are diverted by more recent events – the fire at the Haymarket Theatre, for instance. Do you not realise that the end of America's civil war is fresher in people's memories than your expedition?'

'I understand, but I have limited time left to settle things. And what you said earlier, about my being uneasy in company – there is a reason for that.'

The accusations began immediately after my return to Melbourne. Nora's friend Reverend Bickford, who made me welcome in his house, was inclined to keep the news from me at first. But Macadam had already told me my presence would be required at the commission of inquiry into the expedition. So Bickford and his colleague William Hill, a good-hearted fellow I liked at once, decided I should be kept informed.

'It's yesterday's *Argus*,' said Hill, folding the paper open on the table. 'One of its columnists has suggested you do not merit a "preposterous glorification", as he puts it. There is a broad distinction to be drawn, he claims, between moral heroism and mere physical endurance.'

'Why does he say this?'

'I suspect that this columnist is simply trying to create a stir,' Bickford suggested. 'But look, a leading article in today's *Age* takes *The Argus* and its scribe to task; calls it a dastardly attack demanding a powerful response. See here: "indignant condemnation". And there is more — it suggests you have been stung with wanton malice and maligned without the remotest cause. And it concludes . . .' He paused to clear his throat. '"It is for the colonists to see that Mr King receives every honour which ought to be paid to a brave man."'

'Elegantly stated, I would say,' Hill responded.

I had not sought the attention that had so irked *The Argus*. Nor the fine words in the other newspaper. I had wanted only to resume my life in peace. The unexpected reunion with Nora made the prospect of a new start seem possible. Yet apparently I was condemned to be kicked between opposing forces like a ball in some kind of rough sporting contest.

I had already been called before a meeting of the Exploration Committee. Its members seemed anxious about what I would say at the commission. Especially concerned, too, by what Macadam described as an absence of religious sentiment in the published diaries and fieldbooks. So I told them that we'd each had a Bible and prayer-book and occasionally read them going and coming back. And that on the evening before his death, Mr Burke had prayed to God for forgiveness for the past and died happy, a sincere Christian.

This seemed to be what they wanted to hear.

My appearance at the commission of inquiry took place on a Thursday in December, 1861, close to two weeks after my return. I had been allowed some time to recover my strength, but still felt weak. The commission met in the city, in a hall of the parliament building in Spring Street. Near where the camels had been temporarily stabled after our arrival on the *Chinsurah*. Macadam arranged for a carriage to take me there. My appearance was expected, having been announced in advance by the newspapers that were publishing daily accounts of proceedings. Bickford seemed surprised that I seldom cared to follow the reports myself. Nor did he appear convinced when I tried to explain why.

'Reverend, if you were a survivor of a ship that was wrecked, would you later strive to read accounts of the tragedy?'

'Well, I imagine that if I had been saved I would want to know how the rescue was effected.'

William Hill, who was paying one of his visits to my cousin Mary, interrupted. 'But James, that's not the business of this commission at all. It has concerned itself solely with what went wrong, the so-called lamentable result of the expedition. Not the circumstances of John's discovery.'

'The eternal quest for someone to blame, hmm?'

'Exactly. A lot of money was invested in this expedition. High hopes were held. The loss of its leaders on the return trip, not to mention John's companion Gray and the others, is highly embarrassing for both the committee and the promoters of the enterprise.'

'Seems to me, William, that shamefully few tears have been shed for the likes of Mr Gray. Did y'hear that there is talk of Mr Howitt returning to the interior and retrieving the remains of the leaders? But nothing has been said about Mr Gray.'

'May he rest in peace.'

'Indeed,' I said. 'But what do they want from me now? What should I tell this commission?'

'Just the truth, John,' said William Hill.

The truth. Von Mueller gave me similar advice while I waited for the commissioners to call me.

'Speak the truth, my boy,' he said. 'Answer the questions honestly, that is all anyone can ask of you.' He peered at me through his none-too-clean spectacles. 'You are looking a little better already, I think. *Ja*. Perhaps some more meat on your bones. You are being well looked after?'

'I am. My sister has been very kind to me. And my cousin, another who has crossed the world to come here.'

'A fortunate man indeed, King. Feminine companionship and care is the most priceless thing. Priceless and rare.' He sighed.

I could not think what more to say to him. He seemed mournful. But Macadam appeared at that moment from within the hearing room, mopping his freckled forehead, and diverted von Mueller's attention.

'Ah, Mr Secretary. They have finished with you?'

'For the moment, yes. Though I fear, Ferdinand, that I might have been rather too candid in there. I described a sort of dread in the committee that something was going wrong with the expedition.'

Von Mueller paused. Removed his spectacles. 'Dread, you say? I would think that was quite accurate.'

And then I was called in.

There was no applause this time. No cheering. Newspaper people and members of the public filled the benches, and as I was shown to the front of the room, which smelled musty, there was silence.

I had expected something like a courtroom. Instead, the place had the feeling of a dining-hall, with many more guests than could comfortably be accommodated around the main table. The commissioners sat side by side at one end; at the other were record-keepers, near some landscape paintings on the wall. The light was dim, as if there were insufficient windows. Conversation ceased as soon as I entered. I could feel curious stares upon me.

Von Mueller was right. I looked better than I had, yet still I cringed when I saw myself in the shaving-glass. The colour of my face had lessened, but much of the skin had flaked away and the sores on my lips were proving slow to heal. The aching lingered in my legs. I wondered if I would have to request a chair during the interrogation.

There were five members of the commission present. They called me Mr King and introduced themselves to me one by one. Sir Thomas Pratt. Mr Harvey. Or was it Hervey? I didn't catch it. Mr Sullivan. Mr Haverfield, the secretary. He had an ink bottle by his elbow, and a thick sheaf of paper.

The one I remember best is Sir Francis Murphy. He asked the questions while pacing about, pausing often to consult a number of papers he kept in a box. He wore a wig and had a habit of placing the tips of his fingers on both hands against their twins. When he moved close I could see spidery red marks on his cheeks and nose. His manner was polite and respectful, formal rather than friendly. I was not on trial, he seemed to be suggesting. They would be grateful for any help I could give them – that was all.

He led me over it. All of it. Much as Howitt had done after I was found. Indeed I wondered why Sir Francis wanted to wander over so much old territory. 'King's Narrative', I wanted to say. Read it all there and let me be.

Back and forth we went. To the start, the stay in Menindie, the advance team to the Cooper, then the trip to the Gulf. Patten and his tears. Brahe accompanying us some of the way out and then saying, 'Goodbye, King. I do not expect to see you for at least four months.'

Sir Francis was especially interested in this. 'He made use of that expression — four months?'

'Yes.' I could hear the sound of Haverfield's nib on his paper.

Then the Gulf. Sir Francis, lips pressed tightly together when he composed his thoughts, asking about a vessel of some kind that Mr Burke might have expected to meet there.

'I did not hear him express any expectation of meeting a vessel. We did not expect any help by land or sea.'

Then Charley. The incident with the flour. Mr Burke giving him several boxes on the ear.

'Mr Burke was not in the habit of striking his men?'

'No. It was the first time I knew him to do so.'

Charley's death. The day's wait while we buried him. The return to the depot to find Brahe and the others gone.

Standing in my place, leaning against the table to try to ease the weakness in my knees, all this verbal journeying seemed akin to the slow trip from the Gulf to the depot. Doubling back on an old path, aware of the final destination, I found I did not need to think much on my answers in that commission room.

My attention wandered. A fly circled the industrious Haverfield but never seemed to land. I looked around at the other people present. There amongst the reporters was *The Argus* man with the cravat from Bendigo. Clarke. Looking at me intently again, writing his notes. People were growing restless. One man was slumbering, the top of his head gleaming pink as his chin sank to his chest. These spectators, those reporters, perhaps even also the commissioners, were discovering one of the truths about exploring. It is slow and tedious. And the goal is often not achieved.

'Now,' said Sir Francis, standing close and examining me over the top of his joined fingertips, 'I want to ask you about your last visit to the cache of supplies near the tree, before the three of you attempted to set out for Mount Hopeless.'

The rake. The dung. The tree.

'Did you see the rake?'

'Yes.'

'Did you put it against the tree in the same position as you found it?'

'Having raked the dung over the cache, I left it against the tree.'

'It did not occur to Mr Burke or anyone to leave any mark on the tree?'

'We did not expect anyone to return, and we thought the word "DIG" would serve all the purpose.'

I waited for the question that did not come: *And what if you had left a message, Mr King?*

But Sir Francis went down a different path altogether, the leader's last days. 'Mr Burke, it is presumed, was exceedingly weak when you finally parted with him?'

'Yes, he walked until he dropped.'

'The revolver: did he express any intention in his wish to have it in his hand?'

'He said to me, "King, this is nice treatment after fulfilling our task, to arrive where we left our companions and had every right to expect them."'

This seemed to satisfy Sir Francis. A woman near the front was dabbing at her eyes.

Then he wanted to know about the end. What Mr Burke had said and written. How. And when.

'I...I...' I sagged against the side of the table. I asked for a chair. A buzz of conversation from the seats. Some sounds of sympathy, the commissioners talking one to another. Sir Francis was silent, seemingly embarrassed, like he was to blame.

The one who appeared to be in charge, Sir Thomas Pratt, cleared his throat noisily as a clerk helped me settle into a chair. Then he addressed me. 'We won't trouble you much further, Mr King. It is clear your condition is still delicate, your emotions very fragile. Which is understandable. Sir Francis, I think perhaps we can move on from the mournful circumstances you were touching on?'

'As you wish,' said Sir Francis, consulting some pages. He turned again to me. 'The last letter of Mr Wills, Mr King. Had you known of its contents?'

'I had. It was read over to us. Either one of us, Mr Burke or myself, might contradict its contents if necessary. We should see it was the truth.'

I was aware that this letter, kept by me for so long, had now become a most public document. Doctor Wills had seen fit to release it to the newspapers. Its publication, Bickford had told me, caused quite a stir. Damning those who had left the depot. And also the committee, which was accused of neglect.

I told the commission of the letter. And W's journals. How he had been the record-keeper, though much of what he wrote was read to Mr Burke for his assent. Then I let my head rest in my hand. The gesture of a weary man.

'The commission will not trouble you further today,' said Sir Thomas. 'We are exceedingly obliged for the clear statement you have made.'

Sir Francis resumed his seat. The clerk returned to help me out. 'There,' he said. 'All done.'

Not quite.

'I desire to state that there is an impression abroad that Wills was virtually the leader of the party,' I said firmly.

The commissioners looked up at me in surprise.

'That opinion, sir,' said Sir Thomas Pratt gently, 'is by no means generally entertained. Indeed, sir, the very contrary.'

The man called Harvey or Hervey, who had been mostly silent, said, 'If any such impression exists, it has arisen from the circumstance of Mr Wills keeping the journal. And you have explained the reason for his doing so. That will be all.'

Silence as I left the room. Eyes following me as I passed the reporters' benches. Then one of them — I cannot be sure if it was the fellow called Clarke or not — saying to a colleague, 'There goes a man who has been in Hades.'

From outside the room, I could hear Haverfield speaking.

'The commission will take a ten-minute recess. The next witness will be . . . ah yes, Mr Alfred Howitt.'

He is standing in the room in which I had waited myself before I was called. I have not seen him since he entrusted me to Welch in Menindie some six weeks earlier. He has changed from his customary gear of boots and heavy shirt into city clothes: a long black jacket with a matching waistcoat, his watch-chain secured to one of its buttons. He also has a pair of fine leather gloves, which he has taken off and carries in his right hand. But his beard seems not to have been trimmed and his hair is awry, like he has only just removed his wide-brimmed bush hat. He greets me warmly, his eyes scanning all of me, up and down.

'Good day to you, King. You would appear to be a little stronger. Welch tells me you have found some family.'

'Mr Howitt, sir. I am recovering, though am still not what I was.'

'It will take time. You were in a bad way when we located you. To be frank, Doctor Wheeler doubted whether you would have held out for longer than another two or three days.'

I take a seat, feeling drained by the questioning. 'I had not expected to see you here.'

'They have cast their net wide, King. As many as they can find with a connection to this wretched enterprise have been dragged in. And it's all politics, of course.'

'Politics, sir?'

'Competing forces, King. Rival camps trying to sheet home the blame. The committee members maintain the expedition achieved what it set out to do. They argue that the leaders died as heroes, having been let down by their own comrades. Then there are people, who are finding voice in some of the journals, who insist the whole affair was botched – by the committee and others. They believe the deaths are attributable to error and ineptitude.'

'Where do you stand, sir?'

He swings his gloves against the open palm of his left hand. 'I stand where I am asked to stand by those who pay my way. And I keep my opinions to myself. In there –' he gestures to the hearing room – 'I intend to answer their damn fool questions but say no more than necessary. A more interesting proposition is what *you* think, King.'

'I have said what I think. I told you, sir. I have now told the commission.'

'You have said what *happened*. Without offering much opinion on events. There is a difference, as I said.'

'I was a hired hand, sir. Before that a soldier. It has never been my place to question orders.'

'Your *place*.' He strokes his moustache. 'I suspect that much of what happened stems from unswerving observance of place. The dangerous assumption that commonsense is the province only of a select few. You know I am to return to the interior?'

'Something was mentioned to me of that. When will you go?'

'As soon as preparations can be finalised and this charade is done with. They have decided they need the bodies of the leaders, though what may be left if the wild dogs have got to them remains to be seen. Personally I think it would be more appropriate to let them lie where they are, but doubtless a grand kind of public penance is planned.'

The commission secretary, Haverfield, bustles into the room.

'Ah, Mr Howitt. You're required in just a few minutes, if you please.'

Howitt nods and gives his hair a careless brush with his left hand. Once Haverfield has returned to the hearing room, he says, 'The bodies, King. One thing does intrigue me about them. Do you recall that you were able to guide us to the spot where Wills lay? But then, although we let you recuperate a further few days after that, you professed yourself unable to take us to where you had left Burke.'

'I was very poorly, sir.'

'Course you were. But I wondered at the time if you simply did not wish to go there again. Was I right?'

I remain silent. He raises an eyebrow in farewell, removes a card from a waistcoat pocket and hands it to me.

'Here. The address of my place in town. I shall be there a little while longer. We should talk further. Do you play billiards?'

He is gone. I sit there alone again, very tired. Not looking at his card. Relieved that at this commission Alfred Howitt is a witness, like myself, and not the one asking the questions.

Twenty-seven

Nora said she couldn't reach me. Said it was like I was someplace else still. I couldn't dispute it. In the weeks after my return I wanted only to sit quietly out of the way, feeling in my pocket the toy soldier Nora had returned to me before I met the Governor. Its touch seemed to connect me to a former life. Before India. Before I'd ever seen a camel. Having Mary there helped too. She reminded me of our time in Dublin, Nora and her sharing a bed and me dossing in the hall. And Mary, better than any of them, knew how to interrupt my reverie.

'Hey, John-boy,' she'd say. 'Back from dreamland!' Then she'd shake me by the shoulders. The others were hesitant to touch me, as though fearing I might bruise or even break, but not Mary.

John-boy was what she'd called me in Ireland. I didn't mind her using the name still, though she could only have been five or six years the older and me a boy no more. Mary with the freckles and flame-coloured hair had grown up too. There was a fizz in her.

I wasn't the only one to think so. William Hill came often to the house and I could see the shine in Mary's eyes when he paid attention to her. Nora noticed it also.

'Be off with you,' Mary replied to our teasing, her face the colour of her hair, 'or you'll be putting a hex on him!'

It was Hill who seemed most interested in any expedition

news. After my appearance at the commission he would ask my opinion of proceedings as recorded in the newspapers. I told him I wasn't a regular reader, having seen how my own evidence was reported. *The Herald,* for example, had referred to me as a 'man who would mind his own business and not given to ask very many questions, which, as things have turned out, is to be regretted'.

Whoever wrote that didn't understand that my job was not to ask questions. 'Obedience is the first duty of a soldier' — that's what it says near the front of my regimental account book, which I have still.

But I wasn't indifferent to the commission. I wanted to learn its conclusions. I hoped it would refute some of the claims I had heard about my leader, and put an end to questions about the expedition. But there was nothing more I could do. I had said my piece and been dismissed. Now I was not even a spectator. And when the commission finally finished its hearings, near the end of 1861, people had already found other distractions.

Thousands went to the docks to welcome the first cricket team from England to visit Melbourne. The cricketers arrived on the steamship *Great Britain* and were conveyed into the city on a coach pulled by grey horses. The crowds were extraordinary, Bickford said. He tried to get me interested in the new arrivals, but I had no knowledge of cricket. I'd never played or seen it, though some of the Englishmen soldiers had talked of it in India.

There was another reason for my not venturing out to see the visitors play a Victorian team in a match at the cricket ground. I was uneasy about being recognised. I had not become accustomed to people staring and pointing and muttering when I passed, and was weary of attention after all the receptions. Weary in general: I tired very quickly. It seemed like something had been taken from me in the interior that could not readily be replaced.

One of the gentlemen involved with the cricket tour was

George Coppin, a theatre owner. Through Macadam at the Royal Society, Coppin put a proposal to me not long after the English players had embarked on their return voyage.

'I assured him I would pass on the suggestion,' Macadam said. 'I have grave doubts about it, to speak plain, but the money involved is such that I would be derelict in my duty not to convey the invitation.'

Coppin wanted me to appear in a travelling theatrical presentation describing a panorama of the route taken by the expedition to the Gulf. A cyclorama, he called it. The pay: twenty pounds a week over a year. In all, a thousand pounds. A remarkable sum.

But I knew I could never be a performing puppet, appearing before crowds and recounting incidents I was trying to forget. And I sensed that Macadam was not disappointed by my reply. The Society, too, was keen to put the expedition behind it. So he raised no objection to my reply. 'Be so good as to tell Mr Coppin I am grateful for his invitation but am content to leave myself in the hands of the Government, to be rewarded as it may seem proper.'

Then I smiled, which perplexed him until I explained myself. 'I'm the wrong man for it, you see. Charley Gray would have leaped at such an offer. He felt sure the expedition would bring him a measure of fame and some money besides. It was his way of pushing himself on. Charley would have made a fine one for Mr Coppin. Up on stage, telling his lies...'

I had to turn away then.

The commissioners' report was published late in January, by which time Edwin Welch had come to an arrangement with George Coppin to share with a paying audience his stories and the native artefacts he had brought back from the Cooper.

On the day the report was released William Hill arrived on

Wesley with a newspaper, to be met by Mary, who had contrived to be beating the mats outside the door. I was on my usual seat on the porch, from where I could watch the doings in Octavia Street. Hill removed his hat soon after alighting, wiped his forehead with a white handkerchief, and then, after a quick exchange of greetings, got straight to business.

'Well,' he said, addressing me. 'It's official, my friend. You're a genuine hero! See here, on this page, the concluding remarks in the commissioners' report.'

> *While we regret the absence of a systematic plan of operations on the part of the Leader, we desire to express our admiration of his gallantry and daring, as well as of the fidelity of his brave coadjutor Mr Wills, and their more fortunate and enduring associate Mr King; and we would record our feelings of deep sympathy with the deplorable sufferings and untimely deaths of Mr Burke and his fallen comrades.*

'May I see it?' I had to scan this for myself.

Mary and Hill let me be on that leaden morning, the clouds heavy with rain they couldn't release, studying what the paper published. The names of people and places were all there. Menindie, Landells, Torowoto, Wright, Beckler. Yet much seemed unfamiliar. The commission spoke harshly of Mr Burke, referring to 'an error of judgement' and 'a far greater amount of zeal than prudence'. But others were also blamed. Wright. Brahe. The committee itself. Though not me. There was very little about me.

It was odd. The crowds and bands and speeches on my return had all suggested a triumph. Yet now, in cold print, the commission deplored 'the lamentable result of an expedition undertaken at so great a cost to the Colony'.

When Mary came to bring me tea she found me with my

head sunk on my chest and the newspaper lying on the ground. She picked it up and tried to straighten the crumpled pages. Asked me my reaction. I could say only this: 'They weren't there.'

Some good did come of the report. I fancy that the Society, which had been slow to pay my wages from the expedition, applied some pressure in high places. For the Parliament of Victoria announced it would make a grant to me in excess of three thousand pounds. Like most things to do with the expedition, however, it wasn't as simple as it first seemed. Bickford, who studied the documents, told me that the money would be invested on my behalf in debentures, with the interest paid to me. They calculated an income of one hundred and eighty pounds per year, more than sufficient for my needs. Though much less than the sum proposed by George Coppin.

Then came the awards. A gold watch presented by the citizens of Castlemaine, where Mr Burke was stationed as a policeman before the expedition. And another watch, this one from the Royal Geographical Society of London. A watch for me; a gold medal presented posthumously to Mr Burke. But nothing for W.

'Doctor Wills is none too pleased about this,' Macadam told me at the ceremony. 'No medal for his own lamented son, even though his scientific achievements have been acknowledged. Apparently the Geographical Society has a strict policy of only one medal per expedition, and that goes to the leader. So you've done well to get yourself a watch, King.'

The Governor, Sir Henry Barkly, was guest of honour. He gave a smile of greeting to Nora, who thought that something was weighing on his mind when he made his speech. He spoke as if reciting a script prepared by somebody else. And he never looked my way, even when addressing me directly.

'In such a trying position as that in which you were placed, and with the bonds of discipline relaxed, the instincts of self-preservation have often led men to act selfishly,' the Governor said. 'But you, a Christian, knew it was your privilege to minister to suffering humanity; a soldier, you never dreamed of swerving from the unalterable fidelity which you owed your leader.'

What could I possibly say in response to these fine-sounding words? That I was a Christian who had lost his faith? A soldier without anyone to give him orders? No. I expressed my gratitude for the handsome watch and said I had done my duty. I said that I believed I would do so again if similarly placed. I did not say that the prospect of ever being in such a situation again sometimes caused me to wake shivering and sobbing.

I cannot deny that I was especially pleased by this award. To think that the expedition and my part in it were known about in London. Quite something for a lad from Moy. And if pride is a sin, as it is said, then I sinned that same night.

I was sitting up late, putting off the time when the dreams might come on me again. Hearing some sounds, Nora rose and looked in on me. She found the pair of watches laid before me. I didn't resist when she picked them up, first one then the other, to read the inscriptions by the candlelight.

'Look,' she said, ' "heroic deeds" and "meritorious conduct".'

'Two watches,' I replied. 'How curious it is. I kept two watches with me all the time I was with the natives. And now, once again, I have two watches.'

Nora touched my head for a moment, urged me to get some rest, and retired.

I know she found me remote. She tried to keep me abreast of events, they all did. The cricket match. The new zoological gardens at Royal Park. The death from typhoid fever of Queen Victoria's consort, Prince Albert. I told Nora that Mr Burke would have been especially interested in this, though I didn't explain my meaning. Yet to me, all these things were like distant objects seen from a moving train.

But I did join in the celebrations when William Hill and Mary announced that they planned to wed within six months. I was happy for them both. They seemed a good match. And when Hill asked me if I would act as his best man, I told him I would be honoured. For the pair of them I would willingly be a participant rather than a bystander.

Then, in December 1862, a year after the commission had held its hearings, came two remarkable pieces of news that pierced the reserve into which I had retreated.

Howitt had recovered the remains of Mr Burke and W from the interior and was expected soon in Adelaide, carrying with him his grim baggage. And Stuart, the South Australian explorer, was also due there around the same time. After several failed attempts, he had at last succeeded in crossing the continent from south to north. His condition was said to be poor, but he had achieved his goal and was returning alive.

It was only a day or two after this news reached Melbourne that I went missing once again. I left a note for Nora, who was wont to wake me in the mornings. I didn't write much, just a few lines to leave by my bed so she wouldn't worry too much about me.

I left before dawn, when even the nearby fowl were not stirring. Making a start in the dark once again. Taking little more than I could carry in a clutch bag, I stirred a slumbering carriage-man near the Esplanade and engaged him to take me to the coach depot in town.

And I never told Nora or Mary or anyone else where I'd gone.

I had to see him. This man who had been like a ghostly presence on the expedition, never visible but always there. Whose name alone could cause my leader to lose his composure.

When I learned he had returned to Adelaide, I knew I must go there – on Mr Burke's behalf if nothing else. I told nobody of my intent because I had no desire to explain myself. I was done with answering questions. And I believed that mention of the destination alone would lead to false interpretation of my plans. Assumptions would be made: of course, I was travelling to bear witness to Howitt's return with the mortal remains of the leading men in the expedition.

That wasn't it. I had seen more than enough bones in my life. Bones with shreds of uniform on them in India. The bones of W, well over a year previous. I had led Howitt to where they lay. We stood in the sun, Welch picking at his boils and Doctor Wheeler suitably solemn, as Howitt read a chapter from the Bible: '"The trumpet shall sound, and the dead shall be raised incorruptible, and we shall be changed."'

There would be time enough to pay my respects to the leader's remains. Already plans were being made for a public funeral in Melbourne, an event that promised to be more splendid than anything ever seen. Thousands would come, but I knew that one man who had played a crucial role in our enterprise would not be there.

The trip to Adelaide took three tedious days by coach. Several coaches: I had to change more than once. It was the first time I had been anywhere since my return. If anyone in the booking office or any of my fellow passengers recognised me, they showed no signs of it. I was just another traveller, thinner than most, who preferred a corner seat and seldom offered much by way of conversation. When they asked my name for the passenger list I told them Wilfred Ponting, in honour of my young drummer friend from the regiment. Mr Ponting dozed much of the way, confirming his suspicion that there are easier ways of traversing a country than trudging behind a camel.

The coach made its final stop in King William Street. The coachman seemed surprised when I sought directions to the Governor's house. Still, he pointed the way readily enough. I walked slowly, as I was yet easily fatigued, glad that I had brought with me nothing more burdensome than a single bag.

If I had stopped to consider the improbability of my assignment, I might never have undertaken it. Yet throughout the long journey from Melbourne I sustained myself with the belief that mention of my name, coupled with the object of my visit, would ensure success.

So it proved. At the Governor's residence, which I recognised by the splendour of its façade, my way was blocked by a fellow wearing a blue uniform with brass buttons. He eyed me scornfully, supposing, I guessed, that in my bag I carried samples of products for which I sought His Excellency's endorsement.

'What's yer business?' he demanded.

'My name is King. John King. Survivor of the Victorian exploring expedition. I am here to see Mr John McDouall Stuart.'

I think he was about to laugh, or berate me for my insolence, when he paused to consider me more closely. Perhaps he noticed the gravity of my manner, perhaps something about me reminded him of a sketch he had seen in one of the newspapers. I cannot say. But his tone was less aggressive when he told me to stay where I was and adjourned inside the main building, leaving a companion to study me curiously.

It can only have been five minutes, no more, before the guard in the blue uniform returned, followed by a man in a tail-coat whose manner of walking suggested boots a size too small.

'I am Arbuthnot,' he said to me, beginning his speech without offering his hand in welcome. 'Equerry to His Excellency the Governor. You say you are King?'

'Yes, sir. John King.'

'King from the exploration party?'

'The same, sir.'

I fancied that his lips curled somewhat as he asked, 'Can you prove this?'

I produced from my vest pocket the gold watch from the Royal Geographical Society of London. Arbuthnot's eyes bounced from the writing on the watch to me and back again.

'This is irregular,' he said. 'Quite unexpected. And something of a coincidence, too. You are aware that Mr Howitt was here just recently?'

'I heard something of it.'

'But that's not your business here? Neither Mr Howitt nor his, er, grim consignment?'

'No, sir. Just to see Mr Stuart.'

Although he had handed the watch back to me, he made no move to invite me further than the gatehouse. I wondered if the Governor himself were watching from behind one of the many broad windows of his residence. 'What's your business with Mr Stuart?'

'I, I have a message for him that the late Mr Burke asked me to deliver personally.' A lie. But a most plausible one.

It had the desired effect. 'Very well, then,' said Arbuthnot briskly. 'You will find Mr Stuart at the Queen's Hotel. Around the corner there and no more than two blocks along. I will give you a card to ease your entry.'

The card was very stiff, with a crest on top and the name Hubert Arbuthnot spelled out in raised letters. 'You appreciate that Mr Stuart's condition is poor?'

'That is to be expected.'

'Hmm. To a degree, yes.' He looked at his own watch. 'Nearly three. I suggest you go there directly, or else you may find Stuart, ah, unable to receive you.'

I located the hotel without difficulty, and Arbuthnot's card smoothed the way with the room clerk. Indeed, he seemed to be more impressed by the card than by my name. Perhaps it was the crest. I waited in the hotel foyer until the clerk returned, trying to hide what seemed a wry smile. He told me that Mr Stuart could be found in room seventeen. Up the stairs and along the corridor. The door would not be locked.

So it proved. I knocked twice then pushed it open, my boots creaking on loose floorboards.

I couldn't see him at first. He was seated in front of the window, its drapes all but closed, and my eyes needed time to adapt to the dim light. I also had to accustom myself to the smell, which near smothered me as soon as I entered. It was a room that had not known fresh air for several days. The smell of whisky and a chamber-pot in need of emptying.

'Arbuthnot? That ye? Ye brought me more from the Governor's cellar?' A voice rough as Fife sand.

'Mr Stuart?' I ventured. 'I am King. John King.' My eyes discerned white hair. A white beard hanging limp and wild, like a bleached creeper on a massive tree trunk.

'Ye're not Arbuthnot? Daft fool said ye were Arbuthnot, from the Governor's place.'

'No, sir. He directed me here. I am King.'

'King? We'd all like t'be King, but I doubt Her Majesty would have us!' Then a more mournful tone. 'So ye've not brought me anything?'

'No, sir. Just news of the Victorian expedition. I was a member, you see.'

He raised himself up a little at that. I could see now that he was in an armchair by the window, more lying on it than sitting.

His legs were propped on a stool before him. What I had taken to be a long coat was clearly a dressing-gown. Worn over a set of full-length underwear which looked none too clean.

'King, ye say?' He had turned towards me.

'Yes. The survivor.'

A pause. As if he were struggling to remember something. 'Aye. King. I heard summat about ye. Come closer, so I can try to make ye out.'

I crossed the room to stand by his chair. His head seemed to follow the sounds, but even when I was near to him his face was not directed at mine. His eyes were looking somewhere else.

Jesus. His eyes. One was near shut, the other a milky pink. Stuart was almost blind.

The whiteness of all his hair emphasised the colour of his skin. Weathered and burned the same as mine had been when I looked in a glass for the first time after my recovery. And on his lips and neck the same scars of scurvy. When he spoke I smelled whisky. Also something stale and rotten.

'There ye are. I can just make ye out. Damn these eyes. Doctor said they would recover if I stayed out of strong light for a time, but I'm beginning to think he spoke nonsense. Give us yer hand, laddie.'

He extended his. It was like a claw, the nails yellow and broken. I had to place mine in his, as he was groping uncertainly. His skin was dry, his grip strong, like he was clinging onto something.

'What are ye doing here?'

'I wanted to see you, sir.'

He grimaced. Or perhaps it was a smile. A split in his beard. 'See me? Aye, of course. The hero of discovery. Pride of South Australia. Conqueror of the continent. That's what the blatherskites are saying. Now look at me. A fine kind of hero! Y'ken I barely rode or walked any of the way back? I couldn't.'

'I know you rode a train into Adelaide from Kapunda.'

'That was but the end of it. When I left the coast I was at death's door. I dared not tell any of my party how ill I was except for Thring, my scout, for fear it should dishearten them. I was too weak to ride, King. Too weak. I was carried most of the way here lying in a stretcher tied between a pair of horses. Felt every bump every step of the way.'

'At the coast – did you see the water yourself?'

He leaned forward in his chair. 'See it? I *bathed* in it, laddie. Dipped my feet and washed my face and hands in the sea, as I'd promised the late Governor MacDonnell I would do if I reached it.'

Bathing in the ocean. What I'd dreamed of doing and never did.

Those strange and sightless eyes turned towards me. 'Yer man Burke. Did *he* reach the water himself?'

'He said he did, sir. Said it would be well to say he had reached it, though he could not obtain a view of the open ocean.'

The old Scot snorted. 'Not even a view of it! Aye, I'd thought as much.'

'But I cannot say for sure, you see. I waited behind at the Gulf. With Charley Gray. While Mr Burke and his surveyor went on ahead. They said it was slow going.'

'True enough. Those vines and mangroves and tree roots are buggers to cross. When I could see we were getting close, I said naught at all. Wanted to surprise them. So when Thring finally got through the forest and saw the mud washed up with the waters of the Gulf, he had to shout, "The sea! The sea!" several times before the other men understood we'd arrived at our destination.' Stuart had grown quite animated. 'That wash was the most welcome I ever had. We were covered in scratches and stings and dreadful stuff. Leeches'n'all.'

'Mr Burke imagined you doing this. He feared you getting to

the ocean ahead of him.' I told him about Mr Burke's conversation with me; his vision of Stuart celebrating his arrival at the ocean.

And now John McDouall Stuart, the wreck of him, was laughing. A throaty cackle suggesting derision more than mirth, before it became a fit of coughing. When he regained his breath he said, 'That's how he pictured it? A muckle flag? There wasn't one. Nor any champagne, though by Christ I'd have welcomed it. I can tell ye the beach wasn't white either. Grey, it was. Grey sandy mud. He got one thing right, though – I probably would have laughed at him.'

When I said nothing in reply his tone softened. 'Och, I'm too harsh. I shouldn't speak ill of the dead. Burke was a brave man. Brave but headstrong, from what I've heard tell of him.'

'You pushed him on, sir,' I told him.

'I never met the man!'

'But it was like you were always in his thoughts. Urging him forward.'

Stuart turned his face towards the window, as if seeking the light. 'He believed all that talk about a damn fool race, then? Ye can't rush these things, King. Ye've seen the horrors of the interior. Ye know what it's like. Ye have to be slow and steady and careful. Slow and steady. Or ye'll never beat it.'

'But didn't you have an expedition out at the same time as our own?'

'Aye. That was my second attempt at it, but we turned back in July. Staggered back into Adelaide late in September last year.'

September. The month Howitt's party had found me.

'I got a gold medal from the Governor for that,' Stuart continued. 'A gold medal and no end of speeches, though I hadn't even made it across the continent. We set out again several months later, by which time I'd heard news of yer lot. Burke was said to have reached the Gulf, but still I set out. Why? Because I'd sworn to myself that I would.'

His hand groped across the top of the nearby table until he found a half-full whisky glass. He closed his eyes as he sucked at it greedily. Then, as if remembering he was not alone, he asked, 'Ye want some yerself?'

'No, I have no head for it.'

'No head? I've a head and a heart and a stomach for it. Still, I'll not press it on ye. Little enough left as it is. How old are ye, King?'

'Just past twenty-four.'

'Twenty-four! Can barely recall it. Think I turned twenty-four the year I came to South Australia from Edinburgh. Was twenty-eight when I first went exploring with Sturt, looking for the inland sea. Near killed us but I learned a lot, not least about the blacks and surviving in a land without water.' He drained the last of his glass. 'Nothing beats experience. Burke, from what I know, had never been on such an expedition before, let alone as leader. Nor any of yer main men, am I right?'

He took my silence as assent.

'Asking for disaster! Understand this, King. This last journey of mine was my third crack at crossing the continent. My third! The same year yer lot set out, with all yer wagons and stinking camels, I made it to the centre. Central Mount Sturt, I called it, and planted a flag there as a sign to the blacks that the dawn of liberty, civilisation and Christianity was about to break on them.'

'*Are* you a Christian, sir?'

He frowned. 'Why do ye ask? I just said I planted a flag for God and civilisation.'

'Because . . . because I think I lost my faith there. When I was lost. Abandoned. I called out to my God but saw no signs of Him.'

'Aye, He can be awful hard to find. I tell ye this: I cursed Him in the agony of my return. Yet the Governor has told me to my face that all I achieved is attributable to Divine Providence. And perhaps he's right.'

'What *did* we achieve, sir, any of us?'

'I've been wondering myself, laddie. Ye would think it must add up to something. All who come after understand more than those who ventured first. Burke has been both praised and derided, but know this: he did *not* fail. He made trails others will follow.'

'For what, though?'

There was a long silence before he spoke again. His legs were bothering him. He rubbed and stretched them constantly.

'I've heard talk of an overland telegraph, clear across the country. *I* never expect to see it. But I'd like to think that we toiled, and that good men died, for something more than telegrams.'

He turned his face to me, his better eye seeming to scan my face. 'Is this all ye wanted of me – a lot of talk?'

'It must appear strange. But it has seemed to me that the fates of Mr Burke and yourself were somehow entwined. You were inland before our expedition. Then you set off again after us, causing Mr Burke to hasten. Perhaps more than he should. You sought the sea too. And now you've come back just as Howitt is returning with the remains of Mr Burke and his partner.'

'A pathetic business, that. I promise ye the ceremonies will be designed to divert attention from where it ought to be . . . I'm in for plenty of that myself. Dinners. Presentations. A parade, I'm told, in honour of the so-called Hero of Exploration. Who is now half pickled, can't walk and can barely see. Still, a man won't go thirsty, so I'll go along with it all.'

He clutched my arm. 'Tell me. They looking after ye?'

'My health, you mean?'

'Money, laddie. Money. They paid ye?'

'I've a pension. And two watches.'

'Watches! I'd rather the money. I know how things go, I was a forgotten man after the Sturt expedition. Near twelve years before the next journey. I've heard the talk. They say the hero could drink a well dry. That toady Arbuthnot let slip they're proposing a reward of two thousand pounds. Two thousand! But here's the rub – it's to be paid into an account from which I'll be allowed just three pounds a week. There's gratitude, lad. I can near kill myself leading men across the country and bringing 'em all back alive – *all* of them, mind – but I'm not to be trusted with money. A fine thanks indeed.'

He closed his eyes, like the dim light was hurting them. His chin sank onto his chest, the white beard spreading. He looked ancient, though I believe he was then only seven years older than Mr Burke had been at the end.

I thought he had nodded off, when he said, 'Is it true what they say about yer man, King? That he did it for the love of a lady?'

What could I say?

'Part true. Though not, I venture, the lady they think.'

'Good enough. We all need a reason. A powerful yen for fame and fortune, King, that was mine. Not least the fortune. Perhaps love is a nobler thing.'

And that was it. He looked quite spent now, though whether this was due to fatigue or the drink I could not say. He said nothing more when I shook his hand and left him, propped in his chair by the window. I wondered whether this was what Mr Burke would have become had he survived. Had he come back alive rather than a bag of bones wrapped in a Union Jack.

I was about to close the door to his room when I heard his voice, little more than a croak. 'Here,' he said. 'Have it.'

He was holding a small glass jar, such as apothecaries use. In it, I saw when I approached him, was a quantity of something dark. 'Sand from the Gulf,' he explained. 'May as well have it, seeing as ye never saw it yerself.'

The sand was grey and seemed like ordinary stuff to strive for. Like mud. But I took it from him – the old man whose body was so wasted, whose hair was so white.

Twenty-eight

The remains of Mr Burke and W were brought back to Melbourne on the steamship *Havilah*, escorted by Howitt. They arrived in Melbourne the day after I returned from Adelaide. The vessel docked before dawn on the last Sunday of 1862. From Port Melbourne, all that remained of the leaders of the Victorian Exploring Expedition was taken in darkness through silent city streets to the hall of the Royal Society in La Trobe Street. There they rested for three days until a coffining ceremony set down for Wednesday evening at eight o'clock. Macadam sent word that I would be welcome to attend if I so desired. I replied that I would wait to pay my respects when all appropriate preparations had been made. He said he understood and hoped my health was improving.

I told Macadam I felt fragile. So, it seems, was he. The newspapers reported that Macadam was very late for the coffining ritual. Some suggested the secretary was overcome when confronted by the tragic finale of the grand enterprise organised by his Society. Others claimed that 'overcome' was just a polite way of saying he was drunk. Macadam himself denied this, but he couldn't deny that by the time he arrived a locksmith had been summoned to open the special case in which Howitt's burden was carried by sea.

All I know of the ceremony is what Macadam told me later. But I recall that the day itself was furnace-hot, made even worse by a fierce northerly wind that blew from an early hour in the morning. The wind brought with it dark clouds of dust, thick as smoke, as if fires were blazing beyond the bounds of the city. Horses panted pitifully in their harnesses. Birds fell from the air to lie on the ground, beaks open, craving drops of water. Late in the evening, when thermometers still registered a temperature of over one hundred degrees, mothers laid their children down in dampened sheets to keep them cool, and the dignitaries assembled in the Royal Society's hall to lay out the bones of the deceased explorers.

Medical men were there. And Howitt, who stated that the remains were as he'd retrieved them from the Cooper. He thought wild dogs, not natives, were to blame for those bones that were missing. Also present was a recent arrival in Melbourne, an old woman in black. Mrs Ellen Dougherty, Mr Burke's former Irish nurse, had come to put him to rest one last time.

The case was opened. The flags unfolded. Twin black cloth packages were loosened and the bones arranged by the medical men. W's skull was gone, so too Mr Burke's hands and feet. The newspapers were discreet on this, but Macadam told me it was so and I recalled what I had seen when I led Howitt to the place where W died.

The bones were laid on sheets, Mrs Dougherty attending dry-eyed to her task, and placed in metal canisters with glass in the tops of them. It was near midnight when the Lord Mayor declared the ceremony concluded and announced that the official lying-in-state would commence the following Monday. Not Friday, as had initially been reported.

The delay was for me, so that I could attend before members of the public were allowed in. It was Macadam who had suggested this.

'Best you come quietly,' he told me. 'You would almost certainly be recognised if you waited in line, and your presence could be an unwelcome distraction.'

So we arrived like secret visitors. Myself and Nora, Bickford and Hill. They came because they thought I might need their support. Mary said she found the notion ghoulish and chose to stay behind. Macadam, who didn't look well, let us into the Society's building and then retired, saying he had preparations to attend to. Crowds of people were expected to queue on the Monday, when the hall would be open from ten in the morning until ten at night, and then for a fortnight after that until the day of the state funeral, for which arrangements were almost complete.

I remember a dusty dry smell: the smell of an empty hessian bag. The windows of the hall had all been covered with black curtains trimmed with white. The only light came from two gasiliers, turned low, and some candles. But I could make out a huge dais with steps to it, covered in black cloth with crimson on the sides. On top of this was a bier, four or more feet high, supporting a pair of coffins. Resting inside were the canisters, each the size and shape of a man, containing the remains. The glass enabled limited viewing of the contents. Above all this was an elaborate canopy made of black cloth trimmed with white satin and silver and adorned with feathers and ferns at each corner.

The coffins lay side by side, though the men had died separately. Above the coffin of my leader was a crest for the Burkes of Galway and an inscription in Latin which Bickford translated: 'One king; one faith; one law.'

One King, I thought, and no Queen.

At the far end of the room was a platform mounted with black plumes which was to carry the coffins during the funeral. Placed on this were the coffin lids, bearing the men's names and their ages: forty and twenty-seven. They had each been given the same date of death: June 28th, 1861. I wondered how they could have reckoned this. I could not recall the date of Mr Burke's death, and nobody had any way of knowing when W breathed his last.

A Union Jack hung above the hall's entrance. A plaque recorded the names of all members of the Exploration Committee, headed by Sir William Stawell. Around the room were panels inscribed with place names from the expedition: Cooper's Creek, Swan Hill, Balranald, Torowoto, Carpentaria. More panels carried the names of expedition members: Burke, Wills, King, Gray — Charley had not been completely forgotten. Then other names. Howitt, Walker, McKinlay, Norman, Landsborough.

Howitt I knew, of course, but who were the rest?

'Other explorers,' Bickford explained. 'Several relief parties were sent out. Captain Norman took the steamship *Victoria* north to the Gulf country.'

'And Ambrose Kyte — who is he?'

'Mr Kyte was one of the original sponsors of the expedition,' said Hill. 'Donated a thousand pounds, I believe. And as a trader in provisions he doubtless did well for himself supplying necessities.'

Now here was his name on a wall along with men who had died for much less. Charley Gray was on an assistant's salary similar to mine: one hundred and twenty pounds. But there was no coffin for Charley.

I saw it written later that I became distressed on viewing the remains of my leaders and had to be led out. But that's not how it was: I felt empty, nothing more. And in that dimly lit hall, decorated like a rich widow's fancy hat, I thought of Charley's words to me on our way back from the Gulf: *I've earned any reward that comes with every sorry step I've taken and all of them yet to come.*

What reward had he got? His name on a wall. It made no sense. None of it.

Outside, we stood blinking in the sunshine. Nora seemed

especially ill at ease and did not explain why until later, when we had returned home and she had brought me some tea.

She felt in her apron pocket and held out her hand. 'See this, John. I found it by the curtain, at the base of the platform. I thought it were one of my tunic buttons come loose and fallen. But look.'

A single human tooth.

'An unfortunate occurrence,' Macadam said when I gave it to him the next time I saw him. 'And I cannot say whose it is, to be blunt. Some came loose in the laying out, you see. And a few more were knocked free. There were committee men wanted some as keepsakes. Best we say no more about it.'

He placed the tooth in a drawer of his desk.

The funeral. Like nothing ever seen in Melbourne. The weather was still stifling, especially so in mourning black. At least the wind and dust had died, but in their place was a dread stillness. Not even a gasp of breeze for relief.

There were people everywhere, packing the blocks near the Royal Society's building. Reverend Draper sent word through Metherdew that Nora and Mary should not seek to attend. He had observed the preparations, the setting up of barricades and the hanging of black bunting in windows.

'It will be no place for ladies,' he warned. 'It will be a mix of circus and parade, all the way through the city to the cemetery in Parkville. If any swoon in the heat, there will be precious little opportunity to seek aid.'

As a senior member of his Church, Draper himself was obliged to attend. He was given instructions concerning his designated place in the procession, along with the consuls of foreign countries, representatives of the Legislative Assembly and the

Corporation of Melbourne, the Lord Mayor, members of the Melbourne University and the Ancient Order of Rechabites, who had been told they would follow the Grand United Order of Odd Fellows. Mrs Dougherty, the old nurse, would ride upon a mourning coach. I was to walk behind the funeral carriage, drawn by six black horses, as a pallbearer for Mr Burke, along with Sir William Stawell and other men to whom I was introduced. One of them was Kyte, the sponsor. He carried a cane tipped with gold. Howitt was in W's party. I saw him checking his watch near the start, as if fractious about the delay. I also recall von Mueller looking hot and damp even before the long march began.

The lids to the coffins had been screwed down. The gasiliers around the bier in the hall were extinguished. And then, a little after one o'clock, the procession began. A gun was fired at a volunteer battery in Rathdowne Street. Slowly, slowly, the carriage wheels began turning. Leading the sombre convoy were representatives from Mr Burke's former posting: the band of the Castlemaine Rifle Volunteer Regiment, playing 'The Dead March in Saul'.

Spectators crowded every patch of pavement. They clung to lamp-posts, clustered on the roofs and balconies of buildings. Police tried to maintain order but failed absolutely near Elizabeth Street, where a crowd attached to the scaffolding of the new Post Office building stopped all progress until the people were cleared back.

I was hot and craved water. All the planning had neglected what would have been most welcome: boys with water-barrels and ladles along the route. Once again I was marching through a seemingly endless dry land. Looking at the ground in front of me and at the back of a carriage draped in black. Time had slowed to a crawl. I checked my watch: it had taken an hour to progress the few blocks from our starting place.

As the carriage turned the corner into Elizabeth Street, to

begin the climb up the hill towards the cemetery, Sir William Stawell looked back and uttered an oath at odds with his august position.

'By Christ, will you look at that!'

All the way back, a sea of black hats and pale faces.

I was feeling faint but forced myself to keep walking. Watching the wheels of the carriage turning. Artillery men had assembled near the cemetery: the sound of their guns signalled our arrival at the gates. The clock on the cemetery building showed a quarter before four. Two and a half hours of shuffling and straining forward, sweating under my too-tight black hat.

Apart from those in the official parties, few people were allowed into the cemetery for the burial. This was welcome, as the crush was reduced, but the sun was no less relentless as we stood in the Church of England section on the southern side. Listening to the Dean of St Paul's read from the first epistle to the Corinthians. By the Cooper, Howitt had read from the same chapter for W: 'And the dead shall be raised incorruptible...'

But the leaders of the expedition were gone. Nothing could be plainer. Dead and turning to dust.

When we took the coffin of Mr Burke upon our shoulders to carry it to the grave, I braced myself for the weight. But it was not heavy at all. Were it not for the metal case inside the coffin, one man alone could have borne it without strain, so little of him was left.

Mr Burke was lowered first. Then, beside him, the man he called Will. I would have welcomed a quiet moment for reflection, but as the coffins were lowered order broke down again. A surge of spectators pushed through to the graves, causing evident dismay to the Dean. Even this last scene of the expedition was not to be played out as planned.

Police with muskets assembled, not to deal with the crowd,

but to fire volleys over the grave. Once. Twice. Thrice. The sound echoed between the headstones, though there were none yet prepared for the men being honoured. Smoke from the guns hung low over the cemetery.

It had been decided the coffins should be left uncovered by earth so that members of the public unable to gain entry for the burial could come in to see the explorers' final resting place. This was done not only out of respect to the departed: pandemonium would have ensued if, after that last musket volley, everyone had sought to leave at once.

Yet even so there were unsavoury scenes as hot, thirsty, leg-weary people tried to move out of the gates while others pushed in. I saw Sir William Stawell remove his top hat and stride further into the cemetery, as if he knew a side exit. Members of the Castlemaine band unhooked the shoulder straps to their drums and sat on their instruments in a meagre patch of shade by some headstones. Near the cemetery office I saw Macadam and von Mueller — the latter pink-faced, though he'd loosened his tie — studying a sketch of the planned monument for the grave: a massive, rough-hewn block of granite. But all I really wanted to see as I trudged along the perimeter of the university grounds was Metherdew, Bess and the carriage that would take me home.

It was not until late in the evening, I understand, that the last of the spectators were moved on and the graves filled in. At last it could be said that the leaders of the exploring expedition were at rest. The earth had closed over them. Their bones would be disturbed no more.

A public meeting was held at St George's Hall in the city that same night. The Governor was to speak, as well as members of the Exploration Committee. After the protracted ordeal of the funeral,

I was too tired to attend. I was also weary of speeches and tributes, and people referring to men I knew in a way that made them seem like strangers.

William Hill went to the meeting. He had come to believe that the emotional response to the outcome of the expedition said much about the young colony – striving to achieve, he said, yet still finding glory in failure.

'There are religious resonances also,' he claimed. 'White men venturing into the uncharted heart of a continent. Some seeking comfort from the original inhabitants while those who scorn them perish. And much that has happened since exemplifies the stratification of society. The gentlemen get a state funeral; working men are left to lie in the desert.'

The meeting was very lively, Hill told me the following day. Several speakers were shouted down, amongst them George Landells, the worse for drink, who cast slurs against Mr Burke's leadership and courage.

'Look here, John,' Hill said, his clothes still smelling of tobacco smoke from the gathering. He was scanning the long account of proceedings in *The Age*. 'Mr Howitt mentioned you. Here's what he said:

Some rumours have been circulating concerning a statement said to have been made by King. I wish to say that the whole statement written by King at Cooper's Creek is correct in all its circumstances and, I have no doubt, is a perfectly truthful one.

'He said that?' I asked. 'I could have wished for nothing more.'

On the same day that the funeral took place in Melbourne, tens of thousands also gathered in the streets of Adelaide to pay tribute to John McDouall Stuart and his men. I read later how the South Australian Governor acknowledged the strange workings of

Almighty Providence, which saw one State honouring a leader who had successfully achieved what he undertook while its neighbour simultaneously paid tribute to brave men who had fallen in the attempt.

A laurel wreath was placed on Mr Stuart's brow. A band played 'See The Conquering Hero Comes'. The Governor proposed a toast to the health of 'the Prince of Explorers' and his gallant associates. It was drunk three times in a row.

Then the cheering began.

Twenty-nine

Nora

Mary and William Hill were married late in April 1863, three months after the funeral of the explorers. Mary insisted there should be a decent interval between the marriage and that gloomy public event. Lest John should still be unsettled, she said. But I think the funeral gave him an ending of sorts. The commission of inquiry had done its work and now Mr Burke and Mr Wills were buried. Preparations for the wedding provided a welcome distraction for John after all he had been through.

It were a lovely service. The church in Fitzroy Street decorated with flowers from local gardens, Mr Bickford beaming with pride and keeping to his word that he would not speak longer than half an hour. Mary looked glorious in the dress I made up for her. Full-length, in fine blue cotton to match her eyes. But she wouldn't hear of a crinoline, though the ladies were wearing them in town.

— Get away with you, girl, she said. I doubt I could stand in one of them hoops! And sure I couldn't sit.

I made do with a bustle in a different shade of blue. Mary fair glowed, everyone said so. And has there ever been such an audience for a wedding? Because of his work at the asylum, Mr Hill wanted some of the residents to attend. He said it would do them a world of good to participate in a happy occasion. Mr Bickford were concerned at first, then gave his blessing when the orderlies Rupert and Henry said they'd attend and supervise.

— As long as we get some cake and brandy, said Rupert.

All of them, Henry and Rupert included, had their hair brushed and wore clothes I'd never seen before. They sat near the back, Mr Tregellas and Simon Winslip, Michael Hazeltine and old Martin Foley, with the orderlies at the end of the aisle keeping an eye on them. But they were no trouble, and Mr Tregellas proved himself to be an enthusiastic singer of the hymns.

When I think back on it, considering everything that came after, this seems like the happiest of days. We were together, all who were closest to me. Mary and Mr Hill, eyes bright with their love and hope. Mr Bickford amongst friends in his church. And John standing beside Mr Hill in front of people who hadn't come to point or stare or try to ask him questions. He looked frail and small beside most of the other men, but across his waistcoat were the chain for the watch from the Geographic Society. And at the little ceremony afterwards, in the forecourt of the church, he made a little speech. I hadn't expected that at all.

John said he wished his friends joy. He spoke of the curious string of events that had brought his cousin Mary and himself together, first in Ireland, now once again in Melbourne. Then he turned to Mr Hill and said he were honoured to stand beside him. Said he wanted to thank him for his friendship and support of the previous sixteen months.

— I have known only a few men who are sure what they want to achieve in life, John concluded. Men with the strength of spirit to inspire others to follow them. Men so sure of their own vision that they care not when doubters speak out against them. One of these men is not long gone, but I am proud to be with another, William Hill, here today.

Mr Hill embraced him, his strength of feeling taking John by surprise.

After the ceremonies, we had one last surprise for Mary and Mr Hill. Mr Metherdew were waiting outside the church with Bess and his carriage. He would take them to the seaside village of Sorrento for a brief honeymoon. It could only be for a few days, Mr Hill being busier than ever with his work at the asylum and Pentridge. He had also undertaken to act as editor of the church's own paper, *The Wesleyan Chronicle*.

Mr Hill himself suggested that John assist him with the editing of the *Chronicle*. John were always quite handy with words and we had all been casting about for work he could do. Because of the government pension and his modest needs, money were not a great concern to him, but we wanted to see him occupied. Mr Bickford had thought he might wish to assist with some teaching in St Kilda. John weren't keen, however. Such teaching as he'd done with the regimental school were years before, he said. I think the real reason were that he couldn't abide being the centre of attention, even in a classroom of children.

We had another concern – his health. Though much stronger than when I first saw him in the Governor's residence, John still tired easily. He ate well, yet always had a scrawny look to him. The scurvy sores on his skin had healed, leaving only faint scars, yet he were prone to bouts of coughing and his long silences. He'd sink into places where it were hard to find him.

— It's understandable, Mr Bickford said when I raised this with him. Our Lord was a changed man after his forty days and nights in the wilderness. Your brother was lost in the desert for twice that period. Only he knows what he endured. All we can do is offer him care and love.

We all tried to do that. But Mr Hill fared best with him, even better than Mary, who were happy setting up their home in East

Melbourne. Mr Hill sought to involve John in his work, not just with the *Chronicle*, but also at the asylum and even the prison, where I were forbidden to go. After seeing the way John talked easily with Michael Hazeltine and Martin Foley at his wedding, Mr Hill suggested he join us on one of our visits to the asylum.

It were a fine July day the first time we went. John seemed content to do as I did. He moved amongst the residents, chatting with those in need of company, while Mr Hill attended to some business. When I asked John how he were managing, he said the conversation were better than at most receptions he'd attended. Rupert and Henry invited John to join them at one of their card games. He were going to play but Mr Hill interrupted, saying the game would have to wait for another visit.

— I'd like to take you on a walk, he told us. There's something I want you both to see.

He led us outside the asylum, along the splendid bluestone wall of the Cremorne Gardens, then down a path towards the Yarra River. But he didn't turn like I expected towards the jetty, where steamers tied up at weekends. Instead he walked in the opposite direction, around a rocky promontory. The track grew less distinct. When I lost my footing John took my hand.

The thing I noticed first were the smell. A rotten, sour human stink. And something burning. There before us, set back a little distance from the river bank, were piles of rubbish propped against trees. A broken carriage wheel covered in canvas, wooden packing cases with stones on the top to weigh them down, lengths of timber tangled together as if by a flood. The only patches of colour were pieces of cloth, old shirts and aprons by the look of them, in amongst all this refuse.

— It's a tip, I said.

— A tip of humanity, Mr Hill replied.

Then I realised that what we were viewing were crude hovels, shelters secured together in every way, and every one of those poor structures a home for someone. As we drew closer I saw a pair of legs in filthy trousers protruding from a canvas shanty. And there, by a sputtering fire, a grime-smeared figure with a face that might have belonged equally to a man of twenty or forty.

— People live here? John asked, looking about him.

— All year round, Mr Hill said. This is the other side of our city. Mr De Silva has his mansion in St Kilda, but others must live like this. If I have one goal, it is to ensure some respect for such people.

I were moving towards the fellow by the fire, stepping over a bundle of rags beside a tree. But then the bundle moved and made the noise of a man roused from slumber. Shaking his head like a hound freeing itself of water, this man unfolded himself to a great height. Close to six feet, I guessed, and broad. His hair and beard were both quite grey and had not been washed for some time. But his most alarming feature were his eyes. Each seemed to look in its own direction. With one of them he were now contemplating me.

I shrieked. John moved smartly to my side, standing between me and this extraordinary figure. Who bowed deeply and then spoke.

— A lady! This is an honour. You are welcome.

His voice were rough and rasping, like something dredged from the river. I looked at Mr Hill. To my surprise, he were smiling at this hairy man.

— Hello, William, he said. You're out again?

— Aye, said the fellow, sounding mournful. No work to be done for some considerable time. But they know where to find me.

— Indeed they do, said Mr Hill. Then he turned to us.

— Nora, John, I should like to introduce you to Mr Bamford. William Bamford, late of the British Army and Van Diemen's

Land, more recently finding occasional employment as Her Majesty's Common Executioner.

— Not so common, Mr Bamford grumbled.

— Executioner? John said, examining him with interest.

— Aye, the hangman. That's me. Mine's the last face many a soul has seen before they feel the hemp's rough caress.

— Mr Bamford has been fulfilling his duties for — how long is it now? Mr Hill asked.

— More than five years 'twould be, the man replied, enjoying a new audience. Since 1858. March 1st, 1858. That was me first job. I remember them well. Edward Brown and William Jones, a pair of murderers. Two for one. I was in the Melbourne Gaol meself, serving twelve months for being a rogue and vagabond, as they called it. Heard they needed someone to do the job and offered me services to the Sheriff's office. Seeing I had experience and all from the army.

— And was this true? asked Mr Hill, though he seemed to know the answer.

— True enough. Between the army and Van Diemen's Land I'd seen me share of men dancing the jig in the air. And it worked! I did the job, then got five pounds for me trouble and the remainder of me sentence remitted. Were out six months early thanks to Mr Jones and Mr Brown. Nice employment indeed. I am grateful.

Mr Hill turned to us.

— And ever since, when there's work to be done, Mr Bamford is called in. If he's not already in the Melbourne Gaol or Pentridge, where I first made his acquaintance, they'll pick him up on a vagrancy charge or some such, and he'll attend to his business. How many customers now, William?

— A handful. He shrugged. Lost count after them first pair. But I'll tell you this — not a single complaint! He cackled, revealing a mouth with many teeth gone.

John seemed much less disturbed than me by this man.

— You say you were in the army? he asked him.

— That I was. The 49th Regiment in Ireland.

— And how long were you a soldier?

The hangman laughed again. A ghastly sound.

— How long? Not long enough! I deserted. For which crime I were transported to Van Diemen's Land for seven years, a passenger on the *British Sovereign* in 1841. An involuntary passenger of said Sovereign like all t'other poor sods. He fixed his left eye on Mr Hill. You didn't bring any baccy with you, I suppose?

— No, Mr Hill replied, but I've better than that. Some food.

He opened a canvas bag from the asylum he'd hefted on his shoulder, producing some bread as well as apples, potatoes and packets of tea and sugar. All at once he were surrounded by folk who came from their shelters, taking what they could but being careful not to snatch from Mr Hill. Most retreated on gaining their food but Bamford the hangman stayed close by, paying careful attention to all that took place. I found it hard to look away from him. Crumbs of bread stuck in the grey hairs of his beard. A grumbling sound in the back of his throat.

Like he knew I were looking, he turned to me, though one eye were on the river.

— Fear not, me lovely, he said. I've never had a woman customer yet. Chinamen, yes. And an American nigra who came here for gold and found only a noose. But never a woman. All things in time, I suppose.

He studied me up and down like he were judging my weight to assess the length of the drop. The day were not cold, yet still I shivered.

— Stay civil, William, Mr Hill said. Or I'll tell the Pentridge authorities you've gone on the swag up to New South Wales. And then they'll have to get some other wretch to do their dirty work.

At once Mr Bamford's expression changed from sly to submissive.

— You wouldn't be doing that, would you?

— Not if you behave yourself.

Again the hangman cackled. Then he tipped his head in farewell and moved away, showing a strange, uneven gait.

It being close to two o'clock, we had to get back to the asylum. Mr Hill led the way. John were behind me, lost in his own thoughts.

— How horrible that people should have to live like that, I said when the big wall were again in sight.

— Of course, Mr Hill replied. But the greater horror is that many, including some in government, refuse to believe such places exist in their city. Some of these people have no choice. To others, like our friend Bamford, it is almost a preference. You could offer him decent accommodation and he'd still opt for a shanty here by the water.

— But don't you think him a barbarous man?

— The barbarity is not in him so much as in those who sanction the punishment, Nora. Hanging's an art, I'm told. A botched job is a dreadful thing. Which is why they come looking for him. He knows his business.

— If he was in the army he would know all about barbarity, said John, who seemed to be puffing from the effort of coming up the hill. I saw things in the army far worse than hanging. Far worse.

I were surprised by his comment. He seldom talked about his past. But it were even more startling when he continued as we approached the gates of the asylum.

— You brought something back to me, William, when you dispensed the food. It reminded me of Howitt handing out trinkets to the natives.

John paused for breath. There were sweat on his forehead and his manner were agitated.

— And those raggle-taggle huts near the water. The smell of them, the smoke from sputtering fires. Had there been some dogs and naked children playing in the sand, I might almost have been back in the blacks' camp on the Cooper. I —

He would have said more, but I brought him to a halt when I clutched at his arm. For I'd turned and seen something both strange and frightening. There were a lone figure on the river bank below. Mr Hill had now noticed it too.

— Bamford! he said. That can only be his shape and shuffling walk. The beggar must know we can see him from up here. But what the blazes is he up to?

Bamford, if indeed it were him, were now doing it again. What I thought I'd seen just shortly before when I looked back. A weird kind of movement. Standing with the river behind him, his whole body seemed to be shaking, his arms and legs flailing about and jerking horribly. And his head were on the strangest angle.

— Heavens! I exclaimed. Is the poor man ill, suffering a fit of some sort?

— No, said John, calmer now. I imagine that's his macabre version of the dead man's dance.

— Of course, said Mr Hill. I've heard tell of that. The last involuntary motions of the limbs of a hanged man.

Thirty

Nora says I came into the world like a pink-skinned rat, too timorous to make much of a squeal. That was December 5th, 1838. But since I returned we have marked September 15th as my birthday – the day of my rescue by Howitt and his men.

Anniversaries matter. Dates should mean something. So I wonder who was responsible for choosing April 21st, 1865 for the unveiling of the official statue to the expedition. Was I the only one who appreciated that this was four years to the day since we had returned from the Gulf to find the depot deserted? Because nobody mentioned it, I must assume it was a coincidence.

It puzzled me it should take that long to put up a statue. But everything had happened so slowly. Mr Burke and W had their funeral a year and a half after they died, and then the block of granite for the monument on their grave lay untouched in the cemetery for many months more after that.

'It's all about funds,' Macadam told me. He'd been elected Vice-President of the Royal Society shortly after the funeral. 'The bills still keep coming. This statue, you know, will cost over four thousand pounds! And the government won't foot all of it. If we had our time over, I swear the Society would never have given the commission to this pernickety fellow Charles Summers. None of us understood that when he talked of bronze figures he would need a blessed workshop built here in Melbourne just to do the job. Over two years it's taken him. To speak plainly, I wouldn't have cared had he made the thing out of sandstone.'

The expedition and its aftermath had aged Macadam. There were now streaks of silver in his red hair and his fingers shook. He told me that Summers, an Englishman who'd won a design competition for the statue, planned a pair of huge figures of the leaders. I said I'd be prepared to meet him to help with his sketches, but the sculptor wasn't interested.

'Summers says his intention is to create representative figures rather than likenesses,' Macadam said, scratching at his beard. 'Look, here's his note to the Society: "My aim is a tableau evoking the timeless spirit of heroic endeavour." Whatever the hell that means, King.'

After such a long wait, I was intrigued to see what Summers had produced when his statue was shown for the first time. Another ceremony. A sunny afternoon with a breeze rippling the corners of the sheet covering the statue – a mighty thing, higher than a house – within the intersection of Collins and Russell streets. Seats had been set up for ladies in the yard of the adjacent Scots Church.

'What are you smirking at?' Mary asked as we found our positions on the official platform, close by the statue.

'The church! Mr Burke was never fond of Scotsmen. One in particular. And now his likeness is to stand within spitting distance of the Scots' own church.'

'Behave yourself,' Mary chided me. She seemed determined to enjoy the occasion, saying she seldom got out to fancy dos. And she'd promised Nora, who was minding Mary's baby Albert, born just six months earlier, that she'd tell her what was said at the ceremony and who was there.

Not Macadam. After all his troubles with the statue project, the Society's vice-president was missing for its conclusion. He'd been to New Zealand, giving specialist evidence as a chemist at the trial of a fellow charged with poisoning his wife, and fractured his ribs in rough weather during the return voyage. This developed into a problem with his lungs. Von Mueller said the outlook was grave. And Macadam wasn't yet forty.

The Governor was gone, too. Sir Henry Barkly, who'd met me on my return and then officiated at the state funeral, had left the colony.

'Nora says he's moved on to Mauritius,' Mary whispered to me. 'Perhaps he won't have explorers to fret about there.'

She said this just as the new Governor's carriage arrived, bearing Sir Charles Darling, Lady Darling and even a little Miss Darling, dressed up in pink bows like a porcelain doll. They came shortly before four in the afternoon, greeted by a salute fired by members of the Williamstown Naval Brigade and a Castlemaine infantry guard. I scanned the crowd – not as big as for the funeral, yet still filling the block – thinking of all those people I could not see.

No Howitt. I hadn't heard of him in several years. Nor Landells, who was rumoured to have taken to the bottle and returned to India. Brahe wasn't there either. He'd gone bush again, preferring it to the city, where he'd been made to answer too many questions about leaving the depot on the Cooper. Some blamed him for what had happened afterwards.

It seemed that ripples from the expedition were still spreading on that April afternoon four years after the three of us had returned from the Gulf. But there were only two of us represented on the statue, unveiled finally after too many speeches.

Governor Darling, whose hand when it shook mine was soft and damp, had described me as 'the latest civilised companion of the dead explorers'. But not civilised enough, apparently, to feature in bronze. Indeed, when the sheet was removed with a flourish and Charles Summers bowed to the applause that swept around the intersection, his dark hair flopping down over his eyes, I had difficulty recognising either of the figures depicted. The names on the base were clear enough, Robert O'Hara Burke and William John Wills, but it was not them on the statue. I didn't know who they were. It was as if Summers had asked a pair of bearded actors to assume this pose of heroic endeavour: one sitting, pen in hand, the other standing. The only thing he'd got right was having Mr Burke – I assumed it had to be him – gazing into the distance.

The Governor stood next to the monument, the size of which made him look very small, when he spoke. 'I rejoice to say that Mr King is present to hear from my lips the assurance we offer to him that a full share, a *full* share, of the honour we are rendering to his lamented chiefs here today is due to his distinguished fidelity and courage.'

'Quite right!' cried a voice in the crowd.

Mary, looking ahead, elbowed me in the side.

'He may well take for his motto now, and for his epitaph hereafter, these words among the last written by the hand of Burke.' Here the Governor paused, squinting, before reading, '"King has behaved nobly."'

It rang true.

'On yer feet, John-boy,' Mary said.

I stood as the clapping began. And knew not what else to say but 'Three cheers for the Governor!'

The crowd responded. Then came a call: 'Three cheers for King!'

Summers, I noticed, remained silent. He seemed irked. Upstaged by a man not even on his statue.

After the formalities were concluded and the Governor's carriage had departed, Mary and I walked east up the Collins Street hill, hoping to find a vendor selling drinks. For we were hot and once again the organisers of the ceremony had not thought to provide refreshments. Our path took us towards the new Parliament House. Before we even caught a glimpse of the site, where workmen still toiled, Mary took my arm to halt me before a building on our left.

Half a dozen steps led up from the street to a pair of grand wooden doors with glass inserts, through which a clock could be seen in a marbled hall. The entrance was framed by a pair of columns topped by elaborate cast-iron gas lanterns. All along the front was an iron fence; behind the windows, each at least the height of a man, the curtains were closed.

'What *is* this place?' Mary wondered. 'So splendid and yet so secretive. With nothing to say what it is, only the brass number by the door.'

'Number 137 Collins Street. The Melbourne Club, Mary.'

'So *this* is it. Have you ever been inside?'

The air is stale with smoke. Howitt has placed his cigar in an ashtray on the mahogany sideboard, next to his balloon of brandy, which reflects the glow of the chandelier overhead. As smoking is not permitted over the billiard tables, Howitt confines himself to deep puffs between shots. He says the club is especially proud of this new blackwood table, which has the manufacturer's plaque at one end: 'Alcock & Co.; Melbourne'. A notice on the wall near the rack for cues advises that any player damaging the surface will be charged the full cost of repairs. A Mr Edward Bell has been fined a guinea for cutting the cloth. I have no cigar of my own; the smell of Howitt's is more than enough for me. It has made my head feel fuzzy, or perhaps it is the few sips of brandy I have taken. From the coffee-room, a little way down the corridor, I can hear the low buzz of conversation and a clinking of glasses.

I know the game. There was a table in the regimental headquarters in India, though it was always the officers who were given preference. But I have never played on a table as splendid as this. And I am no match for Howitt.

He has removed his jacket in order to play and wears metal clips around his shirtsleeves to keep the fabric off the table. In one of his waistcoat pockets he has tucked a cube of blue chalk. Between shots he applies this to the tip of his cue, which he has trimmed with his knife. And when he lines up a shot he leans so low over the table that his beard is parted by his cue, though this doesn't seem to distract him. He plays quickly, registering a successful cannon or pot with a satisfied grunt. He plays with force, balls thudding into the pockets like cartridges being snapped into the breech of a gun.

The clock over the fireplace shows the time is approaching 8:40, so we have been playing for little more than half an hour. Yet already Howitt's lead appears insurmountable: sixty-seven to eighteen. Billiards is a game of confidence, and every shot Howitt makes inspires him to build new breaks: coasting his cue ball off the red into the far pocket, ricocheting his ball off mine and then into the red for another cannon. The clink of ball on ball seems as pleasing to him as that of gold coins in a purse. Grunt.

As his score mounts, the little skill I have ebbs away like a puddle in the sun. I do not want to shame myself; in this gentlemen's club I have no wish to seem an oaf. Yet it appears my cue is warped or my eye untrue. The angles are wrong. Twice already I have played foul shots, my ball missing its target altogether. Other than emulating Mr Bell and scarring the cloth, there can be no greater embarrassment. But all Howitt has done in response is nod curtly and deduct points from my already dismal score.

Now, at last, I have an opening. Howitt has narrowly missed an ambitious pot, his ball coming to rest over a centre pocket. Even for me it seems an unmissable shot. An easy two points, then perhaps the chance of something more with the red. I can feel Howitt's gaze on me as I line up the balls. But he waits until I am well over the table before speaking.

'A dilemma, I would say, King.'

'Dilemma?'

'That shot. Cheap points but unethical.'

'A legal pot, is it not?'

'Legal, certainly. But there is an understanding among billiard players that potting an opponent's ball is unacceptable.'

'I didn't know. In India...'

'Ah, but here it is different. A question of honour, you see. I have seen gentlemen walk away from the table if such a thing is even contemplated during the game.'

I stand back, leaving the balls as they lie. 'How is it different from any other pot?'

'It takes your opponent's ball out of play, to start with. And it is a question of how things are done. A matter of principle, in essence. An understanding that there are correct ways of doing things. Or,' and his eyes move from me to the table, 'of *not* doing things.'

'So I cannot play the shot?' I feel confused.

'Oh, you can, King. You can. That's the thing – it's your choice. But ask yourself a question. Is a gentleman's honour, his name and reputation for honesty, worth more than a couple of points?'

I can hear the clock over the fireplace. The cue is heavy in my hand. I look again at the three balls on the table, one so close to a pocket, and I hear Howitt addressing me as if from a long way distant.

'Come on then, King. Your shot.'

The balls seem to be shifting slowly of their own accord on the baize.

'Come on then.' And now he is tugging at my arm.

'Come, John.' The touch has grown gentle, the voice quiet.

Mary is holding my sleeve, looking at me, as we face the entrance to the Melbourne Club.

'Come, John. I swear that sometimes you seem miles away.'

Had the statue been unveiled earlier, I might have been more dismayed by its falsity. But by 1865 I could see that the expedition was bigger than anything I understood. Perhaps Summers was right after all. I remembered sweat and smells, camels and the bitterness of dried meat. But Summers perceived something timeless and heroic. The leaders were gone, replaced by symbolic figures on a monument.

Before the year was out Macadam was gone too. He died at sea from his illness while returning to New Zealand. I liked the man; he never sought to dismiss me like some of the others. President Lincoln was also dead, shot down in a theatre the very same month that Summers' statue was unveiled. And kind Daniel Draper, the religious gentleman who had helped Nora, soon became a hero too, though only in death. In January 1866, as he was returning to Melbourne after a year in England, his ship the *London* was lost in a storm in the Bay of Biscay. Survivors told of Reverend Draper comforting those doomed to be drowned beside him, exhorting them to trust Christ the Pilot who would lead them all to the Port of Heaven. Even old Metherdew's composure cracked when he heard this.

Within six months John McDouall Stuart was also dead. Deprived of his pension in full, the white-haired explorer's final journey was to visit a sister in Scotland, and from thence he had gone to London. There the drink got him. The newspapers used a French word, *ramollissement*, to describe the cause of his death.

Doctor Treacey told me this was a polite way of describing a softening of the brain.

Stuart. And Barkly, Macadam, Lincoln and Draper. All departed now. And me still the survivor, though sinking.

November 1867. Memorable for the first visit to Melbourne by a member of the Royal Family: Prince Alfred, second son of Queen Victoria. Such crowds hadn't been seen since Mr Burke's funeral. We all journeyed into town to see the parade for the Prince. It was the first excursion for Mary's new baby, Grace, then just a few months old and dressed in a pinafore of red, white and blue. Mr Hill hoisted his daughter up onto his shoulders so she could see. Young Albert, named by Mary in honour of Alfred's late father, had a flag of his own to wave.

I should remember that day for the excitement and all the people. Instead I recall it as my last outing before Treacey told me I had the consumption. Since then I have been like one of Draper's associates aboard the stricken *London*, waiting for water to lap over me.

Did Treacey tell me direct? He must have done. Though what I recall now are his words to Nora outside my room as I lay clammy and spent after the examination.

'How long the illness has been present I cannot say for sure. You have noticed some coughing, perhaps, and increasing fatigue? Hmm. I thought as much. Doubtless his condition has not been helped by the privations he has endured. Still, I am not without hope that a remedy will yet be discovered. And I would say that with appropriate care John could still be with us for some time yet. Here, take these for him.'

I heard him snap shut his medical case like a man finishing a book.

I tried to maintain that things could continue as before, but I knew Doctor Treacey's diagnosis would force some changes. Nora was adamant she would attend to me full-time in the house we now shared in Octavia Street, no more than ten minutes' walk from Bickford's church. She would cease her visits to the asylum, though she had grown fond of many residents, and her work for the reverend. This worried her. With Mary a new mother in East Melbourne and William Hill busier than ever, she fretted that Bickford might feel abandoned. But the man himself insisted to us that I had to be Nora's primary responsibility.

'Have no worries on my account,' Bickford said, patting her shoulders. 'None! I shall find a new housekeeper. And increasingly it seems that the line between my parish and my private world, such as it is, becomes ever more blurred. Rarely a day passes by when I am not playing host to one of my flock or a visiting churchman.'

We met one such visitor in the first half of 1868. I can reckon the date from what came after. Nora and I walked slowly in the autumn sunshine along Octavia Street, then down the hill to the church. The day was mild; I felt strong enough to take a little exercise, and Nora wished to give the minister some flowers from our garden. The door to the bluestone building was open and we found Bickford seated on a pew inside, deep in conversation with a young man whose hair and beard were a lustrous black. Black as a crow's feathers, Nora said later.

'My dear friends,' said Bickford, rising to his feet in welcome. 'A pleasant surprise indeed, and what a splendid array of blooms! Allow me to introduce my guest, Mr Andrew Scott from Ireland and, more recently, New Zealand.'

The young man stood and shook my hand warmly, his dark eyes sweeping over me. Then he turned to Nora and seemed at first, to her astonishment, to be contemplating kissing the back of her hand. But he contented himself with a bow.

'Honoured to meet you both,' he said. His voice smooth as honey.

'Mr Scott is a lay preacher,' Mr Bickford explained. 'A protégé of Bishop Perry himself. Mr Hill told me about him. Said he'd heard Mr Scott speak in Bacchus Marsh and insists the man has a gift of the tongue.'

'You're too kind,' said Scott, before turning back to us. 'It is well known throughout church circles in Melbourne that there are few finer speakers than Mr Bickford here and William Hill. I have been assured that the late Reverend Draper himself extolled their powers in the pulpit. Whatever eloquence I possess is nothing compared to their own.'

'I was just telling Mr Scott of some of my favourite texts,' said Bickford, well pleased by this praise. 'You cannot top Psalms, I always say. Nor can you underestimate the importance of tone and rhythm. That's the key, tone and rhythm. Now, John – and do sit down, man, please – it seems you have much in common with our guest. An Irish background, some military training, even a stint in the classroom.'

Scott made a dismissive gesture with his hands, which were much larger than mine and very pale. 'I taught only briefly, in New Zealand. Before a period with the Auckland Volunteer Engineers Corps.'

'Quite a mixture. But what took you to New Zealand, Mr Scott?' Nora asked.

'My father was an Anglican clergyman. We sailed out in November 1861 to Auckland, where he took charge of the Christ Church.'

November 1861. The month of my return to Melbourne. I asked the visitor about his plans.

'I have been stationed at the Church of the Holy Trinity in Bacchus Marsh. Bishop Perry has raised the possibility of another posting, perhaps in the Bendigo region, where I hear the gold fever has not yet abated. I have indeed done several things in my time, but am confident I have now found my true calling.'

'You've certainly been a man of many parts,' I said. 'And how old are you now?'

'Soon to turn twenty-six. With much still to achieve, I'm sure.'

I looked at this man, only a few years younger than myself but so much more robust in appearance. And fair crackling with energy and plans.

Nora appeared so distracted by Scott that she had quite forgotten to deliver her flowers, and had to be prompted to hand them over to Bickford. Having done so, and because we had interrupted the two churchmen, we then took our leave. Nora coloured as Scott wished her well.

'Goodbye, Mr Scott,' I said. 'Perhaps sometime I'll have the pleasure of hearing one of your much-admired sermons.'

'Perhaps you may,' he replied. 'There's simply no telling how things will turn out.'

No telling indeed. I had called Andrew Scott a man of many parts. But none of us — neither Nora, myself nor the Reverends Bickford and Hill, who admired his way with words — appreciated just how many sides there were to Scott until slightly over a year later, a few months after the gold nugget called the Welcome Stranger, bigger than any yet found, was dug out of the Dunolly fields, sparking fears of another exodus to the diggings. It was May of 1869. The month of the tragedy.

We had gathered together in our Octavia Street house for Monday lunch. Roast pork, a rare treat. My appetite, which fluctuated with my temperature, was good. I felt able to eat a decent portion and had helped cut some wood for the stove.

Bickford, who liked his food, was already present when we heard the jingle of a bridle signal the arrival of William Hill and Mary and their children. It was Hill who entered first. Barely pausing to greet the rest of us, he tossed a newspaper before the startled minister.

'Have you seen this remarkable account, Bickford?' He thumped the paper with his forefinger, pointing to a headline: BANK ROBBERY AT EGERTON.

'Hmm,' said Bickford. 'A brigand calling himself Captain Moonlite. What a strange spelling. Is there to be no end to these bushrangers? But why are you showing me this, William? Have you developed a new interest in rural crime?'

'Look at it!' said Hill, before impatiently retrieving the newspaper himself and reading aloud:

> *Mr Ludwig Bruun, agent for the London Chartered Bank at Egerton, near Bendigo, told police that when returning to the bank late at night he was approached by a masked man, also wearing a cloak. Mr Bruun was threatened with a pistol and instructed to hand over all the cash being held by the bank. Notes and coins amounting to six hundred and ninety-seven pounds, five shillings and threepence. Mr Bruun was then tied up after signing a note, dictated by the masked man, certifying that he, L.W.J. Bruun, had resisted the taking away of money from the Egerton branch of the London Chartered Bank. Signed: Captain Moonlite.*

'An extraordinary tale indeed,' Bickford said. 'But what's your point, William?'

'The point is that this fellow Bruun told police he recognised the voice of his assailant. A very distinctive voice. Belonging to Andrew Scott, a lay preacher in the parish.'

It seemed it took Nora and Bickford and myself most of a

minute to comprehend what he'd said. Then, as one, we were speaking over each other.

'Andrew Scott, the preacher!'

'The young man with the coal-black hair?'

'Surely not!'

'Apparently there is little doubt,' averred Hill. 'Bruun is sure of it. And Scott himself has disappeared. Vanished – most likely with the bank's money.'

I found it hard to believe this. 'Andrew Scott, Captain Moonlite? I can scarcely credit it. A bank-robber!'

'Violent, too. He threatened to shoot the unfortunate Bruun if he didn't hand over all the money.'

'But he seemed like such a polite and pleasant man,' I insisted.

Mr Hill smiled at me. 'I should take you with me to Pentridge one time, John. There is no shortage of polite and pleasant men there, all of them prisoners. Which is what I suspect our friend Captain Moonlite will be himself before long.'

'I'd like that,' I replied. 'To come to Pentridge with you, I mean. I've been to the asylum, so why not? Besides, it would close the circle for me. Seeing as while I was on the expedition I probably used harnesses and the like that were made there.'

Hill put the paper down and took Grace from Mary, who had her hands full with a fidgety Albert. 'Well then, let's do it,' he said. 'If your health allows, that is. I'm sure I can convince the conscientious Doctor Treacey that no harm can come from a sedate ride across town in the fresh air.'

Balancing little Grace on one shoulder, he consulted his leather-bound pocket diary. 'I am due to go there on Thursday next, May 13th, for my usual ministering. You can be my guest. I'm sure there are many in the gaol who'd like to meet you. I'll come by early, as it's a considerable distance.'

And so it was done.

Would anything have turned out differently if not for Andrew Scott or my interest in prisoners and one last link to the expedition?

I cannot say. Nothing can be changed now.

Thirty-one

When I think of William Hill I see bluestone. The high towers of Pentridge Prison like turrets over the Sydney Road. Bluestone is hard and dark and cold. It hides all that happens within.

The morning was overcast. Dull and grey. He called for me a little after nine. I assured Nora I was fine to go, but she insisted I cover my lap and legs during the journey. I carried extra handkerchiefs, in case of coughing.

Hill wore his full clerical garb, all in black and with his collar on. Noting my surprise, he explained, 'I go to the prison, officially, for religious instruction. Though I find that most of the men are happy just to chat, often about women and children they haven't seen for years. And food! Amazing how much prisoners talk about food.'

'What about God – do they talk much about Him?'

He considered this as our carriage made its way past the Christ Church School in Punt Road. 'They certainly have time to ponder such things, and in my experience prisoners tend to go one way or t'other. Either they reject God completely, in which case they want nothing to do with me, or they think of little else. I had one man, condemned to hang, who refused to meet with his wife the day before his execution. Said he must decline to speak of worldly things as his time was short and he had to keep his attention on the world to come. Nothing I have ever said in a sermon can have prompted such impressive concentration!'

He allowed the horse to choose its own pace, and apart from pointing out occasional landmarks – a glimpse of the asylum soon after we crossed the Richmond bridge, and the Victoria Parade, which led to his home – we journeyed in silence. I always liked this about Hill: he was a renowned speaker but comfortable with silence.

We'd gone as far as Fitzroy, passing by the Edinburgh Gardens, before he asked me, 'What of yourself? You attend services and help our friend Bickford in his church, but I sense a caution there. As though you are trying to keep a distance between yourself and God.'

He was looking at me. Curious. Awaiting an answer. The carriage wheels splashed through a puddle.

'I have tried to believe, but I . . . cannot trust Him any more.'

'Because of the expedition and what happened?'

'Especially the way I was abandoned. I looked for Him, but it felt as if I were in a place where God had never been.'

Looking ahead over the horse's rump, the reins loose in his hands, Hill said, 'But you *were* found. It took time – an eternity, it must have seemed, but it happened. You were saved while others perished. Can you not see God's hand in that?'

'I see man's hand more than God's. Unless you regard Alfred Howitt as an instrument of Divine Providence.'

'I'm not sure he would fancy that role. Let alone his surveyor, Welch, who made a career of being the one who found you. Or so he said.'

'I can't much blame him for that. Charley Gray said you must grab every chance you see to get on. His tragedy was never getting that chance himself. As for me, I ended up believing that although you wait for God, He can forsake you. Sometimes you have to make things happen for yourself.'

'Ah, elementary determinism. I fancy Mr Bickford would enjoy a debate with you on that score. And you might find that our friend Captain Moonlite took the doctrine to extremes when he robbed the Egerton bank. Incidentally, it's probably best you don't mention the Captain to anyone you see here at Pentridge. Lest it give them ideas.'

The gaol. I'd never seen such walls before. Bigger even than those of the asylum. Massive timber doors with iron hinges, and a far smaller door around eye level. It flipped open when we knocked. Someone within appraised us. Then a voice could be heard.

'Right you are, Reverend.'

We were let in. It was cooler than outside. And darker, though there were some narrow windows let into the walls up high. An aroma of damp stone and men shut up too long, like the smell beneath decks of the ship taking soldiers to India. Hill shook hands with the fellow who let us in and then with a warder named Moran, who carried a fan of keys on his thick leather belt. Moran led us down a bleak corridor to a sign: 'A. Division'.

Hill looked at his diary. 'Seems I have two I can see before lunch, which is at noon, I believe. Edward Feeny and then James Ritson. It's probably best you stay here with Mr Moran in the meantime. Prisoners are not always well disposed to surprise visitors, they suspect police meddling. But I'm sure you can meet the governor later and converse with some of the men in the yard or workshop. You may even see where some of the expedition gear was made. Now, if you wouldn't mind, Mr Moran . . .'

The warder used one of his many keys to open a cell door. I heard Mr Hill say, 'Morning, Edward,' and then the door was closed behind him. Moran and I sat on a wooden bench just a little way along the corridor.

'A good man, him,' said Moran. 'He's got courage, no doubt. They're tough nuts, but the Reverend shows no fear. Says he sees some good in them. More than I can manage. Treats 'em all the same, too. Pickpockets, thieves, murderers.'

'Are there many murderers?'

'We have our share. That second fellow he mentioned, Ritson – nasty little weasel. Shot an inspector at the Eastern Market just last year. Lucky not to swing for it, too. Now he's got life ahead of him here.'

'What does Mr Hill do with them?'

'Reads the Bible. Prays with them. Talks. Y'ask me, some of 'em will try on anything for a change in routine, even make out an interest in religion. Though I reckon the Reverend sees through 'em.'

We sat awhile. Moran sucked at his teeth. There was a knock on the door from inside Edward Feeny's cell. Moran opened it, stood close by to prevent the prisoner rushing out along with the minister, then escorted Hill down the corridor in the other direction.

'You hungry, John?' Hill called out. 'We'll take some lunch directly. Nothing fancy, mind. Potatoes and gravy, it tends to be.'

The ritual again. Moran opening the door. Mr Hill entering. I heard neither his greeting nor any reply this time. The door was closed and the warder and I retreated to our bench, thirty yards or so from the cell.

'You're him from the expedition, aren't you – him who was with the blacks?'

I nodded.

'Reverend's mentioned you before. Said he suspects you endured worse than these prisoners can imagine.'

'I couldn't say, really . . .'

I thought a heard a scream. Or a muffled shout. Moran noticed something too, but he just shrugged and said there were always noises in a gaol. Often prisoners shouting in their slumber.

I noticed Moran looking at me. A shameless stare.

'Did yer reckon you were done for?'

But before I could answer there was another noise. No denying it this time, a thumping sound from down the corridor. Ritson's cell.

Moran moved quickly for a man of his size, running to the closed door, fumbling with his keys. I was some way behind him, gagging as I tried to keep up.

Again. Repeated thuds. Ripe melons being thrown against a wall. Moran reached the door, had it open and pushed in all at once.

'Stand back inside!' he yelled.

The door was ajar when I got there. Moran was against the far wall, grappling with a smaller man under a narrow barred window beside a bed that looked to have been wrenched apart.

'Drop it!' he was screaming. 'Drop it, yer filthy villain!'

And on the floor in front of them... I had thought I would never confront such a scene again. So much blood. Spreading like oil over the rough stone floor. Reeking. A figure in black in the midst of it, his head towards the door. The back of his head gone. Turned to a red mess.

William Hill.

I bent down beside him, careless of what I was kneeling upon. His skull weeping. The eyes open. But nothing there, no life in them. Misting over even as I cradled him.

There was a clang near the corner. Something had fallen from Ritson's grasp, a metal hinge of some sort. Hair and gore stuck to it. I could hear Ritson breathing heavily but struggling no more.

'You'll hang fer this fer sure!' Moran yelled. He blew his whistle, a shrill blast that set more feet running.

A pair of black boots in the doorway. A voice: 'Oh, Christ! The minister's been murdered!'

In my arms a figure quite limp. All the life leaked out of him. Was this my fate – to watch good men die?

I believe I was taken to the gaol infirmary. A fit or a faint or coughing – something that had left me prone and close to senseless. My clothes were taken away and never returned. I assume they could not be cleaned. I went home in the rough garb of a prisoner. How did I get there? I do not know. Maybe it was Metherdew. But I recall hearing Moran's voice, as if far distant.

'A bad business . . . I warned him of the risks. But he was never one to listen.'

Something else I recall. A figure on a corner bed in the infirmary. All covered by a sheet. But I couldn't look at it.

And so there was another funeral. The cemetery again. The Wesleyan section, much further in from the entrance. And no crowds this time. No bands or members of parliament or military guards or mayors. Just a small group of us on a dark afternoon. Spitting rain. A chill wind tossing back the veil that Mary wore to try to hide her grief. Nora close beside her supporting her arm, holding her up. The babes, Albert and Grace, too young to understand but knowing it was something bad. Whimpering. Bickford barely able to read the service due to his breaking voice.

Again I helped carry a coffin. Along with Metherdew, with cracks in his stony face, and Walter Tregellas and Simon Winslip from the asylum. They did their job wonderfully well.

This time there was weight in the coffin. He had been a big man, William Hill. With so much still ahead of him.

The trial was held in July 1869. Doctor Treacey warned me against it, but I had to attend. I owed it to William Hill to learn why his life had been cut short. Why Mary had been widowed and his children orphaned.

Vindictiveness. That's all James Ritson would say by way of explanation for his brutal act. The same reason he gave for shooting the market inspector, Kinsella, a year before. He said Hill had angered him on an earlier visit by asking about Kinsella. He thought a minister had no right to speak of a crime for which he was already suffering, so he'd waited for his next visit, bed hinge tucked in his shirt.

It had come off the bed easy, he boasted. The screws simply worked loose in his fingers. William Hill had entered the cell and started writing something in a book. Ritson struck him over one eye, then smashed in his skull. He claimed he would have struck him many more times had he not been stopped.

He said all this calmly, as if describing hewing stone in the yard. He was an Englishman. Only twenty-five. Looking even younger. He had been brought up by an uncle, then shipped out to the colonies on a twenty-pound passage when sixteen.

His guilt was assured. The only question was whether he'd escape the gallows due to insanity, but he prided himself on outsmarting experts.

'I was perfectly aware of the object of the medical men in visiting me,' he told the jury. Smirking. Pleased with himself. 'Had I so wished it, I could easily have feigned madness, but I hate hypocrisy and prefer to be honest.'

He said this as if the jury men would admire his candour. For them, there was no doubt about it. Their finding was wilful murder. The prisoner was condemned to death.

On hearing the sentence, James Ritson showed little more emotion than if he'd been told of a move to a different cell.

William Bamford again. The fellow by the river. The hangman. Shuffling onto the wooden scaffold with his odd limp, a crumpled calico cap over greasy grey hair. Because of his squint, he had to turn his whole head around so that his better eye could appraise the noose, the knot, and the spectators standing down below at the Melbourne Gaol. Another bluestone building.

Bickford said he could not come. 'My brethren, the Reverends Dare and Watkins, have attended to the prisoner. I simply could not. I don't believe I would find it in myself to forgive him.'

I could go. After India, after the Colonel's firing practice on the parade ground, I could attend anything if I had to. And I had to do this. See it to the end. For William Hill's sake.

Ritson was brought out of his cell followed by two ministers – Dare and Watkins, I presumed. They were praying. Ritson seemed not to be listening. He looked around, interested to see who else had shown up to witness his final performance.

He stared straight at me but he didn't appear to remember. Then his eyes moved on, to the men from the Sheriff's office, the governor of the gaol, some reporters. In amongst them a familiar figure, slightly built, the only one with a cravat and cane. Clarke. Again scribbling with his pencil. But I don't think he saw me. His attention was solely on Ritson, who was rubbing his nose with his manacled hands and continuing to scan the crowd. There were warders. I recognised Moran, and a medical man with his bag. Ritson appeared pleased. Quite a crowd, just for him.

Bamford the hangman used a cord to pinion Ritson's arms to his body. He pulled the knot tight with a jerk that caused the condemned man to wince briefly. Guiding Ritson so that he stood over the trapdoor, Bamford put the noose around his neck. Fixed it like he was tying a parcel. When he went to place a cap over his eyes, Ritson spoke. A young voice, yet loud and clear.

'Don't be in such a hurry,' he said. 'I want to look around again. Lift up the hood, I shan't keep you long.'

Bamford shrugged, muttered something, then tugged the cap back a little on his forehead.

Ritson gazed up to where the sky would be. Then smiled slightly, sighed and said, 'That will do.'

Bamford pulled the cap down and limped over to the wooden

lever, clutching it with both his hands. One of the ministers began reading from a black-bound Bible, but he had only just intoned, 'Man that is born of —' when the trapdoor was sprung with a thudding clatter. Much louder than I had expected.

Ritson was gone. In his place a quivering rope, swaying slightly round and round.

Then Bamford was beside it, leaning over the drop, looking crookedly down to where the rope disappeared behind a black cloth curtain. He nodded once and signalled to the medical man to inspect his handiwork. The doctor wasn't long. After disappearing behind the curtain, he returned, stethoscope in hand, and whispered to the governor, who gave him some papers to sign.

We could leave then. Before I departed, I felt Bamford beside me. Sensed him, smelled him, before I saw him. He was nodding, grimacing. I imagine it passed for a smile.

'I saw you from up there,' he said.

I didn't reply. But he wasn't deterred.

'You were his friend. A decent man, him.' Bamford gestured with a thumb at the scaffold and said, 'But he were a cool one, that Ritson. Some of them can't even stand up. Or they piss themselves. But the governor says this one slept like a babe last night. They had to wake him for breakfast. Can yer imagine? Sleeping! He kept down his porridge, too.'

Then he leaned forward to share a secret, his breath like a cesspit. 'Before the drop, when the reading began, that weren't no mistake. The bastard weren't going to live a second longer than I could help.'

As I left the gaol I heard the bells of St Patrick's strike six, seven, eight times. Again I thought of the Colonel. Here, too, they did their killing in the morning.

Thirty-two

Nora

Mr Hill's murder knocked much of the life that were left in him out of John. It became ever harder to interest him in things. He returned from Ritson's hanging and said, It is finished. Nothing more.

Before, when John fell into one of his long silences, I believed he were thinking about the expedition. Now I couldn't be sure. He'd become close to William Hill, admired him. And once again he'd seen a man he loved slip away before him.

Not long after the execution, he started on his journal, like he knew he must get things reckoned out. He tried to keep it secret but couldn't manage it. He'd fall asleep halfway through a page and I'd come in when it were morning and find him with the scrawled pages on the bed. Pen sometimes still in his hand, ink on the sheets. Ink and blood. But I let the papers lie. Never read any properly. Until after.

Not only John were different with Mr Hill gone. Mary grew older overnight. White hairs amongst the red. Her fire went out. She were like a child's kite with its string cut, one that drifted aimlessly for a time and then fell to the ground, barely moving. They came to live with us at Octavia Street, Mary and Albert and Grace. It were best for all of us. Mary did not want to stay in East Melbourne without her husband, and I were glad of her company.

John too. He welcomed the distraction of the children, it did him good to hear their laughter. Though oftentimes I saw a look of pain when he watched Albert, the boy being the image of his father.

Doctor Treacey couldn't tell us much on the outlook for John.

— All depends on the individual, he said, on his strength, his disposition, his willingness to fight.

We tried to keep him diverted. If the weather and his health permitted, we had outings. Mary took a job in the new Royal Arcade in the city, in the Café Bohemia, and we'd all go in there sometimes. The children would eat pastries, then skip on the squares of the chequered floor. John and I would sip tea or coffee, look up at the vaulted ceiling, then wander amongst the other shops. Schlager Jewels, Robinson's Sweets, the Empress Cake Stall, with its sponge fingers thick with jam.

Mr Bickford invited John to his church often, but John would not go as regular as before. It seemed Mr Hill's death had eroded his faith even further. Mr Bickford showed no sign of being offended by this. Mayhap he'd had to confront some questions himself, and he were still a regular visitor at Octavia Street. Mary told me I were daft not to know he came to see me. In his awkward way he were courting me, she said. Maybe this were so but I couldn't think about that with John ill.

We could have just sunk in on ourselves if not for Mr Bickford trying to keep us up with events. Like the death of the poet Adam Lindsay Gordon, who'd written verse about John's expedition. This were in the middle of 1870, just a year after the death of Mr Hill. Mr Bickford said Gordon shot himself in scrub outside a hotel near the beach in Brighton, poor man.

Then he brought more news of Captain Moonlite, delighted he could surprise us.

— Our old associate has been apprehended, said Mr Bickford.

In Sydney, where it appears he has been for most of the time since absconding from Egerton after the robbery. He has apparently been living the high life in Sydney society, passing himself off as a wealthy squatter with a property in the western district.

Hair so black. Voice so soft.

— I wonder if Reverend Taylor ever saw him, I said.

— My old friend Theophilus? I doubt it. I don't think Mr Scott has moved in clerical circles for some time. Not since the coming of Captain Moonlite, at least.

— How did the police apprehend him? John asked. He were sitting forward, seeming genuinely interested in the ending to this strange tale.

— Ah, he overreached himself at last, Mr Bickford replied. Grew arrogant, or careless. Or both. Perhaps his ill-gained money was finally running low. He started passing bad cheques, including one he used to pay for a yacht in which, strange as it sounds, he apparently planned to sail to Fiji. Accompanied by a young lady.

— Heavens! And now?

— Now he's to stand trial in Sydney for fraud, and authorities in Egerton are keen to question him about that bank robbery. I venture to say the sun may soon be setting on bold Captain Moonlite.

John appeared captivated by the many turns in this story of the smooth-talking young Irishman, but it were rare to see him thus involved in conversations or events. His condition were gradually worsening, that were clear. He became weaker, ever more detached from whatever else were happening. His writing took up most of his diminishing energy. Doctor Treacey said it were unsettling him, wearing him out. But I think even he understood this were something John believed he had to finish.

I were glad Mary had found work at the café. It gave her a new interest, got her out of the house. It meant I had some time of my own in Octavia Street. Mary's Albert were a schoolboy at the St Kilda Park school, not far from Mr Bickford's church. And Grace were a cheeky little girl now, only a year away from going to school herself, yet blessedly too young to understand all that took place. But children sense things. Her father were gone, and then, just a few years on, her ma took a new partner, a man we all knew.

I could try to make it out as a happy ending, a love story like you might see in a music-hall. The sort where two people find themselves alone, sing a duet, then leave together hand in hand. But that's not really how it were.

John and Mary were married in September, 1871.

It were just a simple ceremony with Mr Bickford presiding, keeping proceedings brief because of John's condition. He managed well to stand up as long as he did, though he did have to lean on Mary's arm.

I couldn't call it a love story, though they were fond of one another. They were cousins and had known each other most of their lives. But this were about companionship more than love. Two people scarred in different ways, both hurt by the loss of Mr Hill, who could offer each other a measure of comfort.

Something else, too. John made it clear to me he had thought on it, but I do not know if ever he voiced his concerns to Mary.

— My pension, sis, he said to me. From the expedition. I fear it may cease altogether if I am gone and have no dependants. But if I have a wife, and have been as a father to her children, I feel sure they will maintain support. Honour would say they should.

He took my hand, with his so slight, and looked at me like he were trying to remember everything.

— It is the most practical thing I can do for her. For all of you. And for William, too. Something good and lasting out of all I endured.

So it were done. Each of them, in their own way, supporting

the other. John with his pension and whatever he might do for the children, Mary giving him some care and warmth near the end of his time. For it were clear he didn't have long to go.

Perhaps this were a love story of a different kind. They were linked by their love for the one man. A man gone too soon. The real surprise to me were John's choice of best man, the one who would bear witness to his wedding.

Mr Howitt.

Thirty-three

It must be natural, this need to sort things out. I saw W compose his last letter. Even Mr Burke, never much of a one for writing, made some jottings in his little book. But William Hill never got the chance to total the sum of things. He should have lived another thirty years and seen his children grow up. Instead I saw the life seep out of him on the stones in James Ritson's cell.

A condemned man has time aplenty to ready himself for death. He can write letters, pray, consider all he has done. So Ritson was better prepared for death than Hill, even if Bamford the hangman did reduce his expected span by a minute or two. Springing the trap as the minister began his prayer. Now, like Ritson in his final weeks, I live with a sentence of death. And I have no more chance of a reprieve than him. Yet I have been granted what was denied to William Hill – a chance to set things right.

So. The wedding. I told Nora my reasons. I never said it to Mary in such terms, though she might well have guessed. She was always a shrewd one. Perhaps her acceptance of my awkward proposal was the greatest gift she could give me. Though she didn't put it like that.

'You and me, John-boy? Why not? Quite a pair we are, like two pieces of wreckage washed up on the same beach. *Mrs* King –

I like the sound of it. Then Nora and I will be Miss King and Mrs King. That'll confuse them at the store.'

We had a wedding night. Nora made up trundle cots for the children in the front room, where I normally lay. I went to Mary's room. She was in her nightgown, her hair like burnished copper after a brushing. I'd seldom seen her smiling so since William Hill had died.

There was something in my throat. Something halfway between happiness and tears blocking the words. 'Mary, you don't have to ... I'm not even sure if I ...'

She got into the bed beside me. 'Hush now. Don't say anything. Just give me a hug, John King. Been too long a time since a man's held me.'

She put her head on my shoulder. I felt the wonder of her hair. Then she was crying. Quiet sobs that shook all of her. I pulled her closer, put my arm around her side. The soft swell of a breast. And it happened. Warm and surprising and finished too fast. A feeling of closeness I'd never experienced before. Then Mary was smiling at me, propped up on her arms, her hair hanging down all over me.

'Well. There's some life in you yet. Now, don't anyone try to say we're not legal and all. Con-sum-mat-ed. That's what we are.'

She laughed. I was weeping now, holding onto her while she was saying once more, 'Hush now. Hush.'

I must have slept then. Until the coughing woke me again. As it did the following night. So Albert and Grace went back to their mother's bed and I returned to my retreat in the front room. Which is where Howitt found me when he came calling the last time.

Doctor Treacey had helped me get in touch with Howitt. He left my note for him at the Melbourne Club, where they were both members. It was a simple enough note, advising him of my forthcoming marriage. I said I would be honoured if he would be my best man, should the date be convenient.

I cannot say what I expected. I did not know if Howitt was even in town. Some time had passed since our last meeting – at the Botanical Gardens with von Mueller. That had not ended well. But he was the one who had given me new life. He had been in the interior; he knew what that vastness can do to a man. He understood what I had experienced better than anyone. It had to be Howitt. There was a reckoning to be made. I had enough of the original faith left in me to want a settling of sorts. For more than a decade Howitt had been tracking me down. Now it was time to be found again.

His answer came directly. Curt and to the point, as was his way. He would be pleased to assist, he wrote. He confirmed the details and undertook to see me at the wedding.

Turned out smartly, I have to say. No traces of egg in his beard or on his waistcoat, and his boots were polished. He even remembered to remove his hat inside Mr Bickford's church and smoothed his hair across the top of his head. He greeted me with his customary firm handshake. I sensed that he was quickly evaluating me, running his eyes over my face and body, sizing me up. But he said little more than a few words of greeting to me and Nora, and Mary as well.

Only once did he appear ill at ease. That was immediately after the service, when he seemed uncertain whether the best man was obliged to kiss the bride. It was odd to see him flustered, his cheeks colouring, if only for a minute or two. I'd never seen him like that before. Then he offered Mary his hand again, very formally, like he was meeting her for the very first time.

I saw him chat briefly with Bickford and exchange some words with von Mueller, who had brought seeds from the Gardens as his gift to Mary and me. Then Howitt was gone. Departed without waiting for any refreshments.

'Farewell, King. I wish you well. I wish you both well. I have some matters I must attend to in the city directly. But I will come calling in a day or two, before I head back to Omeo. So, until then?'

The footsteps on the verandah once again. Not unexpected this time. But not so soon after the wedding as he had said – I didn't see Howitt until several months later. Into the new year, it was. His plans must have changed, but he was never one to explain himself.

Still, I knew he would come, in his own time. He understands, we both understand, that the expedition has linked our lives. We are like creeks in the desert that join, then separate again. Running to the sea.

Here he is. The handshake. The appraising look. Polite to the others but leaving no doubt it is me he has come to see. He pulls the chair close to my low bed. Checks his watch, then snaps it shut. Sits in silence for a while, unhurried. Then says, 'I was surprised to get your invitation to the wedding, King. Surprised because I know that some of my questions have upset you in the past, but honoured all the same.'

'Surprised? You rescued me.'

'My men found you. Welch, and the black trackers.'

I sip some water. Feel dried out.

He looks straight at me with his emu eyes. 'You've not long to live, King.'

Put as baldly as if he were mentioning the weather. 'There is no value in messing about,' he continues, leaning closer. 'Collis

Treacey has told me how it is with you. Told me that if I planned to speak with you, I should not dally. He says it can be a matter of weeks, no more.'

Treacey has never been quite so frank with me. 'A few weeks? That's more than I expected to see when I was left on the Cooper.'

'But there's no relief party this time. You know me as a blunt man, King. I deal in facts; that's the way it is. You've little time left. So, is there anything you must tell me? Because I have a suspicion that more than social niceties was behind your wedding invitation – as if you felt there were unfinished business. Well?' He leans back as I sip more water. Slowly, lest it spill on my nightshirt.

When I do not respond Howitt sighs and stands up again. Paces restlessly. Glances out the window to check on his horse and then scans the contents of the room. Flips through the books he sees. A Bible signed and given to me by William Hill. The Wilson and Mackinnon volume, much thumbed. A copy of Gordon's *Bush Ballads* belonging to Mr Bickford. He picks up an *Australian Journal* from the table.

'You reading this?' he asks.

'Only the serial in it. A convict tale. I find it diverting, though often I slumber before I finish reading.'

'I know it. *His Natural Life*, I've heard it discussed. This Marcus Clarke, the author, fancies himself as a bohemian. He has sampled all kinds of intoxicants, I believe. Member of the Yorick Club. Were you aware he used to write for *The Argus*?'

Clarke. Could it be – the man with the cravat and notebook? Andrew Scott was right: there is no telling how things will turn out.

Howitt tosses the journal down on the table, then resumes his seat, reversing the chair and leaning forward on its back. Changes his course.

'Was *he* much of a reader – Burke?'

'He had no time for fiction but he liked poetry. In foreign languages – Italian and German. He could read them both. Carried books with him for some time, before we shed things. He was more than the ignorant policeman many have made him out to be.'

Those eyes are fixed on me again. 'There you go again. You've been his greatest defender, unswervingly loyal all this time. I heard that you even offered to defend Burke's character if Landells slurred it during his examination.'

'Landells had it in for him ever since they parted,' I reply. 'But the commission wouldn't hear his evidence.'

'And now nobody has heard of Landells in years. It's an ever-diminishing number, those who were involved in your expedition and its aftermath. Curious that you, the youngest and least experienced of all who pressed on to the Gulf, should be the solitary one to endure.'

He has pushed forward in his chair, so his face is near to mine. 'Have you wondered why that was so, King?'

I can feel the warmth of his skin. 'Of course. Four of us left for the Gulf, and only I returned to civilisation. I have never been able to escape that. But when the leader died, I did not know for certain I *was* alone. We had left food with Wills. He could have lived. The blacks might have tended him. Over the two days I stayed with Mr Burke after he died, that was the course I settled on. I would look for his deputy. He was now the senior officer.'

At first it is as if Howitt hasn't heard what I said.

He leans back so that his arms are no longer resting on the chair. He is still facing me, but his eyes are seeing something else, looking far into the distance. He runs his fingers through his beard.

'*Two* days? You say you stayed with Burke for two days? That's not what you told me after we found you. Not what I put down on your behalf at all.'

He is out of the chair now, taking large strides around the room. Then, like a falcon dropping on its prey, he grabs the Wilson and Mackinnon and flips through its pages.

'No, you told me — yes, this is it: "I found him speechless, or nearly so; and about eight o'clock he expired. I remained a few hours there, but as I saw there was no use in remaining longer, I went up the creek in search of the natives."' He discards the slim volume. 'You said you found some gunyahs and stayed *there* before going back to Wills. That's what you told me!'

'And it was true. I came upon shelters along the way. I had to rest in them awhile to try to recruit my strength before looking for him.'

'But not so soon as you told me. Now you're saying you lingered with Burke for two days after he was gone. That wasn't your original account to me. Not what was published. "King's Narrative" — I vouched for its accuracy, man. Stood up in public and attested to your honesty!'

He is standing over me now. I can smell the tobacco seeped into him, see the yellow stain in his moustache and one of his eyebrows twitching. I even wonder if he will strike me. But there is nothing more I can think of to say.

Strange — it is relief I feel now, rather than shame or fear.

Howitt steps back, lets out a long breath. When he continues, his tone is much gentler. 'What else, King? What else didn't you tell me? Or *did* tell me that was wrong?'

In his dock I have nothing to say. He can find his own way there.

'And what, in God's name, did you do those two days?'

When again I do not respond he snorts and seems to dismiss me as he turns away. 'Still silent? Saving it all for your journal, perhaps?' And he picks up the most recent pages from the floor near my bed.

I had obscured them somewhat with a blanket, but his eyes miss little. I knew that. He moves over to the window where the light is better.

It doesn't take him long. He looks across the room at me. Flips one page and scans another before returning to the chair. Places the pages down where they were. Gently, face down. Offers me some water solicitously, then uses his own monogrammed handkerchief to wipe it away when I splutter and make a mess.

He sits back, quite calm. Rubbing his eyes and sounding very tired when he speaks. 'I think I see it now. Think I see it. And it's been there all along. So obvious, really. All this time I've been wondering what you've been setting down, but it's not the content that matters most at all.'

He takes out his snuff case and examines the lid. As if this helps him to think. 'It's only just become clear to me, King. Something about your scrawl is very familiar. The large letters, sometimes just a few words to a line, the crossings and flourishes. Almost exactly the same as the handwriting of the late leader of the Victorian Exploring Expedition.'

Thirty-Four

Howitt was not the first to see the similarity between the leader's handwriting and my own. Mr Burke remarked upon it himself, that last night with the fire and dinner of crow. A piece of its flesh stuck in one corner of his mouth. The picture of the Queen. Telling me he could not last much longer. Giving me his watch. His notebook.

He slumbered, muttering in his rest, twitching. I settled down near him, thinking to sleep too. There was nothing more to be done.

Then he was awake, trying to prop himself up where he lay. Said there were still matters to be sorted. I roused myself. Placed more branches on the dying fire. They crackled and sparked, the smoke drifting over us both. The tang of burning leaves, orange light on his face.

Writing the letter to his sister Hessie. Straining to make sense of his words until he indicated he was done and asked to see what I had put down. I had to hold the paper close to his eyes.

'Extraordinary,' he said, his voice very soft. There was drool in his beard.

'What, sir?'

'Your writing, King. It could pass for mine. Uncanny.'

Then he seemed to lose interest. He let the paper fall from his hand. Closed his eyes, turned his head away, his breathing rough. A possum squealed. I placed the pistol in his right hand, though I could not make him hold it. His hand was very cold.

I sat beside him for some time, lest he came to again. If he did, I was not aware. For I slumbered myself, and when I awoke he was still lying against the tree, his breaths coming shallow and soft. There was a clicking in his throat.

He died that morning, as I wrote before. There was no final speech or instructions. Just his restless mutterings in the night. He sighed. Then only a stillness.

It was when I closed his eyes and kissed him that I saw the letter I had written for him the previous night. It lay on the ground where it had fallen. I retrieved it and went to place it, for safekeeping, inside the notebook. Mr Burke's pencil — one end chewed, the other crudely fashioned to a point with a knife — was tucked into its side. Because of missing pages and dates out of sequence, it was hard to tell which were his last entries. Near the end it seemed he had made several attempts to write much the same thing, the lettering sprawling and faint.

There was this:

I hope we shall be done justice to. We fulfilled our task but we were ~~abund~~ not followed up as I expected and the Depot party abandoned their post —

R O'H Burke

On the next two pages there was this:

for the Committee.

Cooper's Creek
26th June 1861

Have travelled up creek.
Think well
James confronted the enemy face on.
Wills has been

Nothing more. I compared this with what I had written in the letter to his dictation. Just as he said, the resemblance was uncanny.

I took my time. I had more time than anything else. If W still lived, he could endure for another day or so. If he had already gone, as I suspected, there was nothing more I could do for him. I wondered what Mr Burke had begun to write. 'Wills has been...' What? But W could speak for himself. He always had.

I had my leader's notebook and pencil. I practised. Just single words at first. The extravagant loops on the tails of letters. The crossing of 't's, sometimes across whole words. As I was wont to do myself. I noted his signature. He varied it, sometimes signing 'Robt Burke', also 'R O'H Burke'. Any inconsistencies would surely be attributed to his extremity.

William Archer, who had the task of transcribing Mr Burke's notebook for the committee, commented on its poor state. Some leaves had been torn out, he observed. I should apologise to Mr Archer for this, though Mr Burke had already removed some himself. For fires. And I didn't take many pages in all, simply enough to get it right and have a sense of what I should say.

First I finished the letter to the leader's sister Hessie. After the farewell to Annie Elizabeth and Mrs Taylor, I added just a few lines:

> *King has behaved nobly and I hope if he lives that he will be properly rewarded.*
>
> *Robt. Burke*

Nothing more in meaning than what my leader had said to me on his last night: 'You have been very loyal, King.'

I nearly put it that way: 'King has been very loyal.' But I liked the sound of the other. Then I added a postscript. As if he had thought more upon it:

June 28th 1861
Dearest Hessie King has staid with me till the last. He has left me at my request unburied and with my pistol in my hand good-bye again dearest Hessie my heart is with you.

I thought of my own sister Nora, who I hadn't seen for many years. So the last words were true. All of it was true, though I had to guess at the date. I doubted Mr Burke had known either, but hoped the gap between entries might give them weight.

That was all the writing I meant to do. It had taken three of us most of a day to lay Charley Gray in the ground. Now there was only me, and I was very weak. But if remaining unburied was Mr Burke's final request, nothing would be said of it. No questions asked about why I had left my leader uncovered, abandoned to the animals and blacks.

I folded the letter to Hessie into Mr Burke's notebook. When the letter was found — and I was unsure then whether to keep it or bury it with some of W's journals, if I got to them — it would surely be read before being sent on to the leader's sister in Ireland.

But if it wasn't?

This doubt gnawed at me like the hunger all the second day with my leader as I struggled to determine my course. Mr Burke had assured me somebody would have come after us. But I was merely a hired hand, the camel man who had lost all his camels. I could be left unrecognised. Unrewarded. My part in it all unknown. Worse, I could be blamed. I was a soldier whose officers had perished.

I needed a testimony.

Mr Burke had already begun his last message to the committee. And he had told me of the power of his words on the day he saved me from drowning in the Cooper. Standing tall, he described how he pictured himself addressing members of the Royal Society and moving them close to tears as he read from the scuffed and torn pages of his notebook.

I looked at it again. The first entry on the final pages, about the depot party abandoning their post, I left as it was. Also the next page, which clearly indicated it was meant for the committee. I liked that. No doubting who it was for. Then I tore out the following entry, the four lines about James and W, and replaced them with this:

King has behaved
nobly and I
hope he will
be properly
cared for
R O'H Burke

Very similar to what I had written to Hessie. Then, with the pencil almost worn away, I concluded:

and he goes
up the creek
in accordance
with my
request —
June 29th 1861

That was all. My leader sending me on my way.

I thought to excise some of it, or perhaps the postscript to the letter, after seeing how they looked on paper. Then I decided the repetition and muddled dates made them seem more real. Like the leader had one pressing thought in his mind near the end.

I finished writing, then put the notebook in the small canvas bag I kept around my neck, along with the watches and W's letter to his father, which does not mention me at all. I barely looked at the notebook after that. I knew its contents and thought it would suffice.

Only much later did I learn what happened to it. *The Argus* had a small entry:

MEMORANDA IN MR BURKE'S POCKET BOOK
BROUGHT DOWN BY KING, AND HANDED TO
SIR W. STAWELL

At a meeting of the Exploration Committee on December 5th, the Chairman (Sir W. Stawell) produced a private memorandum book belonging to Mr Burke, which, he stated, he intended to forward to Miss Burke ... The book contained primarily instructions to his sister, but on some of the leaves there were memoranda for the committee evidently. These he would read to the committee ...

And he did.

In print they seem clumsy. But nobody has ever questioned the notebook. Last words are treated reverently, not held up against a light. Until Howitt — and I always thought he would be the one — nobody thought to ask about the writing. The commissioners were too polite. They nearly got there, asking what Mr Burke had said and written, and when. I requested a chair. I sagged against the table in the hearing room. Then they moved on to something else.

On the bank of Cooper's Creek, his eyes wide and agitated,

Mr Burke had asked, 'Who will tell my story if I am gone?' That was my job now. Mr Burke said that people would follow us up. I believed him. And he was right. Brave and reckless and rash and right.

Howitt wonders why I did not accompany him and his men to where my leader lay. I could not go back. Could not face Howitt's questions at the place where I had written in Mr Burke's notebook. One other thing: returning would have meant leaving him again.

W believed in figures, Howitt in facts. Now he knows they can change like the time of sunrise. Howitt took down my narrative in his own hand, affirmed that it was truthful. And so it is, in most respects. But there is what I said and what I left unsaid. What I wrote was barely more than what Mr Burke had told me himself. But he was always reluctant to put things down.

I have lived with what I did for longer than all my time in India and the interior. Longer than I expected to survive when I crouched not far from Mr Burke's body, practising his signature with the only pencil left.

They have all wanted to know about the end. Nobody more than Howitt – my saviour, my confessor. He has lectured me about honour, but is it dishonourable to claim what is due? The committee was slow to pay my salary. Without the endorsement of the late leader of their own expedition – 'I hope he will be properly cared for' – I might well have been discharged and forgotten.

Charley put it plainly to me near the Gulf: 'We've done whatever they say we've done.' And who better to say it than Mr Burke? Who better to grant me absolution than Howitt? My secret is now his. A transferral has taken place.

The wafer on my tongue tastes of dust.

I am very tired now. Here in Octavia Street, St Kilda, with the voices of Albert and Grace cheery in a back room, it is as if I am again in a gunyah with the blacks. Weak. Alone. Waiting.

I check my watch, the one from the Royal Geographical Society of London. The time is ten minutes after four in the afternoon. Some hours have passed since Howitt left. Abruptly, making no farewells. The watch is a good fit in my hand. Its case is pleasingly cool to the touch.

Would I have got it, or any other reward, if not for the leader's final words? I have often wondered. There is much about the expedition that I still do not understand.

It would be well to say that we reached the sea.

As a soldier, I followed orders. Only when my officers had gone did I choose my own path.

It is nearly done.

Farewell, Nora and Mary. God bless you both. And the children. I would like them to have the watches, one for each.

Farewell, once again, Hessie. Sister to Mr Burke. Howitt wonders that I have been so loyal to him. He was my leader. He saved me. Respected me. And at the end, just as he predicted, he needed me. As I needed him.

King has behaved nobly.

If I say so myself.

Epilogue

My brother died about seven o'clock on a Monday morning, at home in Octavia Street.

I were with him, reading the Bible. He'd asked for Corinthians. Mary, who sat up most of the night, had retired. I summoned her just in time.

It were sudden, though expected. I think John himself knew his end were near. For the last few weeks he had scarcely been able to get up or take any food. He just gradually sank down, but I believe he had found a kind of peace.

He tried to speak some words before he subsided, but Mary and I cannot agree what he said. Myself, I think it were something about the sea.

He had not written anything for several days. I am yet to sort all his pages, which are not numbered, so do not know if he were just too ill to go on or had put down all he wanted.

Some reporters came. I thought they had forgotten him. *The Age* published this:

> *The man whose name must be indelibly associated, along with those of the ill-fated Burke, Wills and Gray, with the greatest event in the annals of Australian exploration — the first crossing of the continent — has at last rejoined his comrades.*

I think he would have liked that, 'rejoined his comrades'. But not all in the newspaper were good.

On the 22nd of August last he was married to Mary Richmond, a widow, at the Wesleyan Church, by the Rev. Jas. Bickford. He has not left her in very prosperous circumstances. He was in receipt of a pension from the Government of 180 pounds a year... but this sum reverts to the Government by his death. The expenses contingent upon his constant state of ill-health prevented him from making any provisions for her.

Seems that John had too much faith in the charity of them in authority. We do not know yet what we will do. Mayhap if John's writings are published, this could help those he has left behind.

Mr Bickford conducted the funeral service. It were not fancy. John had indicated he wished to be buried in the Wesleyan section of the Melbourne Cemetery, close as possible to Mr Hill. They lie but twenty feet apart. It will make the visiting easier for Mary and me.

Baron von Mueller were one of the pallbearers. He looked old and weary. We asked Mr Howitt to come but did not get any word back from him. Doctor Treacey could not say if Mr Howitt even received the urgent message he sent to him at his club.

Around John's grave is a low metal fence. We hope to plant some flowers. The headstone we ordered is simple, nothing like as grand as the monument for the expedition, which is no more than five minutes' walk away in the cemetery.

This is what we had written:

TO

THE MEMORY OF

JOHN KING

SOLE SURVIVOR OF

THE BOURKE AND

WILLS EXPLORATION

PARTY LEFT TO

RECOUNT THE

EVENTS OF THAT

EXPEDITION

DECEASED 15 JAN 1872

AGED 31 YEARS

We didn't see it until our third visit. It were late in the day. Most everyone else had gone from the cemetery and Albert and Grace were getting fidgety. Mary put her hands to her lips and rushed away from the grave. I thought grief had got to her, so I didn't follow.

After long enough for me to wonder where she'd gone, she came back. Hot and sweaty, like she'd been hurrying, and flustered.

– Oh Nora, she said. There's a mistake!

– A mistake?

– On John's stone. The spelling is wrong. I've just checked – on the monument. It should be Burke without an 'o'. Not B-o-u-r-k-e.

She bit her lip. I thought she were holding back tears, then I saw her eyes and realised she were trying not to smile.

Bourke. We looked at the stone again. And this time it were me who saw it.

– The age, also. He were thirty-three last December, not thirty-one. Two years gone.

Mary took my hand, gazed around to look for the children.

I thought to have the headstone changed.

But now, after all that's happened, I'm inclined to leave it be.

Author's Note

King, though usually reticent about the shortcomings of his once leader, would occasionally unbosom himself about the past...
A *Ballarat Courier* correspondent,
quoted in *The Age*, 18 January 1872

In 1979 I was part of a group that followed Burke and Wills' route as far as Cooper's Creek. I recall being struck by the eerie beauty of the region, but if I thought about John King it was only in passing. Nine years later my father gave me a facsimile copy of the 1861 Wilson and Mackinnon volume about the expedition. When I finally read it, several things about King intrigued me: his personal involvement in the key scenes; his survival, not only on the Cooper but for ten years after his return; and the fact that I knew so little about him. Thus began a slow journey with many unexpected detours. King's published 'Narrative' was a starting point, along with some intriguing newspaper references such as the one above. Another described him rushing from a room in tears after Burke's name was mentioned. Yet he has only a bit part in most accounts of the expedition.

In this novel I have been faithful to the basic facts of King's life. He was born in Ireland in 1838, was orphaned early, attended the Hibernian school in Dublin, enlisted in the British Army at fourteen, served in India, and was recuperating from illness after the mutiny when he met

George Landells, who was gathering camels for the Victorian Exploring Expedition. After his rescue by Howitt's party in September 1861 he lived quietly with his sister in St Kilda and died of consumption at his home in Octavia Street in January 1872, having never fully recovered from what he'd endured. Ferdinand von Mueller was a pallbearer at his funeral, which was described as 'unimposing'. Apart from what King told Howitt, his evidence to the commission and some letters, he had little more to say about the expedition. The National Library of Australia holds what it describes as King's journal, but it is fragmentary, seems to have been written retrospectively, and covers only December 1860 and January 1861.

All the main characters in the novel connected with the expedition did exist. Considerable licence has been taken with their thoughts, words and actions (to my knowledge, for example, King and Stuart never met), but quotations from journals, documents and contemporary accounts are accurate. A greater degree of invention is present in Nora. King was indeed cared for by a sister, who learned about the expedition after she arrived in the colony. Her name is given variously as Mrs Anne Bunton or Bunting; she is described as having worked as a matron or wardress at the asylum, and is believed to have died in Melbourne in 1890. In August 1871, less than five months before his death, King married a Mary Richmond, reported as being a widow and possibly his cousin, at the Wesleyan Church in St Kilda with the Reverend Jas. Bickford presiding.

In May 1869, three years after the heroic death of the Wesleyan minister Daniel Draper in a shipwreck, the Reverend William Hill was murdered by James Ritson during a prison visit. Ritson was hanged by the common executioner, William Bamford, three months later. Though Marcus Clarke did write for *The Argus* in the 1860s, there is no evidence that he attended Ritson's hanging or had anything to say about the expedition. But as the serialisation of *His Natural Life* began in *Australian Journal* in March 1870, it is possible King could have read some of it. Andrew

Scott, the Anglican clergyman who became the bushranger Captain Moonlite, came to Melbourne in 1868 and served as a lay reader in Bacchus Marsh before heading to Egerton and its bank. Following King's death, Scott served time first in Ballarat Gaol, from which he escaped, then Pentridge. He was released in 1879, reoffended, and was hanged in 1880. After retrieving the remains of Burke and Wills, Alfred Howitt was a magistrate for twenty-six years, and later held several senior public service positions. As an anthropologist he wrote many scientific papers and a book, *The Native Tribes of South Australia*. In 1904 the Australasian Association for the Advancement of Science awarded him a medal named after von Mueller. He died in 1908, aged seventy-seven, after what is described as the only illness of his life.

In addition to newspaper accounts and the estimable Wilson and Mackinnon, which includes Wills' journals and Burke's notes, for background on the expedition I am indebted to Alan Moorehead's *Cooper's Creek* (1963), Frank Clune's *Dig* (1937) and Sarah Murgatroyd's *The Dig Tree* (2002). I found the insights of Manning Clark in Volume IV of his *A History of Australia* (1978) especially useful. King, wrote Clark, 'looked up without envy or malice to those placed in authority over him'. Marjorie Tipping was with me in the group that travelled to Cooper's Creek. Her lovely book, *Ludwig Becker: Artist & Naturalist with the Burke & Wills Expedition* (1979), was useful for its reproductions of Becker's illustrations and letters. The most comprehensive account of King's life is by John McKellar in the December 1944 issue of *The Victorian Historical Magazine*.

The 2002 exhibition curated by Tim Bonyhady, 'Burke & Wills, From Melbourne to Myth' (which is also the name of his fascinating 1991 book), displayed side by side Burke's notebook and King's own handwriting: what had been conjecture on my part suddenly didn't seem so fantastic. Sidney Nolan's wonderful Burke and Wills paintings boosted my courage to see things in my own way. I also spent much time poring over *Aboriginal Photographs of Baldwin Spencer*, edited by John Mulvaney (1982); and *Sun Pictures of Victoria: The Fauchery-Daintree Collection*

1858 (1983). Also of help were the third volume of Michael Cannon's 'Australia in the Victorian Age' series, *Life in the Cities* (1975), as well as his *Melbourne After the Gold Rush* (1993); Miles Lewis's *Melbourne: The City's History and Development* (1995); Andrew Brown-May's *Melbourne Street Life: The Itinerary of Our Days* (1998); *The Early Story of the Wesleyan Methodist Church in Victoria*, by the Reverends W.L. Blamires and John B. Smith (1886); *The Indian Mutiny*, by John Harris (1973); *Beside the Seaside: Victorian Resorts in the Nineteenth Century*, by Andrea Inglis (1999). John Keats' letters gave me insight into the consumptive patient; Dava Sobel's *Longitude* (1999) had an excellent description of the symptoms of scurvy; Robyn Davidson's *Tracks* (1980) was a useful primer on camels.

A great many people helped in different ways. I am grateful for the assistance of staff of *The Age* library, the State Library of Victoria, and the Manuscripts Section of the National Library of Australia. Michael Gawenda, editor of *The Age*, showed admirable forbearance despite my distraction. Joyce Richardson made me welcome at the Royal Society of Victoria. Sally Bouvier read an early draft and offered several suggestions, especially concerning Nora. Professor Geoffrey Blainey also read a draft: I appreciate his advice and the fact that he was not too offended by the liberties I have taken with history. Katherine Kizilos and Michael Harvey have long been supporters and sounding-boards; Les Carlyon was always encouraging. I thank them all.

This book would not have happened without the energy and enthusiasm of Lyn Tranter, of Australian Literary Management. She was one of the first to believe in it. At Penguin, Clare Forster picked it up and Bob Sessions saw it through. In Meredith Rose I had an editor with great patience, keen insight and unfailing good humour. Her contribution was immeasurable.

Above all, I must acknowledge my wife Kerry O'Shea and our children Lucy, Max and Gus. For too long they have put up with me living in another century. I am unsure if they deserve an apology or thanks. I can only offer them both, with love.